THE *handless* MAIDEN

THE *handless* MAIDEN

LORANNE BROWN

Doubleday Canada Limited

Canadian Cataloguing in Publication Data

Brown, Loranne

The handless maiden

HC ISBN 0-385-25702-3 Pbk. ISBN 0-385-25854-2

I. Title

PS8553.R68732H36 1998   C8I3'.54   C97-93I897-I

PR9199.3.B76H36 1998

Cover design by Heather Hodgins
Cover photo by Julia Margaret Cameron/Hulton Getty-Liaison Agency
Text design by Heidy Lawrance Associates
Printed and bound in Canada

Published in Canada by
Doubleday Canada Limited
105 Bond Street
Toronto, Ontario
M5B 1Y3

TRAN 10 9 8 7 6 5 4 3 2 1

To my parents,
Michael and Laurie Babic,
in whose home love was the given,
imagination the gift.

$\mathcal{A}$CKNOWLEDGMENTS

Heartfelt thanks:

To my husband, Lorne Douglas Brown, and our children, Ian Mitchell and Hilary Claire: my tripod of support, blessings in triplicate.

To my writers' group – Diana Mohrsen, Penny Duane, Terry Shaw, Lyn Blackwood – for friendship, feedback, and weekly whip-cracking.

To my other readers – Lorne Brown; my parents, Mike and Laurie Babic; my brother, Michael Babic, Jr.; Muriel Brown; Karen Campbell; Janet and John Dickin; Susan Barber; Ed Griffin; Margaret Deefholts; Eleanor Brown; Tom Elton; and Paul Goyan – for astute insight and generous input. To Jack Hodgins and the members of the workshop in which I unveiled the first thirty pages when that was all there was, for your enthusiastic response. To the Federation of B.C. Writers and the Writers' Union of Canada whose competitions gave impetus to my emergence.

To Elinor Barr, whose book *Silver Islet: Striking it Rich in Lake Superior* (Natural Heritage/Natural History Inc., 1995) has become a psychic Bible. To Arthur Black for directing me to the Saxberg family of Silver Islet; and to Joan Saxberg for victuals and lore.

To all the ethical lawyers with whom it has been my privilege to work (and of whose number 'Sully' is *not* the last), especially Bruce W. Davies and Ronald A.L. Coward.

To the staff at Doubleday Canada for their generosity and fervour; to Susan Broadhurst for her careful copy-edit; and especially to editor Lesley Grant for long-distance friendship, brain-storming, and gales of laughter.

Not least, to my agent, Carolyn N. Swayze, LL.B., for believing.

And for the leap of faith made by editor-in-chief, John Pearce, who – having handed me pruning shears, shovel, fertilizer, *and* the space in which to employ them – taught me just how creative the editorial process could be.

Part One

Overture

Change one thing.

The sanctioned family memory, even the police report, states that the gun went off by accident. I know better.

Perhaps the rest of the family looks at that first gunshot as the pivotal point of our lives. I don't. When I examine this 1960s photograph, the smiling eight-year-old has a hint of panic in her eye already: it isn't a game any more.

My father and I used to play the game. He'd take a photograph or a picture from a magazine. "What do you see?"

"A quiet forest. Trees. Sky. Animals playing happily," I'd say.

"Change one thing."

"Rain. Animals take shelter. Lightning strikes. Fire breaks out. Animals run for their lives. Forest destroyed."

For every action, a reaction. Alter one element and an idyllic forest scene becomes a cataclysm. "What happened to the dinosaurs?" One thing changed; cause and effect took over from there.

My dad believed his parental duty was to instil a strong moral sense in his children. Teaching me to see that every action has a consequence was his method. Oh sure, our games often had happy endings, but I learned the lesson so thoroughly I couldn't walk into a room full of strangers or board a plane without laying out a worst-case scenario. If we'd been in Dallas on November 22, 1963, we would have anticipated the shooter on the grassy knoll. Hell, we'd have been waiting for Oswald in the Book Depository.

But hypervigilance produces a myopia of its own.

Take this photo of the Standhoffer family – my family – circa 1963: Virginia and Gabriel, mater- and paterfamilias; Mariah, age eight; little Luke, age four. All posed in front of the fireplace under the watchful gaze of the portrait of Gabe's sister, Zoshka. Off to one side, just slightly removed from the group, is Grandfather Lucas Standhoffer.

We all have family snaps like this: smiling parents, happy kids. Normal family life, mid-20th century.

To see the big picture requires distance. Look at a Seurat painting. Step forward to examine its composition and you see each of his dots and brush strokes. The patch of violet is composed of red and blue; the eye reassembles it to make purple. There is the appearance of a whole which, on closer examination, disintegrates into a reality of tiny components.

Bring this grainy black and white photo closer to your eyes. Change one thing — even your perspective — and the happy family dissolves, revealing painfully separate fragments. Change one dot, one pixel — a change so minute it's invisible to the naked eye — and you've for ever altered the destiny of that nice, normal, nuclear family.

Will they ever be able to look at a timeline of their lives together and finger the point — "This is where the change took place. This is the axis; everything after is skewed."

We have secrets we keep from other people; we have secrets we keep from ourselves. My own best-kept secret is the answer to the question: Did I do it on purpose?

Despite replaying my personal Zapruder film daily — despite reliving it waking and sleeping, slow-motion, speeded up, backward and forward, for two decades — I still can't tell if I pulled that trigger deliberately. Sometimes the replay drones by just below the level of conscious thought — like having the TV on in the background while making dinner — when something seemingly new will catch my attention and I'll run it from a different angle. So elusive, those ghost-images: all too often the new detail turns out to be just fly-shit on the lens.

We fed everyone the official party line:

> While changing the sheets on her parents' bed, Mariah Standhoffer, age 17, somehow dislodged the revolver her father always kept tucked between the box spring and mattress. She fumbled for it; it went off, shattering her right hand, which, despite extensive bone and skin grafts, was subsequently amputated at the wrist.

I always thought this story was as full of holes as a pair of cheap pantihose. That anyone bought it has been a lifelong source of amazement to me. At first I thought everyone was stupid or gullible; later, I realized people will accept the incredible when reality is too painful to entertain.

The bald truth:

> While changing the sheets on her parents' bed, Mariah Standhoffer, age 17, was assaulted by her grandfather, Lucas Standhoffer, age 73. She somehow retrieved the revolver her father always kept tucked between the box spring and mattress. While brandishing the weapon, she shrieked, "If you ever touch me again, I'll kill you." A struggle for the weapon ensued and the pistol was discharged at close range, shattering her right hand, which, despite extensive bone and skin grafts, was subsequently amputated at the wrist.

In the aftermath of the gunshot I was so drunk with power that I was deaf to my own screams and oblivious to pain. I'd won! My grandfather would never bother me again. Like an animal caught in a trap I'd chewed off my own paw to win my freedom.

But the question remains: Did I do it on purpose?

"The so-called traumatic experience is not an accident, but the opportunity for which the child has been patiently waiting." I felt the hairs stand up on the back of my neck the first time I read W.H. Auden's words. *"Had it not occurred, it would have found another, equally trivial — in order to find a necessity and direction for its existence, in order that its life may become a serious matter."*

Do we choose our accidents — or do they choose us?

Even now, when I dream of "home," my subconscious takes me to that house. We moved there when I was eight, after Grandma died, from our little house not two blocks away. Doug's first reaction — "Wow, it's a castle!" — embarrassed me. He thought we must be rich; I had no such illusions. By the time I was a teenager I'd learned something of how much it cost my parents to keep.

I think the house itself was the trap.

If so, it was set even before I was born. Perched on the ridge overlooking Lake Superior, three storeys, neo-Victorian, complete with tower room and gingerbread trim, it lured my Czechoslovakian grand-mother, Anna Standhoffer, across town away from her friends in the Slovak ghetto with a promise of Canadian-style respectability.

Change one thing: with that house she could reinvent herself, her past. Not an immigrant seamstress who'd saved the family from starva-tion during the Depression by bootlegging, but a *businesswoman*. From a base of such respectability her daughter, rechristened Zoë, could be anything – beauty queen, debutante, socialite; her son – a hotelier to the gentry.

Never mind that the hotel was in the wrong part of town, that the "gentry" it served was all landed – face down in a skid-row gutter. Never mind that the house itself was in the wrong part of town, that the neighbourhood demographic had already shifted sufficiently to *allow* an immigrant businesswoman to buy into it.

It did seem huge when we moved, in 1963, but not alien: it was Grandma's house, after all. Over the years my brother Luke and I had spent endless hours there amusing ourselves. We'd play hide and seek on the back stairs. We'd howl and hoot up and down the laundry chute at each other. One of us would send bits of toilet paper drifting down from the second-floor washroom while the other would try to catch them from the kitchen before they landed in the huge laundry hamper in the basement.

Until one visit: "Please, Marička," Grandma scolded, "don't play with paper. Big mess in vashing machine!"

Grandpa Standhoffer launched into a tirade in Slovak – pleading our case, I assumed – while Grandma shouted back, "Big mess! Big mess!"

At this point our father, Gabe, entered the fray as referee. Luke and I quaked through it all. Such a lot of noise over some pieces of toilet paper! I vowed never to be the cause of such commotion again.

With Grandma gone, we all moved in with Grandpa. Despite the size of the house, there were only three bedrooms on the second floor. Luke and I had to share. Mom repapered our room, the perfect non-threatening forest: sleeping fawns guarded by fawning does; bunnies peeping out from behind trees; skunks sniffing pastel flowers.

While I don't remember the first time I awoke to find Grandpa star-ing at me in the darkness, I do remember it became a regular occur-rence – so regular that upon waking in terror to the sound of his breathing at my bedside I'd calm myself with a litany: "It's only Grandpa; it's only Grandpa."

At first, I think, he wanted only to watch me sleep. He would loom there in the dark, exhaling beer fumes, swaying slightly like a boozed-up guardian angel. "Go back to sleep," he'd murmur if I sat up. He'd shuffle down the hall to his room, to resume the chair by the window where he could be found at all hours smoking and drinking – sentry over the back lanes of the neighbourhood.

After these encounters, I'd kneel by the window beside my bed, crossing myself over and over, repeating bedtime prayers for good measure.

My window afforded a perfect view of the Sleeping Giant. Didn't we all know the Indian legend? It was part of the mythos of a Thunder Bay childhood. How many of us were threatened with his resurrection if we misbehaved? "Be good, or the Sleeping Giant will get you!" Guarding the silver mines seemed like a boring occupation for the noble savage compared to the excitement of "getting" little kids if we were bad. My prayers were, eventually, directed more to the recumbent geographical formation than to our father who art in heaven.

Years later with my son in an airplane: "When will we be high enough to see God?" he asked.

Most kids think of heaven as "up" – some mysterious place in the clouds, higher than imagination. I'm sure the nuns who taught me at St. Andrew's School would have been shocked. My heaven was a heaven of vista, of waterscape, of horizon. Heaven was the harbour of Thunder Bay stretched out below me, bounded by the peninsula of which the Sleeping Giant formed a part. Grain elevators perched like castles on its shore; bathtub-toy freighters steamed past the lighthouse whose monotonous beacon pointed a finger of accusing light across the dark water.

Heaven was Silver Lining – my misinterpretation of "Silver Islet," the treasure over which the Sleeping Giant supposedly keeps watch. The Sleeping Giant guards the Silver Lining, so "his eye is on the sparrow and I know he watches me." Despite the confused theology I was comforted by his presence, able to unfold my knees from the cool hardwood and climb back into bed gratefully.

But if I pictured a heaven lined with silver, then its antithesis was a muskeg swamp.

Fort William and Port Arthur were the only urban centres of note between Winnipeg and Sault Ste. Marie. The rest was bush. "It was *hell* out there," I heard Dad say once, upon his return from a fruitless days-long search for a hunter missing in the endless wilderness that clawed the northwestern flank of the twin cities. "If he tried to cross that slough in the dark, he's a goner," he said, face grim. "It's bottomless."

It seemed to me that the reclining stone god I prayed to demonstrated a bewildering treachery in the natural world he'd created. A peaceful harbour one moment could be stirred into a storm-tossed lake; a serene forest was man-trapped with fly-ridden bogs.

"You can never let down your guard," Dad said, packing away his bush gear and shotgun. He never went hunting for anything – animal *or* man – without it. "It's dangerous out there."

"Don't wake Lucas."

I awoke to find Grandpa clambering into bed with me.

No worry. Nothing could wake Luke; the little traitor slept like the dead.

The smell of beer and cigarillos. Something warm and hard in my hand. I had no idea what it was. Some kind of stick? Some kind of animal?

"Rub it," he whispered, moving my hand for me. Confused, frightened, I did as I was told. I always did as I was told.

Grandpa got out of bed a few minutes later, holding a crumpled handkerchief in his hand. "Don't tell Mommy and Daddy," he said.

Over the hammering of my heart I listened for his footsteps, tracking him in my mind. He went into the bathroom, opened the squeaky door of the laundry chute, closed it, then went back to his room. When I heard him snoring, I slipped out of bed and crept down the long staircase.

I went looking for my mother – whether to "tell" or merely for comfort, I still can't say. The TV droned; I called, "Mommy!" as I went through the French doors into the living room. No Mommy, but a babysitter – Mrs. Vanetti from down the street. No Mommy!

"Mommy's out with Daddy. She come home soon," Mrs. Vanetti said, trying her best to comfort me.

Betrayed, inconsolable, I cried, I screamed. Despite my vow never to sleep again, I awoke in my father's arms as he carried me up the stairs. "Poor baby; such a bad dream," he murmured.

Ah, my Dad! Such a relief! So safe in his arms, the smell of his after-shave against my cheek. And my mother — her "going out" perfume a tangible presence, the scent of comfort; her embrace the circumference of my need. They both sat on my bed while she sang softly to me, stroking my forehead. Something about God sending guardian angels to watch me, all through the night. Picturing a giant, sleeping guardian, I wondered just how much it would take to wake him up.

Reruns: I'd wake in the dark to find the "thing" in my hand, still not knowing where he kept it or what it was. Hopelessly naïve child that I was, I even peered around on the shelves of Grandpa's basement work-shop, looking for the stick that needed rubbing in the dead of night. Perhaps, like Aladdin's lamp, I'd get three wishes.

During dinner one evening, I almost pinned it down.

Grandpa worked as day desk clerk at my father's hotel; Dad usually manned the bar on the evening shift. Dinner frequently included a debriefing.

"*Počkaj*, Gabe!" Grandpa launched into a spirited Slovak descrip-tion of his day. Gesticulating wildly, he took a compact weapon from his pocket and demonstrated how he had floored a drunken would-be assailant.

My heart lurched when I saw it: covered in black leather, it was the size and shape of the "thing" in the dark.

"What's that?" I asked, astounded by my boldness.

"A billy club," my dad responded matter-of-factly. "The police use it to whack bad people when they make a fuss going off to jail."

"Can I see it?" I asked. Grandpa passed it to me.

It was hard, yet soft; warm from Grandpa's pocket, but somehow not quite right. I rubbed it experimentally a few times in the way in which I had been instructed.

"Marička!"

Grandpa scowled at me across the table, held his hand out for the return of the implement. I burned with shame as I passed it back to him silently. *Don't tell Mommy and Daddy.*

I was a naïve child, but not a stupid one. My parents didn't go out often; still, the pattern established itself: grandpa and "thing" in my bed, no mother downstairs; Mrs. Vanetti less tolerant of my tears, par-ents less sympathetic to finding me asleep in the living room. The warm group cuddle and lullaby gave way to a perfunctory, "Now, now. Enough silliness," accompanied by that tight-lipped expression of displeasure on my mother's face. I knew what *that* meant.

The perfect child was not performing to standard.

God, how I hated that look! Those rigid lips and the edge in her voice. Even when it wasn't directed at me it was enough to inspire contrition. I'd do anything to avoid being the cause of her irritation.

The next time she steps out of the bathroom steamy from her bath and fragrant with her going-out perfume, I withdraw to the solarium, hoping no one will find me huddled under an afghan with a book. I beg Mrs. Vanetti to let me stay up later than usual; rebuffed, I obey her command with silent dread, alert for the board that will creak as Grandpa bisects the Persian rug diagonally from his room to mine; his scent overpowering that of sunshine on the fresh pillowcase I press to my face; his laboured breathing in my ear.

My expectations are not unfulfilled.

Once the snores resume, I slip downstairs, hoping my parents have returned. There's Mrs. Vanetti on one side of the French doors with the droning TV and its flickering monochrome figures. On the other side, a weeping child peers through the glass rectangles, then turns to the stairs.

"Daddy and I brought you popcorn from the movies," Mom announced gaily. "You and Luke can share it while you're watching cartoons."

In the glare of the morning after, it's dry as ashes. I've hated popcorn ever since.

Why do *I* remember everything? Legions of abuse victims forget so thoroughly they spend their whole lives trying to leap the chasm between synapses of memory to make the connection. Scores of people who've never been abused dredge up false memories, muddying their lives hopelessly.

When I consult the mall directory of memory, the floorplan indicates: "You are here." No matter how much distance I achieve with age and maturity, through language and knowledge, my emotional orientation is preserved — for evidential purposes, perhaps — in present tense.

My earliest memory: It's raining. At the window in the kitchen of the third-floor apartment of Grandma's house, I sit in my high chair with a piece of paper and a pencil on the tray in front of me, trying to draw raindrops by tapping pencil on paper. I'm happy when I make perfect dots, but the pencil keeps hitting the ridge between the boards of the wooden tray, causing streaks. Unable to express my frustration, I burst into tears when my mother asks what's wrong.

Entirely interior, it's not a memory planted by parental reminiscence. The most vivid recollection is my inarticulate rage against physical limitation.

I judged myself even then — measuring my abilities against my expectations — and found myself lacking. My internal judge was at the bench before the age of two. Court has been in session ever since.

Now when I hear it, the voice of my conscience is my father's voice. It's not altogether a bad thing. Luke once told me it was "abject terror" of Dad that kept him from committing some of the youthful idiocies his friends had. It wouldn't surprise me if his internal judge also bears Dad's tone. But if we both assimilated Dad's voice, neither of us acquired for ourselves Dad's own unspoken but unassailable conviction: that if only one were sufficiently vigilant one would be, by extension, always, unquestionably *right*. It never occurred to us to question this logic, or even the source of his confidence. Whose voice did *he* hear?

This internal judge has been a double-edged sword in my life, setting me up for continual conflict, criticizing me harshly, weighing my self-judgements in a balance against what I might, rightly or wrongly, perceive to be Dad's judgement on any given matter.

My life's work, as first-born and only girl, has been to be Daddy's Perfect Daughter.

Look at the photograph again: it's in her eyes, directed at the camera's lens. Eight-year-old Mariah has spent most of her life defining herself in terms of other people's expectations. All her powers of deduction, reasoning, and observation have been employed to collect evidence from all available sources. Every conversation, every expression, every action has been analysed for clues.

What do you want her to be? She'll be it. What do you want her to do? She'll do it. What makes you angry? She'll never do that again. She is a *tabula rasa* for every person she meets. She will decorate this blank slate with your favourite colours, your favourite things. And when you look at her you will be pleased by what you see: everything you ever wanted, the perfect child.

But, no matter whether this pressure to be the perfect child was internal or external, I now see there was no way I could be both Daddy's Perfect Daughter and myself at the same time. The two are mutually exclusive because, quite simply, *I am not perfect* — an awful realization made after a lifetime of striving and failing to achieve the goal.

"You can do anything if you try hard enough."

My parents believed; I believed, too. Over the years we spent eternities practising the things at which I was totally inept: skipping, hurdle jumping, volleyball, tennis. They hated to admit failure and I hated to disappoint them.

We all had our Crown Royal bags full of marbles. We'd draw circles and dig little holes in the snow against the wall of the school. Eager play ensued. Only one thing: I was lousy at it.

I loved the marbles themselves: small ones with eyes the colour of a Siamese cat's; big crockers opaque with magical flecks of colour. I wouldn't play with my favourites because I loved them too much. But I'd lost all the others! I'd either have to risk my favourites or get new ones. Somehow.

The Kresge store just down the street from school was off limits. Mom didn't allow me to go there with other kids, many of whom came from the poorer environs of town and were therefore — by some parental leap of logic — suspected of shoplifting.

There was money in my pocket. I was alone. There was motive and opportunity. I went into Kresge's and chose the biggest, cheapest bag of marbles I could afford. There were no beauties in the bag, but no matter. These were for playing — that is, losing — with.

My heart thumping in my ears as I went out the side door, I stopped just in front of the firehall, opened the plastic wrapping, and dumped my cache into the Crown Royal bag. It had a thrilling heft to it. As I ran home, I practised my speech. Where should the emphasis go: *Look* at all the marbles I won? Look at *all* the marbles I won?

"Look at all the *marbles* I won!" I reported triumphantly.

Mom examined the proffered handful. "Where did you get them?" she asked quietly.

"I won them!"

"Where did you get them?"

"I told you, I won them!" I repeated, the conviction fading from my voice.

Her lips thinned; that look replaced her smile. "Why are you lying to me?"

How could she know? Was I wearing the price sticker on my forehead? Was I such a bad marble player there was no margin for even a miracle win?

My miserable admission: "I bought them."

"Why did you lie about it?" she asked.

"Because I'm not supposed to go into Kresge's," I blubbered, choking back the words I wanted to say: "Because I wanted you to be proud of me. I hate losing."

I got the wooden spoon for lying. I deserved it. But some part of me still whispers, "You got the wooden spoon for failing." Perhaps I deserved that more.

Whether by accident or by design, I was a solitary child. Despite playing roles for the family, whatever life my true self lived was an internal one. I'd talk about some of the things that bothered me — my parents expected it — but I kept all the suspect stuff inside. It was safer.

It was safer not to tell my parents Grandpa came to my bed. When Grandpa came to my bed, it was dangerous to think about what he might be doing there with me. There was shelter in the woods, in the wallpaper woods of my bedroom, with the little animals and the pastel flowers. I'd go there when he came, to hide behind the stylized trees, peeking out with frightened fawn eyes until he was gone. The rabbits, the deer, the skunks, and I: we were all safe in the woods.

"Where're you going?" I asked, watching my father load gear into the station wagon. The canoe was already secured on the roof.

"Hunting!" he replied. "With Uncle Piirko. Want to come?" He tweaked me under the chin. "You're a pretty fair shot at the target range. Just like your mom."

Panic edged in. *Don't leave me behind.* "Is Mommy going too?"

"Oh, no!" he laughed. "Mommy will be right here to look after you. I'm leaving early in the morning, but I'll be back in a few days."

Something to do with guns and meat in the freezer. Something he did for fun, to relax, my mother said. The lullaby that night: "Bye-bye Baby Bunting, Daddy's gone a-hunting. He's gone to get a rabbit skin to wrap the Baby Bunting in."

Was that supposed to be comforting?

Days later, I came home from school to find the station wagon in the driveway, coated with mud from stem to stern.

"Daddy's home!" Mom sang as I flew in the door. "He's in the basement."

As I thumped down the stairs I could hear him rattling around in the laundry room. I tore around the corner, expecting to throw myself into his arms for a bear hug. Instead, I ran right into a deer.

A five-point buck hung from the ceiling by a rope cinched around its hind legs, stretching virtually from ceiling to floor; it seemed to take up the whole laundry room with its massive flanks.

I screamed and screamed.

"It's okay, baby; it's okay," Dad tried to console me, bristling beard scratchy against my cheek, wood smoke pungent on his clothes. "It's just the deer I shot while I was hunting. It's going to hang here for a few days; then I'll take it to the butcher to be cut into meat."

Bambi! This was worse than Baby Bunting's rabbit skins; this was a wallpaper deer in the flesh. The woods weren't safe if a nice man like my father could go out clean-shaven and come back — bearded and smelly — with a deer to hang in my basement.

Staring at my wallpaper woods, I cried myself to sleep grieving for the beautiful animal hanging downstairs, grieving too for the lost sanctuary. Where could I go if there were hunters in the woods and predators in my bed? If I were banished from the living room with the TV's comforting campfire glow? I looked out the window and prayed to the Sleeping Giant.

Of course, I dreamed of the deer that night, a biblical dream.

"This is my beloved son," intoned a stentorian voice I assumed to be God's, "in whom I am well pleased."

The deer clicked his heels, unbinding them from the ropes, and stood facing me in the laundry room — which had turned into a church. At least, the windows were stained glass. "It's not safe in the woods," he whispered to me before turning and disappearing into a coloured sunbeam.

"Go down to the pantry and bring me two cans of corn," Mom asked before dinner the next day.

Reluctantly, I got the corn from the pantry. Instead of going directly upstairs, though, I felt pulled into the laundry room. Bambi. I stroked his soft fur, the flesh under it cool and solid. Walking around the carcass, I peered into the exposed ribcage. A clean, wild smell, a neat bullet hole.

"A nice clear shot to the heart," Dad had boasted. "No needless suffering. One second he was walking through the clearing, the next he stumbled and fell like a ton of bricks."

Fingering the bloody circle: *"Thomas, do you believe?" the Lord asked. "Yes, Lord; I believe."*

My mother's voice broke the spell. "Mariah, can't you find the corn?"

I raced back upstairs, almost dropping the cans on the way.

After that I looked for any excuse to visit the laundry room. I stroked the fur; I sat on the floor staring into the creature's sightless eyes; I talked to it; I sang it "Baby Bunting." It was my deer and as long as it hung in my basement I would hold my strange vigil.

"What are you doing here, honey?" Dad's voice startled me out of my reverie. "Don't sit on the concrete; you'll get piles."

He started to untie the rope from the ceiling. "What are you doing?" I asked, trying to keep the panic out of my voice.

"It's time to take it to the butcher."

"No!" I burst out. "I mean, can't we take some pictures of it, or something?"

He looked at me strangely. "Why?"

"I need it," I began, knowing I sounded ridiculous, "for a science project!" came the blinding inspiration.

He looked as relieved as I felt.

"Can I keep something for the science project?" I begged.

"How about a nice package of steaks?" he teased. I laughed uncertainly. "I'll see what I can do," he said.

Some days later Dad reversed the station wagon into the driveway, then hefted a ton of frozen butcher-wrapped packages into the deep freeze: Bambi-bits. I wondered how I would ever be able to eat them.

"I've got something for you, Mariah."

He handed me a cardboard box. The five-point rack of antlers. A tail. And a hoof. My vision lurched, as if the horizontal hold on my world needed adjustment.

"For your project," he said. "That's the right foreleg. Look, if you make a print in the dirt you can see how it curves out to the right."

"Thanks," I mumbled.

It was hard for me to breathe at dinner that night, let alone eat. I kept glancing at the gun cabinet, the centrepiece of the dining room, where the gleaming rifle with its telescopic sight was housed with its mates. I picked at the vegetables on my plate; I could hardly bear to look at the chunks of meat.

"It's venison," my mother said.

Call it anything you want, it's still deer to me, I thought.

"You have to try it, Mariah."

The unwritten law of the dinner table: you must try some of everything on your plate. Truth to tell, that statute involved cleaning the plate. And if you cleaned it too quickly, there was a good chance Dad would toss something else onto it. "Here, have some more!" Pokiness was a defence against his generosity.

"You have to try it, Mariah."

Nodding, I stabbed a morsel so violently the fork screeched across the plate, out of control. My hand collided with my milk glass. Splash.

"Jesus Christ, Mariah!"

Almost nothing could set Dad off into a rage at the dinner table as quickly as someone overturning a glass – this overreaction a holdover, no doubt, from his own childhood during the Depression, when milk was hard to come by. He would turn often to the china cabinet, pointing to the tiny mug with a bear on it that had been his as a child. "And damned lucky I was on the rare occasion when it was filled!" he'd say. His passion over spilled milk and the extravagance of his rage led me to believe milk was more rare, more valuable, than sacramental wine – than the very blood of Jesus himself.

Over the mop-up operation, the standard litany: "Can't you be more careful? How many times do you have to be told?" Hands and cloths and serviettes flying, dishes lifted, milk dripping through the crack between the table leaves onto my knees. I glanced at my brother – and saw one more hand added to the mêlée.

Splash.

"Oops!" Luke chirped, gleefully assuming the attention.

"*Je-sus Cher-rist!*" Dad exploded, so furious he had to leave the table to cool off.

With the focus thus deflected from myself, I stared at the meat submerged in spilled milk on my plate and brought the speared morsel slowly to my lips. The lump in my throat was huge and oppressive, but I reverently placed the meat on my tongue.

"Behold the Deer of God." Words from Mass tumbled in my head while I chewed. It was good. *"Happy are those who are called to His supper."*

I can do this, I thought, as I swallowed bite after bite. The Deer of God must be eaten. My head spinning with the words, the lump and the meat closing my thoat; my fat body falling from my chair. . . .

High fever, severe tonsillitis: "Never seen such badly infected tonsils," the doctor said. I had them out as soon as possible.

I attributed my A+ on the deer project to the visual aids. After I brought it home I gave the antlers back to Dad. "Don't you want to hang them in the rec room or something?" I asked. My brother appropriated the tail.

But that hoof I kept for myself. I don't know if it was tanned or just thoroughly desiccated, but it lasted a good many years.

"Do animals go to heaven?" I asked my mother once.

"I like to think so," she said. "There aren't too many truly evil animals and the ones that behave badly must have been hurt or mistreated."

"How will my deer survive in heaven without his right foot?" I asked.

She thought briefly. "Doesn't the Creed say, 'I believe in the resurrection of the body and life everlasting'?" I nodded. "Well, if we believe in the resurrection of the body, that means it'll go to heaven whole and well."

"Even if the hoof is missing?"

"Even if the hoof is missing." She spoke with such conviction I was reassured. Still, thinking it over later I realized the "resurrection of the body" wouldn't take place until after the world ended. Did that mean my deer would be limping around in heaven until the end of time? Surely not, not if he was the Deer of God.

❧

"What does this mean?"

"What do you think it means?" Dad shifted the *Oxford Dictionary of Quotations* more comfortably between us.

Sunday afternoons were quiet oases in my father's week. The hotel bar was closed, the pressure was off. We'd curl up together on the overstuffed couch next to the built-in bookshelves and leaf through the books: Winston Churchill; the *Odyssey* and the *Iliad;* the *Bible,* the dictionary. We'd read to each other, or he'd just talk. I didn't care what the topic was; listening to him was a way to be with him. If we had company he could be his most charming and entertaining self: recounting tales of his youth, telling picaresque stories. He'd forget I was within earshot until –

"Gabe," Mom would interrupt, inclining her head in my direction. The story would come to an untimely end, or limp along after editorial surgery.

" 'A man's home is his castle,' " I read, then ventured: "You don't have a home unless you live in a castle?"

Smiling, he shook his head slightly. "Not everyone can live in a castle, yet we all have homes," he said. "Every man is the king of his own castle and he tries to keep it — and everyone he loves — safe. That's my job," he said, giving me a hug.

If that was my father's job, then it was Mom's job to keep the peace. She was the conciliator.

"Don't wake Daddy," she'd tell us. "He needs his rest, or he'll be grumpy."

Luke and I would play quietly until it was time to get him up for the day. "Don't wake Daddy" — an unnecessary warning. He was *difficult* to wake; so difficult Mom had resorted to carrying a tray in to him, late every morning.

"*Now* you can wake Daddy."

And we'd pounce on the sleeping giant. Sometimes he'd feign sleep for a few extra seconds as we pummelled his lifeless form. Then he'd sit up suddenly, roaring and tickling. He couldn't be grouchy when faced with an inviting breakfast and the piping voices of his children. Perhaps our mother used us as her shield.

Mom tried to make our home a haven for him from the bedlam of the hotel with its drunks, the fights, the long, late hours he worked. When arguments broke out between the volatile Slovak factions of the family, she'd try to turn down the volume.

I'm sure my father truly believed his job was to keep everyone in his castle safe. That's why accidents were always someone's fault — failures of vigilance.

The few times I went into hospital there were always whispered — or not-so-whispered — assignments of blame.

At age two, with pneumonia. My parents told me they'd almost lost me then. Viral pneumonia, no one's fault — yet ultimately hers.

At nine, with tonsils. Again, somehow my mother should have been paying more attention.

At ten, with a broken leg. Whatever befell us was Mom's fault. Random chance could play no part in it, because random chance couldn't shoulder the blame my father needed to assign. If the price of peace was to accept the blame, she would. Sometimes I wonder if she was atoning for something – some failure, some mistake.

Six weeks in hospital with my leg in traction: surgery, metal pins, the works. I was scared at first, uncomfortable, and in pain. And alone a good deal, despite everyone's best intentions. But there were far fewer terrors in the hospital than in my bedroom at home.

Away from the dangerous woods of my bedroom I let down my guard. It was like a vacation for me – a vacation from myself and my incessant observation. I wasn't interested in what went on around me. In that private room I was an island unto myself, becalmed in a sea of terrazzo flooring. People could drift up to visit, but I couldn't leave – nor did I want to. That island was my universe.

Not having to waste time interacting with other students, I did my school work quickly each day. For there were stacks of books to read and virtually unlimited time in which to read them. At first I pigged out on popular pap like Nancy Drew and the Hardy Boys. But, like eating too much chocolate before breakfast on Easter morning, those sweets soon gave me a headache. I needed meatier stuff. When I got it, I devoured it voraciously: *The Chronicles of Narnia; The Hobbit; A Wrinkle in Time.* The complete works of Mark Twain. Steinbeck, even the ones that were too old for me. Everything I could lay my hands on.

Reading was all-consuming. I read late into the night; I read while eating. I itched – like my skin under the cast – for visitors to leave so I could get back to those worlds that I could visit in my head.

Two books I'd been given languished on the bedside table. One, from my maternal grandparents, on the lives of the saints; the other, from Grandpa Standhoffer: the *Complete Grimm's Fairy Tales.* Brought up on a diet of Disney, I thought the fairy tales would be too babyish. I avoided the saints for much the same reason.

When I'd virtually run out of other material, I picked up the large volume of Grimm and tested it, jumping in at random. The first tale I read was "The Robber Bridegroom." The miller's beautiful daughter was betrothed to a man she didn't trust. At his house, which, she'd been warned, was a den of murderers, the girl hid – watching as the robbers dragged in a young girl, plied her with three kinds of wine, then tore off her clothes, put her on a table, chopped her beautiful body into pieces, and seasoned them with salt.

Wow! This was great stuff! To think my mother had confiscated a contraband copy of *The Carpetbaggers* I'd acquired. It was tame by comparison.

I met several other characters in that sitting. The wizard who stole pretty girls to chop into pieces. The father who cut his daughter's hands off with an axe. The dreadful stepmother who served her stepson to his father in a stew.

When Dad came, I read "Godfather Death" to him. The physician, given the healing herb that makes him famous, tries to outwit Death and is himself struck down.

"Serves him right," Dad mumbled.

"Why?"

"I don't have a lot of faith in doctors," he said absently. "They all try to outwit death to make themselves look good."

He saw me — confined with my leg in the air — struggle to sit more upright and changed tack. "They do a good job, don't get me wrong!" he assured me, hastening to plump up my pillow. "I'm just not sure they all do what they do for the right reasons."

The holiday was over. Seen through my father's cynical eyes, my hospital world took on a sinister aspect. Here I'd been, screened off from the rest of the world by a wall of books. Everyone who'd come through my door had been invariably cheerful. I'd accepted the invasions of privacy — the bedpan, the sponge bath, the constant stream of nurses and doctors — as necessary, but benign.

But now: my father had issued a judgement and I needed to test its validity.

I asked the nurse to pull aside the screen. Instead of reading I watched the traffic go by, making eye contact with some of the commuters, even mumbling a shy "hi" to a clump of kids.

"Hey, there's a new girl in here!" one gregarious girl announced to a lagging companion. To me, "Can we come in?"

"Sure."

Motioning to her comrade, she settled gingerly in a chair at my bedside. "Been here long?"

"A few weeks," I shrugged, embarrassed by my previous lack of hospitality. "But I don't get out much," I joked, pointing to my encumbered leg. "What are you in for?"

"Appendix. I'm Alice, and this," she added, gesturing to the threshold, "is Jason."

I turned to greet Jason, my intended "hi" almost choked off by shock. He stood in the doorway on crutches, one striped pajama-leg with slippered foot on the floor, the other — out of sight above the hem of his bathrobe — missing.

"Mariah," I coughed. "Broken leg." We all laughed at the obvious.

Did I stare in horrified fascination, betraying my dismay? I tried to focus on Jason's face as he sat in the other chair. "Cancer," he said.

Somehow, I picked up the gist of the conversation through the buzz of static in my head, words floating in and out on the ether like WLS from Chicago on a clear summer's night.

Alice and Jason eventually left me alone to draw an obvious but startling conclusion: this was a place of life and death. My immobility had been a buffer against that reality.

Adult conversations I'd overheard without comprehending came flooding back to me. Women trading stories on the delights and horrors of childbirth, someone's botched gall-bladder operation, someone's hysterectomy. At the lake the previous summer, my mom had had coffee with the lady from the camp next door. The neighbour lifted her shirt to expose a web of scars. Shocked, I thought, *if she lifts her shirt much higher she's going to show her boobs!* Mom's commiserative hand on the woman's arm, the tsk-tsking, the "You'll be fine!" I suddenly understood there were no breasts under that shirt to be seen.

From the physician who tries to outwit death to a hospital full of physicians who chop people into pieces — it wasn't a spectacular psychic leap my dreams took that night. I awoke screaming, straining to escape.

Where I'd quietly enjoyed the first weeks of my stay without complaint or curiosity, now I questioned everything. Blood pressure, temperature, blood tests: "Why are you doing that?" I monitored every drug they gave me, noted everything they took away. I suffered the procedures with less patience, gagged on the food, hated the smell of the place.

To some extent I was homesick — and my parents took my fretfulness and complaints for just that. But it was more.

The last straw had to be the enema.

For whatever reason, I became so constipated that eventually, I could no longer deny my extreme distress. My mother comforted me while I explained my predicament, then left to speak with a nurse. They returned with all the equipment.

"Can't I just eat more bran?" I begged.

"Too late for that!" the nurse said cheerfully. "We'll have you fixed in a jiff."

Oh, strange child — no woods for you in this antiseptic room, no safe place to retreat, no darkness to hide your face. Bright lights and strangers and your mother holding your hand. With your head full of fairy tales and nightmares of doctors with their knives — the better to cut up little girls. Can you die of this? Bunged up to your eyeballs with shit and secrets? Can you die of shame as you suffer one more invasion? Can you drown in warm water as it fills you? Hold it, hold it!

How many parts can you live without, little girl? How many things can they take from you — those buds of breasts, that womb? Can you live without that leg, that shattered, pinned, useless thing that keeps you here?

And you think of the boy — will he die? He showed you his stump one day. Your heart beating in fear and fascination, something new setting all your strings vibrating and your crotch buzzing like a tuning fork. Something new. Like longing, like release.

I stand back from the little girl in the bed, watching from the doorway, through the screen. If I could avert this stone flying into the windshield of her soul, if I could change one thing, would it be this?

No. People have had enemas before and survived. If I could still her hand I'd keep her from picking up the unread book on the bedside table: *The Children's Little Book of Saints.*

Why did I not try to tell someone? Why didn't I bar the door? Or yell? Or scream? Or lock myself in the bathroom?

At the time I began to discern the pattern of my grandfather's visits I wasn't upset by what we were doing in my bed: the thing was still alien and unexplained. I was more upset by *who* was in my bed: I hated my grandfather.

He was a short man but large in girth. A family outing some time before we moved into Grandma's house: I walked with my parents while Grandpa walked ahead with his little dog, Fifi. The dog scampered along on short legs.

"Look at that little keg!" my dad exclaimed.

"Which one?" my mother laughed, "they're both as tall as they are round."

"A perfect example of the dog looking just like its master," Dad agreed.

Grandpa stooped to pick up the fat, panting animal, waited for us to catch up. He smiled; the dog smiled. My dad was right — they did look alike. I felt proud, certain we were speaking the same language.

Language was a barrier between us. Grandpa spoke English well enough, with a thick Slovak accent, for general purpose conversation. But to me, Slovak was the language of anger and exclusion.

When Grandpa and Dad were angry, they spoke Slovak. Slovak was fast, Slovak was loud, Slovak was scary. I hated conflict as much as my mother did, but the arguments were magnified because I didn't know what they were arguing about. Discussing politics. Ranting about my aunt Zoshka's latest demands. Disagreeing about the way things should be managed at the hotel. If I'd understood they weren't going to kill each other at the climax, it might not have seemed so threatening.

But when the volume rose and the language changed, when their faces flushed and their gestures broadened, there was danger in the air. *Don't wake Daddy*. My father, whom I loved, was someone else. I hated Grandpa for disturbing the peace, for turning my dad into an angry, incomprehensible, shouting stranger — threatened and threatening — who seemed capable of anything. Murder, even.

If the argument was not resolved to Grandpa's satisfaction, he'd walk away from it, purple in the face, sweating. "Paah, fooey!" he'd say, mopping his brow with his omnipresent handkerchief, "Crazy bastidd!"

If it went the other way, Dad would be left volleying the departing figure with one last barrage of words. Mom would try to calm him: "Gabe, come on; leave it alone."

How many times did I hear those words: "Ginny, I swear: someday I'm going to kill him!"

Cause and effect. I knew what would happen to our family if my father ever got angry enough to kill the old man.

"You take the breadwinner away from the family," Dad had said to his brother-in-law, "and you have chaos. You've got a man in prison, chewing out his guts, while his wife and kids are on welfare. Or the wife goes to work. There's no one home to look after the kids, so they wind up shoplifting at Kresge's after school. A vicious cycle: a new generation of felons, the destruction of both the family and of society."

Uncle Piirko had nodded sagely; it went without saying.

So, whatever threats my grandfather might have made to ensure my silence were magnified by my own projections of doom. Grandpa didn't have to say, "Don't tell Mommy and Daddy because your Daddy will kill me and the whole family will go to hell in a hand basket." I knew instinctively that breaking my silence would mean the total destruction of my family.

Yet, for the longest time, I didn't know *why* what we did in my bed was such a secret, because I didn't know what it was I was rubbing with such intensity. I'd never seen a grown man's penis.

How could I have been so naïve?

An extraordinarily modest man, Dad always locked doors. I never saw him naked or half-dressed, never surprised him in mid-pee, never walked in on a primal scene between my parents.

My brother Luke, of course, I saw naked all the time. But his tiny spigot of a penis hardly deserved its name.

It was the boys next door who changed my knowledge. They were twins, a few years older than I. Since there weren't many kids in our neighbourhood we were reasonably tolerant of each other when we wandered into each other's yards during the interminable summer vacations.

Casimir and Stanislaus were nice Polish Catholic boys, altar boys at St. Andrew's Church. They'd discovered (or created) an entrance into the shady substratum of their back porch. It was their clubhouse. They hooked up an extension cord with a light-bulb dangling from the low ceiling, dragged concrete blocks in for seats.

"Come inside," Cas invited, drawing aside the screen of unkempt ivy.

I stood outside the little patch of weeds and flowers bordering the porch, surveying the entrance to the "cave": a ragged hole in the lattice.

"Come on, Mariah!" Stan urged.

I hesitated, not from fear of the dark or the bugs and spiders I knew would be lurking. I was afraid to get my clothes dirty. To the child who could play for hours in the sandbox in her Sunday best and stay clean, this possibility was dismaying.

Temptation won out.

Cool in the shadows and dark – despite the naked bulb – underfoot, but secret. As if no adult had been there since the foundations of the house had been laid. It stank of dampness and sweating boys.

"Shhh," Cas whispered.

The screen door screeched above us. Mrs. Stachkowski thumped across the porch to the clothesline, took down some laundry, then stomped back into the house. We shushed each other and giggled behind our hands, thrilled by the danger of discovery.

I heard my mother calling. "Come back after lunch," Stan invited as I ran off to eat.

When I returned later, the boys weren't around. I hesitated, unsure if I should stay. Then one of the twins spoke. Reassured by the familiar voice, I stooped to draw back the ivy at the entrance of the cave.

A voice I didn't recognize, deeper than either of the twins' — almost the voice of a man — "No, no; like this," it said. "Haven't you ever done this before?" he asked derisively. "You have to rub it hard."

Rub it. My stomach lurched, the blood rushed in my ears. I drew the ivy aside gently, suddenly more intrigued than frightened.

They knelt in a circle as if praying: Cas, Stan, and the older boy from across the lane. He wasn't part of the usual group. Gradually, in the gloom, I realized they were kneeling because the roof was too low to stand. That they had their pants open and were worshipfully rubbing their penises. That the older one's equipment seemed different than the younger boys'.

"You have to rub it," he murmured, "rub it."

An intake of breath and a blinding explosion in my head like a flash bulb popping. The stick, the thing, my grandfather.

Shocked by the discovery, I lost my balance. Crashed headlong through the ivy, through the lattice, into the entrance of the cave where three altar boys knelt serving the god of puberty.

Screaming, shrieking. I don't know which of us was more surprised. Four bodies in such a small enclosure, all fumbling: the boys with their pants, me to make my escape. Adult footsteps clomped across the porch. I emerged into sunlight just as Mrs. Stachkowski came down the steps. I didn't stop. Not a graceful child — but I never ran so fast, down their driveway, through the back lane to our yard, and up the steps of my own back porch.

Now what? Hesitating with my hand on the knob, I heard Mrs. Stachkowski yelling, Cas and Stan pleading with her in Polish. Time to disappear. Bang! In through the back door and into the bathroom in one movement, not stopping to take off my sandals.

"What's all the racket?" Mom called.

"Nothing! I just have to pee," I shouted back, heart beating, head buzzing, breathless. Suddenly I did have to pee. I sat on the toilet, panting and thinking. Seeing the older boy's penis, seeing my grandfather's: "Rub it, rub it!" Not a billy club, not Aladdin's lamp. "Rub it, rub it!"

I vomited my lunch into the toilet; I vomited my breakfast. I thought I'd never stop heaving and weeping, even after my mother came to hold my head and clean me up.

"Poor baby. Too much sun. Let me cool you down."

She washed me, gave me a damp cloth for my head, found a fan to set up in my room, and put me to bed. I bit my lip to keep from starting all over again as I turned my head to the wallpaper forest. Somehow, mercifully, I fell asleep to a tattoo of hammering in the Stachkowskis' yard.

The nails in the new lattice next door had hardly stopped ringing under the hammer before the mothers had, obviously, conferred. For when I got up the next morning, still shaky and pale under my tan, Mom confronted me gently over my corn flakes.

"Mariah," she began, "did something happen yesterday with the boys?"

I could deny it, but experience – and the way she'd worded the query – told me she already knew.

"Nothing, really," I started. "The boys asked me to come back to the cave after lunch." I thought that explanation sufficient. She didn't.

"Did they take their pants down in front of you?"

"I was supposed to come back after lunch, but it was late," I wailed, bursting into tears. "They didn't know I was there! I kind of fell in. I didn't know the other boy."

"Who was he?"

"The big boy, from over there!" I gestured wildly, launching into a detailed but confusing narrative.

She sighed, reached for my hand across the table.

"You have to be careful with boys," she began reluctantly. "I'm not saying Cas and Stan are bad boys; you just caught them at a bad time, when the big boy was being a bad influence. But, as a general rule, girls shouldn't be with boys – especially older boys – in a situation where there's no one else around. Not in caves, not in bedrooms; an adult should be somewhere near." She looked at me intently. "Do you understand?"

I pondered a moment. "What about playing badminton with

Dwayne?" I wasn't particularly good at it and would have been glad of an excuse to say "no" the next time he came down the lane, racquets and birdie in hand.

"That's okay," she assured me. "That's in an open space, in the back lane, where I can keep an eye on you. I'm talking about *alone,* in a place where a not-nice boy could take advantage of a pretty little girl."

Take advantage. Now, what did that mean? Didn't Dwayne "take advantage" by thrashing me mercilessly every time we played?

Sensing my confusion, she pulled her chair closer to mine at the breakfast room table and put her arm around my shoulder.

"Sweetheart," she said, stroking my cheek, "it's a confusing world out there. You're growing up and you're going to have strange feelings about boys, just like they're going to have strange feelings about girls. You know, you can always talk to me about your feelings. If something happens that confuses you, come tell me and I'll help you get it sorted out. If someone does something that you don't like, you tell me. You don't have to put up with anything nasty from anyone."

Did that include my grandfather? Could I really tell Mom what Grandpa and I did in my bed? She brushed the tears from my face.

Hope sprouted briefly, then withered and died: my grandfather stood in the doorway.

"Morning, Pop," she threw over her shoulder.

"Good mornink, Geeny; good mornink, Marička."

Pushing my chair away from the table, I grabbed my uneaten bowl of corn flakes. "Morning, Grandpa," I muttered as I pushed past him, leaving my bowl by the sink.

A bower of cedars abutted the fence on the opposite side of the yard from the Stachkowskis', yielding a shady hiding place. I knew all the hiding places. Still cool there at that early hour, almost too cool for me in my shorts and tank top, it smelled pungently of bleeding cedar.

I sat on a stump and rubbed my goose-bumped arms. I should have brought a sweater. I thought about the things my mother had said, about boys being dangerous. I thought about what my grandfather might do to me if I told, what my father would do to him. Mom said I didn't have to put up with anything "nasty" from anyone. But surely it was my nastiness, wasn't it? He wasn't doing nasty things to me – I was doing them to him.

To touch a man's penis was so revolting I could scarcely breathe for guilt as my mind raced, torn between two logical possibilities. Running immediately to confession. Or never setting foot in church again. The priest would shout at me through the screen, breaking the whispery silence of the confessional: "You did *what!!*"

Revolting child – touching yourself "down there" was forbidden. "Nice girls keep their hands out of their pants," my mother had always admonished. "Pull your dress down – don't let anyone see your panties."

But to touch a man's penis! This was unforgivable. I'd have to carry my secret alone.

"Hi."

I nearly fell off the stump. I'd been so absorbed I hadn't heard someone approaching from the other side of the fence.

It was a child's voice. I could see pink slacks and shoes: a girl. I couldn't yet see her face for the branches between us. "Hi," I said to the shrubbery. "Just a minute; I'm coming out."

Like ours, the house next door was a big elegant one that had seen better days. And better occupants, too, for Dad forever complained about the foster kids who sheltered there: the mischief, the property damage. "Put all your toys away," he warned, "they'll walk off with anything that isn't bolted down."

But they had a swing set and a slide, monkey bars, and a basket-ball hoop. I played there occasionally when there was a girl my age in residence.

Pushing through the cedars, I stood by the fence and waited. The girl hung shyly back by the branches, then stepped out.

An intake of breath to say "hi," an expectant smile of greeting on my lips. I stopped breathing.

Dizzy with shock, I grabbed two metal fence spikes for support.

What kind of face was this? A Hallowe'en mask, hideous and rubbery. Scarred, twisted, varicoloured. A patchwork face. The eyes: clear brown and gentle. The eyes. Focus on the eyes. Smile. Don't show shock. Smile. Breathe. Say "hi."

"Hi," I said. "My name's Mariah."

"Corey," came a voice from behind the rictus of teeth and lips. Lips that weren't lips. Nose that was no nose. *Focus on the eyes.*

"I see you two have met!" came a cheery voice from across the yard. Mrs. Parsons, who ran the foster home, was what my father referred to as a "grass widow." Though I'd never seen her in a hula skirt, the possibility that she might someday demonstrate this talent was never far from my mind. She lived in the "Waverley House," as Dad always called it – referring to the old man who'd built it, lived there, and died there – with her son, Stafford. Staff Parsons was quite a bit older than I was, a quiet, studious boy who would "go places" – perhaps to Hawaii with his mother, the grass widow.

"Of all the houses in the city," my father complained, "Pandora Parsons has to turn the Waverley House into juvenile hall. She just wants a good address for Staff to put on his college applications."

"Not unlike your mother's wish for Zoshka?" my mother asked wryly.

"That's different, Ginny," he scowled. "At least my mother bought this house with her own money; she didn't get the city to pay for it."

Despite his complaints, he liked Mrs. Parsons. We all did.

Crossing the yard now, she wore her usual smile. "Corinne, this is Mariah. Mariah, this is Corinne." She put her hands warmly on Corinne's shoulders. "Corinne was in a terrible fire, Mariah. She was in the hospital for a very long time and has had many operations. She's a real fighter, aren't you, Corinne?" She gave the girl a little hug. "Would you like to come over to play?"

It would be impolite to refuse.

"Come around by the gate," she said.

She waited for me while Corinne went off to the swings. "Thank you, dear," she said, unlatching the gate. "Corinne's had a very hard time of it. Both her parents were killed when their tent caught fire. They were Indian trappers, you see."

I nodded, as if this explained everything.

"Corinne could really use a friend. Everything's very strange for her after being in the hospital for so long. I know you'll be her friend, despite the way she looks." Mrs. Parsons smiled again. "Now, run along and play, dear. Come any time."

I drew my feet through the playground gravel, listening to the sound of the stones tumbling against each other. Corinne sat on a swing, dragging her toe back and forth.

"Would you like me to push you?" I asked.

" 'Kay."

"It won't hurt you?"

"Naahw," she said, making it a long word. Her eyes crinkled up, the rest of her face hardly moved. I realized she couldn't smile much, if at all. Her face was a mask, useless for all but ceremonial purposes.

I was grateful to stand behind her, where I didn't have to make eye contact. Despite her assurance, I was certain I'd hurt her. I pushed gently, afraid of knocking her off the swing, for she had no grip on the chains. Her hands, too, had been badly burned, the fingers mere stumps, virtually webbed together by scar tissue. I gawked in fascination and horror. The network of scars continued up her arms where the skin was shiny, puckered. It still looked hot, as if the flesh might melt like a candle, leaving only a wick of bone.

Higher and higher she went, up to the treetops, up past the roof, as I pushed. A horrible sound escaped her lips. It took me a shocked moment to define it as laughter.

"Hlying, hlying!" she shouted. She half-turned to me. "You hly, too!" she commanded.

Flying. Yes, I would fly, too. I clambered onto the other swing and pumped for all I was worth. Flying. We were two birds, soaring into the sky. Freed from the ground — away from grandfathers, away from burning tents and hospitals, away from foster homes and gingerbread trim. Flying.

In bed that night my imagination soared. What sins had Corinne committed to deserve such retribution? Surely, God must have been very angry with her. Could Corinne's sins possibly have been worse than mine? Or had I not yet been visited with my own punishment?

My punishment. What would it be? A face like a mask, too hideous for people to look at? That would surely be a fitting punishment for "a pretty little girl." My mask was my smile: I wore it all the time. A mask of submission, like a puppy rolling on its back to bare its vulnerable stomach to a larger dog. Look at me, I'm no threat. I'm just a little girl. See how cute I am when I smile? Go ahead, rip my guts out with your fangs: I will smile. Without this smile I'm vulnerable to your anger. Without it, I'm not cute. I'm hideous, my sins on display for all to see. Without this smile you won't protect me. You'll let me die. Or you will kill me.

By the glow of the street lamp in front of the full-length mirror, I contorted my body. Curled my knuckles under in a vague approximation of Corinne's ruined paws. How could I play the piano with hands like that? No amount of grimacing, or sucking in my cheeks, could make my face like hers. It was only in the shadows, beyond the reach of reflected light, that my face began to lose its cuteness, lose its smile. A child who did such nasty things with her grandfather deserved to hide her face in shadow. I fell asleep with the pillow between my legs.

By most standards it wasn't much of a friendship, Corinne's and mine. We didn't do much. I'd invent little songs, or tell her stories: our in-flight entertainment. We didn't converse. Her carelessly sculpted lips might as well have been wooden. I knew nothing about her other than the little Mrs. Parsons had told me. But, despite the practical barriers to friendship, we flew together when we could – pumping for dear life.

One day, she was gone. "To another foster home, dear," Mrs. Parsons said. I shrugged. Kids came and went from Waverley House all the time, kids whom I knew better than I ever knew Corinne. But I never missed any of the others the way I missed her.

⟋⟋⟋⟍⟍

Mom's perfume that evening was so nauseating I was sure I'd throw up. I even tried to *make* myself throw up, thinking that, perhaps, if I were sick, she and my dad would not go out.

My mind raced with impractical plans: I would hide in the basement at bedtime; stay awake all night; keep the light on. When the time came, I trudged upstairs without argument. Would Mrs. Vanetti make me go to bed if she knew she was staking me out like a goat in lion country?

Luke snoring across the room. So peaceful; so safe. I had an idea: I crawled into bed with him.

When I woke to arms lifting me from my brother's bed, I thought I was done for. I struggled and squirmed, shouting, "No! No!" But it was only my dad, putting me back into my own bed.

"What's she doing in there, do you think?" he asked my mother.

"I don't know," I heard her whisper, "but she needs her own room."

My own room! Those words reverberated through my head well into the night. Where would they *find* another room?

There'd been a string of student boarders from the university occupying the "maid's room" whose rent had helped augment the family income. My parents decided they would not let it again. It would be mine.

My own room! What a prospect. Mom and I shopped for wallpaper, drapes, and a new bedspread. No namby-pamby wallpaper forest for me: I chose a grown-up floral print. I was excited by the "maid's room." It was small, compared to the room I shared with Luke, but it had its own toilet and wash-basin, its own staircase to the breakfast room, and *two doors*: one from the midway landing of the central staircase, the other between it and the back stairs. Such privacy, such luxury!

I craved privacy. I loved both the vast spaces and the little nooks and crannies the house afforded. I could usually find somewhere to be alone. In the "maid's room," I would be away from my pesky little brother, away from everyone else. Surely I'd be safe behind two doors.

Lulled into a sense of false security, I moved in. The trouble was, Grandpa followed me there.

Insidiously, the room's isolation from the main bedrooms worked in his favour. Everyone was used to him roaming the house at all hours, making himself a midnight snack, fetching yet another midnight beer.

All this nocturnal rambling took him past my doors – which my mother preferred I keep open. The room was always cold. Mom thought open doors would improve the circulation of heat from the rest of the house.

In through those open doors he came, shutting them behind him. I was not safe in my own room and I couldn't tell anyone. Because it was my fault. *I* was the one touching his revolting penis and compounding the sin by continuing to take Holy Communion without confession: I was not in a state of grace. I was unworthy. If I died in my sleep I would go straight to hell.

"Don't tell Mommy and Daddy."

Then, one time, he added: "Good girl. I bring you something special."

Something special? What could he bring me that would make me feel better?

I dreamed of Jesus. Well, I dreamed of the Sleeping Giant, rising from his reclining position. He walked across the bay. "I forgive you," he said. "Let me wash away your sins." A basin and a bar of soap. He washed my hands, the way he washed Mary Magdalene's feet, dried them tenderly and said, "Go, now, and sin no more." My hands were shining white, like beacons in the dark; never had they been so clean.

Grandpa kept his promise. Coming out of the garage the next after-noon after parking his car, he handed me a cardboard box. "Something special," he said, winking broadly.

It was a puppy. A tiny golden puppy, a wee handful of panting dog. "Jesus, Pop! We don't need another dog!" my dad exploded.

"Sasha will have it for breakfast!" The German shepherd wandered over, sniffed the tiny animal, and decided it was no threat. "It's not even a dog," Dad exclaimed, rubbing it behind the ears. "It's a glorified rodent."

"What kind is she?" I asked.

Dad examined her all over. "See these hind legs? She's part Chihuahua. Except for her colouring she's a dead ringer for old Fifi. You sure know how to pick 'em, Pop," he snorted.

"Partcha wow-ah!" Luke repeated gleefully.

When Dad put the animal down, she began to chase her tail frantically, making a complete circle of herself.

Mom joined the throng. "She looks like a doughnut," she said.

"Doughnut," I repeated. "That's her name."

Dad waved his hand dismissively. "What kind of name is that for a dog?"

Doughnut she became.

Grandpa came to my room again that night. The ritual proceeded. "You like the dog?" he asked.

I nodded.

"Don't tell Mommy and Daddy," he said, as usual, then added, "or something happen to the dog." He made a throat-cutting gesture.

The next morning was a Sunday. The house was quiet. I thought of Doughnut, whom Mom had placed in a basket in the back entry. I started dressing to take her out for a walk. There was a noise below me, like a yelp, then a funny rasping sound I couldn't figure out. I finished dressing, then went downstairs to see my puppy.

She wasn't in the basket. I looked all around the entry, checked the washroom adjoining it; I even checked all the shoes on the mat. No Doughnut. I opened the back door and stepped onto the stoop. No Doughnut. But her leash was there, tied to one of the spindles of the banister. I peered over the edge. There, on the end of the leash, was the dog, hanging some two feet off the ground.

I ran down the steps in my stockinged feet and quickly unsnapped her collar from the leash, laying her gently on the ground away from the stream of feces she'd let loose. Then I dashed back up the steps into the entry and shouted into the house at large, "Quick! Come quick! Something's wrong with Doughnut!"

Back outside I ran. I rubbed her chest. She coughed.

My dad came thundering out the back door, still tying his robe. "What's the matter?" I told him. "Another minute or so and she'd've been dead," he said. "You saved her life."

"Will she be okay?" I stroked the dog's tiny head.

"I think so."

Grandpa appeared at the door. Dad explained what had happened. "Don't tie the dog on the porch," he said and went inside. Grandpa nodded and waddled down the steps.

"I put doggy out this morning."

So he was responsible. He hurt my dog! He'd broken our pact.

I glared at him. "I didn't tell Mommy and Daddy," I said, "but you hurt my dog anyway."

He was alarmed. "No, no! I no hurt doggy. It was accident. Accident!"

Something hard clanged shut in my heart. I couldn't be bought with a dog; I wouldn't let myself love it. I helped Dad clean her up, but I didn't consider her my dog any more.

Just as well. She must have been a little brain-damaged by her brush with death, for she proved to be the stupidest dog we'd ever had: hard to house-train, deathly afraid of thunderstorms, snappy, and generally disagreeable. She attached herself to Grandpa, who fed her under the table despite orders not to. Within a year she was a fat little keg on short legs, as round as she was tall.

⌒

"A woman should have something to fall back on."

The images conjured up by this statement changed over the years as a barometer of my maturity. A pillowed *chaise longue* into which she would sink? A trampoline – in which case she would bounce back from whatever misfortune had befallen her? It was always "something to fall back on," never "able to stand on her own two feet."

My parents' expectations for me were traditional. Marriage was both expected and sacrosanct. The "D" word – divorce – was never mentioned. It wasn't an option. "Something to fall back on" entertained two possibilities: widowhood and, God forbid, spinsterhood. It was drilled into me that, in the event of marital calamity, one should have plenty of life insurance or be prepared to take up the world's oldest profession: giving piano lessons.

To that end, I embarked on piano lessons at the age of five. I plod-
ded along in a pedestrian manner, no prodigy, but no dunce either,
progressing through the graded levels, one a year, to match my grade
at school.

I was taught by various nuns who were not particularly gifted themselves. They were adequate teachers of technique and theory, sufficiently schooled in a fall-back profession to pass it along to young
ladies who would, eventually, pass the knowledge along to yet another
generation. These nuns were examples of the fall-back theory taken
another step: one could always become a nun, as a fall-back to the fall-
back. Provided, of course, that one had no children.

Doughnut had just been "spaded" (as I misheard the word): a mysterious operation that somehow precluded the arrival of puppies. Since
children and puppies were gifts from God, surely the convent should be
overrun with babies. Were nuns "spaded" too?

"Why don't nuns have babies?" I asked Mom.

"Because they're not married," she answered.

If I'd been searching for biological proof that nuns were somehow
more or less than human, if I'd been seeking advanced sexual information, the seeking stopped there. My mother's answer was inarguable –
sufficient for both my age and the times. It wouldn't wash with any
three-year-old these days, but it held for me then, in the early sixties.

I went to the convent, once a week, for my half-hour lesson.

"Time to go, Mariah," my classroom teacher would nod to me.

I'd silently leave the room, close the door behind me, and slip into
boots and coat and scarf and hat and mittens to trudge across the tun-
dra of the play yard to the convent, immediately behind the school.
Crossing the school grounds was like leaving the country. My music
books were my passport.

The convent door had a sanctified squeak which I tried not to aggra-
vate. Inside, it was quiet, despite the strains of distant music emanat-
ing from the teaching rooms. The gleaming hardwood floors reflected
even the candlelight from the chapel. Beeswax, floor wax, chapel flowers, peace: their combined scent was a heady relief from the classroom
smells of wet wool and imperfectly bathed children.

I loved to be either early or late for my lessons.

If early, I'd perch on a chair outside the room and listen to the lesson in progress. An older student could provide a preview of delights

to come in the Royal Conservatory stream; a younger student might be berated for lack of practice or attention – then I could feel good about my own progress.

If late, I might catch Sister at practice herself. I'd watch her fingers fly over scales in complicated key signatures: merry major scales with many brilliant sharps; minor scales like dirges, funereal with flats. And if I were very lucky, Sister might actually perform a piece. Bach. Beethoven. Mozart. I thrilled to them all, an unattainable goal. I was certain I'd never play that well, for, basically, I was lazy.

With enough innate ability to catch on quickly, I learned to read music as easily as I read books. A fair talent at sight reading, I could fake my way through a piece I'd hardly practised. The half hour a day I did put in was with little heart and not much inspiration.

The lessons in general were uninspired. "I'll hear your scales, now," Sister would say. Or it might be technical exercises, or an old piece, or sight reading a new one. Toward the end of the year we'd decide which piece from each category I'd play for my exam and I'd concentrate on those: memorizing, refining, perfecting. Come examination day I'd be in terror of failure but – somehow – I managed to pass each one.

I liked playing but hated to perform, even for the family. My mother loved to sing and always wished she'd learned to play the piano. She liked to sit in on my practice sessions, encouraging me, praising me. But she was untrained and easy to fool, her praise too extravagant for the amount of work I put in.

"I'd rather practise alone," I told her eventually.

It was easier alone. Easier to whip through the lesson, to hide my vague dissatisfaction with the process. The nuns' pace was probably too slow for me. I was never pushed; I never pushed myself. What I needed was motivation. I liked to noodle at the piano, to pick out little tunes of my own, to make up my own lyrics. I wanted to play the Bach and Beethoven that seemed so far out of reach, but I was too inexperienced to know that hard work and application would be more satisfying than just sliding by. I didn't know I could aspire to brilliance – and, perhaps, achieve it. A woman should have something to fall back on, but she shouldn't be so good at it that it might handicap her chances of getting married: brilliant women live alone.

"Thank God that's over with."

Nothing could kill a fledgling interest in music more effectively than

Sister's theory classes – unless it was the musical history classes to which the older kids were subjected.

I met Martina Leicester at the convent, prisoner of the same Grade 2 Theory class. We learned musical notation, key signatures, time signatures, mysterious Italian instructions for velocity and volume: *con brio, allegro vivace, lentamente, fortissimo*. Even the word "piano" had another meaning: softly. It was all extremely dry and seemingly pointless. If only Sister had made it fun, somehow; if only she'd told us, "Learn this and you'll be able to write your own music."

As it was, the biggest challenge of that theory class was to keep Martey from giggling. She'd burst into a stream of equine laughter at the least provocation. Repelled and entranced in equal measures by her lack of restraint, I never knew what would set her off. Her high-strung laughter was dangerous; being with her made me edgy and alert. We were instant friends.

"Perhaps you girls would like to play a duet in the festival this year," Sister suggested.

We looked at each other. The logistics were complicated. We went to different Catholic schools and lived miles apart. We were Saturday friends at theory class, but never saw each other otherwise.

"You can work on the music separately at your lessons. We could rehearse together for a few minutes after theory," Sister said. Our toothy grins were confirmation enough; our respective waiting mothers were consulted. We had a deal.

"But I didn't *want* to play in the festival this year," I wailed in the car on the way home, once I realized the enormity of the commitment.

"You can't back out now," Mom said. "You can't let Martey down. You'll just have to do your best."

I didn't know how good my "best" would have to be until the first Saturday practice. Until then, I'd never heard Martey play. Theory was strictly paper and pencil.

Sister had assigned me the treble section of the duet. It was light and airy, the staves like empty telephone wires with a few birds perched here and there. In contrast, Martey's bass score bowed under the weight of flocks of crows. The music was full of thundering chords and deep scale runs, dense with incidentals. Even my unschooled mother realized the bass was complicated. "My goodness," she said, "what a lot of notes!"

We had both studied the music at our lessons for several weeks. "Mariah, please play the treble first." Stiffening over the keyboard, I grimaced and plunged in as if I'd been thrown off a diving platform. I went down a few times and spluttered, but just about managed to keep my head above water.

Martey, on the other hand, not only played without drowning, she played with grace. Compared to my dog paddle, hers was the high dive with triple gainers, followed by a synchronized swim. She moved with the music; she didn't fight it the way I did.

"Wow, that was great," I managed to blurt when she was finished. I was completely outclassed.

"All right," Sister said brightly, "let's try it together. Listen to the rhythm: one, two, three; and a one, two, three. Count two bars and – begin!"

Several false starts and we were off.

It's a funny thing about duets: the whole is greater than the sum of the parts. My treble alone was high and insipid; Martey's bass was flashy and low. But together, even at that early stage – mistakes and all – the music was truly three-dimensional, popping into marvelous relief as if heard through an aural View-Master. I was delighted.

We left the lesson twittering and giggling. "You were great," I told her. "How much do you practise?"

"Oh, hours," she said.

"A week?" I asked.

"A day." She leaned in close. "Don't tell anyone, but I think I'd like to be a concert pianist," she whispered.

A concert pianist! I could hardly imagine such a thing, let alone dream it. I'm not sure I even knew what a concert pianist did.

"My mom's taking me to the symphony next week. Maybe you'd like to come?"

Again, the waiting mothers were consulted and plans were laid.

"Looks like a friendship is emerging here," Mom said, smiling indulgently. "Mariah doesn't have many friends."

Angry and embarrassed, I blushed furiously. Maybe Martey wouldn't want to be my friend if she knew I was such a wallflower.

"Neither does Martey," her mother confided.

We looked at each other. Martey whinnied. Maybe we'd be okay, after all.

The fledgling Lakehead Symphony Orchestra had been taken in hand by a flamboyant conductor who — by dint of his personality — managed to make, if not a silk purse, at least a suede one of the sow's ear he'd been given. Many people thought it was pretentious nonsense to attempt a symphony season in a blue-collar town. What need had woodsmen — or men employed in the paper mills, grain elevators, shipyards, or Hawker-Siddley plant — for classical music? Others felt culture was sorely lacking. There wasn't even a proper venue for such a production.

But I couldn't have been more excited if Martey and I had been headed for Carnegie Hall that Sunday afternoon instead of the high-school auditorium on the other side of town, its acoustic ceiling tiles watermarked like a Rorschach test.

The program that day? The pianist? I don't remember. But — for the first time — those Italian words took on meaning: *con brio* — with life! *adagio* — slowly, but so beautiful, so sad! *allegro* — lively and graceful! It was Helen Keller's water; it was a tactile understanding of the language of music, a breakthrough of the senses.

I boosted my practice time for the music festival. I worked hard at my piece; memorized it so thoroughly it kept me awake at night; paid attention to the dynamics of volume and speed. When I was certain I was alone I tried to move to the music like Martey did: hunching over the more complicated bits, swaying to the rhythm, stretching out with the expansive flow of the longer passages. I tried to *feel* it. I tried to let it move me.

Sister was pleased with my progress. Our Saturday practices went well. Martey and I coordinated our wardrobes, planned to drive to the festival together. The mothers would take us out for lunch after the event. We were nervous, but excited. I, who hated to perform, was caught up in the spirit of the competition.

At the auditorium we waved to Sister over the heads of other giddy and excited children dressed to the nines, and scanned the program anxiously for our names. We would play last in our age group.

"That's good," Mom murmured. "The judges usually remember the last performance they see." She squeezed my hand.

We listened to the others with a critical ear, winced at each mistake, shook our heads at hopeless botch-ups. We were better than that.

"Do your best," our mothers whispered as our names were called.

An endless walk to the stage. I felt sick with anticipation, but we smiled, poised our hands over the keyboard, counted to each other, and plunged in.

We started a little faster than we generally played. The spotlights were hot. I could hear the noise of the audience over the buzz in my head, the buzz that said I had no business showing off. Part of me wanted to retreat to the forest where I'd be safe from the invasive lights and staring faces. Another part wanted to use that nervous adrenalin to boost me up and over the top: to fly.

I'm doing it, I thought; I'm doing it.

That threw it: the centipede consciously thought about which foot should come next. I stopped short. Martey shot me a glance but kept going. My heart bumped around in my chest, an India rubber ball dropped from a great height.

"One, two, three," she counted, "and a one, two, three." I nodded, counting along as if at prayer, "and a one, two, three." Do it by rote, don't think. Autopilot kicks in and my fingers join Martey's on the keyboard to find their way without further incident to the flourish at the end. Amen.

We rose from the bench, bowed to the audience, and hurried back to our seats.

"I'm sorry," I whispered to Martey, ignoring my mother's attempted hug. "I'm so sorry I wrecked it for you."

"It's okay," she whispered back. "It was good except for that."

Yeah, good except for that. My fault. I bit my lip, chomped down on my tongue. Twisted the program into a tight tube while we waited for the judgement. Life imprisonment? The death penalty?

"Martina Leicester and Mariah Standhoffer should be commended for their poise during a difficult moment," read the adjudicator. "Their interpretation was sprightly and assured. They must not be put off from competing again."

We placed fourth.

At lunch I could hardly eat. It was supposed to be a celebration. Everyone overcompensated: Martey giggled even more recklessly than usual; I grinned until my cheeks ached.

On the way home I wept silently. Martey squeezed my hand. "It's okay," she said, "really. We can still be concert pianists."

Why had she included me in her fantasy? *I* hated to perform. Wasn't this failure proof that I was right? I couldn't get up in front of a crowd of people and leave myself behind, so blatantly unprotected. The lights would pierce through the unguarded husk while I was away, revealing the things I hid: my sins, my shame. I couldn't fly, after all. It would be the same every time. *We* couldn't be concert pianists. Only Martey could.

We passed our theory and our Grade 6 piano exams. We'd go to the same school in September.

"It's too bad we don't live closer," her mother said as she piled Martey into the car one day. "We have to nurture this friendship, don't we?"

And then, suddenly, Martey quit calling. I'd phone, but she'd have some excuse. My imagination ran riot. Somehow, Martey had found out about the things I did with my grandfather. Had I talked in my sleep? That was it, surely. I didn't deserve to have a friend. Now that she knew me better, she didn't like me.

"What have I done?" I asked. "Doesn't she want to be friends any more?"

Mom made sympathetic noises. "Her family's just busy," she said. "It's vacation time."

In the neighbourhood one day, "Let's drive by Martey's house," I suggested. I could see it before we pulled alongside the curb: a "for sale" sign with a "sold" sticker slapped over it. Martey was sitting on the front step. She stood up and brushed the seat of her shorts as I got out of the car.

No Martey giggles now.

"We're moving," she said. "My mom and I are going back to Saskatchewan."

"What about your dad?" I blurted before I could stop myself. It was obvious: they were getting a divorce. "Are you taking all your furniture?"

She shook her head. "They sold my piano."

"I'm sorry," I babbled. "Maybe you can get another one, when you're settled."

That same expressionless shake of her head.

"You can still be a concert pianist," she said with more urgency than she had thus far exhibited. "You can."

I nodded, not believing it — and, yet, needing to believe it for Martey's sake. As if, by keeping her fantasy alive as my own, I could keep hers from dying.

"I'll send my address when I know it. We can write."

I didn't wave as we drove away, but I stared out the window long after she was out of sight.

Mom quizzed me. "What was that Martey said, about being a concert pianist?"

"She thought we could both be concert pianists," I mumbled, without elaboration.

A mistake. The next time we had company, my mother insisted I play for the assembly.

"Mariah wants to be a concert pianist," she said gaily.

I couldn't have been more shocked if she'd announced, "Mariah wants to be an axe murderer."

No, no! I wanted to shout. *Martey* wants to be a concert pianist; it's Martey's dream, not mine!

Martey's dream. At the piano, I riffled through my music book until I found a piece I'd learned for that spring's exam. It was an *adagio*. I played it *lentamente*, *doloroso*, like I'd never played before.

⌁

Figure this: "What is the distance in psychic miles between Statement A and Statement B, where Statement A equals 'Mariah *wants* to be a concert pianist' and Statement B equals 'Mariah is *going* to be a concert pianist'. Factoring in the weight of parental expectations, calculate their accelerative or decelerative effect on the subject and predict her ETA at Statement B."

I had only to cave in once to my mother's demand that I perform for company before it became a regular occurrence. The subtle shift in language from desire to expectation of achievement was in place: Mariah is *going to be* a concert pianist.

There was no point in arguing the semantics of the transition, nor in denying that I even wanted to be a concert pianist.

"Don't be so modest!" I was told. "You can do anything if you try hard enough."

We'd been through this before. This was a hurdle I could jump, a volleyball I could return. If I'd shown no competence on the playing field, I couldn't plead incompetence at the piano — I'd already set myself up for the next crusade.

Suddenly, the nuns were not good enough for the budding prodigy: they were glorified (if not sanctified) amateurs.

Enter the university and the symphony, a symbiotic relationship. With the nascent university came a shoal of professional musicians; with the musicians came a fetal orchestra. Suddenly the plodding provincial amateurs who filled out the ranks were not good enough any more. Professionals must be enlisted; new professionals nurtured. Concert pianists were not trained by nuns.

If I'd thought the convent was a foreign country, the music department of the university – where my new teacher had his studio – was a different planet.

Its architecture was so modern the concrete had hardly set. It was all angles of brick and stone, hollow and echoing. No welcoming music drifted through the halls; only slices of sound escaped the soundproof studios when doors opened and shut.

The students were old compared to the mousy little girls and boys who skulked around the convent. They were brash and loud, with determined strides and confident smiles. They knew what they wanted to be when they grew up.

My mother ran me through the gauntlet for my first lesson, otherwise I would surely have fled in terror. We knocked on a studio door bearing only a number. It was answered by an alien creature with long hair, a beard, and unchannelled energy: the Tasmanian Devil himself.

"Welcome! Welcome!" he bellowed, pumping our hands and whirling us into chairs. "I'm Jim Altman and you're Mariah. What grade are you going into? Seven, isn't it?"

He grabbed the Grade 7 music book from my hand, twirled, and slam-dunked it into the trash can. "Seven's a lucky number, so lucky we'll probably skip it entirely. We're going to have a blast."

Without taking a breath he launched into his philosophy of musical education. "I don't believe in one grade a year. I'll assess your capabilities, but I don't do anything by the book. If your technique needs work, we'll work, but we'll have fun doing it. That I promise."

He grinned at us. Mom looked taken aback. With one fluid movement he turned, picked the music book out of the trash, and handed it back to me with a flourish.

"Keep it for a souvenir; we may actually play something out of it. Now, let's shoo Mom out of here, shall we? Then we'll get down to business."

He opened the door for my mother and bowed her through it. "See you in fifty minutes. There," he said, brushing his hands together, "it's always better with the parents gone, isn't it?"

I nodded uncertainly.

"You can call me Jim, or you can call me Jimbo, but you must never, never call me Mr. Altman. Are we straight?"

"Yes, sir," I mumbled.

He thumped his forehead dramatically. "That's another thing: you must never, never call me Sir. Okay?"

I nodded again.

"Okay. Play me something from memory. Anything. An exam piece, 'Twinkle Twinkle Little Star.' I don't care."

Less nervous for my last exam than for this lesson, I shook badly but managed a decent rendition of my "best" exam piece. He paced the room behind me while I played, then straddled a chair and sat down for the first time.

"You don't like performing, do you, Mariah?"

I shook my head, lowered my eyes, muttered, "Sorry to waste your time."

"No! No! That's not what I mean! Listen to me."

As if I could only understand him by lip-reading, I stared intently into his kind, furry face.

"Right now," he said, "you're an untrained performer. Oh, sure, you've played a few recitals and you've hated it. You're embarrassed and frightened. With good reason: you've learned how to play, but not how to perform. They're two very different things. You couldn't get up on the stage and do justice to *Hamlet*, let's say, without learning how to act, now, could you?"

I shook my head.

"Same with music. You speak the language, you read the language, but that doesn't make you Vladimir Horowitz. But you can learn!"

He nodded earnestly. "I'm going to teach you." His voice fell to a whisper. "We're going to find the part of Mariah that likes to twist people's emotions, the part of Mariah that likes bright lights and standing ovations, the part of Mariah that wants to be a *star*."

By the time he'd finished I was leaning forward, straining at every word. Listening; listening. And wanting to believe.

I knew I'd fallen into a good thing with Jim Altman. He was still young and idealistic enough to want to "make a difference" in the field of musical education. He had a holistic approach. He believed in musical immersion.

As his student I would receive free admission to all the concerts. Handing me a symphony schedule, he said, "There's no such thing as a free lunch. By way of payment you'll learn everything there is to know about the music to be played at each concert."

He loaned me records; he gave me books to read; he told me anecdotes about composers. In short, we would cover the entire syllabus without ever breathing the words "Grade 3 History."

One day, he shooed me away from the piano bench and waved me into a chair.

"Next to the piano, I love the oboe best," he enthused. "For me, it's the instrument closest to the human voice." He took it in pieces from its case and assembled it quickly, quacking like a duck through the reed. I laughed.

But when he started to play the "Adagio" from Bach's *Oboe Concerto in D minor*, I could scarcely believe such a compact instrument could produce such a beautiful sound.

He smiled at my awed expression. "I'll be playing the "Largo" from Dvořák's *New World Symphony* at the next concert. If you need any books, let me know."

"Dvořák!" exclaimed my father, breaking into a whistled rendition of one of the *Slavonic Dances*. "Now you're speaking our language, eh, Pop?"

Even Grandpa could whistle Dvořák. "Yah, yah," he winked at me, "too bad he was Czech, not Slovak!"

The house vibrated with the *Gypsy Songs*, the *Dances*, and the *Rhapsodies* for days, belted out by the record player in the living room. But I resisted borrowing the symphony from the library, wanting to hear it for the first time at the concert.

I'd never worked so hard on a school project as I did preparing my paper for Jim. It ran to almost twenty stiff, formal, extremely careful pages. An act of love in its truest sense, I poured my soul into it, learned so much I could hardly keep the project within reasonable bounds. I would have produced the *Grove Encyclopedia of Music* for him if I'd had enough time.

Turned out I had heard the *New World Symphony* before. It carried both a hint of anticipation and the surprise of familiarity. But Jim's

Largo – the program notes called it a lament for the beautiful Indian girl, Minnehaha – a love song of such breathtaking simplicity, such heartbreaking loveliness, it spoke to every drop of estrogen pumping through my almost-adolescent body. Jim's Largo was all for me.

If he'd been my shrink, it would have been a classic case of transference. But it's not called "transference" when you fall in love with your piano teacher. It's called a "crush."

I was sleepless with anticipation that whole week between lessons.

"An excellent report," Jim said. "You've obviously done a lot of work on it."

A ferocious blush – nothing dainty about the BTUs of pleasure radiating from my face.

"Next time, though," he continued, "I'd like it to sound less like the *Encyclopedia Britannica* and more like Mariah. I want to hear it in your own words, in your own voice."

"You mean, you want me to *sing* it?"

"If you want to," he laughed. "Certainly it doesn't have to be snobby and formal. Surprise me."

"What's the next topic?" I asked, my mind racing ahead.

"The Romantics. We'll focus on Robert Schumann," he said.

Although I soon learned the musical definition of the word was far more broad than I imagined, I was hooked at the first breath of it: *Romantic.*

Schumann's story was a love song. He fell in love with his piano teacher's daughter, Clara Wieck. The hapless lovers were kept apart, absence forging their bond ever stronger. Good thing Schumann had studied law before he took up music, for he was forced into protracted litigation with her father before the old man eventually relented.

By that time, Robert was finished as a concert pianist. The fourth finger of his left hand was paralysed – due, perhaps, to misuse of a device he invented to increase the spread of his hand for intervals. He turned to composition, and in both his writing and his music began to explore different aspects of his own character. Bold, extroverted Florestan; sensitive, introspective Eusebius.

Gobbling up Schumann's biography like a novel, I cheered for the lovers during the first idylls of marriage; prayed during Robert's years of mental disintegration; wept when he attempted suicide by taking a header off a bridge into the Rhine; felt helpless and distraught as he spent the last two years of his life in an insane asylum before his death at forty-six.

Mom caught me sobbing into my weighty tome while the second symphony announced his torment. "What's the matter, baby?" she asked, proffering a tissue.

"It's just so sad!" I told her the whole story.

She gave me a hug. "I suppose it's a good thing when history comes alive," she sighed.

Her words suddenly struck a spark against a nugget of information I'd acquired: that Schumann's works are like pages torn from his diary.

Here was a way to organize my presentation to Jim in a novel manner. Since Schumann was an intensely literate musician who possessed a poet's imagination, I would dig into my own soul to recreate his diary — in my own words — and sing it *in my own voice*.

It was a lot of work. If I'd been more experienced — and less enamoured of Jim Altman — I'd have been daunted by the task I'd set myself. I cleaned out the library's Schumann collection, arranged it chronologically, and listened to it with tape recorder, books, and notes at hand.

The early piano works reflect his youthful exuberance and his despair at not being able to marry the woman he loved. I chose a theme, all *Sturm und Drang*, and set words to it, along the lines of, "Oh Clara, your father despises me; when will I win your hand?"

After his marriage, he was happy for a few intensely productive years. I employed a joyful theme from the *Spring Symphony* and put inanely uxorious words into his mouth.

Taking poetic licence with the beautiful theme of *Träumerei*, I used it as a lullaby for his eight children. And so on, through his mental decline and tragic depression, suicide attempt, and subsequent death.

I called it "The Diary of Robert Schumann" and presented it to Jim with fierce trepidation. He was gracious enough not to laugh at my unintentional howlers. In fact, he applauded with great good humour.

"That's wonderful!" he pronounced. "Are you sure you don't want to cross over and study voice, too?" He laughed gently at my blush. "Seriously, Mariah, that's just what I wanted: your imaginative response to the music and the research. Robert Schumann's come alive for you. That's splendid!"

He strode around the small room like a captive baboon, stroking his beard and gesturing largely. "In fact," he said, halting in mid-stride, pointing a long finger at the bridge of my nose, "you've given me an idea for the student recital: we'll do your 'Diary of Robert Schumann'."

"What?" I squeaked, blushing a shade of purple between pleasure and terror.

"You can all learn a Schumann piece; there's enough variety of style and degree of difficulty for everyone. You'll be the narrator, of course – "

And so "The Diary of Robert Schumann, based on a concept by Mariah Standhoffer" was born. We reworked the narration together. All of Jim's students played in it: his piano and woodwind students, his voice students, everyone.

The introspective part of Mariah – Eusebius – stayed at home that day, hiding in the forest with the animals. Florestan, the extrovert – the part that loved applause – played *Träumerei* flawlessly while singing the words she'd written for Robert's lullaby, in her own voice.

One fringe benefit of the student recital was the chance to meet some of Jim's other music students. I shyly fell in with Jennifer Larson. We were in different eighth grade classes at St. Ignatius, but a familiar face was comforting in a sea of precocious strangers. A tenuous friendship was forged on campus; I was pleased and hopeful when she started to appropriate my company at school.

It surprised me that, as one of Jim's performance students, Jennifer had time for a social life. At least, she spent so much time talking about boys I assumed she had a social life.

I, on the other hand, breezed through my homework for school and, spurred by devotion to Jim, spent several hours a day practising the piano or frittering away my "free" time in pursuit of the megaprojects that would win me his regard and – dare I hope? – love. I would win Professor James Altman's devotion the way Clara Wieck had Schumann's, only *I* would be able to save my musical genius husband from despair and madness.

Compared to Jim, the boys at school were idiotic creatures, uncouth and uncultured. Most of them were shorter than Jennifer and I, essentially objects of ridicule.

"Isn't he cu-ute?" she would gush, hiding her giggling face behind her locker door, while I craned my neck and gaped in search of a boy who matched her description.

"Which one?"

"Joey!" she'd admonish, as if he were the only specimen rare enough to attract her eye.

In order to keep Jennifer's favour, I felt compelled to feign an attraction I didn't feel, to assume a vocabulary of admiration I didn't possess. As with most games, I was inept.

"Don't you *like* boys, Mariah?" she asked one day.

"I like *boys*," I hedged, "but I'm not fond of these, these *children*." I tried sophistication. "I like *older* guys."

"Like who?"

Jennifer's vaguely awestruck tone both pleased and frightened me. Like *Jim*, I wanted to say.

"Like," I grasped at a straw of truth, hoping to spin it into a bale, "Jason Burns. We call his parents 'uncle' and 'auntie,' but we're not related. Now, he — *he* is cute."

"How old is he?"

"Sixteen," I said, wondering how long the interrogation would continue.

"And does he like you?"

Does he even *know* me? I'd grasped at family friends, but I hadn't seen this particular son in years. An enigmatic smile, a raised eyebrow. It was enough.

"Wow," she breathed. "Sixteen."

Now that I had somehow achieved the upper hand, what was I supposed to do with it? And how in the world could I keep it?

An almost-sleepless night, trapped in a web of lies — what had I done? I remembered the marbles. I remembered third grade: porky little Mariah who hated being overweight, who endured the ridicule visited on the class klutz with as much grace as she could muster. But who wished — how she wished! — that she could be slender like the others, that she could skip double-dutch, that she would not strike out at baseball.

I'd had the flu. "I bet you've even lost a few pounds," my mother said. What a bonus! I walked around in a cloud of slenderness all morning.

"How are you feeling, Riah?" Rosa asked in the cloakroom as we dressed for recess.

"I feel fine now," I said, "but I threw up so much I lost five pounds."

"Wow!"

Rosa looked so impressed I couldn't stop myself. "The *first* day. I was so sick the next day I lost *ten* pounds." She was gullible, so I continued, "And another five pounds the day after."

The teacher entered the cloakroom.

"Mrs. Manfred," Rosa babbled, despite my hand signals, "Mariah was so sick she lost twenty pounds!"

"Did she?" A long look, a little smile. "Isn't that nice?"

I could read that look. It said: "Pitiful child; overweight, ugly, and a liar to boot!" Faint with humiliation, I wanted to sink through the floorboards. How many times had my dad read those words from the *Oxford Dictionary of Quotations*: "What a tangled web we weave." Hadn't I learned anything?

Trussed up like a fly for the spider's dinner, I lay awake concocting an elaborate fantasy love affair suitable for reporting to my boy-crazy friend. Poor Jason. To be the subject of such deceit!

I never volunteered any information, released details reluctantly when pressed. I even tried to avoid her — but Jennifer pursued me relentlessly, forcing me out of my anonymous group into her "cool" group. It was flattering but terrifying: as if I didn't have enough secrets, here I was waiting to be exposed as a fraud.

"Would you like to come to my birthday party? I'm having a sleep-over," Jennifer asked.

Mom's radar could generally be counted on to discern my mood. If I needed an excuse to get out of a particular invitation, she'd provide one: the good old parental veto. In this case she failed me. She was delighted that one of the "cool" crowd had invited me to sleep over.

Couldn't she read my mind? That I'd prayed she'd say "no"? It was the thing with Martey all over again: "We have to nurture this friendship." As if I was socially backward. Which I was; which I deserved to be. If friendship was so difficult, I preferred to be a hermit.

Friday night arrived. Terrified, I tried to make myself sick after dinner, wishing I could just be tucked into my own bed.

I clung to my father. "I love you, Daddy," I said, warm within his embrace, perched on his knee.

"I love you, too, baby."

"Daddy's girl," Mom smiled at us across the kitchen.

I kissed him. *Daddy's girl.* I kissed him again.

Was it practice for when I'd kiss a boy? It was nice, it was warm, it was comfy. Would it be different with a boy? How? Why? Self-consciously, I flooded his face with kisses, thinking, yes, I'm practising. I'm practising how to kiss a boy.

"Boy, am I ever lucky tonight!" he grinned.

"Time to go," Mom announced. I let myself be dragged off to the party.

An impostor entered the Larsons' house that night to mingle with Jennifer's friends. Girls I hardly knew, girls for whom I was expected to be cool. We got into our pyjamas, talked, giggled for hours and played records in her bedroom: songs about love; holding hands; kissing.

What did these children know about romance? I thought, thinking of the Schumanns. Now *that* was love: Clara never composed another song after 1855, the year before Robert died. As if all her creative powers died with him; as if he'd been her inspiration, her life.

Almost asleep, nudged by an elbow: "Mariah's been kissed by a boy; isn't that right, Mariah?"

"I was practising with my father before I left the house."

Off guard, I'd spoken my thought aloud.

"What?!"

"Practising with your father?"

"Were you *frenching*?" someone asked. "Geez, isn't that *incest*?"

The *coup de grâce*, delivered by Jennifer: "What do you need to practise with your father for, if you've been kissing Jason?"

Indeed. She had me there. "Practice makes perfect," I managed. Faking a yawn, I rolled over and pretended to sleep, all the while hoping to be struck by lightning.

Jennifer's cousin jumped on the bed.

"Ow! Watch it!" I mumbled.

She clambered in beside me and pulled the covers over both our heads. "Oh, did I hurt you? Let me kiss it better, Mariah," she teased. "Let me kiss your boo-boo." She made a smooching sound on the back of her hand, then another. "Practise with me, Mariah," she crooned. "Practice makes perfect!"

We both laughed. Came up for air, greeted by silence.

All eyes were upon us. "Hey, what? We were just joking!" I looked wildly around: there was not a smile in sight.

"Let the two lesbians sleep together," Jennifer said, "we'll sleep in the other bed."

My heart thumped wildly. I wasn't entirely sure what a lesbian was, but I knew it wasn't good, judging from the looks we got.

"Lezzy, lezzy!" came the chorus, building to a crescendo.

"She kissed her own hand!" I howled miserably.

A quote I'd never quite understood before came to mind: "The lady doth protest too much, methinks." I shut my mouth and prayed for the night to end.

"Have a nice time?" Mom asked.

"It was okay."

Jennifer waved from the doorway. "See you at school, Mariah!" Her words were no farewell; they were a threat.

"What's a lesbian?" I asked.

Mom shot me a look. "Where did you hear that word?" she asked. "At Jennifer's?"

I shrugged. "Just around." I regretted the question.

"In what context?" she pressed.

"In the context of she called me a lesbian!" There would be no end to this now. Why, oh, why had I opened my mouth?

"She did what?" Mom shouted, braking at a green light.

"Is it so terrible?"

Silence. She drove on calmly, trying to collect her thoughts. "A lesbian is a woman who doesn't like men," she said eventually.

A woman who doesn't like men. My mind churned around the definition. I slipped away to the bookcase at the first opportunity, pulled the Oxford dictionary down from the shelf.

Lesbian, adj. & n. of Lesbos (~ vice, Sapphism); (n.) female homosexual. Little enlightenment in that entry.

Homosexual, adj. & n. having a sexual propensity for persons of one's own sex. Had to look up "propensity."

Turned rapidly to "S." Couldn't find "saphism." Ah ha; two p's. *Sapphism, n. unnatural sexual relations between women.*

That was clear enough. I felt sick. My imagination could not encompass unnatural sexual relations. Nor could it even grasp *natural* sexual relations. From my limited and perverse experience, sex had something to do with penises: secret penises in the dead of night, accompanied by the stench of grandfather's beer and cigarillos and old man's body.

What could be natural about something so disgusting?

I knew enough to understand my parents must have had natural sexual relations at least twice during their marriage. Robert Schumann must have done it at least *eight* times with his beloved Clara; small wonder he'd died insane. Johann Sebastian Bach had had twenty-odd children! Had he died of insanity, too? Or had his wife?

And if I were to marry Jim Altman I'd have to do it with him.

I barely made it to the washroom in time. I emerged, with trembling knees, to a round of Assignment of Blame.

"What do you know about these people?" my father demanded. "How could you let her go to a stranger's house for a slumber party! She's just a child. At her age she should be at home, safe in her own bed, not out cavorting with perverts!"

"She has so few friends; it *is* possible to shelter her too much," my mother defended.

"No" – a thump on the table, the clink of leaping cutlery – "No; you can't shelter a child too much. A drawbridge and moat wouldn't be too much. Our duty is to protect! We have failed in that duty! We've exposed her to inappropriate language and an inappropriate situation."

My mother's voice, inaudible.

"Ginny, if you can't do it, I will. I'll get on that phone and blast them from here to kingdom come. I've half a mind to go over there with the shotgun, put some fear of the Lord into all of them. Little girls with sewer mouths, and they call themselves Catholics!"

Mother's voice, conciliatory.

"No," he roared. "If we don't champion her cause, who will? I'm going outside. If you haven't spoken to that little harlot's mother before I come back in, *I'll* make the call."

Sound of door slamming. Silence. Sound of phone dialling. Mother's voice: apologetic.

I supposed that Jennifer would now be duly sentenced and incarcerated for her crimes.

But Jennifer had a truly nasty streak. Jennifer had power, both in school and out. She could make things rough for me with Jim's music students around the university; she might even tell Jim!

A sleepless weekend followed. What could Jennifer do to me? How bad would it be?

It was worse than I had imagined.

Jennifer must have spent the entire weekend on the phone. Everyone knew. Kids who'd never before noticed me now giggled behind their hands and pointed when I walked through the halls. Boys smirked derisively, whispering, "Lezzy! Lezzy!" just loud enough for me to hear. Notes were left in my homeroom desk, in my locker, stuck to my back: "Kick me: I'm a lesbian." If I'd been a nonentity before, now I was a social pariah. Even the geeks didn't want to sit with me at lunch, so I skipped it.

My desk in homeroom was positioned right by the door. In order to avoid making eye contact with anyone, I took to reading whatever I could lay my hands on, usually the dictionary. There was something comforting about it. It was my only friend. All those words: nuances, shadings, economy, precision of meaning. Always something new to discover, something exciting to learn. If I amassed enough words perhaps I could prove my innocence.

Since I'd stopped eating lunch in the gym, I needed someplace to go. I approached the music teacher and received a papal dispensation to use the classroom piano during the break. It was found time. I worked feverishly for Jim; always for Jim. So far, Jennifer had proven impotent in tarnishing that relationship. Jim treated me as he always had. My whirling dervish. My romantic genius. How could I be a lesbian if I harboured such mad fantasies of Jim?

Jim's music studio at the university – just the thought of it – became a haven, like the wallpaper forest used to be; where part of Mariah could go when she needed to hide. The hurting Mariah, the private Mariah, went there so she could play like Clara Wieck, in a little room where Jim would love her and hold her and tell her she was beautiful. Away from bright lights and prying eyes, where her secrets were safe, where no one would laugh and call her ugly names, where a genius would call her "Beloved." Away from herself.

With her feelings thus compartmentalized, Mariah, the performer, began to walk the halls, ignoring the stupidity around her. When she was on stage, she was invincible. It didn't matter if the audience threw tomatoes, or booed, or crinkled candy wrappers, she could not be touched. She was Florestan; she would survive.

Those horrible clouded months had a silver lining: they precipitated the development of my performing persona. I don't know if I would otherwise ever have achieved it.

Jim was astounded and delighted by the change, by the fierceness with which I grasped the music, the hunger with which I consumed it. The distance beyond myself I travelled to reach it.

"Yes, yes!" he exclaimed after one particularly thrilling run-through of Grieg's *Jeg elsker dig* into which I poured every ounce of frustrated, unrequited love; every ounce of rage and impotence; every adolescent longing. *Jeg elsker dig*; I love you. In that transcendent moment, I used the energy, the sickly excited feeling in the pit of my stomach. I pumped myself up and over the top: I flew.

"You've got it! Whatever it is, you've got it." He danced me in a little jig around the room. "I don't know how you've done it, but I wish you could bottle it."

Just when I thought I'd faint from happiness, he kissed me.

A big fuzzy-caterpillar kiss. A fatherly kiss, a chaste kiss. Full on the lips; brief, but strong. Like lightning; like love.

He stood before me, grinning hugely, his moustache twitching with pleasure. "Sit down," he commanded. "You just did *Hamlet*."

I could hardly wait to get to that room at noon every day to throw myself into the music, the music that brought me close to Jim. The anticipation set me vibrating in waves. Now that I'd learned to fly I was addicted; needed the thrill of it like a drug that would take me out of myself and up so high that the oxygen was thin, leaving me giddy and breathless.

As I brought the piece I was playing to its climax, there was applause. I whirled in surprise.

"Sorry! I didn't mean to startle you."

A boy. He leaned against the teacher's desk as if he belonged there, long legs crossed at the ankles. I'd seen him around, but we had no classes together.

"I'm Dan McAllister."

"Mariah Standhoffer."

"I know who you are," he said. "Everyone knows who you are."

Flushing, I looked down at my hands to avoid his eyes. He was taller than most of the other boys; looked older. He wore motorcycle-type boots and a black leather jacket, altogether too slick. I was hazy on social distinctions: did he qualify as a greaser?

"That was beautiful," he said. "What was it?"

"Bach," I offered. "*Goldberg Variations*."

He nodded as if he knew what I was talking about. "Don't let me stop you." He gestured to the keyboard. "Do you mind if I stay? I'd like to listen."

I minded greatly. I'd lost my concentration, my persona. No longer Mariah Standhoffer, concert pianist, beloved of Jim Altman, I was Mariah Standhoffer — social pariah, piano geek — flustered in the presence of a strange boy. I was too embarrassed to tell him to leave. So he stayed.

By my new standards I played badly. It certainly wasn't *Hamlet*. But Dan didn't know any better; he said it was wonderful.

"Variations, eh? One song done differently in each piece?"

I nodded.

"Show me."

He sat beside me on the bench. "This is the main theme," I said, playing part of the Aria. "And this is how he changes it." I played snippets from a few of the variations: fast, slow, major, minor.

"How many are there?"

"Thirty. Then you play the main theme again."

He gave a low whistle. "How long does it take to play the whole thing?"

"Almost an hour and a half, if you don't play too fast."

"Or too slow!" he laughed. The bell rang. End of lunch hour. "Come on," he said, "I'll walk you to your class."

Unable to think of an excuse, I walked beside Dan McAllister through the school halls, blushing crimson, certain all eyes were upon us.

Dan came to the music room on a regular basis. Not every day, just often enough that I came to expect him. And, subversively, to miss him when he didn't show.

Sometimes he'd sit in the first row of desks, lanky legs stretched out into the aisle. Other times he'd sit beside me on the bench, invading my space, inhibiting my movement with his presence. I'd blush if he sat so close I could feel the heat of his thigh pressed against mine; was alert to his aftershave, the tobacco smoke on his clothing.

He treated me respectfully; asked questions that demonstrated a glimmer of intelligence. I was both flattered by his attention and put off by it: I didn't know what his motives were. And I was too shy to tell him to get lost.

"Just a word of advice, Mariah," said one of the girls who hadn't spoken to me in months. "Dan McAllister doesn't have a very good reputation," she whispered.

"What do you care?" I asked, surprised by my own effrontery.

"I don't," she huffed, slamming her locker door.

Jennifer Larson approached me. "Hi, Mariah," she gushed, all sarcastic sweetness.

"What can I do for you?" I asked coolly.

"I've got a message from Dan." She leaned conspiratorially into my locker. "He wants to talk to you during fire drill today."

I shrugged. "It's a free country."

"No, you don't get it," she insisted. "He wants you to find him on the field during the drill."

"Why?" I asked, suddenly alarmed and suspicious.

"Listen," she hissed. "Your reputation's been shot to hell by this lesbian thing. Everyone's seen you and Dan together. You can clear yourself, just by taking a stroll across the yard." Leering at me, she said, "You're in no position to say 'no'," her voice dropping to a whisper. "Unless it's true, of course. That you're a lesbian," she added, for clarification. She winked broadly, then turned and left.

What did all this mean? That I could regain my reputation by getting mixed up with a guy who had a bad one? What kind of simpleton did she take me for? On the other hand, it was just a stroll across the yard, a cakewalk.

I was a bundle of nerves all afternoon, and jumped like a cat when the fire bell finally rang. My class was near the exit. Ours was one of the first groups on the field, I saw with some relief. If Dan wanted to see me he'd have to find me.

He did. He actually waved to me like a guy in the Clairol commercials: "The closer he gets, the better she looks." My traitorous heart did a little flip-flop. (What would Jim think? I felt somehow unfaithful.) The crowd parted — as if by prearrangement — as he made his way through the throng, leaving a little circle of privacy around us.

Standing close to me, Dan tipped his head down to speak. "I'm having a little get-together on Friday night. I'd really like it if you could come."

"Gee, I don't know," I started inanely. "I'll have to ask."

"I'll call you tonight," he said. "I really hope you can make it." He looked sincere, if dangerous, in a James Dean sort of way. James Dean; J.D., Juvenile Delinquent. I almost giggled.

What would my parents think? It was impossible. Why had I not said "no"? What did I care if the whole school thought I was a lesbian? *I* knew I wasn't. At least, I was pretty sure I wasn't. Or was Jennifer right? Was my reluctance to play the game indicative of "unnatural" tendencies?

Extremely uncomfortable under the watchful eye of the entire student body, I tried to smile and laugh and fling back my hair in that appealingly feminine way the Breck girls had. I was never so happy to hear the "all clear." Dan walked with me as far as he could.

It was strange: the thawing of the chill around me was almost palpable. People smiled at us approvingly, as if we'd passed some sort of test. Girls who hadn't spoken to me in months stopped to chat. Boys who just yesterday had hissed "Lezzy" at me in corners and on staircases were suddenly thumping Dan on the arm and greeting me by name. I was sure it wasn't my imagination. We were enveloped in a fog of goodwill the likes of which I'd never before experienced.

I dropped a bombshell into the dishwater that evening: "Dan McAllister asked me out," I told my mom.

"What did you say?" she asked, looking at me, reading me.

"I said I'd have to ask."

She nodded. "When?"

"Friday night."

She cleared her throat. "Well, sweetheart, I'm afraid you can't go. You have your music exam on Saturday morning."

Of course! My line of retreat, without dishonour.

By the time he called I'd convinced myself I was crestfallen; I managed to turn him down politely and convincingly.

"I won't keep you late!" he protested.

"Maybe not," I said, "but I really need the time to study. Otherwise, I'll be a wreck."

A white lie. I was as prepared for the music history exam as I'd ever be; Jim's preparation had been unconventional but thorough. I spent that evening with the notebook on my lap virtually ignored while I doodled on sheet after sheet of loose-leaf: *Mrs. James Altman. Mariah Altman. Mariah Standhoffer Altman.* It would look good on the marquee at Carnegie Hall.

Having run out of paper, I languidly reached across to the metal ashstand and scrawled "Jim Altman" with my ball-point. Realizing what I'd done, I sat up hastily, spat on my finger, and rubbed furiously. The ink came off on my finger, but the words were etched into the chrome: "Jim Altman," large as life, in my finest hand.

Now what? There was nothing for it but to hope my mother wouldn't notice, a futile hope at best. I forced myself to relax. No point in worrying now; I'd catch hell eventually.

I should have ended the autograph session then, but I wasn't done fantasizing. I pushed my watch up my right arm as far as it would go, took my ball-point to the little untanned circle it left and marked on it a stylized "JA," the "J" forming one arm of the "A."

A tiny tattoo would be nice, I decided. Too bad the ink wasn't permanent. But something else might be.

Taking the compass from my pencil case, I examined its tip. Not too dull after a year of geometry. I poked myself experimentally, scratched at the outline of "JA." Bearable. I applied more pressure, gratified by a few drops of blood. If I could just achieve a nice outline, pick off the scab a time or two, I might create a nifty little scar. I'd done worse to my knees learning how to ride my bike. Just a discreet scar in the form of "JA": a symbol of my love and devotion.

"The exam's three hours long," I reminded my mother at breakfast, "but I might be done sooner, if you want to come a little early."

"That's all right," she said casually, "Mrs. Larson will bring you home."

"What?!" I shrieked.

"Jennifer's mom called yesterday. She thought it might be nice if you girls could get together after the exam. So she offered to bring you home later."

"You didn't even ask me!"

"I'm sorry; I thought it'd be a nice surprise. And it would be more convenient for me today. I've got lots to do."

I shook with rage. Here I'd endured six months of hell at Jennifer's hand and I was expected to make nicey-nice with my character assassin for the sake of convenience? I felt betrayed. But I said nothing.

Nor did I say much on the drive to the university. Mom attributed it to nerves. "Don't be scared, sweetie; you'll do fine." She reached over to pat my hand, tried to kiss my cheek. For the first time in my life, I deliberately pulled away.

"Not here," I muttered.

She smiled; a little hurt, maybe? "I forget; you're growing up. Good luck, honey. See you at home later."

I watched her wheel away. My throat closed; I had to blow my nose three times before I found the examination room. Hay fever, I told myself.

The exam went well. How could it not? I had the knowledge and a new vocabulary to complement it. I was only assailed by butterflies when I was finished writing: I was nervous about going home with Jennifer. There was bound to be a quiz and I hadn't studied for that. I was certain Dan McAllister would figure heavily in the examination.

She waited for me by the door. "So, what did you think?"

I shrugged. "Piece of cake."

Jennifer prattled all the way home, as if nothing had ever happened. I spoke in monosyllables when comment was expected. Her mother fed us a dainty lunch.

"C'mon," Jennifer said, wiping off a milk moustache. "Let's go to the park."

The Larson house was a few blocks from the Leicesters'. I stared longingly at Martey's house as we walked past, wishing I could be with her instead of Jennifer. Our letters had been brief and difficult. I couldn't tell her the whole school thought I was a lesbian; couldn't tell her I could fly; couldn't tell her about Jim's kiss.

Jennifer kept glancing at her watch. "Hurry! Let's sit on this bench by the fountain," she urged.

I saw his boots first, pointy black boots. One heel dug into the soil for support, the other crossed over the ankle. My stomach lurched as Dan stepped into view from behind the big balm of Gilead where he'd been lurking.

Exhaling a cloud of cigarette smoke, he said, "Good afternoon, ladies. Fancy meeting you here."

Jennifer giggled. "Give me a smoke, Dan." He flicked his lighter for her chivalrously; she inhaled the first drag like a pro. "Ta ta," she said, waggling her fingers coyly. "I'll see you in half an hour."

Checking my own watch nervously – half an hour! an eternity – I adjusted the band, revealing a little tangle of scabby calligraphy. "JA."

I hid it again quickly, momentarily fortified by the sight of it. Jim was with me: in the flesh, so to speak.

"So," Dan began. "How was your exam?"

"I think I did well," I said, nervous stomach churning.

"I'm sorry you couldn't come to my party," he said. "I really wanted to see you."

"So, you brewed up a little conspiracy with Jennifer?" I asked.

He nodded. "Yeah. Jennifer's cool." He stretched one arm out along the bench behind my back, blew some smoke over his opposite shoulder. "Smoke?" he offered. I shook my head. "Didn't think so. That's good. Don't start." He looked at me intently. "Maybe I'd even quit. For you," he added.

I leaped from the bench, heart pounding. Why was I here? "It won't work, Dan," I heard myself saying. "You're a really nice guy but we don't have anything in common."

He stood up. "Don't say that. We could get to know each other."

I shook my head. "I'm sorry." I fingered the scab under my watch. "My heart's not in it. There's . . . someone else," I blurted.

Oh, God! What was I saying? It all sounded like a B-movie plot.

His eyes narrowed. "Jennifer told me all about this Jason guy. She thinks you cooked up the whole story. You'll have to do better than that."

"There *is* someone else," I insisted. "Someone even older than Jason. Someone I love," I whispered. He looked unconvinced. I played my trump card: "Someone who really, truly kissed me." Spoken with the conviction of a pathological liar who finally had truth to tell.

A glimmer of doubt in his eye. "Who?"

I shook my head rapidly. He grabbed my arm.

"Who?" I pulled away. "I'll believe you. Just tell me," he insisted. "I won't bother you any more, I promise. And," he threw in for good measure, "I won't let anyone call you a lesbian, ever again."

Too good to be true: just the whisper of a name would free me. The name of a man — not my father — a grown man who'd kissed me full on the lips. Like lightning, like love. *Jeg elsker dig*, Jim; *Jeg elsker dig*.

Tears streaming, Judas whispered: "My piano teacher. Jim Altman."

Dan's head bobbed minutely, repeatedly. "All right." He exhaled for a long moment. "I'll keep the bargain. Can we still be friends?"

"Sure," I conceded. Had we ever been friends?

He stubbed out his smoke with the toe of his boot. "See you around."

I sank to the bench like a convalescent, relief mixed with sorrow. I'd left an important clause out of our contract: I had not enjoined Dan to secrecy.

Jennifer smirked. "Did you have a nice visit with Dan?"

"Yes."

"So?" she pressed, stirring the air with her hand.

I stared at her. "We've decided to be friends."

"Still a lezzy, eh, Mariah?" she breathed, leaning close. "Can't cut it with a real man."

I slapped her; hard. "Tell your mother, 'thanks for lunch.' " And set out of the park on foot.

The door of St. Andrew's Church was open when I drew near. I climbed the familiar steps, blessed myself at the font. Slipped into a pew, kneeled, and covered my face with my hands. What had I done?

Alerted by a cough behind me, I noticed a light in one of the confessionals. A priest lurked in the darkness, waiting for another soul to save. Should I confess? What would I tell him – that I was in love with an older man? That I harboured lustful thoughts for him? That I'd betrayed his love by speaking of it to someone unworthy?

I tried to classify these sins: venial or mortal? Or indeed were they some or all of the Seven Deadlies? I tried to remember them: Gluttony. Lust. Sloth. Dopey, Sneezy, Grumpy.

Pride. I'd betrayed Jim for the sake of pride. I could have survived another month in that school with the lesbian label. Then it would be high school and a clean slate. But no; for the sake of my pride I'd spoken the name of love in vain, thereby tainting it for all eternity.

Compounding my sins by leaving them unconfessed, I left the church and took a meandering route home, self-loathing weighting every step.

"Mr. Altman wants to see me at today's lesson, too," Mom said.

Only a few weeks before summer vacation; only a few sessions left with Jim.

"Why?" Alarms went off in my head.

"Maybe my cheque bounced this month."

I smiled weakly.

"End-of-the-year wrap-up, perhaps." She patted my leg.

Jim was leaning against his desk when we knocked, talking to several men with their backs to the door. "Come in; come in!" he greeted us, his usual energy overflowing the vessel of his being. "Mrs. Standhoffer, Mariah, I'd like you to meet my bosses: the chancellor of the university, the president, and the dean of music."

The big guns! Hands shaken, pleasantries passed, Jim seated us all comfortably, rubbed his hands together, and said, "I'll just leave you alone, shall I? Mariah, I'll see you next week for our last lesson. Right? Good! Bye-bye," and was gone.

I stared out the sliver of window after him. What was this all about?

The chancellor began. "I don't wish to alarm you, but we've received an allegation of impropriety on the part of one of our teachers. We must take all such allegations seriously, despite the hearsay nature of the complaint, or we'd be remiss in our duty to you, as student, and to the teacher as well."

Blood drained from my face. Did "impropriety" mean what I thought it did?

"This isn't a trial, Mariah. It's a sort of fact-finding mission. We'd like to ask you a few questions. I'm certain you'll answer truthfully."

I nodded, unable to speak for alarm.

"Do you like Mr. Altman?"

"Oh, yes," I answered.

"Has he been a good teacher?"

I bobbed my head enthusiastically. "The best I've ever had."

"Would you say you have a good teacher/pupil relationship?"

"Yes."

He cleared his throat. "Would it be accurate to say you have a little crush on Mr. Altman?"

I took a deep breath. "Yes." I exhaled.

The chancellor smiled. "There's nothing wrong with that, my dear," he said gently. "Many girls of your age develop crushes. It's perfectly natural. I was the flattered subject of a crush or two in my own time, if you can believe it." He looked to the other gentlemen; they chuckled jovially.

My mother flashed a nervous smile, took my hand. I let her hold it.

"Tell me, Mariah. Has Mr. Altman ever led you to believe that your relationship is anything other than teacher and pupil?"

Jeg elsker dig, Jim. "No," I answered.

"Has he ever hinted that you could be more to each other, that you could carry on a relationship outside of the university?"

Only in my dreams. "No."

"Has Mr. Altman ever touched you inappropriately?"

"No."

"Or spoken to you in a suggestive manner?"

"No."

"Mariah, has Mr. Altman ever kissed you?"

"Yes," I whispered, hanging my head. My mother pressed my hand.

The chancellor cleared his throat. "And can you tell us the context of that kiss?" he asked quietly. "Do you understand what I mean by context?"

"I'd just done *Hamlet* for the first time." I turned to my mother. "That's what we called a real performance, 'doing *Hamlet*.'" She smiled. To the dean of music I said, "I'd just played the Grieg like I'd never played before. I put everything into it. I *flew*."

He nodded as if he understood.

"It was as if I'd become a real concert pianist. It was exciting. It was wonderful."

"Go on," he urged.

I bit my lip. "I was so excited. And Jim – Mr. Altman – he was thrilled. He was proud, I'd played so well. He took my hands and we danced a little jig around the room. 'You've got it!' he said; 'You've got it!' And then," I gulped, "he kissed me." My mother's grip tightened. "Just one kiss." I swallowed. "Just a great, big, fuzzy, proud kiss." Tears filled my eyes, washing away the fantasy, the romance, leaving only truth: "Just like my dad would have done if he'd been there."

The chancellor flashed a small smile. "I see. Did he swear you to secrecy, or ask you not to tell anyone?"

My grandfather. He'd ordered me not to tell anyone; he'd threatened to hurt my dog. How innocent Jim was by comparison.

"No," I replied emphatically. "He did nothing wrong, so he didn't ask me not to tell."

"But you did tell someone? That Mr. Altman had kissed you?"

"Yes." I was in for it now. "A boy who liked me. I told him there was someone else, so he'd leave me alone. Because I didn't like him the way – " I paused, weighing words " – the way I like Mr. Altman."

A clearing of throats. "How do you suppose we found out about this incident, Mariah?"

There was no "suppose" about it: I knew precisely. "That boy, Dan, must have blabbed to Jennifer Larson," I said fiercely. "She's one of Jim's — Mr. Altman's — other students. She's been mad at me for months. She knew she could hurt me by hurting Mr. Altman."

Oh, God! By hurting Mr. Altman. I turned, panicked, from my mother to the chancellor. "She hasn't, has she? Is Mr. Altman in trouble because of this?"

The chancellor patted his knees, then stood, his speech formal: "Mr. Altman is on suspension, pending a satisfactory report by the disciplinary tribunal." He winked. "That's us."

The president turned to my mother. "Mrs. Standhoffer, do you have any words on the matter?"

Mom nodded. "Yes, I do. I hope you'll conclude there was no impropriety in this case. I'm sure Mr. Altman meant no harm."

"I'm certain Mr. Altman would thank you for your vote of confidence," he said, shaking hands all around, "as we thank you for your time. Come to my office next week just before your lesson. I'll have a copy of the tribunal's decision waiting for you. I assure you, your anonymity will be preserved."

"And, Mariah," said the dean, turning from the door, "keep up the good work. Mr. Altman tells me you have star quality." He smiled. "Good day."

Alone with my mother, I buried my head in her bosom and wept. "Shh," she said, "it's okay. Just let it out."

"He didn't do anything wrong, Mommy! It's not fair. This is such a mess!"

"No, it's not fair. But everything will turn out all right."

"Suspended! He must hate me for causing all this trouble!"

She squatted down to my level. "No," she said, "you mustn't think that! You did nothing wrong. Nor did he. He won't hate you; you'll see."

Mom went with me to pick up the promised report. We sat down on a deserted bench, opened the envelope, and drew out a parchment document.

"My goodness; it looks so official!" she exclaimed.

[Coat of Arms]
Report of the Disciplinary Tribunal, Lakehead University,
dated this 18th day of June, 1969.
In the matter of Lakehead University v. James Altman

THE CHARGE

In this matter, James Altman is accused of committing an
impropriety upon the person of a female minor music student, hereinafter referred to as "Miss X," aged 13 years.

INFORMATION IN THIS MATTER

This information was delivered by the parent of another
female minor, Miss Y, also a student of Mr. Altman. Miss
Y had hearsay evidence of a conversation which led her to
believe Mr. Altman had kissed Miss X during the course of
one of her music lessons. Mrs. Y, the child's mother, was
concerned that Mr. Altman might be preying upon his
female students and demanded the matter be investigated.

Under questioning, Mr. Altman did not deny that he
kissed the subject student, Miss X. He explained that she
had demonstrated a sudden intellectual grasp of the music
and an ability to perform it at concert level. In their mutual excitement at this breakthrough, they joined hands,
danced around the studio and then, as a demonstration of
avuncular or paternal pride in his student's ability, he kissed
her once.

Miss X, in the presence of her mother, confirmed this
story. She denied that Mr. Altman had ever enjoined her
to keep the encounter secret. She denied the occurrence
of inappropriate touching or suggestive language. Miss
X confirmed the source of the hearsay evidence, saying
she was certain that a young man – the only person to
whom she had ever confided the story of Mr. Altman's
kiss – must have reported the conversation to Miss Y.
Miss X characterized Miss Y as a troublemaker capable
of setting out deliberately to injure Miss X by discredit-
ing Mr. Altman.

OPINION OF THIS TRIBUNAL

Some child psychologists consider a "crush" on an older man safer developmentally for a girl of tender years than a love affair with a boy her own age. Within the social confines and strictures of a decorous relationship with an unattainable older man, she can explore her romantic yearnings, develop social and/or professional skills under his mentorship and bolster her self-confidence – all the while forging ahead with strong ego development.

The key word here is "unattainable." The mentor must remain a mentor and teacher. At no time can that relationship be breached, physically or verbally.

While it is true in this case that the kiss given Miss X by Mr. Altman was, by all accounts, a "chaste, fatherly, congratulatory" one, the fact remains that Mr. Altman is not Miss X's father – unattainable by virtue of blood relation and societal taboo. Mr. Altman is a young, attractive male on whom the subject is known to have a crush. In the context of Miss X's romantic yearnings, the kiss, no matter its innocent intent, can only be seen as encouragement: a first step toward a more fully realized romantic relationship. The boundaries of the teacher/pupil relationship have been crossed, the bulwark of decorum breached.

Mr. Altman's behaviour has encouraged this young girl to entertain fantasies of a romantic nature, fantasies strong enough to impoverish the considerable charms of a young man more appropriate to her age.

In his defence, Mr. Altman contends that "Miss X's use of her feelings for [him] demonstrated great good sense. She felt safe enough within the confines of the mentor/pupil relationship to use it as a buffer, a shield, from unwelcome and unwarranted pressure visited upon her by an unsuitable suitor."

With all due respect to Mr. Altman, Miss X did *not* employ the teacher/pupil relationship as a shield. She took shelter behind the romantic component of the relationship. Her words to the young man were, "There is someone else; someone I love; someone who really, truly kissed me." Had she used the teacher/pupil relationship in her defence, her choice of words might have been in the nature of: "Buzz off, Charlie, or my piano teacher will beat you up." But she did not: she chose the romantic nature – or, rather, her perception of the romantic nature – of the relationship to hide behind.

While no one can control the subject or nature of a child's crush, one can posit with fair accuracy a positive correlation between the child's degree of sensitivity and the depth of her susceptibility to such encouragement. In this case, the child is an extraordinarily shy and sensitive one, precocious in her grasp of musical technique, its language, its emotive power. Her extreme sensitivity is, in large measure, responsible for both her prodigious display of talent and the quandary with which we are here faced.

RECOMMENDATIONS OF THE TRIBUNAL

Mr. Altman is *not* accused of molesting this child nor of causing her any physical harm. We, all of us, accept the innocence of his intent, given his exuberant and demonstrative nature. We will not ask a teacher to curb all praise for his prodigy.

Our recommendation is, however, that all teachers ensure their behaviour is absolutely circumspect. The University hereby serves notice that there will be no tolerance of impropriety between teachers and students.

By publicizing this case, by demonstrating the emotional ripple-effect of an innocent action – upon the child, upon the teacher and his career, upon the community – we hope to encourage our teachers and students to "look before they leap" into hasty and regrettable action.

JUDGEMENT OF THE TRIBUNAL

This Tribunal finds James Altman innocent of impropriety toward a student. The Tribunal is empowered to and does hereby dismiss all charges, rescind Mr. Altman's suspension, and make full monetary restitution for back-pay during said suspension.

Signed,
Chancellor
President
Dean of Music

"AD AUGUSTA PER ANGUSTA"

I've kept that document all these years, read it so often I had it memorized for a time, its dispassionate words a sobering contrast to the
tumult of thought and feelings that surged within me. The crested
parchment is watermarked and smudged from the tears rained upon it:
tears of remorse for my adolescent stupidity, tears of anger to have my
love so trivialized by its formal language and paternalistic tone.

The shame of secret knowledge burned within me like a blast furnace, forging and tempering the steel of my resolve. No secret would
ever again escape my lips. If I'd been tempted to tell my mother about
my grandfather, I suffered no such temptation now. If so much potential for damage could be unleashed upon an innocent man and his innocent actions, how much more damage could the revelation of a guilty
secret like my grandfather's wreak? It was like possessing a nuclear bomb.

The parchment I held in my trembling hand crackled like autumn
leaves. "Does this mean everything's all right?" I asked my mother.

She nodded.

I fingered the embossed initials under my watch like Braille. I both
dreaded and anticipated my final lesson of the year.

"Shall I come with you?"

"No."

She patted my arm. "I'll wait here, then."

My heart leapt to spy his dear bearded face through the glass of the
door. I watched for a moment as he took books from the shelf and
packed them in cardboard cartons. I tapped cautiously. His face creased
into the familiar welcoming grin when he saw me. He waved me in.

"Packing up for the summer?" I ventured.

"No," he stroked his beard thoughtfully, examining the floor at my
feet. "That's what I meant to tell you today." He steered me into a chair.
"I'm packing up for good."

"For good?" I looked around the room wildly. "You mean, like,
for ever?"

He pulled his chair around to face me, straddled it, and rested his chin on his folded arms across its back. "Yes" — a little smile — "like, for ever." He looked into my eyes. "I'm sorry to be leaving now, Mariah, just as your talent is unfolding so wonderfully."

Leaving! My mind leapt over a chasm of possibilities, jumped to a single conclusion: "Because of what happened?" I asked.

He touched my arm gently. "No; oh, no!" he said with real concern. "Don't think that. The decision was made months ago; I just recently received confirmation. But, I must admit," he added wryly, "if I'd questioned the wisdom of the decision before, I won't — after this."

"Where are you going?" I managed to ask.

He put his fist to his face, did a trumpet fanfare: "To the University of Toronto," he said, gesturing with mock solemnity, "my esteemed alma mater, where I will continue my staunch refusal to teach — " he repeated the trumpet fanfare " — by the book!"

I laughed. He rose, resumed his normal pacing. "It's a marvellous opportunity," he said earnestly, "and I stand a chance of getting the oboe chair with the symphony. Maybe one day I'll see your name, Mariah, on the program as soloist in a concerto."

A knock at the door. A woman stood by the window.

"I'm not interrupting, I hope?" she asked.

"Not at all." He took her by the elbow and drew her close to me. "Mariah, I'd like you to meet my wife, Lesley Jones."

His wife? It hit me like a blow to the solar plexus, completely winding me.

"Lesley's the brains of the family," he continued proudly. "She's been on the faculty at U of T for several years now. Not like me," he winked, "plodding away in the hinterland, luring the finest students away from the convent." He smiled at her fondly.

She was beautiful. Strawberry curls framed her face like a pre-Raphaelite angel. Jim seemed calmer with her near, less frenetic, as if she were the ground wire for his undirected electricity.

"I have the results of your history exam," he said, stepping to his desk. "You should be proud. You got 92." He handed me the paper.

The words blurred. "It's because of you," I whispered.

He shook his head. "You taught yourself, you know. You did all the work. You took your love of music and put your soul into it."

So wrong! I thought. I took my love for *you* and put my soul into it. I did it for you! But that was a secret I would not speak.

"What will I do without you?" I asked. Such a very small voice.

"You've done *Hamlet*," he smiled. "You can fly. The music will take you wherever you want to go." He went to the desk again. "I've something else for you." A photograph: the two of us, together, smiling; smiling. "One of the other students took it after 'Schumann's Diary.' I thought you might like to have it."

Look at this photograph. What do you see? *Change one thing.*

⌒◞

If I'd known the expression "pathetic fallacy" at the time, I'd have applied it to the weather that summer: thunderstorms — in quantities excessive even for a harbour named after them — ricocheting like billiard balls banked against the ring of low mountains; rain; rain; endless rain; temperatures so chill there wasn't a two-week period all summer during which the furnace didn't kick in.

All reflective of my own palpable adolescent misery: a kinetic unhappiness that seemed to strike against every object in its way, transferring my destructive pain and rage to every thing, every person.

My parents were uncharacteristically distant with each other for a few days. I must have missed a classic round of Assignment of Blame following the Altman incident. I could only begin to divine the nature of their argument from the content of parental lectures.

Mom: "Someday you'll meet someone your own age, someone who'll be just right for you, someday when you're ready. . . ."

Dad: "The world is full of predators. You must keep your wits about you at all times. . . ."

Grandpa and Dad argued endlessly at the dinner table, so upsetting me that one night I spilled my milk.

"Mariah, for Christ's sake! Look at this mess!"

Mea culpa. I would have left in tears if I'd been able to get out. It was a tight squeeze around the breakfast room table where we took most of our meals. As if on cue, Luke added the last inch of his own milk to the mess.

"*Does he do it on purpose?*" Dad growled through clenched teeth, following Mom to the kitchen.

"Gabe, you and your father get us all so agitated, the glasses just leap with tension!"

Luke grinned at me, as if confirming his guilt. *Did* he do it on purpose? *Don't think you're doing me any favours!* I warned him telepathically. *It's
my fault.* Everything.

My emotions were cyclonic. Guilt and grief, rage and fear. All the
boxes I'd designed to compartmentalize my feelings spun free of their
lids, spilling into each other in a deadly mix, like chlorine and ammonia.
I was snappy with my brother and intolerant of my parents; prone to
tears for the least criticism. Frantic for solitude but so unnerved that I
was equally desperate to share the warmth of the hearth with my family.

My unhappiness was a magnet for further misery.

It seemed as if Grandpa was drinking more that summer. As sentry
of the backyard, if not the whole neighbourhood, he'd sit at his window and keep watch. The smallest movement in the bushes and he'd
pounce: "Marička! Lucas! Bring Grandpa a beer!"

Whichever of us was nearest to hand would race into the house, grab
a beer from the fridge, and charge up the stairs to his room. It was Luke
who devised the ingenious plan of bringing him *two* beers at a time. I
don't know if the ploy served to lengthen the interval between inter-
ruptions or merely caused the old man to increase his consumption.

"Gabe," I overheard, "you really must speak to your father. He's
drinking way too much. I won't put up with it."

Grandpa, in foul humour at dinner one evening, picked at Dad,
needling him in Slovak, provoking him so mercilessly my father
slammed his fist down on the table, jumped into his car, and screeched
off to the hotel for his evening shift without a word of farewell to the
rest of us.

Mom was furious. "Finish your dinner, Pop, and get out of here. I
don't want to see your face."

He shoved his plate across the table and stomped away, all the while
muttering what I knew to be bad words in Slovak.

"What were Dad and Grandpa arguing about?" I ventured over dishes.

Mom sighed. "I don't know; I don't care to know. I just hate what
he does to your father."

It had been some time since Grandpa had come to my room. I'd begun
to hope he was too old to bother any more. But, that evening, the smell
of alcohol on his breath was different; stronger than beer, sharper.

"Go away," I whispered, emboldened by his long absence. "I hate
you. Everyone hates you."

He slapped my face. "You do vat I say," he hissed. "You no tell Mommy and Daddy. Or I *kill* your daddy!" And he let off a stream of invective in Slovak which, despite my lack of understanding, left no doubt that he meant what he said.

More drunk; less delicate. He was different this time. Where he'd made special attempts to hide his connection to his organ in the past, he made no such effort this time. Instead of slipping into bed beside me, he straddled me, attempted to force his horrible thing into my mouth. Terrified, I tried to protest. He drove it home behind the barricade of my teeth. I gagged; struggled; vomited all over everything.

"Son of a bitch!"

He shook me roughly, turned me over. Drew up my nightgown and slapped my buttocks.

"Do vat I say!"

Face in the pillow, praying to die, to be smothered, to have it over with. No time to escape to a haven. All havens destroyed in any case. No Jim. No forest. No hope. Only a branding iron of pain. And an act for which I had no words.

Mute with dismay at the mess, as much as anything, my first thought was how to keep this a secret from my mother. Dawn's first grey tentacles had already roused the robins to the rain-soaked lawn. Such a hideously happy sound! I shut the window to block it out, rolled all the bedclothes into a ball, and limped to my toilet. After attempting to clean myself up, I put on a fresh nightgown and lay down on top of my naked bed.

Sleep? Or shock? The sky was bright when my mother entered my room.

"Oh, sweetheart!" she rushed to the bed. "Were you sick?" I nodded. "You should have told me!" She bustled around, opened the window. "Grandpa says he was sick last night, too. I wonder if it was something you ate?" She felt my forehead, left the room; returned with clean sheets. "Just sit on the chair for a minute while I fix your bed."

I tried not to wince when I sat.

"All done. Lie down now, I'll tuck you in." She followed me to the bed. "Just a second." She stopped me before I sat again, bringing the back of my nightgown around so I could see it.

Blood! I felt sick all over again. How could I explain this?

She smiled at me fondly. "Poor baby. You're growing up. Looks like your period has started. We've talked about it; you know it's a natural thing."

I tried to think. No, no! Not that.

On the other hand, she would believe what she wanted to believe. It was *natural* that her thirteen-year-old daughter should bleed menstrual blood eventually. That she was bleeding from a sodomite's wound was unthinkable and, thus, unthought.

She ran to the other bathroom to retrieve a belt and pads, the paraphernalia of womanhood; fished fresh underwear and yet another clean nightie from my drawer; showed me how to use it all, how to dispose of the evidence.

"There now; just relax. Come down for breakfast when you feel like it." And left me alone.

Alone in a maelstrom of pain and confusion radiating like a storm front from my bleeding asshole through my entire being. My body disintegrating, my thoughts and emotions out of control. Friendships dissolving into puddles of anger and innuendo; beloved teacher walking out of my life under a cloud of gossip and dishonour that my very fantasies had induced. Family threatened with extinction because of my unconfessed sins.

I stand at the mirror and examine my diabolical reflection, my budding woman's body. *Temptations of the flesh*: the words pass through my mind unbidden. The little breasts, the widening hips, the little stomach pouchy and soft like a puppy's.

What will this body become? I stuff socks up the front of my nightgown. Tits. As big as my mother's? Another pair on each side. *Blessed is the fruit of thy womb.* A baby: add a pillow to the upholstered figure in the mirror — a madonna's hand supporting the weight, another beneath the breasts.

Turn to the mirror in profile. Breasts and hips and baby. How much I look like my mother! Is that how she looked carrying me? A lovely young woman in love with a handsome young man, carrying his child.

Heat spreads to, from, around the locus of the pain.

I am momentarily confused with the multiple images in the mirror: the child Mariah, pregnant with her self, impregnated by — her own father? Looking from the mirror to the bed behind her, the child imagines the grandfather. Ugly, smelly old man, stench of alcohol on his breath. Thinks of her father, her handsome, beloved father. For one

fleeting moment a breath of words whispers at the ear of consciousness: *let it be Daddy. Let it be Daddy instead.*

My punishment! This very pain a punishment for all the terrible
things I've thought and done. *Mea culpa; mea maxima culpa*: through my
fault, through my most grievous fault.

And so I pray: every prayer I've ever learned – in Latin, in English.
Prayers from Mass; hymns; Christmas carols. Prayers to every saint in
The Children's Little Book of Saints and every other one I've ever heard of.
Every litany, every benediction. *Lamb of God who takes away the sins of the
world, have mercy on us; Lamb of God who takes away the sins of the world, grant
us peace.*

Words upon words upon words. And in the repetition – like a
mantra – an emptying of the mind, a draining-off of the excess, a
calming of the whirlwind. *Grant us peace.*

With the peace comes the clarity to realize that I will have to carry
on, to function according to custom and expectation; arouse no alarm;
cause no unseemly scrutiny. The Perfect Daughter must "pick herself
up, brush herself off, and start all over again."

Practical matters have to be addressed. Such as how to sit without
grimacing, how to walk without hobbling. How to shit without
screaming. I know there will be suppositories – glycerin and
Preparation H – in the other bathroom for my hemorrhoidal father;
laxatives to soften stool.

Still, for several days, the fear of applying bottom to toilet is intense,
the pain fierce. And with the healing comes an itch – both physical and
psychic – unacceptable to scratch in either case: a focus for fear, a focus
for desire.

"You haven't touched the piano in weeks."

I glanced up guiltily from my corn flakes. I'd hoped she hadn't
noticed.

How could she not? For two full years I'd practised virtually every
waking moment I'd been at home. Now, the silence was reproachful:
not an absence of noise but an oppressive presence. I hadn't touched
the piano since the day Jim said goodbye.

"You've worked very hard," she continued. "You deserve a rest." She
collected dishes from the table. "I'm not saying you have to practise for
hours. Just try to keep your hand in."

Interpreting her suggestion as an order, I dumped my cereal sludge down the drain, then went to the living room.

The piano stood against the wall, closed and threatening, its grinning ivory hidden behind tight disapproving lips — like my mother's: the Perfect Daughter was not performing to standard.

I approached the lowering beast gingerly, pushed back the lid. Ran my fingers in a *glissando* from treble to bass, back to treble; the strings roared in protest.

An alien creature, this hulking instrument I'd once tamed. How had I ever thought to befriend it, to employ it in my fantasies of love and flight? The true power of the beast had been revealed as destructive: its gaping maw and bellowing noise had nearly destroyed a man and his career.

I prodded it with a stiff finger. It spat back a doleful "C." The noise grated; I poked it again. A raucous "G" issued. Whipped at it with a chromatic scale; it snarled back.

Who has control — the lion tamer or the lion? Does the beast yield to the mastery of the trainer, or the trainer to the beast? I asked the musical questions, beating against the ivory.

Can I force my will on you? I asked. Can I make you do my bidding? Do I even *want* this kind of control?

The savage response — *no*. I am unwilling to fly.

Whatever I'd accomplished had been achieved under false pretenses. I'd appropriated Martey's dream, letting it become my parents' dream for me, even Jim's. I'd flown on borrowed wings, lifted beyond myself on the current of misery and the updraft of my feelings for Jim, to a freedom to which I dared not aspire.

This is not my dream! I shouted through the finger motions. *This is not my dream!* came back the echoed roar. Back and forth we struggled, theme and variation resolving, the motif restated conclusively.

A contrary thought: *I was good at it.* I loved doing it, for Jim. If I could hold onto the feeling, perhaps I could hold onto him. Or, at least, something of his essence, his energy. His love.

Done. Lifting my fingers from the keyboard, I let the last notes vibrate through the strings to infinity, carrying with them a sorrowful ambivalence.

"What was that you were playing?"

Is there nowhere I can be alone? Anger tempered quickly by common sense: it's impossible to be alone with such noise if anyone else is in the house. *Don't wake Daddy.*

"What were you playing?" she asked again.

This is not play; this is assault. "It was nothing."

"Nothing? It was fantastic!" she enthused. "A bit discordant, maybe, but quite wonderful. Stravinsky?"

I shook my head and jumped up from the bench, annoyed. "I was just doodling."

"Just doodling?" she smiled in amazement, gave her head a little shake. "Well, now that you're back up on the horse again, I hope to see you in the saddle a lot more." She turned to leave the room.

"No," I said.

"No what?"

I cleared my throat, amazed at my effrontery. "No, I'm not 'back up on the horse,' and I'm never going to 'ride' again. I just closed the lid on the piano for the last time. You might as well sell it."

Totally astonished: "Sweetheart, what are you talking about?"

Had she not heard a note I'd just played? Was it not obvious? Trembling with rage, "I'm not going to be a concert pianist," I hissed. "I've never wanted to be a concert pianist. I refuse to play the piano ever again."

Crossing the room between us so quickly I thought she might strike, she gathered me in an embrace instead. My arms hung stiffly at my sides, fists clenched. She held me a moment, then tilted my head, stroked my cheek.

"Honey," she said, "you have a God-given talent. You can't bury it, or turn your back on it. You've said it yourself: you can 'fly.' How many people do you think that ever happens to in a lifetime? How many people take lessons year after year, study their whole lives through, and never approach the level you've achieved?"

I resisted with every sinew, held my tongue firmly between my teeth, desperate not to cry.

"You're not a quitter," she said, fussing with my hair. "You're confused right now. You've had a rough year and you've lost your favourite teacher, but you mustn't quit. You can't quit. I won't *let* you quit," she said fiercely. "You'll thank me for that some day."

I shook my head, hard.

"You will," she repeated. "It'll take lots of work and total dedication.

But you must. It's your duty. And mine: I'd be the most negligent of mothers if I let you quit now."

She clutched me to her bosom, then released me slowly. "I love you," she whispered.

As I watched her leave the room, my heart filled with an uncharitable emotion: I don't think I ever hated her more.

What now? I know my mother; know her unyielding resolve. She'll never let me quit. Having once glimpsed my cursed talent she'll defend it to the death. She'll pawn the china or sell her hair to keep me in lessons.

I throw myself on my bed, stare at the ceiling. Black thoughts whirl, with them a memory of pain. Punishment for badness. It's not right to hate your mother. Repenting quickly, I pray for forgiveness. I'll be especially nice to her later. She only wants the best for me. Only the best.

Rhyme off some Hail Marys, in honour of mothers. *Blessed is the fruit of thy womb.* Find myself in front of the mirror with a pillow up my shirt. Again. And again, the strange tingle between my legs. I lie down on the bed, clutching the pillow and the sensation to myself.

My hand brushes my breast and I gasp: the sensation below is intensified like a jolt of electricity. But not unpleasant.

Deliberately now, I circle the nipple with my finger. As if by remote control I feel the circle inscribed in my crotch, in my belly, like a brand. Almost pleasure. Almost pain. A sensation of fullness, like water filling a secret place. Hold it, hold it!

I leap from the bed in disgust. Moments ago I was *praying!* Suddenly I feel unclean. Prowl the room in a frenzy, decide to have a bath.

Hot and sudsy: hot to remove the filth; sudsy so I can't see my nakedness. I close my eyes against the harsh lights reflecting off the old-fashioned white fixtures. The tub is deep and substantial. Grateful for the heat and the mind-numbing drowsiness it creates, I relax. Drawing a snail-trail of foam around the rim of the tub, my hand encounters my mother's razor.

Hold it, feel its weight. Examine its edge.

Brush the bubbles from one leg, feel the downy blonde hairs. Surely I should be shaving my legs by now, a girl old enough to have supposedly started her periods. Draw the edge of the razor up my shin. So many little hairs clog the blade I'm disgusted. Swish them away, draw the razor up my leg again.

My hand wobbles; I feel a bite, as if the razor has nipped my skin, but I see no blood. I finger the scars left by the surgery to my broken leg as I round my knee with the razor. That forbidden tingle in my crotch again. What is this? I renew the hot water to make it go away, continue until my right leg is shiny and smooth. I admire its hairlessness, then start on the left.

Scrape and swish; scrape and swish. Warm and drowsy, gratified by the labour: before I quite know what I've done, I've shaved every visible hair from my legs and arms. Hairless as a babe, I stand in the water to examine my handiwork in the mirror, but it's too misty to reveal anything. I realize I've missed a patch — the darkest, coarsest, most offending patch on my entire body. Carefully, bubbles lapping around my ankles, I remove it too.

Before sitting in the soapy water I glance again at my beautiful naked legs. But this time, the right one is not entirely nude. A rivulet flows from the invisible wound, bright against the pallor of my skin, against the whiteness of the fixtures. Fascinated, I sink into the water with that leg outstretched so as not to disturb the ribbon of blood that refuses to congeal on my wet leg. I imagine the water turning pink, then crimson, with an unstoppable flow. This tiny wound could never produce such a transformation.

But the razor could be used.

My veins stand out blue against my white skin. So many of them! But nowhere more clear, nowhere closer to the surface, than at my wrist. I clench my fist and watch the vein swell with its cargo of red, red blood.

Swish the razor free of curly hairs. *I can do this.* I can take this slender weapon and draw it across the dam of my skin. It would be so easy, so painless: a little bite of the razor into the flesh, and the water will turn crimson at my bidding.

At the back of my mind, a whisper of conscience. "It would be a sin," it says.

But surely the sin lies in being so out of control, not in *taking* control. The razor and I will take control, and it will be no sin.

Then the voice once more.

Reluctantly, I return the razor to its position on the edge of the tub. Pull the plug and poke the vortex dragging the water down the drain. With my tears. With my blood. With little bits of hair. I staunch the clotting red wound with a bit of toilet paper: the bleeding is under control.

Part Two

Triple Concerto

The bleeding was under control. But the child was not.

Raging hormones? Or just rage? I wonder if I would have sorted things out sooner if I'd just let myself masturbate in my room all summer, but I didn't realize at the time that the web of stimulation and denial I was weaving had a name, that the pressure could be relieved by orgasm. "Climax" was a word I'd learned in literature, in music, but the sexual concept was an alien one. Or, at any rate, a forbidden one, at thirteen.

The volume of preorgasmic blood coursing through my genitals that summer was attended, every drop, by guilt. I'll do penance, I thought, to atone for my sins. I'll suffer the stone in my shoe, the itching of a tag at the nape of my neck, the gurgling of hunger in my stomach.

It is warm in the church at the eleven o'clock Mass one Sunday morning. Dad is at home sleeping off his late shift at the hotel. Despite his never-ending moralizing, he is a Christmas Catholic, leaving it up to the nuns and my mother to make sure we attend Mass.

Luke is at the altar serving the priest. I envy him his closeness to God, his admission to the inner sanctum. He looks so pious, all robed in white, so serious. To give him credit, just when I'd begun to think the experience of serving the Lord was wasted on him, he'd displayed true feeling.

His class had gone on a field trip to a country church. Somehow, in an unsupervised moment, some of the boys had gotten into the priest's cache of unconsecrated hosts. When Luke came upon them, they were suggesting novel orifices of consumption.

Luke was horrified. "Put those away."

"No way, Standhoffer. Here, have some."

"Put them away," he said, "or I'll tell Sister."

"Fuck off."

Incensed, my little brother took a swing at the larger kid. "You can't treat the body of Christ that way!"

A mêlée ensued, broken up eventually by Sister, who reported the event back to Mom. "You know I don't condone fighting," she said, "but I must tell you: I was proud of Luke for standing his ground, for taking on a bigger boy in defence of his faith. Technically," she continued, "unconsecrated hosts are no more the body of Christ than a bag of potato chips, but that's not the point. Be proud."

I've not broken my fast before communion. I stand, mouthing the words while my mind takes me elsewhere, to a world just beyond focus, all stained glass colours and consecrated motes of dust.

A thread of melody trails through a maze of imagination, the notes resonating in a cavern of memory. If I could grasp the phrase – hold it – I could make it my own. Music that could bring Jim back to play in concert with the symphony on his oboe.

My focus dissolves repeatedly, then fades to black. An unholy noise – a distracting and disturbing crash – the sound of my own body falling against the pew and kneeler.

Mom helps me to sit, pushes my head between my knees. An usher comes to our aid. My embarrassed shadow trails reluctantly down the long aisle. All eyes upon me: the eyes of the priest, the eyes of God. The eyes of my poor brother, bewildered and concerned.

Outside, Mom sat me down on a retaining wall in the shade. "Your blood sugar is low," she said, "because you haven't had anything to eat. You should have breakfast next time."

"Then I won't be able to take communion!"

She patted my arm. "Sweetie, you only have to fast for three hours before communion now. Get up earlier and have breakfast."

"That rule change is for weaklings," I scoffed, thinking of all the saints who had fasted as a way of life. "We'll just go to an earlier Mass, so I don't have to fast so long. I will *not* eat before communion."

My aspirations to sainthood couldn't be thwarted by something so banal as low blood sugar! In the words of Saint Catherine, "Fullness of spirit overflows into the body, because while the spirit is feeding, the body finds it easier to endure the pangs of hunger."

I wasn't foolish enough to attract attention to myself by displays of unnatural virtue. Still, I quietly tried to perfect myself as a countermeasure to my secret wickedness. If I could look at the ledger of my life and tot up more credits than debits, then perhaps I stood a chance of redemption. And if it meant sublimating the "unacceptable" urges of approaching adolescence, so be it. All to the greater glory of God.

I aspired to the Catholic high school where other saintly children would, surely, congregate *en masse*. St. Pat's, the sole Catholic high school, was across town in Fort William. The logistics were insurmountable.

"We'll get you into the Collegiate, sweetheart," Mom assured me.

A consolation prize: it was not the designated high school for our neighbourhood. Supposedly catering to a "better" class of student, it was fed by lawyers' and doctors' kids who lived on "Pill Hill," the preferred address for professionals of the day. My grandmother had miscalculated when she'd moved up to the Court Street ridge from the Slovak ghetto of the Coal Docks. How could she have predicted it would be superseded?

Port Arthur Collegiate Institute was an imposing limestone monstrosity perched strategically on the hill above Waverley Park, as if its crenellated battlements held defensive guns. Entirely artificial – mockcastle, fake fortress, ersatz Ivy League institute of higher learning – it nonetheless commanded a certain respect, if only that its sporting teams were so bad there must have been some merit to its claim of academic superiority.

That fall of 1969, I was nervous but shored by the possibility of new beginnings. I was glad to have St. Ignatius behind me, where everyone knew me and my supposed sexual orientation, glad that few of its graduates would follow me through the Collegiate's looming portal.

My behaviour was friendly but not effusive. My unexpressed motto – "when in doubt, smile" – served me well. If I achieved eye contact with anyone, he or she – from the principal, to the janitor, to the football quarterback – was bestowed the smile.

And, if conversation should ensue, the willing ear. It was my form of protection. By listening to others I could determine what was expected of me. My true talent – to adapt like a chameleon to the colour of my surroundings and the expectations of my audience. I am green, I am blue. I am everything you ever wanted. I am the perfect child; I am the perfect woman.

Since we were arranged in alphabetical order in homeroom, I was placed in front of Wendy Staplin, with whom I struck up a random sort of friendship. She'd attended the neighbourhood elementary school and not only knew everyone but was willing to share her knowledge with me. She drew me into her wake between classes and I followed gratefully.

"So, Sully," Wendy smirked as we came upon him. "When do you report to boot camp?"

I looked anxiously for escape, uncertain if I was meant to be included in her conversation.

If the boy flushed in response to Wendy's jibe, it was impossible to tell. His face was an angry red, peeling in sheets, and strangely expressionless. Dressed in combat boots, fatigues, and an olive-drab shirt — complete with dog tags — scalp shaved to stubble, no eyebrows or eyelashes: he would not have looked out of place reporting to the Marines.

My first reaction: what a hideous specimen!

"I ship out as soon as I get my travel orders, Wen."

His grin, teeth startlingly white in contrast to his crimson face, was so warm and appealing my creeping blush forced me to reassess my judgement.

"That's Sully Riordan," Wendy explained as we walked away. "He's practically my brother; his mother and mine are best friends. He doesn't usually look so stupid," she added.

"What happened?" I asked, following him with my eyes.

"The oil heater back-drafted on him at camp. Singed his hair and eyebrows, burned his face a little." Assessing my interest, "If he'd been wearing a shirt it might've been a lot worse."

"Oh," I shivered, thinking of Corinne. "He's lucky."

"He looks like a dork," Wendy laughed, "but you've got to give him credit for trying to make it work for him."

Sully, I learned, was the class clown: not an unintelligent oaf, but truly amusing and beguiling, with a strong theatrical bent and impeccable timing.

" 'To be or not to be? That is the question,' " he announced on his way into English class. We were studying *Hamlet*. He fingered the numerals on the open door. "Hmm; not 2-B. Must be the wrong room." He exited to laughter, then re-entered, grinning largely.

His wordplay was appreciated by all but the most hard-nosed teachers, for it was generally informed and to the point. I paid him close attention during oral presentations and dramatic snippets, admiring his poise, his ability to make eye contact with the audience. And with me. *He's playing to me!* I realized — and immediately turned my eyes away.

Sully's face was like one of those games, I mused, where a moon-faced outline is brought to life with carefully placed iron filings. What would this face become? I pictured the finished product, watched as the weeks passed and it became ever more expressive — animated and tempered by eyebrows, long lashes, wiry dark hair.

Brows knit in concentration over his combination lock: *there is the face I invented.* Fully formed, complete, just as I'd imagined it.

He looked up from his locker as I drew near. "Hi, Mariah."

"Hi." I smiled reflexively, ducked my head, and opened throttle for my next class — shaken as much by the intensity of his gaze as by my response to it.

Wendy and Sully sat near the back of the classroom during English where she, unlike the rest of us, was privy to his whispered comments.

"He likes you." She laughed at my expression. "He does!" I blushed crimson. "Do you like him?"

"It's nice he has enough self-confidence to be different," I hedged.

Wendy must have reported the exchange to Sully. For he suddenly arrived sporting a new look: postwar prep school. Flannel cricket trousers that had once been white; shawl-collared sweater; voluminous shirt, sleeves rolled up to the elbows. And a tie! for God's sake — who else would wear a tie?

"Where does he get that stuff?" I asked incredulously.

"His father went to Harvard," Wendy replied. "Looks like he's been raiding the attic."

Everything just a bit the wrong size, accessorized with an incongruous element: last term's combat boots with the white flannels; a moth-eaten silk cravat tucked into the neck of an olive-drab shirt. Suspenders with anything. And, for the season they fit him, blue suede shoes! All worn with an insouciant disdain that declared, *This is my little joke.* His bravado was heart-rending: to be so exposed, so open to public ridicule — or regard.

Still, I sensed Sully sought my approval as much as I looked forward to his costume *du jour.* I stopped resisting his attempts to engage me in conversation. I memorized his timetable. And not only met his smile in the hallway with my own, but sometimes actively sought it out.

How bold. I tried to analyse the attraction. Yes, he was appealing.

Any number of girls who followed in his wake would attest to that. Sully was at home with anyone.

Yet I felt he was different with me. As if he needed something more than feminine laughter in response to his jokes: a foil, maybe, to set him up for more complex verbal jousting.

And what did I need? Connection. I felt so energized by our brief exchanges I yearned to soar with him on my flights of fancy. With this engaging Peter Pan and a little pixie dust, perhaps there was a chance I could fly again.

Jim Altman had been succeeded by his antithesis: an ultra-conservative, straight-laced, well-groomed, vaguely foppish man. Mr. Watson was never referred to by his given name, Charles; was never seen dressed in anything but a suit and tie, as if he'd been chosen by the dean of music to be as unappealing to young ladies as Jim had been attractive. He invited no intimacies with his students and was accorded none. Everything was strictly business. He was technically brilliant and a good-enough teacher. But I never caught a glimpse of emotive fire when he played; never honoured him with an incendiary performance of my own.

Our lessons were directed toward one goal: audition for entrance into one of the university schools of music. But I had so far surpassed expectations with Jim that I could coast for a while and still seem advanced for my age.

If Jim had been in the picture, there would have been no time for Sully; I doubt there would even have been a need. I'd fed off Jim's undirected energy like a light-bulb; I'd felt charged in his presence, incandescent, the only acceptable outlet the music and my megaprojects. So I missed Jim diabolically – and craved the excitement like a drug.

Shocked when I felt it in Sully's presence, at first I pulled away. But soon I let myself be drawn to Sully like a junkie. Needy. But scared of addiction.

"Do you think Shakespeare sympathized with Shylock?" Sully asked, falling into step with me one spring day, making an intellectual appeal I couldn't resist.

So began the obligatory walks home (although I lived literally miles out of his way); the thinly veiled phone calls requesting homework information; the casual visits.

Despite my terror, I was receptive to this flamboyant boy. He seemed to sense, though, that I would bolt if he moved too fast. Now that he had my attention and could voice his fashion statement less stridently, his clothing became less affected. His grand gestures and coltish nervousness were broken gradually as we got used to each other; his histrionics tempered and confined to a smaller stage, his raucous laughter and large jokes honed precisely to a trenchant wit: Sully, learning the art of subtlety. Not grandstanding for the world – but *becoming himself*, for me.

Laugh! I don't think I'd laughed so much in fourteen and a half years as I did that summer. To be Sully's perfect girl all I had to do was listen and feed him lines to react against. He provided the entertaining patter, I provided the laugh track. He saw himself through my eyes, reflected back as the charming, the suave, the hilarious James Sullivan Riordan.

My father – one of few people who didn't call Sully "Sully" – referred to him as either "James Sullivan" or "J.S." I thought this foible made him seem hopelessly eccentric.

"Do you mind?"

"As long as he doesn't call me Jamie," Sully insisted, tickled by my father's quaint formality. "Only Jimmy and Sonja call me Jamie." He always referred to his parents by their given names.

Sully never picked up on my father's true objection to his sobriquet – and I never told him.

"Why don't you ever call him 'Sully'?" I asked my father in exasperation one day.

Dad paused a long moment. " 'Sully' is a stupid nickname," he said. "It's practically a licence for a young man to run around despoiling maidens."

I sighed.

"Don't roll your eyes at me, young lady," he said, tapping me on the shoulder. "*Nobody* is going to 'sully' *my* daughter. Understood?"

A little ritual evolved. When Dad opened the door to Sully's knock, he gave a little nod. "James Sullivan," he intoned formally.

Returning the nod: "Mr. Standhoffer, sir. Good evening to you. I request the pleasure of Miss Mariah's company, if you please."

A final nod, then Dad would summon me.

I'd find Sully in the back entry – "God, I love your dad! He's wizard." – grinning as he untied his shoes.

There were times I wondered whether Sully came calling to see me – or my father. Despite Dad's unbridled hostility toward all contenders for the title of son-in-law, he didn't actually dislike Sully as a person.

Sunday dinners were set in the dining room with time and space to linger at the table.

"Listen to those two!" Mom exclaimed as we bustled around the kitchen, cleaning up afterwards.

Engaged in extended debate – his brow creased in concentration, elbow braced against the bow of the chair – Sully could hold his own. Luke, who generally expended his eleven-year-old attention span on the contents of his plate, would place his elbow in imitation of Sully's, his ankle resting on opposite knee the way Sully's was, and hang worshipfully on Sully's every word.

"Do you like him, Daddy?" I asked once, hesitantly.

He wore the "lecture look" on his face – and I steeled myself. But, "The boy's a charming lunatic," he conceded. "Just keep your wits about you."

One definition of "Platonic" I quite like is this: "Confined to words or theory, not issuing in action, harmless."

The moves Sully made were slow and all by design. It wasn't so much that he was shy; Sully hadn't a shy bone in his body. His intent, as I see it now, was to lure me a step at a time from the safety of my distance into the orbit of his love, drawn near by his gravitational field. A process so slow, so inexorable, as to be, finally, inevitable.

His vision, I believe, extended far into the future. He could afford to wait – for ever, if necessary. He would tame me, as he might a wild and exotic bird, with persistence and consistent gentleness.

It worked. I felt safe with him, he was another haven from myself. Sully threw back the curtains on my world, admitting colour and light. Admitting the possibility there was something worth loving in me.

"I'm going to camp with Jimmy and Sonja," he informed me in mid-August. "I won't be back until after Labour Day."

My crestfallen monosyllable: "Oh."

"Let's go for a walk."

We hadn't gone far before he meandered off the sidewalk, stopped, and sat down on the curb – head between his legs.

"What's the matter?"

"Nothing, really. I just feel a little funny." He stood — bent, hands on knees — as if testing his legs for sturdiness.

"Okay?"

He studied me, eyebrow raised. "Maybe you could help."

"How?" I asked, concerned. "There's a phone booth over there; I'll call my mom."

He shook his head minutely, taking my elbow like a blind man, then angled me toward the sidewalk. As I looked down the street, he placed his right arm fully around my shoulders.

I turned my head sharply. His amber eyes, usually full of laughter, looked surprisingly serious. "There," he said, "that's better."

We set off side by side, his arm heavy across my shoulders. The warmth radiating from the spot where I was pressed against his side was electric and carried with it the scent of his freshly laundered shirt. I found myself, to my great amazement, wanting to bury my face against his chest so that I could fill my nostrils with his scent.

For once he was quiet. I returned my attention to the business of walking, wondering if something needed to be said. Unnerved: the silence admitted too much scrutiny of the feelings I'd experienced.

"I'll miss you," he said huskily. "You're the only real girl I know."

What a funny thing to say! "Are you sure I'm not just the *only* girl you know?" I teased — and instantly regretted. He was hurt by my flippancy. Granted, I didn't have much practice at taking him seriously; "serious" was not his strong suit.

"You're the only real girl I know," he repeated, taking his arm away.

I felt suddenly bereft. But he picked up my left hand, brought it quickly to his lips, then held it firmly in his hand. And off we went.

Several letters addressed to "James Sullivan Riordan, Junior" — emphasis on the Junior, bearing the warning "Personal and Confidential" — found their way to General Delivery, Silver Islet, Ontario.

During that two-week power failure the light went on only when I was writing to him. Or reading the long, rambling, hilarious letters that found their way to me. I missed him so much I wept over them, jokes and all. I slipped into Luke's room at the front of the house to stare out at the Sleeping Giant, imagined Sully at Silver Islet, nestled at the Giant's toes.

Flood-lit on his return, all our time together was spent walking. We walked miles every day, just for the pleasure of holding hands. Down the driveway to the end of the lane, then — out of range of Grandpa's neighbourhood surveillance — hands locked, we'd continue.

"How do you know all these places?"

Trails meandered the length of McVicar's Creek; some days we followed it so far I was sure we'd find its source.

"I've spent a lot of time alone," he replied — serious, intense.

We'd walk to Boulevard Lake and stand looking out over the dam, watching the water churn and surge. Sat with joined hands in quiet places near the lake and talked and talked.

Even though Sully and I were a "thing," we were circumspect at school. But walking with him to classes, sharing lunch breaks, just being with him was strangely liberating. I was "Sully's girl." As such, there were no lingering questions as to my sexual orientation — in my mind or anyone else's. I was "okay," perhaps verging on "cool," since Sully was generally beloved.

And he'd also had a growth spurt over the summer. He arrived on my doorstep seemingly a head taller than he'd been two weeks before. Dad, muttering, attributed the spectacular growth to the quality and quantity of Standhoffer groceries James Sullivan consumed. People at school looked up to him, literally. And I was happy to stand in the sheltering embrace of his shadow.

"Will you please calm down!"

Balancing, one-legged, on a wet stone in the middle of the creek, Sully flailed his arms as if to keep from falling, noted my expression, then came — docile — to my side.

That autumn evening, he was unusually restless: swinging from branches, beating his wings around me with the manic intensity of a moth.

"What's with you, anyway?"

He just smiled as he reached into the pocket of his jeans and made a production of trying to find something in it. At last, he pulled out a packet of gum with the flair of a magician.

"Beech Nut," I noted. "Where'd you get it?"

"The States. Jimmy and Sonja went for a jaunt across the border on the weekend. Would you care for a piece?"

"Sure," I nodded. "Thanks."

"As I mentioned," he continued, opening the striped package, "this fine chewing gum was imported all the way from the United States. You can't get it here."

I nodded again.

He cleared his throat dramatically. "Perhaps a little payment might be in order."

"What did you have in mind?"

Grinning, he rubbed the bridge of his nose between thumb and forefinger, then drew his hand down his face, erasing the grin as he went. He stood, all seriousness, staring intently into my eyes. Something inside me did a little flip-flop.

"A kiss?" he ventured.

The little flip-flop turned into a major commotion, as if a small animal might batter its way out of my ribcage. "All right."

We'd read the books, we'd seen the movies. We knew the drill: turn head slightly, close eyes. But who starts? We flopped our heads tentatively; flopped them again the opposite way. Laughter. I leaned my head against his chest, embarrassment shaking my shoulders.

"Shh," he said. "Hold still."

And somehow it was accomplished. Lip met lip so gently it was the merest whisper of a kiss. And yet, and yet! It spoke so much.

We stared at each other in the twilight a long moment.

At last, face earnest, voice low, he murmured, "Give me your hand."

I offered it to him, unable to control my agitation. He bent to touch it with his lips. Retained it while his eyes returned to mine, then folded my fingers into a loose fist. Held it in the warmth of his own palm until its trembling subsided. Then released it.

It took me a moment to reclaim it as my own, a moment to realize something lay within the closed fist. Slowly I opened the fingers – like a flower blooming in time-lapse photography – to reveal a single stick of gum.

Our laughter pealed through the still, leafless trees, shattering silence, smashing tension. We held each other close.

"Perhaps you'd like another stick of gum?"

"I can only chew one at a time."

"No matter. I want you to have the whole pack."

I did go home with the whole pack, in the end, although each individual stick had been traded back and forth like potlatch. When he ran out, I sold them back; when I ran out, he sold them back to me.

On our next walk, he had a fresh pack of gum. Which was fine. But on the third walk, when he pulled the package from his pocket like a prop, on cue – the only thing I felt was annoyance.

I let him manipulate the game for a round or two while I collected my thoughts.

"What is this?" I asked finally, ducking his embrace, "a reciprocal trade agreement?"

He raised an eyebrow. "What's the matter?"

Trying to quell my irrational anger, "Look," I began. "I'll kiss you when I want to, when the moment is right. But you can't *buy* me," I spat, "with a pack of gum!"

He reached for my arm. I pulled away. "I'm not trying to buy you!" he said, alarmed. "It's just a game. An ice-breaker."

I stared at my shoes, poked at leaf mould with my toe. "I don't like games unless I know the rules."

Lifting my chin with his thumb, he whispered, "Let's learn the rules. Together."

"Hey!"

Sully leapt out of the way of the station wagon as Dad reversed at high speed out of the garage and tore down the lane.

"What gives?" he panted, joining me on the back porch. "An ambulance nearly ran me down a minute ago. Was it leaving here?"

I nodded. "Grandpa."

"Geez, what's the matter?"

"He didn't come down for breakfast this morning and Mom couldn't wake him for lunch." I led Sully into the solarium, where we cosied up together on the couch. "Dad thinks he might have taken too many pills."

"He drinks like a fish, doesn't he?" Sully reflected. "That can't be a good combination." To me, "Sorry. Didn't mean to be insensitive. I hope he'll be okay."

I don't, I thought. *I hope he dies.*

A hope so strong can't be right; a hope so strong must be punished, no matter what the old man did to me. See-saw prayers: *let him die/let him be all right.* There would be an omen in the outcome. But how would it be divined?

If he dies, I'm damned. If he lives? I'm fucked.
"Shh, it's okay," Sully murmured. "Cry if you want to. I'm here."
Grandpa lived.

"You'd better watch that boy," Dad said.

As things between us intensified, so too did the "lecture quotient" rise in the odd hours when Sully was not either physically present in our home or connected to it by telephone. My father, given to long-winded treatises on any given peril – racially mixed marriages, communism, unrinsed dishes, atomic fallout in the food chain – became fairly single-minded in his sermons.

"Jimmy Riordan was quite a drone in his youth," he reminisced. "Came courting Zoshka. I sent him packing."

"For his own protection!" Mom sniffed. "Zoë would have eaten him alive."

"True," Dad conceded. "Still, he buzzed around both those English girls, the Flowers – what were their names? Lily and Myrtle?" He turned to my mother. "You worked with them at Eaton's, Ginny. One of them had a deformed baby."

"Now, Gabe," Mom admonished mildly. "There hasn't been the slightest hint of impropriety since Jimmy married Sonja."

"Good. He picked the right blossom – but he might not have recognized her if he hadn't played the field." To me: "Just watch that boy, Mariah. Nuts don't fall far from the tree. And you're too young to be going steady."

My parents never forbade me to see Sully, but they worried about where so intense a relationship could lead. Their sermons on chastity were, looking back on it, quite unnecessary. Sully was pretty much the perfect gentleman. Perhaps, at fifteen, the most noxious of the teenage sex hormones had yet to be dumped into his bloodstream. Sully was really more desperate for a warm hand to hold his and an ear to listen than for anything more overtly sexual.

Come to think of it, maybe talking *was* sex for Sully.

But although he put no pressure on me, I knew from my precocious reading and my father's incessant lectures that one day, Sully would want One Thing and One Thing Only.

I had no trouble picturing the logical consequence of doing One Thing with Sully: I would get pregnant, incur my father's wrath, and ruin my life by marrying James Sullivan Riordan who — at age fifteen, or sixteen, or seventeen — would be capable of supporting his family only by pumping gas (I could see him in his Esso coveralls, oily dirt lodged under his fingernails, reeking of petroleum products) or engaging in petty larceny. I wouldn't be able to complete my own education. Burdened by a child, I'd resort to supporting myself in the only way possible: giving piano lessons.

I had other plans.

Despite the intensity of my affection for him, I knew I had no future with Sully. Imaginative as I was, I couldn't form a scenario in which I would spend the rest of my life with him. I was fifteen years old! How could we avoid the traps and pitfalls of a mature relationship based on what we shared? Because — and this admission came only after much thought and many tears — *what did he truly know about me?*

When I added up the hours we'd spent in each other's company, measured the miles of dialogue that had passed our lips, I realized that for all I'd revealed of myself I might as well have been mute. He knew nothing about the real me — as much as he might have liked to — because I wouldn't let him get that close.

"Play the piano for me," he'd asked on first admission to "Standhoffer Manor," as he called it.

A demure shake of my head, accompanied by a memory of Dan McAllister invading my space. While I could still sometimes conjure up Jim's shade when I was alone at the keyboard, I wasn't sure, that early in our relationship, if Sully was trustworthy enough to share space with Jim, let alone replace him.

"I don't like to play for people."

After repeated rebuffs, he stopped asking. By that time, Contrary Mary *wanted* him to ask — an irony that made me weep.

To think he'd called me "the only real girl" he'd ever known. I was like Pinocchio — a *real girl* only insofar as he, Sully, had created me. I was cut out to be his mirror — and how strong and sensitive and amusing he appeared in it. He needed a sounding board, I was it, returning the sound of his own voice to him, amplified through my laughter. He needed love, I gave it him.

But I never gave him my self. I gave him what he truly wanted and needed: I gave him *himself.*

And when he spoke of love one crystalline, cold, cold, January night

— exhausted, like a wintering deer, with the effort of breaking trail through the crusted snow — I said I loved him, too. Because I wasn't ready to throw it all away.

He opened first my coat and then his own — a voluminous Donegal tweed greatcoat appropriated from Jimmy's closet — and buttoned it around us both. We huddled against each other on the bridge over the frozen creek, sharing warmth, murmuring words of love between the kisses because they were the ones called for in the script.

Despite my reservations, I harboured hope — hope that he might ask, "Let me see your self, Mariah. Let me look into your heart. Show me what you have hidden there."

Of course, I would have bolted if he'd made any such demand. But that would be the true test of love, wouldn't it? For me to reveal the beast within; and for someone to love her.

Despite Jimmy Riordan's reputation as a crackerjack lawyer, despite the big house on Pill Hill, Sully had little money, so we never dated much. There was little incentive: the grub was always good at our place and Mom set an extra plate at the table for Sully as a matter of course.

There was only one occasion on which I was allowed admission to Sully's home. Jimmy Riordan phoned to invite me himself. "I'd be pleased if you would join us for dinner, Mariah." His booming, jovial voice alarmed me. "It's his mother's birthday and I'd be grateful to have my son present for it."

I was impressed with the Riordan house, not because of its size — ours was probably half again as big — but because of its decor. It was the first time I realized just how shabby our old barn was. God knew when last it had been painted. Zoshka had, upon my grandmother's death, taken all the draperies (which were original to the house) for her own down-at-heels fire-sale mansion in Toronto, and they had never been replaced. The furnishings were a mixture of Grandma's things (those Zoshka hadn't pillaged) and my mother's sensible good taste; together, nothing matched. But Sully's house had *design*, fresh paint, and drapes on all the windows. I felt immediately more at home there than I did in my own.

And the dinner! A standing rib roast, rare. *Beef*. Not venison, not moose. My mother was a wizard with game, but that beef practically dissolved on my tongue. Even more astounding, the chef for the occasion was Jimmy Riordan himself.

"Your father *cooks*?!"

I'd never, ever, seen my father produce a meal in our kitchen other than the odd reheated leftover or, perhaps, a scrambled egg. Certainly not an elaborate dinner in honour of his wife's birthday.

Sonja was gracious and Jimmy was cordial. Like the Waterford set at each place, the repartee was multifaceted and brilliant, its polish enhanced by the two glasses of wine Jimmy poured for himself – not to mention the half-glass allowed Sully and me. Father and son jousted as equals; Sonja and I played foils to the men. We were like two couples of a similar age at a dinner party. As long as that tone was maintained Sully was relaxed enough. But as soon as a certain line was crossed – if, for example, his parents forgot themselves and called him "Son" instead of "Jamie" or, as he truly preferred, "Sully" – he bristled and withdrew. It was as if he rejected outright the role of child in his own family.

"*I'll* take Mariah home!" Sully insisted when his dad offered me a lift.

It was cold that evening. I was wearing high-heeled dress boots – those boots *weren't* made for walking – and hadn't risked a hat for fear of wrecking my hair. I would have been grateful for a ride. But Sully was so adamant I dared not oppose him.

"What's the matter with you?" I asked as I picked my way down Red River Road. "It's as if you don't want them to be your parents."

"Exactly."

"What's *wrong* with them? Do they *beat* you when no one's around?"

"Don't be daft," he said grimly.

"They're not lushes; they don't curse each other out at the table in a foreign language; they're not gargoyles. And you have a lovely home!" I pressed. "Why have I never set foot in it before?" I was suddenly floored by the thought: "Perhaps you're ashamed of *me*?"

Sully gaped, astonished. "Of course not, Mariah!" He stirred the air with one gloved hand. "I simply refuse to be moulded to their expectations; I'm not a kid."

Yes, you are, I thought; this little demonstration proves it.

"As long as they follow the rules, we're fine together," he said. And dropped the topic.

Who sets the rules for whom? I wondered. And why do his parents accept it? He was already, apparently, lost to them as a child; perhaps they feared losing their charming boarder outright if they pressed the point. Still, it could be worse, I reasoned. There was an unusual mutual respect at that table, Sully's for them and theirs for Sully. As if they trusted him to be himself. Which – if I admitted it – was the one thing missing from my parents' view of me.

"I prefer ballroom dancing," Sully said – as appendix to his invitation to the school dance. "Wendy and I were dragged to lessons by our mothers when we were kids. She hated it."

"Let's not go, then. I don't much care for rock and roll."

We were a thing; it was expected.

Sully arranged for his cousin to pick us up. Curfew was assigned and agreed to. Mom waved us off reluctantly.

The first intimation of disaster: Fred, sitting alone in the front seat like a chauffeur, handed Sully a small brown paper bag.

"Here, I picked this up for you. What's a dance without some fortification?"

Sully slipped it into the deep pocket of his coat.

The gym was decorated in a jungle motif, alive with strobe lights and coloured spots. The band was overly loud, conversation impossible. Sully pressed his lips to my ear and shouted, "I really hate this noise."

"Then what are we doing here?" I screamed back.

"Maybe we can do a slow dance."

I shrugged. He steered me into a spot against one wall where we stood for some time. Once again, lips against my ear.

"What?"

He opened his mouth in a laugh, mimed walking, and formed the letter "P" with his fingers. I laughed and nodded; he waved goodbye.

The band played a slow dance just after he left. Huddled against the wall, watching the other couples shuffle in place on the hardwood floor – some of them engaged in vertical coitus – I felt anxious, worried he'd been gone too long. "Sully's girl" was no one without Sully. At last I spied him making his way through the throng.

As he bent to kiss me, the smell of alcohol assaulted my nostrils. I lurched back a step. So that's what he'd been up to! He leaned to kiss me again and I tried, I tried to meet his lips, but at the last instant I turned my head. His lips brushed my cheek instead. He shot me a quizzical look but, rather than meet his eye, I focused on a mural, seeking shelter in the jungle.

When the band struck up another slow dance, I hung back against the wall, but Sully held out his hand and led me to the floor. I buried my head against his shoulder, hoping that, if I held on tight enough, I might forestall abandonment. A futile hope: the alcohol gathered him in its grasp and wrenched him away from me.

He stepped on my foot, stumbled. Grabbed me to regain his balance, then threw back his head and laughed — the sound lost in the maelstrom of noise. When he stepped on my foot and stumbled again, I turned and left the gym, my safe haven gone.

"Riah, come on. Whatsa matter?"

No point in explanations, not with this drunken stranger. And no point going home. I'd have to explain why I'd returned well before curfew. I'd wait it out, so I could lie and say we'd had a great time.

"I'm sorry," he apologized in the car on the way home, rubbing his head against my shoulder like a cat.

When he tried to put his arm around me, I stiffened into a tight knot. I caught a glimpse of my face in Fred's rear-view mirror. My lips were a tight line of displeasure: my mother's lips, my mother's expression. The expression she used when the Perfect Daughter was not performing to standard.

You've failed me, Sully.

Wary of him now, looking for an excuse and completely unforgiving: I decided I'd trusted him too much. There was nothing benign and harmless in his love. I'd been duped. He didn't love me; no one could.

During our months together I'd so relaxed my death grip on myself that my grades had fallen; I'd spent too little time practising the piano; I'd lied to my parents. In short, I'd loosened up to a frightening degree. I was, I felt, out of control.

The pendulum swung back toward hypervigilance. I left nothing unexamined. *Look at the way he manipulates me*, I thought. He had even used his dog.

"Her name is Xanthe."

"What kind of a name is *that*?" I'd asked at our first meeting, scratching the aging and odiferous golden retriever behind her silky ears.

"*Xanthos* is Greek for 'yellow'," he explained with a shrug. "Jimmy named her. He calls Sonja Xanthe sometimes, too. Because she's so blonde."

"It sounds like your dad's as bad as mine."

"What can I say?" he scowled. "He had 'small Latin, and less Greek' at Harvard and won't let anyone forget it."

Sully would frequently bring her along on the long walks from his home to mine, whereupon Xanthe would collapse in a heap and sleep, regrouping her forces for the trip home. I thought this was too much for the old dog, but Sully insisted it did her no harm.

During the Winter Carnival at school, a particular game was introduced. Each girl was issued a ribbon to be relinquished if a boy engaged her unwittingly in conversation – the verbal equivalent to losing one's virginity. The ribbons were instantly dubbed "cherries." Many a girl lost her ribbon that day by responding "no" to a boy's coy question: "Can I have your cherry?" There was a similar way for the girls to win back ribbons in a sort of reverse deflowering.

I'd held on to mine all morning and most of the afternoon. I'd even managed to win a few ribbons from the boys. When Sully and I met for one of our few classes together, he said, sadly, "Old Yellow-Dog died last night."

"Oh, Sully!" I choked, brimming with sympathy, "I'm so sorry!"

"I'm sorry, too," he said, eyes downcast. When he looked up, he wore his Sully-smirk. "Can I have your ribbons?"

It took me an awful moment to decipher this non sequitur. "You mean Xanthe's all right?" I demanded.

"Yes," he grinned happily. "Can I have your ribbons?"

Fury competing with hurt, I handed over my ribbons and took my seat without a word.

He charged over to my desk, all mirth drained from his demeanour. "You're not mad, are you?"

The teacher arrived and called the class to order. Sully took his seat with a troubled glance at me.

Promptly upon the ringing of the bell after class, I slipped out, travelling to my next by way of a long detour to the girls' washroom. Sully, as I should have predicted, was waiting for me at the door.

"You're mad," he said, "because I took your silly ribbons?"

A long level look. "I'm mad at the *way* you took my ribbons." He stared blankly. "You manipulated me."

I spent the entire next period formulating a note. "This," I began, "is not about ribbons. You used me. You used my love for you, and my affection for your smelly dog, to trifle with my emotions. Love is trust. I trusted you not to play silly games with my vulnerability. We are obviously not ready for a relationship like this."

"I do not wish to speak with Sully when he arrives," I told Mom. She didn't even question my early arrival; I'd cut half my last class.

There was a half-hour's respite before he came panting to our door; Mom was in the basement. Luke let Sully in, then found me lurking in my room and shouted down the stairs, "Hey, Sully, she *is* here!"

Nothing for it but to talk to him. I grabbed my coat and huffed outside.

"Mariah, you don't want to break up, do you?" he asked wildly when I let him catch up to me.

Yes. No. Traitorous heart, not knowing what it wanted. Control; it wanted control.

"I'm sorry, Riah. I love you."

"Then you should take more care with a relationship we're not mature enough to handle," I warned, believing, *we will now play by my rules*.

The admonition had a predictable effect: it backfired completely.

If Sully had been devout before, he was now totally pious in his devotion and anxious to prove his love. He would have swung from chandeliers or across ravines on vines to prove it; he'd have become a Catholic if I'd wanted him to. (For all his stage Irishness, Jimmy Riordan had let his membership in his own faith expire when he married Sonja, a Danish Lutheran.) Sully was committed to me.

"When we're married . . . " he began one conversation in the rec room.

After those words, I heard nothing but a thunderous deluge in my ears. Hot and nauseated, I wanted to run to my mother.

As trapped by his words of love and marriage as if we'd already spoken our vows, I couldn't see a way out of the situation. I'd be forced to assume lifelong responsibility for an ageless child. Hadn't Dad warned me about boys?

My father. Dad had offered, gladly, to murder Sully on several occasions. My father might yet be a saviour to me. If anyone could get rid of Sully for me, he could.

"Sully's getting too serious," I told my mom.

"Is he pressuring you?" she asked, alarmed.

"Not like *that*," I said, knowing what she was thinking. "He wants to get married."

"What, now?" she asked with that tone she used to respond to the inadvertently preposterous.

"Not *right* now," I said. "But he's planning our whole lives."

"And you don't like it."

"I don't know what I want to be when I *grow up* yet," I exploded, "but I don't think being Mrs. James Sullivan Riordan is it."

We talked it out. Immense relief that we *could* talk about it; knowing I wasn't alone with a problem – for once – was almost as good as having it gone. The conclusion: Dad would speak man-to-man with Sully to discourage him, as tactfully as possible.

My father took to the prospect of a new body to lecture – particularly if he could dissuade the boy from consuming his groceries, boosting his phone bill, and ravishing his daughter – with something like delight.

"Thursday night, after supper," I told Sully. "My dad wants to have a little chat with you."

Thursday came. I watched TV with Mom in the living room, sick with anticipation, while Sully was in the basement with Dad. It took several hours.

"Want to go for a walk?" he asked when he finally surfaced, looking bruised and delicate.

"It's late. We'll talk about it tomorrow."

As soon as Sully left, I ran to my father for debriefing. "What did you say?"

Dad had recounted more parables that night than Jesus – most of them ones he'd already told Luke and me in one form or another over the years.

"Gee, Dad," I said, exasperated. "Did you say anything specific? Anything Sully would understand, like, 'Get lost'?"

"No, I didn't," he said. "That would only push him closer to you. If you want him to get lost, you have to tell him so yourself. But I laid the groundwork; it shouldn't come as a huge surprise."

"Your father doesn't have a lot of respect for me," Sully began when we met at lunch.

"How do you mean?" I asked, picking my way carefully down the icy stairway to the park.

"He thinks I'm just like any other boy," he said, obviously injured, "wanting to take advantage of you. He says it's time for me to sow wild oats." He turned to me, grasped me by the shoulders. "Mariah, I don't want to sow wild oats! I love you. Why don't we get married?"

My feet went out from under me and I plopped down, hard, on my tailbone. "What, now?" I squeaked, using the same words my mother had, not days before.

He helped me up. "As soon as absolutely possible."

That left us a good year, at least, since we weren't yet sixteen. I wasn't sure it was sufficient reprieve.

"Whatever you told Sully, it's backfired!" I tore into my dad. "He wants to prove his intentions are honourable. He wants to get married right away!"

Dad looked at me sadly. "Sweetheart, I've done everything I can, short of murdering the poor bastard. It's up to you. Nobody's putting a gun to your head. You don't have to marry him. And you certainly better not wind up at the point where you *do* have to marry him!" he said, waggling an admonitory finger in my face.

"I told him," he continued, "that you two ought to cool it; that you're not ready for a lifelong commitment. I told him that if he enjoyed his youth, got his education, and played the field a little then, perhaps — someday when he has prospects for a stable future — he might come back and find the time is right for you to commit to each other."

Sighing, "How much plainer could I have made it?" he hugged me. I let myself be comforted against his chest a moment. "It's up to you."

Up to me.

Having handed the problem to my father to fix — despite his ultimate failure to do so — was, nevertheless, somehow satisfying. Reassured that there was an exit to the maze of the relationship should I decide to seek it, I did nothing more to disturb the status quo.

If, as I sometimes allowed myself to think, Sully was selfish, so too did the fear arise: "You, Mariah, are even more selfish; you give nothing of yourself." My mother had noticed the lack of passion in my music-making. I knew she sometimes watched me practise. Not wanting to scare me off, she used the French doors like a duck blind — as if I mightn't see her lurking behind the glass wearing an expression of concern as she analysed me.

I sent silent messages when I caught her eye: See? I dutifully exercise the beast, but I do not ride. I'm sleepwalking.

She must have caught the contradictory messages as well: I want to soar, but I'm afraid to invest too much of myself in the process, afraid to love it the way I did with Jim.

My parents hatched a plan for Mom and me to tour several musical Meccas over spring break. We would attend a concert at Carnegie Hall and an opera (for my mother) at the Met, followed by visits to Juilliard, the Berklee School of Music and Harvard in Boston.

Excited by the prospect of a trip – who wouldn't be? – but conflicted as well, I was leery of being "bought." Afraid I'd sell out to my parents' intentions for me; afraid to accept the dream as my own.

Sully insisted we attend the Spring Break Bash together on the eve of my departure. I tried to beg off. I looked forward to the separation, considered it a test.

"It'll be our farewell," he pleaded, as if I'd be gone forever.

He was attentive and deferential. We danced a few fast numbers and snuggled into the slow ones so thoroughly that I did experience a pang or two. We even kissed a few times on the dance floor.

"Let's go for a walk," he shrieked into my ear. We left the gym, detoured to our respective washrooms and lockers, and met at the appointed door with coats and boots on.

March dampness assaulted us. I shivered. It was colder in the mild pre-spring weather than it had been in January at twenty below. The park, compared to the din we'd left behind, was peaceful and inviting. Sully slid down the handrail with a whoop, shattering the silence. He waited for me at the bottom of the stairs, took my hand with a little chivalrous bow, and grinned.

"I'm going to miss you during the break, you know." He brushed the slushy snow from a bench, indicated that I should sit.

No hat tonight – I hadn't wanted to mess my hair. I thrust my hands into my pockets, hunched my shoulders up around my freezing ears, stared into the trees. Stars overhead; the slush would be frozen solid by morning. No chance the airport would be snowbound for my flight.

"You won't miss me at all, will you?" he asked, as if he'd read my absent thoughts.

"I'll only be away a week."

Putting one foot up on the bench near my thigh, he leaned toward me. "But you won't miss me, will you." It was a statement, not a question.

"I won't have time. I'll be back before you know it."

He stared at me, unsmiling and silent. I could swear I saw tears well in his eyes. My heartbeat stumbled, then raced to catch up, alarmed by his seriousness.

What now? As often as I wished Sully would be more serious, his gravity was unwelcome, unfamiliar. Almost threatening. He turned his head, exhaled with a sigh.

An alcohol-scented sigh.

I leapt from the bench as if I'd been slapped. He bounded through the crusty banks beside me like a deer, stepped onto the rim of the fountain.

"What is it with you?" he shouted, flapping his arms for balance, an enormous bird of prey.

"You've been drinking."

He reached into his coat pocket, pulled out the flask. "Here, have some. It'll loosen you up." I stared up at him, unspeaking. He stepped down from the fountain, brow furrowed. "You're the only one who can make me stop."

"Stop what?"

"Stop me from doing anything," he said.

You're the only one who can make me stop.

What a huge and oppressive responsibility, to keep a headstrong and impetuous boy from self-destruction. It would be like trying to stop a freight train single-handedly.

If I'd thought I wouldn't have time to think about Sully on my trip, I was wrong. "Let your heart be moved! Trembling, I wait for you — come and make me happy!" The baritone voice singing those words from Schubert's *Schwanengesang* — fourteen songs expressing love's longing or its loss — might have been his. I'd expected too much from him. If he cared for me, I rationalized — with time, with love — he *would* learn to take responsibility for himself, wouldn't he? His inability to do so had been caused by *my* failure to love him enough; *I'd* held back too much. Carried away by the romance of it: if Sully had been with me at Carnegie Hall, I would have married him on the spot. This certainty was magnified by the opera. As Turandot tore down the walls of her pride to accept Calaf's love, I let Sully and music mingle in the same chamber of my heart for the first time.

Passing me fistfuls of tissues, my mother was pleased by my unseemly display: "The music really moved you, didn't it?" It had. But not in the way she and my dad might have hoped. I determined that the moment Sully asked "How was your trip?" I would truly open to his love. I would tell him how the music had worked to allay my reservations: I could love them both — music *and* Sully — without losing anything of myself.

We were hardly in the door from the airport when the phone rang.

"Hi, it's me," he said. "How are you?"

"Fine."

That was virtually the only word I spoke. Sully burst into a torrent of news, the flood of his words assailing my ear. He related everything he'd done, every move he'd made during my absence. My parents bustled in and out of the house retrieving baggage from the car; my mother made irritated hand signals.

"I've got to go," I said. "I've still got my coat on."

"That was a one-sided conversation," Mom said sarcastically. "Why didn't you tell him about the trip?"

"He didn't ask. And I couldn't get a word in edgewise."

She glanced at me warily, trying to read my tone. I went to my room to unpack.

Sully was at our door in record time. "Come out for a walk," he urged.

"It's not a good time," I stalled. "I've got to get organized for school tomorrow."

"It can wait."

Off we trudged, our steps accompanied by his incessant babbling. It was as if he hadn't spoken to a single human while I'd been away, as if the log jam of his dammed-up words had suddenly broken apart and swept him away. I followed him along a snowy path, then sat on a bench. How long would it take before he noticed I was gone?

Seconds. Long seconds. He eventually turned his head, expecting an answer from me, then raced back to the bench.

"What's the matter?" he asked solicitously. "Tired?"

I nodded dumbly, my throat aching with unwept tears.

"Let's go back," he said, taking my hand.

The tide of my resolve ebbed and flowed over a number of days. Did he love *me*? Or would a smiling, nodding, deaf-mute suffice? I set up little tests, benchmarks against which to measure the rightness of my decision: If he asks about the trip. If he asks one sensitive, insight-ful question. If I can carry the conversational ball for two minutes without interruption.

If, if.

I decided I was extraneous to his love affair with himself.

Rehearsed and rehearsed, slept badly for nights, but convinced myself of the rightness of my impending action. It was the only way I could regain control. All I needed was an opening, an omen.

"Walk me to the corner?" he asked after we had done our homework together.

Like too-tight earmuffs, my heartbeat blotted out all sound. I steeled myself. Steps from the corner: if I didn't speak he would turn and kiss me and destroy my resolve.

"You told me," I heard myself speak, "I was the only one who could make you stop."

I looked at my boots. When I looked up, his face was drained. He knew. "Stop what?"

"Stop seeing me," I whispered.

With a wounded animal sound, he reached out and rested his head on mine. "Your parents?"

"No."

"Someone else?"

"No." The pressure of his dark head against mine, the warmth. I could feel him tremble.

His face crumpled like a used tissue. "Why?"

I looked away, hoping some of my carefully practised words would come back to me. He wasn't so *hurt* when I rehearsed this! How had I not foreseen how shattered he'd be? Had I expected him to shrug, smirk, and leave with a *bon mot:* "Here's looking at you, kid"? What a fool I'd been.

I felt terrible, but held onto my need for self-preservation. *You're the only one who can make me stop.* How could he abdicate so much responsibility?

"We're too young," I managed. "My grades are falling. I don't play the piano enough. I don't spend enough time with my girlfriends," I rambled. "I hate it when I have to lie to my parents. I don't like what I'm turning into."

He was deaf to the litany. "There must be someone else."

Why did there always have to be someone else? Would it be easier on his ego?

"No," I repeated. "There's no one else." I pulled at his coat. "Can't you see? I love you, but I'm breaking up with you on principle."

Maybe I should have *invented* someone else. Surely that would have been preferable to this face, his face. Desperate tears coursed down my own. "I'm sorry. I'm sorry, Sully. I'm just not old enough for so much responsibility."

He bobbed his head, shoved his hands into his pockets. Looked down at my bare hands, took off one of his own gloves. He wiped the tears from my eyes as if I were the one being left, then – folding my hand into his own – kissed me, and walked away.

He knew I was watching; he didn't turn back. But I'm sure he heard my strangled cry when I opened the fingers of my loose fist to reveal a crumpled, linty, pocket-worn, wrapper of a single stick of Beech Nut gum.

⌒◡

If only he'd left it at that, it might have lived in my memory – along with the closing scene of *Casablanca* – as one of the great romantic farewells. But he didn't.

If I'd expected Sully would go off quietly to lick his wounds, I was wrong. He took every opportunity to remind me of what I'd done. Sure, playing the role of tragic hero suited him. But still, like a hemophiliac, he seemed truly unable to clot and get on with it; might he hemorrhage to death from love of me?

The sound of his footsteps at a discreet distance, following me home from school, day after day.

The times the telephone rang and there was no one there.

His eyes the first time he saw me with Doug.

The way his displays of humour changed from "informed" and "to the point" to "cynical" and "distracting"; the way he'd show up drunk and belligerent at some function where he knew I'd be and glower from a distance until our eyes would meet and he'd as much as dare me to rescue him. *You're the only one who can make me stop.*

He'd drop by, bearing gifts, as if to ask, "Is it time yet, Mariah? Have I done enough penance? Have *you*?"

No, I hadn't done enough penance; I hadn't done *any* penance for quite some time.

If his intent was to punish me, he succeeded. As if my own guilt wasn't enough to bear, everyone blamed me for turning Sully, lovable Sully, into someone else: I'd transformed an affectionate, affable golden retriever into a pit bull.

I rode out the aftershocks of the breakup with increasing alarm, shaken by the forces I'd set in motion. I never felt a physical threat, only an emotional one. The fear I felt was for *him* — so out of control, so irresponsible: an undisciplined child seeking limits. Still, when I read about serial killers and stalkers and women killed by former boyfriends, I'd feel a *frisson* of recognition: *There but for the grace of God*. I was terrified to possess, at fifteen, such responsibility, such power.

Just as I'd almost ruined a man's career with the strength of my fantasies — just as I could destroy my family with the whisper of a secret — here I'd demolished a perfectly nice boy whose only sin was to love me too much.

One day, alone in the house, I took my misery and remorse to the piano. I practised for a while, channelling some of my undirected energy and emotion into appropriately morose music. I pulled back when I realized I'd ventured too far, into dangerous air space — *almost outside myself* — perilously close to re-addiction.

To calm myself, I started noodling tentatively. Eventually I hit upon a little melody, a turgid thing in a minor key. Repeated it a few times to commit it to memory, decided I should scribble it down on manuscript paper.

It looked rather bare. I messed around at the keyboard for a while, trying to flesh it out. But it didn't sound quite right. What if I did this to it, or that? I thought, walking away from the piano with my block of manuscript paper and pencil. I sat down at the coffee table and attacked the little motif like a homework question for counterpoint.

Several dense pages of notes later, I looked at my watch in surprise. When had an emotional exercise become an intellectual one? I took the pages back to the piano, squinted at my hieroglyphs, and started to play. Hmm. There was the motif; and there I inverted it. That's where I sent it into the bass while the treble took off on a little tangent. I had stated the subtheme, played it counter to the melody, and, for the finale, resolved the minor key into the relative major and they lived happily ever after.

I played it over and over, awed and amazed. It didn't sound much like the doodle with which I'd started. It had weight and substance.

It could be read and replayed, improvised upon and mutated again. It was a snapshot of my sorrow and yet it had taken on the depth of a painting.

"How could Beethoven compose such beautiful music," I'd asked Jim once, "even after he'd gone deaf?"

"He heard it in his head," he'd said. "He knew the sound of every instrument, every scale, every chord so thoroughly he knew exactly how to mark it on paper."

I hadn't heard it all in my head when I sat down with paper and pencil, but I'd somehow managed to consolidate the rules of harmony and counterpoint with the motif I'd picked out: a gratifying bit of serendipity, unlikely to be repeated.

"I know it was difficult to break up with Sully," my mother comforted in the immediate aftermath. "But the good thing is, you learned something. You're young; sometimes you can't rely on your own judgement," she said, her words sending up red flags in my mind. "Dad and I have some experience with these things."

I swallowed my retort – angry words that could only cause a confrontation – nodded dumbly, pretending to accept her condescension. Arguing with her would only leave me exposed to parental judgement, by which I would always be found lacking. The unspoken but obvious conclusion I'd reached after fifteen years of their lectures: they were always right. The only way I could harbour my own opinion was to appear to agree and to think my own thoughts in private. Unreasonable as it was, I couldn't run the risk of being rejected. I'd seen Dad make rhetorical mincemeat of worthier opponents than I. To argue with him was to fence with a ruthless adversary. I would certainly lose my sword and stand there, vulnerable, shreds of logic flapping in the breeze, radical and foolish opinion exposed. Where, then, to hide those opinions, once so exposed?

It didn't matter that he sometimes *wanted* me to argue with him. Like our game of Change One Thing, debate was his form of intellectual exercise.

"I'm *not* afraid of him!" Sully insisted once after being defeated. "He loves to play devil's advocate as much as he loves to be proven right; maybe more."

"Then how come you always let him win?"

The Sully smirk: "I'm not an idiot, Mariah! He's your father — I've got more to lose than an argument."

Dad's most outrageous monologues were meant to provoke me into an exchange; I caught his puzzled, slightly hurt, expression more than once as he was forced to babble his way to an eventual conclusion.

But that was one thing I learned not to do: *exchange* thoughts and opinions. Listening was safe, if one-sided. By just listening, I could safely be with him (which I loved) and avoid conflict (which I hated).

I could never understand Luke's style of conflict and argument. He revelled in it, even drew it upon himself when he saw it being wasted on me. My style seemed so much safer and simpler and yielded me my own way more often than I care to admit, but it was essentially deadly to my self and to my relationship with my dad.

The balance of Dad's expectations shifted gradually. He no longer looked for me to argue against him. He would lecture and I would listen. Like Sully, he expected to see himself mirrored in my devoted eyes; to see himself as Daddy: handsome, omnipotent, infallible, all-knowing, beloved.

My grandfather looked up from his soup. "Where's the boy?" he asked, a month or more after the breakup.

Dad looked around vaguely, did a nose count. "Which boy, Pop?"

"The *Irish* boy," he responded.

Sully's presence had graced our dining table three or four nights a week for almost a year and yet Grandpa never referred to him by name. It was always "the Irish boy," spoken with that derisive tone that indicated that, in the mind of this Slovak immigrant at least, the Irish — first, second, or any generation — were lower on the immigration totem pole than even the despised "Polacks."

Everyone looked to me for an answer. "He's gone." On a long sea voyage? Dead? I didn't elaborate, just slurped my soup.

"I miss him!" Luke accused, standing so suddenly that his chair tipped against the wall as he barrelled his way past me.

"What the hell's *that* all about?" Dad asked, mystified.

"I think Luke admired Sully as a substitute brother," Mom said quietly. "A champion."

A champion. Yes; Luke missed him. So did I.

Grandpa hadn't been well, both before and after his accidental overdose. But I preferred to think he understood I was "Sully's girl," that he'd smelled Sully's scent on me like dog piss on a tree: *this territory is marked.* Sully's proprietary protection had extended slightly beyond his tenure, but it now wore off. The old man restaked his lapsed claim.

I didn't offer resistance, knowing it might only provoke him to greater extremes. If this was punishment, I deserved it. For wishing him dead; for destroying Sully. I could get off lightly only with good behaviour.

With maturity had come knowledge and, with knowledge, language. Where once I'd shut off a part of my mind to avoid reality, now I concentrated completely on the task at hand, exhibiting a false sense of control. Disgust was tempered with the sort of grim determination I applied to other unpleasant chores, like dusting, like doing the dishes.

Revolted by the little bits of food floating in the dirty dishwater, I thought if I hurried through the task I might finish before the grunge settled at the bottom, and my fingers might escape the spongy crumbs and wilted lettuce lurking with the last spoon in the basin.

So, too, with Grandpa: hurry, hurry. Do it right. Do it fast. Get him out of my bed before the filth has a chance to settle. And, with his departure, the hand-washing: over and over, like Lady Macbeth.

"You've just had your hands in soapy water for the last fifteen minutes," Mom exclaimed once. "Why are you washing them again?"

How to explain my disgust with the oil slicks, the errant peas, the old man in the night? She must have read my expression as I rinsed the detritus down the drain, for there was something special in the Safeway bag after her next shopping trip: a pair of rubber gloves, just for me.

If only I could have worn them to bed.

Amazing, isn't it? That one can accept the unacceptable when it becomes routine, can accept a sentence of second-degree depravity – a plea bargain – in exchange for escaping greater degradation. I would willingly – well, willingly is too strong a word – I would *reluctantly* provide a hand job for my grandfather if it meant a reprieve from fellatio or sodomy. His wrinkled penis in my hand was a talisman of sorts; I was grateful for small mercies.

And so, one night when he visits an unprovoked attack upon my backside, I feel extraordinarily betrayed, as if an unspoken bargain has been broken. My illusion of control crumbles like a windshield starred into a thousand shards. I wish he'd died. *The devil take him.* Or, if not him, then me.

Managing to feign illness for several days, I stay huddled in my bed, weeping so much in the intervals between Mom's visits that my sheets and pillowcases are sodden as if with the sweat of fever. I eat nothing, my body passing through intervals of dizziness by falling into sleep or oblivion.

On the third day, my mother announces, "I've run you a bath. Go have a nice soak while I change your sheets; I'm sure you'll feel better."

Shuffle tentatively to the bathroom like an old woman, Mom supporting my elbow.

"Can you manage?" she asks, "or do you want me to stay with you?"

Waving her away, "I'm fine," I say, clutching my bathrobe tighter, unable to strip naked in her presence.

"Don't lock the door," she warns. "If you feel dizzy, just call."

Nod, hovering as if I will hang my robe on the hook as soon as she leaves. I wait until I hear her footsteps creaking on the stairs to my room, then quietly turn the lock.

Let my robe and nightgown fall to the floor. I want to look at myself in the full-length mirror. Are the changes visible on my body? My face is pale, dark circles ring my eyes like a raccoon's. The mosaic tile is cold on my feet; the naked skin immediately pops out in goose flesh, my nipples stand at attention.

Thinner, yes; thinner. Three days without food. Three days weeping like a weakling. I brush my hand down my goose-bumped leg; what a disgusting sight. How long has it been since I last shaved my legs? I turn from the mirror, find the razor in the cupboard.

Fingers of steam beckon. I put the razor down on the edge of the tub, lower myself into the water gingerly, all the way to my neck. Despite the depth of the water, though, my breasts poke out of it like twin islands, the nipples flaccid now in the heat, the aureolae flushed pink but not identically, as if the artist's hand had flinched on application of the pigment; certainly a flaw. I crank on the hot water — *Oh, that this too, too solid flesh would melt* — obliterating the imperfect islands in the steaming flood.

The hot water aggravates and soothes my wound. As if the blood has ceased flowing to all other extremities, my pulse beats there and nowhere else, a throbbing bull's eye, surely as bright as a beacon. No wonder my grandfather can find it in the dark.

My hands: a few freckles; a mole; a scar from the time I burned myself on the oven rack. My watch is on the washstand, so the white "JA" on my wrist is exposed. Fingers: long, slender, the nails a uniform length.

"You're a pianist," my mother's voice reminds me. "You must keep your nails looking nice. Everyone looks at your hands as you play."

The nails are in decent shape but the hot water wrinkles the fingertips, magnifying their imperfections. I'm not *allowed* to chew my nails, so I worry the cuticles and surrounding skin; nibble on them sometimes until they bleed; pick at the skin and devour the severed bits like a sacrament. *This is my body.* It's easier when the flesh is soft and pliant.

My hand encounters the razor on the rim of the tub. The first time I found it, in circumstances identical to this, I wrestled my conscience for control of the razor — and my conscience won. Today I hold the razor in my hand and think, *I have no conscience.* The way I discarded Sully and Sully's love: *unconscionable.* Surely, anything I might inflict upon myself cannot atone for what I've done to him.

I shave my legs automatically, having done it some one hundred times since that first time with no further thought of spilling my own blood. Until now. When I'm done, I take the double-edged Wilkinson Sword blade from the handle, holding it firmly by the benign edges between thumb and forefinger, and examine it carefully — as if the pattern of holes down the middle might reveal itself as a foreign language for which I've suddenly discovered a talent.

No revelation comes. I stroke the inside of my left thigh. Fat, I think; flabby and gross compared to the trim ankle, the slender wrist. I press my leg open against the porcelain (cold above the water line, warm below). Take the blade in my right hand, press the edge gently against the dead white skin. It springs to life in a thin ribbon of colour.

Ah, colour! No pain, but the life-affirming colour of blood. Rotate the blade forty-five degrees, bisect the line, and press. A cross, now, of colour. *Christ died for our sins.* Rotate, bisect the angles once, twice: a flaming star, an asterisk of delicate red lines.

Admiring my handiwork, I'm pleased to discover a regular pulse beating in my ribcage again, after all. And a ringing in my ears, very much like music; a song very much like life.

An indefinable sense of peace descends as I watch the blood congeal in the star-shaped pattern on the inside of my thigh. It doesn't bleed as copiously as the accidental gouge I took out of my leg that first time. Drying myself carefully so as not to get blood on the towel, I'm calm, but shaky. For the first time in days I feel as if I could eat.

I was gratified by the fine scabs, then scars. A delicate tracery, gossamer as spider's web, virtually invisible – especially in such a location, where one would have to be looking to see it.

"What's this?" Doug asked once, having spread open my thighs in the intimacy of daylight, which I seldom allowed. He drew his finger-nail down each arm of the figure. "I've never seen a scar like this. It looks," he glanced up at me, his face framed by the V of my knees, "well, *deliberate*."

He returned to his examination, all business now like a doctor, passion quite evaporated by the heat of curiosity.

"This?" – a matching flower on the opposite thigh.

"And this?" – a circle of circles, each the exact diameter of a lit cigarette.

"And these?" – the random marks of a straight edge, where artistry or nerve had failed me. Less than or equal to; greater than or equal to, depending on your perspective; from mine they'd always indicated *less than, not equal to*. One could inscribe only so many asterisks on the creamy flesh of a thigh.

I trembled under his touch, dreading the moment of explanation, the questions. To have allowed myself to be so exposed!

He closed my knees like a book, rolled over, pulled the sheet up over my legs like a coroner over a corpse. He struggled up to the pillow and, leaning on his left elbow, looked at me intently.

"There's a name for that, you know." He knew a name for everything. "It's called 'delicate self-cutting.' It's a clinical term, with a clinical definition. Found quite often in adolescent women."

I was surprised. "I never imagined anyone else would do such a thing," I ventured. "I can't imagine so *many* people doing it that it would warrant a name."

He traced my eyebrow. "Textbook. Tension release?" I nodded. "How old were you?"

I puffed out some air, as if I had to think. "Fifteen. Sixteen. Before you."

Shaking his head, "I can't believe I never noticed before."

"I never let you."

He buried his head between my breasts, kissed them. "Mariah, Mariah."

I stroked his hair with my left hand; he reached for my right.

"And this," he said, kissing the nub of my wrist, "this might constitute 'coarse self-cutting,' if you'd done it on purpose. But self-amputation is more of a male thing."

I remember how I leapt out of bed at those words. Did I leap to escape the words, or his tone, his so detached, know-it-all tone? I'd never seen the words "delicate self-cutting" on paper. Where was the hyphen? *Delicate-self* cutting? – in which case it was the "delicate self" one was attempting to excise – and its flip side, *coarse-self* cutting: surely the excision of demons. Or was it delicate *self-cutting*, in which one cut oneself with delicacy and precision. A civilized pursuit for young ladies, like crewel embroidery.

Cruel embroidery. A sick, perverse thing to do to oneself. And yet, somehow, not nearly as cruel as the event that precipitated it. "Tension release" – yes, I admitted that much to him, but not the cause of the tension. It wasn't a little premenstrual tension I sought to release; nothing so mundane as performance pressure in either music or school. Not peer pressure, not dating pressure. I could never have imagined a sorority of delicate self-cutters at the time, so alone did I feel with my razor and my rage. How many other textbook young ladies were being butt-fucked by their grandfathers, now on an increasingly regular basis? How many others started with one completed symbol per episode, then had to be content with a single ray at a time, or one circular burn in a circle of circles, knowing there was a good chance symmetry could be achieved next month, or next week? Hoping to leave a figure unfinished, or to hold a razor blade again one day with the sole intent of shaving one's legs.

⌒

"What are you doing here, sweetheart?"

Dad shook me gently, waking me where I'd fallen asleep on the living-room couch after the rest of the household had gone to bed. My book fell to the floor.

"I was waiting for you," I said.

Actually I'd been avoiding Grandpa – whom I'd heard prowling the house. On speaking the lie, though, I was instantly convinced of its veracity.

He smiled. "Come into the kitchen, then. It's time for my midnight snack."

Midnight? The kitchen clock revealed the time as 2:30 a.m. Dad had just gotten in after the nightly ritual: he'd closed and cleaned the bar, taken inventory, and left the place in the capable hands of the dozing night clerk.

"How about a cheese and onion sandwich?" he asked, laughing at the face I made. "How about cheese and onion for me, and plain cheese for you?"

We clattered around together, toasting bread, staring into the fridge.

A few minutes later, as I nibbled my cheese sandwich and Dad wolfed down his repast, "How can you eat like that at this hour?" I asked.

"I've put in a full day's work," he said between bites. "It's as if I've just come home for dinner. That's the curse of shift work: even though it's the middle of the night, I still need time to unwind before I go to bed." He looked at me. "So, what are *you* doing up at this hour?"

"You woke me up, remember?"

"Mere details," he gestured with a glass of milk. "You said you were waiting for me. Any reason why?"

I shook my head, blushing a little, as if I'd been caught in a lie or, more accurately, a half-thought-out potential truth.

He patted my hand. "Well, I'm glad. It seems as if we don't spend much time together these days: you're busy during the day, and I'm so — " he paused, grinned, spread his arms wide, and continued in a Transylvanian accent " — so beezy afterr darrk!"

"Yeah, Dad; when was the last time I saw you up and around before sundown?"

He chuckled into his glass, drained it, then examined it as if it might magically refill itself. I went to the fridge, returned with more milk.

"Thanks. Just leave the bottle, barmaid." He refilled his glass, and began one of his stories.

"Are you going to finish that sandwich?"

I pushed it across the table, where it disappeared, like parentheses, in two bites wedged around a stream of words. He talked until he caught me in a yawn.

"As much as I've enjoyed your company, sweetheart, it's time for bed. Every hour you sleep before midnight," he launched into one of his favourite old-wives' tales, "is worth two after."

"What about you?" I asked, yielding to his hug. "You never get to bed before midnight."

He pulled down on his eyes. "That's why I look so ancient. I'm really only twenty-nine."

I went back to sleep with a smile on my lips.

The next morning, a Saturday, found me awake at the usual time. I took some books downstairs and spread them out over the breakfast-room table. Music exams were only a few weeks away. I timed myself to do a sample examination: three hours. Would that be too much or too little on the day?

"Add a part in invertible counterpoint at the fifteenth below the given part. Maximum marks: twenty-five."

There followed three staves of a piece by Handel. Hmm. At least that gave me a clue as to the expected style; it wouldn't do to plug in ragtime.

Then a different quotation. "Continue the lower voice, preserving the style of the opening. Thirty-five marks." Easy enough. But the next question, based on a third excerpt: "Complete the upper part of this piece for piano. Forty marks." Yuck. You could pretty much flunk the exam on that question alone.

I set to. It seemed as if I'd just started when Mom wandered into the kitchen.

"Boy, did I sleep in! I thought maybe Luke'd run away from home, it was so quiet around here." She looked over my shoulder. "Have you had breakfast, sweetie?"

"No," I replied, glancing at my watch. I'd been at it for ninety minutes, was almost finished the difficult third question. I'd saved the easy second one for last. "I'm not hungry. I ate with Dad last night."

"Don't wait too long. We don't want you keeling over."

I wave her away and continue the exam. Oops; hadn't noticed all the incidentals in the last half of the "easy" second question. I'll have to study the questions more carefully when allotting my time. Stare at the little black marks on the page. Intervals of fourths and fifths; progressions; a regular pattern of beats in four-four time: it's all so mathematical! Like a secret code, breakable if only you can decipher the sequence.

"Oh, God," I pray sardonically. "I'm not very good with math. But I'd really welcome some enlightenment as to the mysteries of invertible counterpoint."

I let my focus wander, then disintegrate entirely. Black smudges; what do they have to do with music, anyway?

My stomach growls, alerting me to the fact that I'm hungry, after all. A wave of nausea breaks across my vision. I should stop and eat. But, with an effort of will, I force myself to refocus on the page.

Suddenly it stops being mathematical. These notes on the page are like words in a story; they convey certain sounds, colours, rhythms. The melody is the story line. The visual shorthand integrates with the aural code. I hear the music. I know how the lower voice must sound, revealed in all its complexity. Gratefully, I scribble black marks on the page, convinced of their rightness.

Having completed the exercise in less than three hours, I take the finished paper into the living room to the piano. The part I've done last is definitely better, to my ears, than the others. The hard question is passable, but laboured. It doesn't sound as if my melody truly meshes with the bass provided, despite having followed all the rules.

Back to the kitchen to rework it entirely.

"Have you had lunch?" Mom asks.

"Yes," I answer — vaguely, distractedly. I can hear the Andante now; if only I could hum during the exam! Not wanting to be branded a nut like Glenn Gould, humming as he plays, I force myself to hear it in my head alone.

When I'm done, I take it to the piano, play it through several times with increasing gratification. Yawn mightily and sneak upstairs to my room for a snooze.

That evening I eat lightly, not wanting to tip Mom off to the fact that I haven't eaten since 3:00 a.m.

On examination day, I credit my easy pass to the breakthrough of being able to hear the music I see upon the page. And attribute my new-found faculty to divine revelation brought about by prayer and fasting.

"What can I feed Dad tonight when he comes home from work?" I'd quiz my mother.

Bemused, she'd point out the choicest leftovers, cheeses, coils of garlic sausage, fresh rye bread, mustard, pickled herring.

Well into my new routine, I'd catch a secret nap after school, then set my internal alarm clock to go off at the sound of his car in the driveway. Mom monitored me for tiredness, which I took care not to display. I liked to show off for Dad, proud of my increasing competence in the kitchen.

"What are these?" he asked, gobbling down a damaged, over-baked cookie, one of my first attempts.

"Gingerbread men."

"They look more like the casualties of a gingerbread battle," he teased, "but they taste good."

I blushed, angry at myself for not greasing the cookie sheet properly; the biscuits had stuck at random, leaving the pan littered with fragments. My sole meal of the day had consisted of a spatula's-worth of those crumbs, prised off the sheet. I deserved nothing better than to consume my mistakes: strands of pasta welded to the bottom of the pot; a strip of burnt bacon; gelatinous egg whites, not quite coddled. If the error was too large – like a shrivelled, hockey puck of a meat loaf – I would take a tiny bit for myself and share the rest with the dog, but I would never offer my father defective goods again.

I loved those times, huddled around the kitchen table in my bathrobe. I read all manner of books I knew he'd read so we could talk about them: Hemingway, Shakespeare, Churchill, Marx. Books were safe. They might veer dangerously toward politics – a potential minefield that could trigger an angry explosion – but I felt extraordinarily sheltered basking in the glow of his late-night attention, fed by his love.

My availability to keep my dad company during the wee hours served Mom's agenda. She'd always got up when my dad came home, having decided that if she expected to stay married to this night owl, she'd have to adapt. She'd run out of energy; she wasn't well. She was off the hook as long as I was willing to understudy as my father's nocturnal audience.

I was happy to look after the family while she was in the hospital for the hysterectomy. Shopping, cleaning, cooking. Cooking especially – making wonderful meals for my dad and (only incidentally) Luke and Grandpa – totally in control of the kitchen.

There were a few schedule changes. Dad worked the day shift that week so he could be home at night with Luke and me. The dog, Sasha – used to having the run of the neighbourhood when Mom was around

— was tied to the half-opened garage door so she'd have shade and shelter during the day. Dad was supposed to feed her and leave a bucket of water before he set off for work.

I came home from school that late June day, sweating in the extraordinary (for Thunder Bay) heat, lugging books and a Safeway bag. Sasha growled from the shadowed maw of the garage.

"Poor thing! You're out of water."

Without putting anything down, I turned on the hose and bent to pick up the nozzle to fill the dog's pail.

Crazed with heat and thirst, the German shepherd lunged out of the garage, clamping my mini-skirted thigh in her jaws. Screaming with pain and surprise, I dropped the hose, books, and groceries — broken eggs, apples rolling down the driveway, water spraying everywhere.

The dog was immediately apologetic but so thirsty she lapped water from a puddle while I, trembling with shock, carefully filled her pail.

"Poor Sasha," I wept. "Poor Sasha."

Thirst slaked, she padded over to the pail, guzzled more water out of it, then sniffed my thigh. I hadn't noticed the blood before.

"Okay, girl," I sighed. "Clean up the eggs." And she wolfed down the entire dozen.

I was still chasing apples around the sodden driveway, when Dad pulled in.

"What happened here?" he asked tiredly.

"Sasha didn't have any water," I started, ready to launch into the saga.

"My fault," he rubbed his eyes behind his glasses. "I left the house in a rush. Your mother had a bit of an emergency."

My stomach lurched. "What happened?"

"She's fine; she's fine," he flapped his hand dismissively. "Can you manage here?" And headed for the house without awaiting my answer.

Oh, fine! Rage roils within me. My mother's fine. *She* can have an emergency and he'll race off without attending to his other obligations. A neglected animal can sink her teeth into my flesh and he doesn't even notice. Well, *fuck you*, Dad; *fuck you*, too, Mom. *I wish you'd died.*

I slam my way into the kitchen, drop the groceries noisily on the counter. He's at the breakfast-room table, head in his arms, sobbing.

"Daddy?"

"She almost died; Jesus, she almost died."

He reaches out to me, mumbling *incompetent doctors* and *haemorrhages* and *another round of surgery to cover up the way they'd botched the first.* I take him in my arms; hold him and comfort him while he weeps and tells me how much he loves her and how scared he was of losing her. All the while feeling as if I'd cursed myself with the words *I wish you'd died.*

"Oh, my God!" he exclaims when he sees the circle of puncture marks, the blood congealing on my thigh. "Sasha did that?"

"She didn't mean to."

"Oh, baby," he sobs. "Get the peroxide; I'll help you clean up."

"I can handle it, Daddy," I say gently. "I'll have a nice soak in the tub. Cool off a little; get cleaned up." *Shave my legs.* "And then make you a nice dinner."

"Pickle?" he'd shove a plate across the table. "Cheese?"

"No, thanks. I had a big supper."

And in the morning when I'd take Mom a tray: "Did you get some breakfast yourself, sweetie?"

"Oh, yes."

At dinner: "You've become a great cook, Mariah. Why aren't you eating?"

"I was so hungry, I ate while I was messing around in the kitchen."

So easy to lie! And, yet, not a lie: I was truly not hungry in the middle of the night, truly not hungry at breakfast, at dinner, at lunch. I could control my light-headedness during the day, I'd found, by a small snack, sheer will-power, a quick prayer. If that didn't work, there was always a nap or – that long indolent summer – the chance to stretch out on the couch or the chaise in the backyard with a book.

The scuff of slippers on linoleum, the whisper of a silky robe: if we ignore her, will she go away?

"May I join you?"

Irrational anger wells within me. Why has she come downstairs? It's *my* time, no matter that I've usurped her position as kitchen angel. In fact, *why didn't she die?* With the anger, an electrical charge, such as I'd felt for Jim, for Sully.

Love.

Let it be Daddy.

Jesus.

I stand up suddenly, smacking my chair against the wall.

"What's the matter, sweetie?"

Mutely, I stare at my parents. My silent scream: *This is wrong; this is wrong.*

"Just a little warm," I smile woodenly. "Think I'll have a soak — unless you need the bathroom, Dad."

"No. Just don't be all night."

Oh, you're sick, Mariah! *Why didn't she die?* Your mother isn't a woman, any more; they've cut it all out. Calcified by endometriosis, hard as stone. No womb to bleed from, just as you don't bleed. Have you turned yourself into her? Or has she turned into you? How long before he comes looking for you, little wifey? After all, you'd make him such a fine wife, intellectual equal and all.

No, you don't bleed any more. But you can. Take the razor: yes, you can.

⌒⌒⌒⌒

"That must be Lily Flowers' boy," Dad said.

The family was all together in the station wagon — that summer, after I broke up with Sully — on our way somewhere, when we passed Doug walking on the street. I followed him with my eyes, then peered out the back window of the car over my shoulder until he was out of sight.

"Doug Hassock," I supplied.

"Hassock, pah!" he exclaimed. "His grandfather was 'Hašek.' What's wrong with a good old Slovak name?"

"Like 'Standhoffer,' you mean?" Mom teased.

"It's German, Ginny! We didn't Anglicize it," he exclaimed, aggrieved. "They tossed borders onto the Austro-Hungarian Empire like pick-up sticks," he said, embarking on a magical history tour.

Doug Hassock. What surprised me most about the sighting was my physiological reaction to it. It seemed entirely out of proportion to the encounter. I experienced a full body blush, arrhythmia, and faintness. All on a day when I'd eaten quite well: three grapes, the scrapings of Luke's breakfast yoghurt container, and the tooth-crescents of toast crusts left on his plate.

Perhaps it was the heat. Our annual fortnight of Thunder Bay summer had held over Labour Day. Or perhaps — and here my heart started to race again — perhaps I was attracted to him in a way that, before that summer, I wouldn't have imagined.

September 1969. The first time I saw him was in the lunch room at school. He stood across the room, leaning casually against the wall, holding a can of pop in his hand. Something in the awkwardness of his grasp caught my attention. I refocused, trying to discern what it was that had caught my eye. He turned in profile, put the can down on the table — not by stretching out his arm and placing it on the surface as any of us might, but by bending at the waist and releasing it carefully from shoulder level.

How strange! I thought. How awkward.

He swung his torso back to full standing height. With a rush of blood from my face as if I'd seen him picking his nose or pissing behind a tree, realization hit me like a gong: he had no right arm. A right hand, yes, jutting straight from the shoulder. But no right arm.

Rampant speculation followed: birth defect? Thalidomide? Act of God? And, with the speculation, that forbidden feeling: the moisture between my legs; the screech, like feedback, in my ears; the blindfold passing momentarily across my field of vision, then falling away. The intake of breath: hold it! hold it! Breathe. And try to forget the unacceptable, that inexplicable flash of desire.

He was a strange commodity. Douglas Hassock: science whiz; math geek. Part freak, part god. His was a bizarre charisma. He was shunned by the boys: no interest in sports, too smart for his own good. And loved by the girls for the same reasons. An intellectual boy — just what some of us wanted. And a fascinating freak, to boot, all the more fascinating because of his perfect twin, Kat.

We were all in the same freshman year at the Collegiate, shared various classes and extracurricular activities. I studied him when he wasn't looking, shot him "the smile" when he was. Kat and I were lab partners in science class, our friendship kindled over a Bunsen burner. She was much better at it than I was; I owe my only decent grade in physics to her.

My friendship with Kat allowed access to Doug, access that fostered acceptance and took me beyond the need to stare. He was "Kat's brother" to me, while others referred to him variously as "the guy with the little hand" or, depending upon the degree of imbecility of the speaker, "the Freak."

His easy manner made him approachable. On the surface he was forgiving of the stares and moronic questions.

"Teratologists refer to it as 'phocomelism,' which is a bit of a mis-nomer," he would explain to anyone who asked. "A phocomelic is a 'seal child,' according to the definition: a human with vestigial hands. The bone structure within the appendages of seals, whales, and other marine mammals is remarkably human," he would waggle his fingers, "but, as you can see, my hand is rather more developed than a seal's flipper. It's the arm, in this case, that is vestigial."

The interlocutor would race, blushing, for the nearest dictionary or, if brash enough, would ask, "What is teratology?"

And he'd reply, with a sadistic sort of glee twinkling in his green eyes, "The study of animal or vegetable monstrosities."

What a conversation killer! It didn't take me long to realize he wore his defences like a set of Russian dolls: an inferiority complex within a superior intellect, within a razor wit, within a benign (if malformed) exterior.

He *was* a bit of an exhibitionist. I often replayed that first sighting, and my reaction to it, in my mind – that feeling of having intruded on something that should be kept private. That was his intent. He was, quite deliberately, pissing in plain view, daring anyone to comment. He didn't try to hide his infirmity; he flaunted it.

What was wrong with that first sighting? Not that he used his little hand, but that he used the *awk*wardness of using it. He could as easily have transferred that can to his good hand, then put it down on the table. But no: he bent, released it from shoulder height, and swung his torso back to standing position – with all the aplomb of a flasher tuck-ing his pecker back into his pants.

Was it perversity? Or the sheer strength of his self-confidence?

As the blood faded from my cheeks that day, though, I made a res-olution. *Run run as fast as you can, you can't catch me I'm the gingerbread man.* I would explore this strange attraction to see where it would lead.

It took me over a year. Sully's aura marked me much longer at school than it had at home. I was anathema to the Pill Hill lads: one of their own had been dealt a death blow. They were all perfect, in any case; I didn't deserve them. Doug was an outsider to that crowd (both geo-graphically and fiscally), but even he kept a respectful distance. I was forced to take action.

Did he know? Did he sense that my orbit had shifted subtly from the gravitational pull of friendship with his sister to a potential involvement with him? I was shocked by my own lack of determination in the matter. It was a given, like the moon's status as a satellite of the earth.

Kat and I were "school" friends. The Hassock family, like almost everyone else's, lived on the other side of town, so we weren't likely to bump into each other over the holidays. I liked Kat very much, though; I felt a strong sense of kinship with her, despite our complementary aptitudes at school: hers in maths and sciences, mine in arts. Kat was so excruciatingly shy she made me look downright gregarious; she was as reticent as Doug was brash.

Spending more time with the twins during eleventh grade wasn't difficult. We had a number of classes in common. It was natural to follow Kat into more extracurricular activities, many of which, as Doug's twin, she naturally shared with him: the chorus, the Red Cross club, the church youth group.

By Grade 12, the core members of these groups overlapped, forming a sort of clique of friends – male and female alike – who were largely devoted to Doug. At least, Doug was the catalyst. If he abandoned any of these enterprises, it seemed to fall apart – as when separate iron filings lose the magnet that drew them together.

Since there was nothing at which Doug did not excel except, of course, sports, he was in the "enriched" stream of everything: maths, sciences, English, French. Our twelfth-grade English teacher was generally uninspired, except when it came to Shakespeare. He made us memorize speeches from various of the plays and present them.

Doug and Sully excelled. It became a competition. They goaded each other to ever more complex performances, expanding their range of drama and subtlety. Doug's "To Be or Not To Be" – performed in front of a class of twelfth graders with only the blackboard for a set – was mesmerizing. It unleashed a passionate streak in all of us, particularly the teacher, Mr. Harris.

"Doug," he gushed after class, "That was a wonderful performance. Mr. Widener and I have always wanted to put on a full Shakespearean play, one of the historical tragedies, but we've never had strong enough male leads. Now we do."

"What about this?" Doug gestured, shrugging his right shoulder. "I'm not exactly Romeo material."

"A good actor can make the audience forget anything. But I have the perfect play in mind." He ran to the book shelf, pulled out a slender volume: *Richard III.* "Read this carefully. If you think you'd be comfortable in the part, let me know. We'll talk."

We left the room together. Doug held the Shakespeare in his little hand, tucked his other books under his good arm. " '*Richard III*: the Crookback King.' Sounds like typecasting, don't you think?"

"Some actors have made a lifetime career of one role. Maybe you've found yours," I suggested.

He stopped in his tracks. "Let's skip our next class," he exclaimed, his face lighting with anticipation. "We'll read the play together, see if it's any good. What do you think?"

My heart tumbled awkwardly. Two of the school's best students, skipping class together? But the pay-off: a whole hour alone with Doug. "Sure," I answered, with no discernible hesitation.

He led the way to the auditorium which, despite its reputation as a public place, offered quiet nooks and crannies. There was, inexplicably, a couch in the wings – actually a *chaise longue*, the kind one might see in a psychiatrist's office, with a raised back perfect for reclining.

"Here," he waved toward the couch. "We can sit here."

I perched awkwardly on the end; he assumed a lotus position with the ease of familiarity. "Do you spend much time here?"

"It's a great place to escape. If I don't have a class, I'm here. And, sometimes when I do have a class, I'm here." He smiled. "Don't look so shocked, Mariah! Sometimes it's what you learn out of class that's more important, in the long run. Like Shakespeare," he appended, waving the book at me. "Let's start."

We put our heads together over the book. I could hardly breathe. We'd never been alone together, never mind so close I could feel the warmth of his left shoulder – his good shoulder – pressed against mine; so close I could discern his shampoo, his soap, his deodorant – separately and intermingled – on the warm air current that rose between us.

" 'Now is the winter of our discontent made glorious summer by this sun of York'," he began, his voice rich and close (so close!) in my ear.

> "But I, that am not shaped for sportive tricks
> Nor made to court an amorous looking glass;
> I, that am rudely stamped, and want love's majesty

To strut before a wanton ambling nymph;
I, that am curtailed of this fair proportion,
Cheated of feature by dissembling Nature,
Deformed, unfinished, sent before my time
Into this breathing world scarce half made up,
And that so lamely and unfashionable
That dogs bark at me as I halt by them. . . .
Why, I, in this weak piping time of peace,
Have no delight to pass away the time,
Unless to spy my shadow in the sun
And descant on mine own deformity."

He dropped the book into my lap and leapt from the couch.

My pulse surged in my ears. While he read, I'd felt the creeping blush. Richard's words were so transparent I feared Doug might be insulted.

But when he turned to me, his expression was delight, more than anything; triumph, perhaps.

"This is great!" he grinned. "Can you imagine the impact of those words coming out of my mouth, opening the play? Can you feel the audience squirm in embarrassment? There I am on the stage, one arm flapping in the breeze, spouting Richard's words: 'cheated of feature by dissembling Nature,' " he gestured, " 'deformed, unfinished, sent before my time into this breathing world scarce half made up.' "

I was astounded: he had the speech half memorized on first reading. He paced the space we'd claimed for our own, his thoughts so loud I could almost hear them.

"Let's read some more; there's got to be a part for you in here."

"For me?!" I squeaked.

He sat down beside me, looked at me earnestly. "Oh, yes; the soliloquies you've prepared for class have been great. You have the IQ for Shakespeare. We're going to need all the brains we can get on that stage."

"What about Kat?" I asked, feeling somehow disloyal.

"She has the IQ but, alas, poor shrinking Violet," he shook his head, "she was not made to tread the boards. But you and I shall rule England together, if only for a time."

It was obvious he'd already decided he was going to be Richard. No, in the space of reading the opening lines, he'd *become* Richard. Despite my reservations, he dragged me along in the wake of his enthusiasm.

"Read Lady Anne." He'd scanned ahead a scene or two. "Richard has murdered her husband and her father-in-law, but he's going to woo her and win her."

I poked my head over his shoulder. "How do you know that already?" I marvelled.

"It's here in the *dramatis personae*: 'Lady Anne, widow of Edward Prince of Wales, son of King Henry VI; afterwards married to Richard.' Start there."

Anne's first speech was an extended curse against Henry's murderer: charming. I swam through the flood of blood to my face as I intoned her words, spat at Richard: " 'Blush, blush, thou lump of foul deformity.' "

By the end of the scene, Anne wore Richard's ring by dint of the strength of his personality. And, by dint of Doug's, I had consented to audition for the part. I would be his Lady Anne.

"I've heard he was the black sheep of a Boston Brahmin family. That his family disowned him and exiled him to Canada."

"Probably a draft-dodger."

"He's too old for the draft! But *I* heard he's independently wealthy."

"Then why's he teaching in this dump?"

Richard Winslow Widener III was the kind of teacher who was either loved or hated intensely. He demanded excellence. Too urbane and cultured for a blue-collar town, he was conspicuous in his very conservatism. Very few of his students were ambivalent in their regard for him. Some picked their courses and juggled their timetables to get into his classes each year; others would rather drop out of high school than face the prospect of sitting under his tutelage.

The students who loved him were loyal. Of the others, some were intimidated; some were awed; some felt threatened. Troupes of the more idiotic mimes of the school sashayed down the hall behind him, turning his poised, elegant walk into the visual equivalent of a lisp and limp wrist. There was a corpus of apocryphal anecdotes supporting various theses: he was a "fairy," a dethroned aristocrat, a Kennedy-conspiracy witness-in-hiding.

Mr. Widener, consummate gentleman, never paid attention to the emulation, good or bad. But he knew instinctively which students numbered among his allies and tried to cultivate them.

For us he became a sort of cult figure, a window on the world outside the provincial palisades that imprisoned the Thunder Bay mentality.

Messrs. Harris and Widener wasted no time throwing together a production of *Richard III* once Mr. Harris had "discovered" Doug. Auditions were advertised and held.

"You're a shoo-in for Lady Anne," Doug whispered as I stumbled into a seat next to him at the back of the auditorium.

"I'm not sure that's a good thing," I whispered in return. "Look at my hands!" I held them out, trembling, for him to see. My face still burned from the combined effects of the lights and my own terror.

He inclined toward me like a courtier, took one hand, and gave it the merest hint of a kiss – which did nothing to still its trembling.

"I don't know why you want me for your Lady Anne, anyway," I said with feigned petulance. "You're only going to kill me in short order to marry your brother's daughter."

Doug jumped to his feet as if to hail Mr. Widener. "It's not too late for you to audition for Margaret or Elizabeth; they both have many, many more lines than Anne!"

I pulled him hastily back into his seat. He laughed.

"But soft! what worthy opponent before us takes the stage?"

I turned in time to see Sully step into the spotlight. He shielded his eyes from the light, spoke to Harris and Widener some rows back. "Richmond," he stated, "from Act V, scene iii."

"Ah!" Doug breathed into my ear. "My nemesis!"

Sully took a moment to examine his shoes, then launched into Richmond's oration to the troops, projecting to the back row where, I'm sure, he knew I sat:

> "For what is he they follow? Truly, gentlemen,
> A bloody tyrant and a homicide;
> One raised in blood and one in blood established;
> One that made means to come by what he hath,
> And slaughterèd those that were the means to help him;
> A base foul stone, made precious by the foil
> Of England's chair, where he is falsely set;
> One that hath ever been God's enemy."

"Not bad," Doug conceded. I shushed him.

> "Sound drums and trumpets boldly and cheerfully;
> God and Saint George! Richmond and victory!"

It was all I could do not to applaud. Sully had always been dramatic, but this speech showed true flair. I was impressed, despite myself. As was Doug.

"I don't intend to be felled on the field of battle by the likes of Sully Riordan!" he grunted.

I raised my eyebrows. "Do you plan to rewrite Shakespeare?"

Doug sat back in his seat, sighed deeply, glanced at me from the corner of his eye. "I can't believe he broke up with you," he said.

"He didn't," I answered, a little sharply. "I broke up with him."

"Perhaps knave Richmond plans to woo the Lady Anne," he suggested.

I shook my head. "He doesn't stand a chance."

"Art sure, fair Anne?" His tone made me turn. "I saw the way your eyes glommed onto his." He held my glance a long beat; I said nothing. "We'll see," he said. Then, turning back to the stage, he switched tack: "Keep an eye on the new girl; she's trying to steal your part. You could wind up as Margaret or Elizabeth yet."

Birgitta Andersen, a stunning blonde, had recently transferred from another school. She was beautiful *and* brainy, active in school politics, and had amassed a storehouse of general knowledge sufficient to earn her a spot on the Collegiate's high school quiz show team.

"Thank you, Birgitta." Mr. Widener rose from his place in the auditorium. "Would you mind reading Queen Margaret at Act I, scene iii, line 185? Margaret was banished after Richard killed her husband and son, and now — "

"Yes, I know," Birgitta interrupted. "I've prepared that as well." She cleared her throat.

" 'What! Were you snarling all before I came, ready to catch each other by the throat, and turn you all your hatred now on me?' " she began, launching into Margaret's angry tirade with both venom and dignity.

Doug followed her movements as she took a seat next to Sully, a few rows in front of us. As Sully bent his head to speak, her laughter rippled the silence like a skipping stone. "She'll do well as Margaret," Doug said. "She's not afraid of conflict."

And I am? I thought, but did not voice, thereby proving the truth of the observation. Yes, yes; I'm afraid of conflict. That's how I wound up auditioning for Lady Anne in the first place, despite my fear of performance. I'd fallen into predictable patterns: I'm the perfect woman. To be within your sight, I'll do the unpredictable, the unsafe.

What is performance, after all, but another mask? I'll take the face of "actress" out of my box of tricks and wear it. No matter that it resembles the others I wear: "good student," "pianist," "Perfect Daughter." Similar, smiling, impenetrable masks for Mariah to hide behind.

Mr. Harris held the floor at the first meeting convened to draw the cast together. His opening remarks were welcoming in nature, encouraging, impassioned.

"And now, I give you Richard the Third."

Mr. Widener took the floor with a patronizing smile for Mr. Harris. "While it's true that I'm Richard, the third of the Widener family to bear that name, there all similarity with Shakespeare's 'crookback king' ends. For I have no murderous intent for these proceedings."

A tentative giggle from the cast.

"We, together, will move the audience, providing its members with catharsis and entertainment. We'll work hard, but we'll enjoy ourselves in so doing.

"*Richard III*," he went on, "has frequently been transposed into other eras, in order to make the play more accessible to contemporary audiences. During the first read-throughs, I'd like you to be alert to resonances that might give us such a peg. It will also be necessary to cut a little from the script; *Richard III* is one of the longest of Shakespeare's tragedies. But until we know what angle we're going to take, we won't know what may be cut without unravelling the plot."

The read-through proceeded. Doug had vast quantities of lines to learn as Richard – who was either in every scene or cast his shadow across the action, larger than life.

I tried to concentrate on Lady Anne. What would possess her – not long widowed – to marry her husband's murderer? Her disdain of Richard was evident in her opening speech. In Richard's words: "Was ever woman in this humour wooed? Was ever woman in this humour won?" Why was she so ready to believe the words of a dissembling

murderer? Was the lure of power – power shared, but power nonetheless – great enough to kill her objections to the man himself?

At some point in my studies, an image of Jacqueline Kennedy Onassis
flitted across my consciousness. I remembered asking my parents why a
woman like that would marry such a toad as Aristotle Onassis.

"For power, perhaps. For privacy," my father suggested. "Only someone of his stature would have enough money to protect her and her
family properly."

We'd been young at the time, but who among us could forget the
image she cast at JFK's funeral: the grieving but composed widow at a
November gravesite, holding her children's hands: black coat, black
pillbox hat, little black veil across her eyes?

And the matriarch, Rose Kennedy – she who'd buried so many
children, so publicly: "Was never mother had so dear a loss." The
Duchess of York's words, as she compares sorrows with her son's children and widow.

Discussing my thoughts with Doug, "It's not a direct parallel," I
said, "only a suggestion. They're contemporary figures we can all
relate to."

"You're right," he said, nodding, thinking.

"But who would that make Richard?" I posed disingenuously, not
wanting to risk my own obvious conclusion, in case it was too far-out.

"Well, it's very indirect," Doug mused. "But if you crown a Richard
king, using the Oval Office for the throne room, then there's only one
person he could be," he proposed. "Richard Nixon."

I nodded, pleased.

"The personification of evil, but with a wicked sense of humour,"
he continued, gesturing. "Haldemann and Erlichmann as the murderers: Richard's department of dirty tricks. Perhaps Kissinger as
Buckingham?"

"And who is Richmond?" I asked. "Who is Richard's nemesis? And
over what is the final battle fought?"

"Richmond really only wants peace and unity within the kingdom,"
he said, "an end to the War of the Roses. So," he looked to me for confirmation, "Nixon's war was ended, in effect, by the peace movement."
He nodded his head imperceptibly. "A battle of placards, in front of
the Washington Monument. Yes?"

Yes. And so it was: a modern hook to hang our Richard upon.
Doug, of course, was our spokesman before the teachers. I shrank from

taking credit, but he shared it with me equally.

Constantly together during rehearsals, I would seek him out or he'd seek me. Our point of rendezvous became the red couch which, inexplicably, stayed in position in the wings throughout, as if it were bolted to the floor.

"Are you okay?" Birgitta walked into the wings to find me, one day, head between my knees.

"Just a little light-headed," I admitted.

"Why don't you lie down?" She rustled through her shoulder bag, handed me a box of yoghurt-covered raisins.

"Thanks." Our hands brushed; hers felt like a branding iron.

"Yow. You're freezing!" she exclaimed. "Take my coat." She fussed around me like a mom.

"I'm fine."

"Anyone would take you for a ballerina," she said. "Why do *you* need to be so thin?"

"I'm *not*."

She cocked a knowing eyebrow, smiled a little sadly.

By the time Doug arrived I'd consumed a dozen raisins and felt reanimated. There I was, stretched out full length on our couch, casually studying my lines.

What was more natural than that he should recline beside me? Once the precedent was set, it remained unbroken. Everyone knew either of us could be found between scenes — before, after, and during rehearsal, anytime we weren't actually on stage — laid out on our couch, singly or together. Close but not intimate, separated by a chalk line of absolute circumspection.

A tall stepladder screeched across the floor; a shadowy figure ascended it from the far side. We were running through Doug's lines, oblivious to the activity around us. The figure fiddled noisily with a light fixture, then we were suddenly illuminated.

"Well," intoned the unseen voice from above, "if it isn't Sigmund and Anna, cosied up together on the couch."

We looked up, shading our eyes. The voice was Sully's.

"Anna was Freud's daughter," Doug retorted.

"An unnatural relationship, no matter how you look at it."

The beam of light drifted away from us, wandered about the stage.

"Mariah, Doug; step onto your marks for Act I, scene ii," called Mr. Widener. "Sully, let's refocus that spot. Fine. Richard, at the end of the

scene, when Anne says, 'Imagine I have said farewell already,' you'll surprise her with a kiss.'"

My neck snapped so suddenly toward the teacher I almost gave
myself whiplash. A kiss? That wasn't in the script! I was hardly accus-
tomed to hearing the seductive words Doug, as Richard, must speak to
me. But a kiss!

I allowed my eyes to meet his. He wore a funny little smile. Just as I
thought he might say something – blam! the spotlight fell, exploding
into shards of glass and expletives.

"Are you all right?" we asked each other, were asked by everyone who
rushed to the scene.

Sully leapt from the ladder. "God! I'm sorry!" he apologized. If it
hadn't been for his unnatural pallor I might have suspected that the
light was aided in its descent. "Watch out for the glass," he warned as
he dashed off for a broom.

The kiss was thus forestalled that evening. Considering my initial,
violent response, I was surprised to define my eventual reaction as palpable disappointment. Here I was, ready to be subsumed, on stage, by
sanctioned passion; to let my lips meet Doug's in full view of the student body, parents, strangers: everyone. A declaration of all – or nothing. For what true emotion ever attended a stage kiss?

But at the next rehearsal, Mr. Widener glossed over it. He blocked
the scene in terms of upstage arms and downstage arms.

"I think it will be most effective if the audience is reminded of
Richard's . . . um, handicap. Yes. Stand just so, angled to the prosceni-
um. Dramatic screen embrace. Fine – we'll practise the kiss some other
time. Next!"

And we were hustled from the stage before I could determine what
had hit me: a sort of public *coitus interruptus*.

Rehearsal after rehearsal, the story was the same: no kiss. I began to
suspect it would be dropped completely. The teachers must have
changed their minds.

"Do you want a ride home?" I had the car and permission to go
somewhere for a Coke with the gang after rehearsal, if the opportunity presented itself.

"I'm supposed to meet Kat at Eaton's after she gets off work."

"I can take you both home."

It was very cold. The station wagon sent up clouds of frozen exhaust as we kept it running, parked close to the staff entrance, waiting for Kat.

I plucked up my nerve. "Why do you think we haven't rehearsed the Act I kiss yet?"

The distance across the bench seat was so immense I thought perhaps Doug hadn't heard. Staring at his gloved hand, he flexed it experimentally as if he was surprised to discover an opposable thumb. "Because I asked the teachers to skip it. For now."

"I see." The small voice was my own.

Doug cleared his throat. "Richard is such a monster. When he says, 'Bid me farewell,' that's where the kiss should be. He should force the kiss on Anne, a predatory kiss. And she should slap his face, then say her line: 'Tis more than you deserve.' See?"

I nodded.

"We'll have to rehearse it, of course." He stared at his open palm, then looked up at me. "But I don't want to see Anne's revulsion for Richard on your face the first time I kiss you."

"I see." Same words, different intonation — backed by more resolve than I knew I had, or dared reveal.

Somehow the space between us dissolved and, despite steering wheel and winter coats, it was accomplished. A kiss. Right there, under the cold sodium lights, in spitting distance of Eaton's. We grinned maniacally at each other.

Over his shoulder, I noted a bundled figure walk past the car. "Kat."

Doug fumbled with the door handle and called for her. Frigid air blew in.

"We took for ever balancing," she laughed. "I thought you'd left without me. Hi, Mariah! What a nice surprise."

As his sister clambered in, Doug scooched down the bench seat toward me, his thigh coming to rest comfortably pressed against mine. Placing his finger to his lips he enjoined me to secrecy. I nodded. Kat chattered on, noticed nothing.

"Do you have to go straight home?" I asked. "How about hot chocolate? You can phone from the Grill."

The three musketeers: our pact as a threesome was sworn that evening. It was not unwelcome. I considered Doug and Kat equally my friends and held my hands out to the warm glow of inclusion like someone who'd been left in the cold too long. I wanted to fling my arms around them both.

We were inseparable after that, in whatever form and combination.

"May I speak with a twin?" I'd ask on the phone.

It wasn't as if I was phoning a *boy*. They were a unit, either/or. It didn't matter which of them answered when formulating plans: if Kat wasn't available, Doug was. If Doug wasn't available, Kat was. Or, most often, they both were. All for one, and one for all — I would have thrown myself in front of a bus to save either of them.

That our first private kiss was not repeated seemed hardly to matter: its light shone between us like overlapping haloes in a sacred painting. The most difficult thing about rehearsals became not the public kiss, but having to slap Doug across the face after it — an idea the teachers had bought.

"This way," Mr. Harris demonstrated. "It will make noise, but it won't hurt."

I shook my head, embarrassed. "I can't."

"Try."

"It's okay," Doug coaxed.

"People! Everyone on stage! We're going to have a little exercise here."

Mr. Harris demonstrated the stage slap to everyone. "Got it?" Nods all around. "Booth! Put the 'Blue Danube' on over the P.A."

He positioned us in two circles on the stage, one clockwise, the other, counter-clockwise. "When the music goes 'da da da da da' you walk; then, on the beat, you 'slap-slap' the person across from you. Go!"

Much goofing-off followed, the stage populated with Three Stooges clones. Until the music brought me to Sully. Oh, I slapped him, right on cue. But he wouldn't slap me. Arms at his sides, his gaze remained fixed on mine as he moved on, slapping the next person gently. His pacifism ended, however, when he faced Doug as an opponent.

"Hey!" Doug exclaimed. And though he shook it off, the imprint of Sully's hand remained on his face long after the exercise had ended — as Sully's expression, when I slapped him, stayed with me. *Grow up; get over it!* I couldn't stand that naked gaze: Sully, singed of all defences by the backdraft of first love.

Richard III was far from flawless. It had moments of unintentional hilarity, as lines were flubbed or cues were missed, scenery stuck, or curses emanated from backstage. It was, after all, a high-school production.

Still — and most everyone who saw it will agree — there was something about it: moments that transcended the mundane; moments that soared.

Doug's portrayal of Richard was as good as any I've seen since; perhaps better. His Richard was not all monster, not all evil and ambition. He brought both humour and humanity to the part – and arrogance and humility in equal measure.

No fake humpback, no false limp. Just Shakespeare's words ringing with veracity, magnified by the inescapable demonstration of his own handicap. We could see his Richard as a boy: compensating for his lacunae by burying himself in books, wielding a barbed wit like a rapier and words like "teratology" against the taunts.

We *liked* his Richard better than Sully's righteous, white-bread Richmond. Richard's tragedy was that of a man unable to channel his rage and ambition into anything but evil when, if only he'd asked, we might gladly have handed him the crown.

❧

What a huge gap there was in our lives: no rehearsals, no applause, no excuse for a daily kiss. We were bereft when the three-night run ended.

"The Red Cross club visits the psychiatric hospital on Saturday mornings," Kat suggested. "Join us."

"Sure." I grasped the opportunity greedily.

"You might bring some music," Doug suggested. "Half the glee club is in the Red Cross."

I was armed with sheet music, but not much else, when we assembled in the parking lot outside the pediatric psych unit that Saturday morning. Talk with the kids, sing a few songs, play a couple of games: what could be so difficult?

The hospital smell assailed me immediately as we assembled in the cafeteria: pine cleaner. No, pine cleaner and piss. Pine cleaner, piss, and some horrible concoction being brewed up in a cauldron for lunch. I wanted to barf and run. I was reluctant to touch anything for fear the odour might come off on my hands like a fine layer of grit.

"They'll bring the kids in a minute," Doug assured me.

I nodded weakly.

The kids entered in a stream: some in wheelchairs, some under their own power. It was a Brueghel painting, animated; a Disney nightmare. A grinning Down's syndrome sumo wrestler tackled Doug. "Gug! Gug!" she cried, flinging her arms around his waist.

He crouched down. "Hi, Ellen! How's my girl?" She turned to me.

"Ellen, this is Mariah. She's come to visit today. She might play the piano for us later."

"Hello, Ellen."

She grabbed me by the arm in a moist but steely grip, and dragged me across the room. "Nanno!" she squealed. "Nanno!"

"Piano, yes. I'll play for you later," I ventured.

"Nanno now!" she ordered.

I looked across the room for the twins, but they were already engrossed with other kids. "Okay," I agreed. "What would you like to hear?"

It wouldn't have mattered. Here I was, a pianist, but what did I pick? "Heart and Soul." Ellen joined me on the bench for a cacophonous duet, a gleeful smile spread across her wide features. "Nanno," she said, lifting her hands from the keys at last.

"You like to play, don't you?" She nodded vigorously, then tore off across the room in search of "Gug."

A room full of retarded children. What next? They asked for so little, it seemed to me. Doug had a small child perched on his hip, firm in the grip of his good arm. He tweaked her nose with his little hand, quacked like a duck. Her laughter pierced the noise, her delight carrying across the room.

There was no disgust on her face, no aversion to his deformity. Just total acceptance. They both looked so natural I felt a twinge. *This is what you will be like with your own children*, I thought. Warm. Loving. And accepting. I painted myself into the scenario, but I couldn't picture myself as good a mother as Doug would make a father.

"What would you do if you knew your child would be born retarded?" I asked him later.

"What would you do if you knew your child would be born with only one arm?" he responded mildly.

I blushed. "You're right."

"It's only a matter of degree," he added. "None of us is perfect."

None of us is perfect. I looked out over the sea of imperfect faces, imperfect bodies, and tried to discern one expectation, one single expectation I could fill.

There was none.

This thought distressed me. All my life I'd conformed to expectations: perfect child, perfect student, perfect girl. To be in a room full of people who had none – what perfect torture! I felt empty, colourless, like a chameleon stranded on a sheet of white paper.

What could I give any one of them that would make a difference? Bach, Beethoven, "Heart and Soul" – what did it matter? I had absolutely nothing to offer these children. Not even, I thought – glancing at Doug across the room – not even my total acceptance. Not even *conditional* acceptance, I amended, since my predominant emotion was – say it – revulsion.

But even if the children had no expectations, *Doug* expected I would rise to the occasion and acquit myself honourably. So, circumnavigating the room, I looked for some way to involve myself. Kat's group played "Monkey in the Middle"; I was the guest monkey for a few minutes.

"What's wrong with that girl?" I asked, indicating a solitary figure with my chin. "She *looks* normal enough."

"That's Maria," she said. "She's autistic."

Maria sat in a chair, oblivious to everything around her, it seemed, rocking, rocking. There was something familiar about her, something elusive. Her hair was lank, her face pinched. Her bony arms a self-imposed straitjacket, she gripped her torso as if she might otherwise fall apart. Back and forth. Back and forth. Her lips moved constantly, like an old lady in church praying the rosary.

What was it about her? Intrigued, I advanced toward her laterally, masking my approach. Squatting behind her, hoping to catch what she was saying, I felt not unlike a voyeur trying to sneak a peek between the shutters. The only thing I could make out of the stream of words was "Doug."

I was so surprised I almost fell back on my heels. She wasn't even looking at him; so far as I could tell she was focused on a spot just above the clock on the opposite wall.

I closed my eyes. If I were Maria, what words of my own could I supply to a reverential litany to make his name pop up with such regularity? Free association: Doug like a sort of punctuation and Doug the ticking of a clock and Doug the crest of every wave and Doug the quest of every waking moment.

God! I bumped down on my tailbone, shocked by the intensity of the words running through my mind.

"Doug," I said aloud.

Maria's lips still moved. Was it my imagination, or did she rock faster?

"Doug," I said again, from behind her right shoulder.

Not imagination; rocking beats per bar visibly increased.

"Do you like Doug, Maria?" I asked, boldly.

Faster and faster she rocked. But this time something new: her hand at her crotch, shockingly oblivious to what she was doing in full sight — not that anyone else was paying her a particle of attention. My head swam. If we hadn't been called to lunch, I don't know where I might have gone, where I might have hidden.

As it was, I wound up next to her at the lunch table. Various of the children needed assistance with their food; I was assigned to Ellen, who loved "nanno" music so much. Maria fed herself — still rocking — with a vacant intensity, as if eating was something to be gotten out of the way quickly and efficiently.

Someone in our group brought out a camera; various unnatural grimaces were assumed. I inclined my head toward Ellen. The flash went off, then splash! A tidal wave of milk and I was on my feet, spluttering and dripping, shocked from the cold.

"Maria!" an attendant laughed as she handed me a cloth. "If I didn't know better, I'd say you did that on purpose!"

Maria made no comment, just went on rocking and mumbling, her lips forming the mantra, "Doug, Doug," so only I could hear.

I filled my lungs with frosty parking lot air the next Saturday as if it were possible to stockpile enough to make breathing unnecessary for the next few hours. Dread sat between my ribs like an indigestible meal.

"I've got pictures!" last week's photographer announced when we were all assembled. The snapshots were passed from grubby paw to grubby paw. Someone pressed one, slightly crumpled, into my hand: Ellen and I, heads together. On my other side, Maria — eyes fixed beyond the action, raised glass of milk in one hand.

I passed the photo to one of the nurses. "Nice shot of Ellen," she remarked. "And you and Maria. Look at that — you could almost be sisters."

"What?" I snatched the photo from her hand.

"Sure," she pointed, "around the eyes, the mouth. And you're both so thin."

She passed on casually, leaving me to stare at the photo in my hand. She was crazy as a loon, I thought. There was no resemblance between me and the vacant-eyed waif. No way.

"You're intent."

I laughed nervously. "Nurse says there's some resemblance between us." I offered Doug the photo. "Isn't that silly?"

"Not really. I thought I caught it at lunch last week. Something in the shape of your faces." He passed the photo back to me and moved on.

My lungs deflated, forcing me to inhale the fetid hospital air too quickly. I sat down to keep from keeling over. It was impossible to focus on the picture so I slipped it into the pocket of my jeans.

"Let's have a sing-along now," Doug suggested.

I took my seat at the piano gratefully, opened one of the books. The notes swam before my eyes like alien calligraphy that might take as long as the Rosetta Stone to decipher.

"What's your favourite song, Ellen?"

"Donno!" she trumpeted.

I drew a blank.

"Old Macdonald," Doug translated into my ear.

Much mooing and chirping later, "Donno" was exhausted, as was the general attention span. Abandoned at the piano bench, I fished the creased picture – moulded to the contours of my ass – out of my pocket, examined it stealthily for a moment, then slipped it back.

Maria was in her usual place, occupied by her own vacancy. Gone; gone. Where did she go when she was away? I'd looked up "autism" in my dictionary during the week, but the dictionary definition was more fanciful than useful: "Morbid self-admiration, absorption in fantasy." It seemed to me she was less absorbed *in* herself than *beyond* herself: she was probably the most outward-focused of anyone in the room.

Trembling, I studied her from the safety of my bench. I still couldn't see the resemblance. Possibilities flooded my mind one after another without truly forming, like surf claiming a message written in the sand. What? What?

I walked up to a nurse, a different nurse; not the one who had remarked on the photograph. "What is Maria's surname?" I asked.

She glanced at the girl briefly, smiled. "Standish," she replied. "She's Maria Standish."

Maria Standish; Mariah Standhoffer. Maria. Mariah. Maria/Mariah. MariaMariah. . . .

Uncanny coincidence? Two reactions. Physically, a fainting spell – if only to stop the noise in my head. Mentally, a breakdown of sorts – although I'm careful to mask it with the flu.

What am I supposed to think? There is only one conclusion I can reach and I leap to it immediately: this demented animal-child is Zoshka's daughter, my cousin. My aunt. My cousin-aunt. My aunt-cousin. My father's sister's child and, yet, my father's sister. My grand-father's daughter's child and, yet, my grandfather's daughter. Words, around and around.

A maelstrom of words. But only one conclusion. It doesn't matter if I'm wrong. At the crossroads of sanity, this way madness lies – and I choose it.

Sleep – constant during the day, not a moment during the night. I stand on guard against thee, old man. I am alert. Vigilant. You will not plant your demon seed in me.

Food – none. My periods have long since stopped. Even if you do succeed in planting that seed, it will fall on barren soil. I'm as infertile as my mother – who's had her womb, her ovaries, her womanhood plucked from her body like the viscera of a hen. I admire my boyish figure before the mirror. If I can't be Daddy's Perfect Daughter, I may yet prove to be Daddy's perfect son! No hips, no breasts, no belly. No hunger. But I'm full – full with resolve, full with determination.

After several days of "flu" I must recover. So I do. Gradually. I let my mother mother me. I leave my room and steel myself to her com-pany in graduated increments.

"Where's Dad?" I think to ask, eventually. I haven't missed his con-cern; have felt, indeed, lucky to escape his solicitude.

"He's out with the Search and Rescue. There's a plane down north of town. Idiots; white plane lost in all that snow."

As she provides details, I tune out.

"So, you'll be okay if I run out for groceries?"

"Sure."

Handing me a stack of folded sheets, "Dump these on my bed, will you, sweetie," she asks, "on your way upstairs?"

"No problem."

She gathers coat and keys and boots, leaves me alone.

Only, I realize belatedly, I'm not alone. As I pass his room I hear him coughing. Old man cough, old smoker cough. *Why didn't you die, old man?* I catch a whiff of his cigarillo escaping under the door. Why isn't he working at the hotel today? Why isn't he out killing himself with cigarettes and booze, lording it over the other drunks at the hotel. So superior, I think with rage, on the other side of that desk – separated from drunken homelessness by a pane of glass and my father's filial largesse.

My parents' bed is naked. The blankets, bedspread, and pillows are stacked on the cedar chest, ready to be layered over the sheets I hold in my arms. Perfect Daughter decides to surprise mother, will make the bed while she's out.

I unfurl a sheet like a sail, drop it carefully, evenly, onto the mattress and tuck it in with hospital corners. The smell of fresh linen fills my nostrils like spring. Smooth and fold; smooth and fold; she's taught me well. Separating the pillows – Dad likes the real down one – I walk around the bed to drop it into place.

"Geeny."

His voice at the bedroom door. I look up, startled. He stands there in his long johns, startled, too; he's mistaken me for my mother.

"Marička. Where is Mommy?"

"Shopping." Damn! I curse myself for ten kinds of fool.

He walks away from the open door. I continue my task, relief hammering in my ears so loudly I don't hear him return. As I bend to tuck the spread around my father's pillow, I catch his movement in the mirror from the corner of my eye. I don't look up. I hum a tuneless hum and slide my hand under the mattress.

Where is it where is it where is it? My hand touches cold metal and it fits into my palm as if made for me. I know the drill; I've shot enough tin cans in my life. *You've got a good eye*, my father said. *Just like your mom.*

"What do you want?" I ask without turning, monitoring his progress in the mirror.

"Marička. Come be nice to your grandpa."

Maybe. Maybe if he'd asked me to get him a beer I'd have slid the gun back under the mattress, then crawled away to my own room to throw up in relief. Maybe. But isn't this the resolve I've formed in bed all week, feigning flu? Isn't this where it stops – for Zoshka, for Maria, for me?

Slowly I uncover the down pillow again, hold it in my right hand to mask the gun in my left. I turn. He's closer than I thought he'd be.

"Come. Be nice to Grandpa. I give you twenty bucks."

Twenty bucks! "I'm not your fucking whore!" I scream.

The pillow falls to the hardwood floor. He sees the gun in my hand, looks mildly surprised. In the movies, in my imagination, he would back away from me, hands raised. But he's a street fighter.

"If you ever touch me again, I'll kill you! I'll kill you now!"

He doesn't back away, doesn't raise his hands. He thinks he'll take it from me. I steel myself for his rush. He lurches forward – Shoot! Shoot now! – he steps onto the bedside mat and it scoots out from under me. Falling, falling; I can feel his hands, I feel his hands, but I still have the gun I still have the trigger I still have the trigger. And I pull.

Backing away from me like a mime, his mouth moves, but I hear no words. There's blood splattered across the front of his belly. Victory! I try to shout, "I got you, I got you!" But my vocal cords are already engaged, screaming, screaming, although I can't hear it. His mouth flaps and he points and I wonder where the gun went, I'd like to try again, to stop that flapping mouth. He's pointing, pointing. My eyes follow his finger and I see it – fresh road kill – my own right hand a geyser of blood.

The volume suddenly returns to the program. More screams, not my own: my mother is there, still in her coat and boots, wordless but vocal, capable only of vowels.

She grabs my father's tie from the closet door for a tourniquet, whips a sheet off the bed, wraps it tightly around my hand – "Above your head!" she shrieks. "Up, up!"

I raise it, a bloody salute.

She snatches the bedspread and bumps us both down the stairs on our butts. Impelled by her adrenalin and my own we somehow make it to the car. My stockinged feet are wet with snow. She tucks the bedspread in around me – "Up! Keep it up!" – slams my door and lurches behind the wheel. She drives like hell.

I am silent; she is wailing. When words finally form on her lips they are, "What happened? What happened? Grandpa, don't tell me. Tell me. Grandpa hurt you?"

"Not today," I croak.

"When?"

"Always."

More vowels on a high keening note.

Suddenly I'm urgent. "Don't tell Daddy; don't tell Daddy! The gun fell, it went off, the gun fell. Don't tell Daddy!"

"What are you saying?"

"Don't tell Daddy! Please, please. Promise!"

"All right!"

I see the canopy of the emergency entrance overhead. I let go.

"Seen the X-rays?"

"It's a mess; it's gotta come off."

"Her mother wants to wait for Goodfellow. He's in OR – could be a while."

"Her lytes are way out of whack. When was the last time she had a decent meal?"

"In Belsen, from the looks of it."

"She's what, five-eight?"

"Step right up, guess your weight. Guess your weight here!"

"Chart says one-fifteen."

"No way! Eighty, eighty-five – tops."

"Let's get this blood pressure up or she won't make six hours of surgery."

"Shh, she's awake."

"Hey, you're back, sleepyhead."

Not really. Tongue won't work.

"You know Dr. Goodfellow. He's the best reconstructive hand surgeon around. He's done what he could."

That's nice. Good night.

Snores from the chair. Mom snores; this is a revelation.

Nurse with a needle jabs my butt.

"What is that?"

"Demerol."

I love Demerol. Have I said that aloud? Shh. My little secret.

A wedge of light across the floor. Mom rises from the chair. "Let's find somewhere to talk," she whispers.

To whom?

Blue uniform holds the door open for her, wedge closes up.

"Have you been home yet? No, I guess not."

She embraces a stranger; no, it's Dad, shoulders heaving. I smell wood smoke as he bends to kiss me, feel his stubbly cheek.

"Hi."

"Hi, baby." His breath is a sob.

"Did you find the plane?"

"Yes."

"Good."

"I'll be back, honey, after a bath – and some clean clothes."

"And a shave?" I manage to tease.

He rubs his chin against my cheek. "And a shave."

"You didn't tell him, did you?" I challenge when he's gone.

"No." Mom takes my left hand, brings it to her lips. "Mariah, I want you to know – your grandfather will never hurt you again."

How can I be sure?

"I swear it."

Accepted.

The phone on the bedside table rings. She picks it up.

"Oh my God. I'll be right there."

What?

"Daddy's downstairs in emerg. He just brought Grandpa in, in an ambulance."

I claw at my mother's arm.

"No, no." She holds my face in her hands. "It's not what you think. Daddy found him dead in his bed. You understand? Dead in bed."

"How?"

A flush of outrage, a flash of resolve. "He was old. He drank too much; took too many pills." She kisses my cheek. Words brush my ear, so formless they could be telepathic: "I took care of it."

A brief, fierce pressure of her hand on mine and she's gone. Relief floods through me, relief so pure it is sweeter than Demerol, safer than the arms of Jesus.

My mother looks on, arms folded across her chest. Dr. Goodfellow is explaining to me, to my father, what he's done to save my hand. I recognize him. He's been to our home; has purchased pieces from my father's gun collection.

"So," Dad says, "how long before she can play the piano again?"

Silence. He's serious. We gape at him like a trio of trout on a string. Hasn't he been listening? Hasn't he heard the words "graft," "reconstruct"?

"Gabe, be realistic," Dr. Goodfellow says, quietly. "You're a hunter. You know the damage a slug that size does to soft tissue and bone, especially at close range. Our choices were to amputate immediately, or to *attempt to salvage a hand* – or part of a hand – with, if we're lucky, *some function*. Retaining enough function to play the piano was never a viable option."

He looks at me, at my mother. "Sorry to be so blunt. But you've seen it; *you know.*"

We nod. Our eyes are drawn to the shrouded white thing suspended between us that is the object of such scrutiny. My head buzzes from the prolonged attempt at concentration.

"As it is," he continues, "the odds aren't good. There's a pulse in the fingers, but it's weak. The grafts may not take; sepsis may set in; sometimes the body just can't cope. Mariah's making a good recovery otherwise. We'll know in a few days."

He nods to me and my mother, claps Dad on the shoulder on his way out of the room. Chin up. Rally 'round.

Sinking into a chair like an old man, Dad holds his head between his hands. I feel my first strong emotion – any emotion, actually – since coming out of surgery: I'm angry at him. He's taking this harder than he has a right to. He makes me feel guilty for putting him through this. He needs to assign blame, I realize, and it falls, intolerably, on his own shoulders.

And they're weak.

For the first time in my life I see his weakness, with a surety that brings tears to my eyes where the whole ordeal to this point has caused none. My mother stands behind his chair, rubbing his shuddering shoulders in characteristic pose, and *lends him her strength.* She, I see with both clarity and surprise, is the stronger of the two. Mom and I have entered this conspiracy of silence to shield my father from realities he cannot bear. Because we are strong. This truth floods me with purpose, with admiration, with love. Love for her. Love for him. Love for him, mingled – inexplicably – with contempt.

This thought is so painful I wince and close my eyes. I cannot bear to examine it. Tiredness weighs in my heart like a brick and I will them to leave me alone.

They kiss my brow in turn and slip out of the room.

In the margins of consciousness, like scribbling, like graffiti, I hear music. When I close my eyes, I see the marks as they would be written on manuscript paper. A little melody: add a part in invertible counterpoint at the fifteenth below the given part. Continue the lower voice, preserving the style of the opening. Complete the upper part of this piece for piano. Transpose the theme for a chamber group. Arrange for full orchestra.

Hear it? Hear the little melody, carried by the oboe? Oh! The oboe, as Jim played it: that plaintive singing voice! Hear it swept up and away by all the winds? The strings fight for it, brasses trumpet their victory, timpani thunders in approval. A crashing, swelling, turbulent mass of sound. And then, the little melody again, carried by the oboe: a good night kiss, then sleep.

Pain. I wake to pain, as if to an alarm. This is new. The pain of bones mending and wounds healing is gone. I remember that as clean pain, coloured bright red, intense but tolerable. This, this is different. This is evil pain. It is black and dirty. It eclipses the red pain at my hip, the donor site for the grafts. I know without having to be told that it's gone wrong: there will be no saving this hand.

Pride in his handiwork forces him to remain optimistic, but I know by the squareness of Dr. Goodfellow's jaw. He orders more antibiotics, more anticoagulants in the hope that thinner blood will find a ready route to the extremities. "Extremities" – what an accurate word: my fingers feel the ends of the earth away, my arm feels a hundred miles long. And every mile is a mile of black asphalt, tarry and oozing under the heat of the sun.

The heat of the sun: my face is the sun, source of the heat; sunspots dance before my eyes, burning twin satellites of the sun. It's impossible to keep them open but I fear my eyelids may be immolated if I let them shut. I can almost smell the lashes burning, smell my hair singeing on my scalp.

But no, I'm wrong; it's not the stink of burning hair I sense. It's the stench of my own dying flesh.

"Colour's not good," Dr. Goodfellow says. "Gabe, you should sign the consent form. You know I won't do it unless it's necessary."

Dad shakes his head. "I can't, Tony. Not yet. Isn't there still hope?"

"Not a lot."

Don't I have a say? No one asks me. My father needs to hope, so I hold on.

Nightmares. Daymares. They are my sustenance. I'm gorged with images, pictures, landscapes, hellscapes. Demons with my grandfather's face plunge pitchforks into my hand. Myself as Maria in a prison formed of words from which there is no escape. I'm abandoned, abandoned because no one understands what I'm saying.

An executioner, clothed in black leather: "Your head? Or your hand?"

"Take it!" I scream, holding out my hand. "Take it!" When the axe falls I'm grateful. After all, I still have my head.

Before long I beg him to take that, too.

Even Demerol doesn't take the edge off the black pain, the roaring in my ears. The music in my head is loud, discordant, with an awesome terror: a score for the Last Judgement. The pages behind my eyelids are dense with notes, but I can follow every one.

My father sits in the chair, reading; a small radio plays the classical station. CBC Stereo. It conflicts with the orchestra in my head. The noise is unbearable.

"Turn it off! Turn it off!"

He thinks I mean the radio. He switches it off with a resounding click. He holds an ice-pack to my face but the ice cubes crash together like cymbals. I brush him away with my good hand; try to brush him away with the other one, too.

But something has that hand. I struggle with the monster that has my hand clenched between its teeth.

"Let it go! Give it back!" I pull and pull in a dreadful tug of war. "I want my hand back. Give me my hand back!"

I'm shouting. My father is shouting, something about papers; he'll sign the papers. The monster collapses. I've won. I cradle the swaddled paw against my bony breast, one last time.

I thought he turned off that radio, I think, waking to a mournful dirge. He stares out the window, his lips moving. I realize the tenor rumbling is his, hardly above a whisper. The words take shape in my mind, familiar words, words sung in happy times to a crisp beat. Words sung after nightmares; words sung with fevers, and sniffles, and flu:

> Maria blows the stars around
> and sends the clouds aflyin'.
> Maria makes the mountain sound
> like folks up there are dyin'.
> Maria, Maria! They call the wind Maria!

There are shiny streaks on his face; runnels. He makes no motion to change their course. I glance at my hand, suspended again, but different now. No black pain, not even red pain. Bandaged, but slender. No cast encasing wired bone and patchwork flesh. I feel nothing but relief.

Dr. Goodfellow half-sits casually, one buttock on my bed, knee bent to form an examination table, his other foot planted firmly on the floor. He unwinds the mummy-wrapping. I turn my head.

"It's healing nicely. Do you want to see?" he asks gently.

I look into his kind eyes, vivid with regret. He doesn't like to fail, I can see that. He nods, urging me on. The reconstruction may have failed, but it will have been the perfect amputation: I must approve his craftsmanship.

My jack-hammer heart pulses in my wrist. I look down, expecting to see the stitches split under the pressure. But they're intact, railroad tracks inscribed on a rounded nub of a map.

"We'll take the stitches out in a few days. It'll look better then. The swelling will go down, the scars will fade in time."

"Can I go home soon?" Do I want to? It's expected I should want to.

"As I said, it's healing nicely. There's no sign of infection. But," he inclines his head to meet my eyes, which are still fastened on the alien limb, "there is some unfinished business."

"What?"

"Your weight. You're far too thin for a girl your height. It's caused us some concern; we weren't sure your heart could take two rounds of surgery and everything else your body's been through. You're danger-ously underweight."

Shame. As if I've been caught doing something filthy, something for-bidden, like spilling my milk or masturbating in public.

"There's another doctor I want you to talk to while you're here. She's very nice. You need someone to talk to; she's the one." My wrist rests lightly in his palm. "Nothing you say to Dr. Chenier will get back to your parents. I think that's important to you right now."

Is it? I guess it is.

"I'll leave you alone for a few minutes. Have a good look. Get used to it. I'll rebandage it, then you can graduate to a sling. You can be mobile then; keep it up and out of harm's way, so it won't get bashed around. And we'll talk some more about your weight."

Alone with "it," I cradle it like a newborn. "It" has a life of its own, as if it is a new arrival, rather than a departure. Shiny and red and throbbing, it strikes me as vaguely phallic. This thought makes me light-headed and provokes a most unbecoming tingle that doesn't sub-side until "it" is rebandaged and safely tucked away from sight.

A shrink! Dr. Chenier must be a shrink. This is terrifying. What can I say that will satisfy her and still leave me in control?

Control. I pounce upon the word as it flits through my mind. Control. I savour the sound of it, the flavour of it. I chew it up and swallow it. Control. Two syllables, so satisfying I have to lie back to digest them.

I consciously thwart the process, and turn in my finest performance, better than Lady Anne, better than Perfect Daughter. I tell Dr. Chenier things I think she wants to hear: the pressures of school and piano, my disgust at being overweight my entire childhood. I weep at appropriate moments, weep with a regret I don't feel for the lost hand, weep with simulated regret over a lost career as a pianist. The more I weep, the more I spin out these tales, the dearer does the truth become, the more gleefully do I revel in it.

When she leaves my room, clutching her notes and shaking her head sympathetically, I practically kick up my heels at the deception. *This is freedom*, I tell myself. Free of my grandfather; free of the piano. *I am in control.* I am giddy with power. I can bend my parents to my will with the merest flick of my handless wrist, particularly my dad. He is battered with grief – over my hand, over his father. He would fetch me the moon if I should ask for it.

I clutch my greatest secret to myself, the one that mitigates the loss: the music has stayed with me. The awesome, the beautiful, the terrifying music I experienced in my delirium – where, at one point, I thought I could only hear it in my head while I was hungry, now I hear it all the time: radio waves received through my fillings. But, unlike CBC Stereo, *music all my own.*

My secrets, my sorrows, my anger, my rage: all there. The weight of the gun in my hand – there. The explosive silence of freedom – there. The unshed tears; the sound of one hand clapping; the searing pain of sodomy – there; all there.

Like grains of sand encapsulated in pearl, it's all there in the music I hear in my head. And it's mine. Mine, and no one else's. I will not share this revelation with anyone, least of all the doctor who seeks to peek behind the shutters of my consciousness.

Why must I keep this secret? That's simple. I know what my parents are like, so anxious to grasp at straws. When they concluded I'd be a concert pianist, they trotted out the prodigy for any dog-and-pony show. Now? They'll take the credit; they'll take control. *Oh, yes!* they'll gush – *A compensatory talent for the handless pianist.* There will be no peace. I'll relinquish control to their fantasies, only to find my own desires bent out of shape by theirs.

With the flush of freedom comes a physical hunger I haven't experienced for months, a year, a year and a half. My parents bring in tempting treats, but even the hospital food is delicious. I savour every morsel. It would be no trick to devour everything on my tray and ask for seconds, but I display more restraint. It would be suspicious, unseemly, to recover too quickly.

Besides, then I would have to go home.

"We ought to think about school; get you caught up, now that you're feeling better."

School! I haven't given school a solitary thought, nor have I thought about anyone *at* school. This surprises me; here is a whole avenue of life I haven't thought to turn down during this strange time.

I request a bunch of books from my room and, incidentally, a pad of manuscript paper and my Harmony and Analysis textbooks.

When I look up to see Doug standing in my doorway — a bouquet of flowers clutched at his shoulder in his little hand, an armload of books under his good arm — and Kat peering around his shoulder carrying as many books again, I'm terrified and delighted.

Here two worlds collide: Doug and Kat and my other life step over the threshold into my little hospital sanctuary, the world of blood and the memory of black pain. I'm embarrassed to have them see me this way: *damaged goods.*

Protectively, involuntarily, I draw my stump tighter against my chest. I can feel the thudding of my heart through robe and sling and bandages. Awkwardly we exchange cheek-kisses and embrace, conscious, conscious of the thing between us. They're careful not to hurt me, careful to make eye contact. Kat's eyes well up and Doug's are overly bright. I, too, feel as if I might weep.

"Let's not think about elephants," Doug says.

"What?!"

He shrugs. "Mom used to say that when we'd had a nightmare. 'Don't think about elephants.' It'd take our minds off the bad dream. Unless, of course, we'd dreamed about elephants."

We laugh, we cry; the ice is broken. "How *are* you?" Kat asks urgently, wiping her eyes.

"The elephant and I will survive," I say, smiling. "Wanna see?"

Suddenly reckless, like a kid with a Band-Aid: see my booboo? If we can share this, we can share anything. Except, of course, the unsharable. They bend their heads closer. I unwrap the tensor bandage and proffer it for their inspection. It's not so bad.

"Elegant embroidery," Doug comments, with a dry British accent. "A rather trunk-like appendage."

"You're right."

More elephant jokes pass and somehow, inevitably, the stump becomes "Elly." "Elly's feeling the cold today; Elly thinks it might rain": there's not been a moment in all the years since that Doug's elephant has not been in the room with me.

The three of us fuss with rewrapping the stump in the tensor bandage. We giggle like school children, joke about getting caught by one of the nurses. I hold the sling open while Doug tenderly guides my arm into it.

"An arm with no hand; a hand with no arm. Between the two of us we might make one whole person," he says softly.

He's not joking; his eyes are serious as he bends over me. My face burns. Kat gathers her coat. The kiss Doug places on my lips is far from brotherly. "Be well," he says. "Come back to us soon."

"How about this one?"

"No."

"This one? It's very elegant, although not very functional."

"*No.*"

"The hook, then. Many people develop quite a lot of dexterity with it."

A tempting array of spare parts laid out before me. Choose a model, any model. The Cadillac: top of the line. The Dodge: a nice mid-priced unit. The Volkswagen: ugly, but utilitarian.

Trembling behind a dam of unspoken words, "I had a beautiful hand!" I'm surprised to hear myself shout. "You can't replace it, not with your plastics, not with your metals!" I glance at my mother. She bites her lip but stays silent.

"You don't have to decide today," the prosthetist says, quietly. "These are the options. Think about it."

On the elevator back to my floor I sense Mom searching for something to say. Not so long ago, she would have been full of comforting words. She'd have put her arm around me, shushed me, stroked my cheek. But now, I see it: she's afraid. Of me!

I marvel at this turn of events. My mother is afraid of me. This is new; this is wonderful.

When she leaves, I examine my face in the mirror. What's different here? The edges, the angles, are softer, cushioned by the pounds I've gained. But the edges are merely camouflaged. They're there, sharper than ever I've known them. *I* am sharp; I am flinty, like newly tempered steel.

The old Mariah, I think with contempt, would have chosen the "perfect" hand, the one that would draw the least attention to herself. She'd have chosen the Cadillac, useless but lifelike, down to the petal pink polish on the ersatz nails.

But this new Mariah is not so meek, I'm surprised to find. This new Mariah will hide behind nothing. This new Mariah wants to see the reactions on people's faces when they see this beautiful phallic thing, this perfect truncated limb. It's so powerful! It has the power to make people wince and turn their eyes from it in their unworthiness.

This, I realize, this is the root of the exhibitionism I sensed in Doug when I first saw him: flaunting the difference, revelling in it.

Unwrapping the stump from its concealing bandage, I study the tracery of scars. Spot an old one, one I'd almost forgotten: a neat "JA" where the face of my watch used to rest. But power must be used wisely. I rewrap the bandage around my wrist. What was that aphorism? "Modesty is but a shield from the eye of the unclean."

If I must choose a hand, I will. But it won't be the perfect hand. It'll be the one everyone who knows me will least expect. The Volkswagen: ugly but utilitarian.

~~~

The snow is gone except for a few scabs. I test the air as my dad helps me out of the station wagon: the pervasive stench of defrosting dog shit. Ah, spring.

Mom has gone ahead with the keys.

The paint is peeling on the gingerbread, the back porch seems just a little off plumb, as if time has accelerated since I left, seven weeks ago? Eight?

"What have you got in here?" Dad pants as he lugs in a suitcase. "Rocks?"

"No; books."

He holds the door open for me with a flourish. "Same thing." He tweaks my cheek as I go by.

A flash of my last exit through this door. I'm returning with much more than I had when I left. Extra pounds like ankle weights. Fourteen of them. One stone, as the British say, carefully amassed ounce by ounce. Fifty thousand four hundred calories above my body's requirements to maintain the eighty-eight pounds I'd gone in with. One hundred and two pounds now, including the prosthesis. I don't think anyone realized I skewed the results by wearing it at my last weigh-in. I feel like I've gotten away with something.

As I enter the house, though, I change my mind. Is it too late to rat on myself and go racing back to the hospital at less than the required one hundred pounds? This time I'd spin out those last few ounces —

until I'm twenty, perhaps. No wonder the prisons are full of recidivists; coming out is terrifying.

Luke bobs around me like an eager puppy. At the hospital, he'd been subdued and quiet, unsure how to react to me, to the intimidating surroundings.

"Come see your new room, Riah," he enthuses. "I helped."

"Oh, Luke!" Mom says, "you've spoiled the surprise."

New room? Oh, great.

He shrugs, grins. "Well, come on then, since the cat's out of the bag."

Leading the way, he takes the stairs two at a time, past the landing where the door to my room stands closed. He runs ahead into Grandpa's room. My insides freeze into a block and I stop my ascent. Dad, bringing up the rear, bumps me with a suitcase, forcing me to continue.

Mom's been busy. The room is completely redecorated around my grandfather's furniture, augmented by a new bookshelf. A brilliant, almost psychedelic, flower print papers the walls. The curtains and bed-spread are vivid pink. The room smells of new paint and fresh wax and a whiff of that inimitable "spring" smell blows gently through the open window.

"What do you think?" Mom asks, anxious for approval.

"Very nice," I manage. It's almost pathologically cheerful; I doubt I'll be able to bear it.

"I was torn. Wait, so you could choose – or have it all finished and ready to welcome you," she dithers. Uncharacteristic hand gestures accompany her words.

Why didn't she ask? I'm glad she's had doubts about this because, well, I'm angry. She could have lugged wallpaper sample books up to the hospital, could have brought swatches and paint chips. Could have asked if I *wanted* to move into Grandpa's room. This room won't have the formerly dreaded privacy of my old room: I'll be back in the bosom of the family. *Too late; too late.*

I decide not to indulge in the luxury of anger. Not right now, anyway.

These first hours are tiring for us all: I'm a stranger in their midst. They try gaily to entertain me but they seem to have, constantly, one eye cocked toward the door as if expecting someone to come through it bearing our reprieve from this sentence of life imprisonment together. I acknowledge their effort without doing anything to ease their discomfort. I will *not* be the old Mariah.

Adrift on the tide of conversation I surface to find my dad well-embarked on a morality tale. I can't listen. "I'm sorry," I say, too loudly, rising abruptly. "I think I'll have a nap before dinner." And I leave him with his mouth still open, in mid-sentence.

The stairs loom above me, interminable. I feel a rush of vertigo, reach to the newel post for support. And miss: the hook on my right hand takes a gouge out of the mahogany, leaving exposed wood so like a wound I fear it may bleed. Oh, shit; already making my mark. I stare at it wordlessly, waiting to feel remorse. But don't. Instead: satisfaction. My head clears and I continue up the stairs.

More refurbishment has occurred in my absence. The bathroom doorknob has been replaced with an elegant brass handle. So have the taps at the sink, in the tub. The tub also sports a showerhead and new glass doors. Welcome to the twentieth century: no need to lounge around with book and razor blades. A quick shower and out you go.

I test the new handle at "my" door by pushing down on it with the hook. It opens gently with little effort, swinging open to reveal a blaze. At first I think the room is on fire, but it's just the sun streaming in through the curtains. I throw them back and yank down the opaque roller blind. There. Darkness is preferable to the nauseating pink inferno.

My suitcases are lined up along the wall, full of books. I poke into corners searching for evidence that my grandfather once occupied this room. Closet: a cardboard box on the floor; a few of my clothes on hangers. They'll be less voluminous now than they were a few weeks ago. Shoes. Have to get rid of the laced ones; loafers will be easier.

Desk: my stapler, my tape, my stuff. I open a drawer. His scent rises from its recesses. Cigarillos and Old Spice. I slam it shut quickly, before his shade can escape. Imagine his death dispassionately, curiously incurious as to the details: how my mother managed to arrange it, how she feels about it. Dispassionate, but satisfied. I've made my mark here, too.

The weight of the hook nags at me. I push up my sleeve, remove it, and place it on the bedside table. The stainless steel fittings glitter in the gloom. I *am* tired, I'm surprised to find. Under the new bedspread a new blanket and new sheets wait tidily folded back. I pull off my slacks and slide under the spread, unwilling to disturb the arrangement beneath.

Pressure marks from the prosthesis line the stump like fresh scars. It's such a relief to take the damned thing off. They keep saying, at physio, that I'll get used to it. But I can't imagine it, it's so heavy, so awkward. I can't believe I'll ever wield it like I would a hand. A weapon, maybe; an instrument of torture. I'm half-afraid I could put out my own eye in an unguarded moment, that I might impale someone in my embrace.

Close my eyes, finger the scars like a Braille road map. There's no pain, not any more; just an exquisite ache that replicates itself in my crotch. This seismic activity scares me. Deep beneath the calm exterior of the earth, rumbling toward a fault line where the tectonic plates will grind against each other before a gaping crevasse of need, of desire, opens up.

I stop. It would be like giving in to drugs, to addiction. So easy! So easy. I sensed this with the Demerol – the safety and comfort it offered was illusory, no doubt about it, but tempting. I loved the feeling of Demerol: its peace; its surrender. I craved it, even as I feared it. With a great effort of will I refused it and the other painkillers well before time, while the pain was still a searing red brand.

"You must have a high threshold," my Demerol nurse commented as I waved her away.

No; not at all. But even then I craved the drug more for itself than for the relief it offered.

Now I can "taste" it – like a honey coating on the synapses, lubricating the jagged edges with its sweet, cloying viscosity. I crave it at some level; perhaps at the same level where I crave the pain. There were moments when I was wild with pain, terrified of its permanence. But pain is a sacred thing when I'm in control of it; a holy flame cauterizing my consciousness, leaving soft tissue scarred and callused. And healed.

A soft knock. "Mariah – it's almost dinner time."

I awake to find the stump cushioned between my thighs, draw it away guiltily. Mom pokes her head into the room.

"There's a box in your closet, junk I wasn't sure about. You'd better go through it and toss anything you don't want."

I pull on my slacks, straighten my hair, open the closet door. I drag the box out into the centre of the room, bring the waste-basket over. Mostly paper. I flip through a few pages to refresh my memory.

This isn't junk! This is all stuff from my bedside table, from my bottom desk drawer. My private things. Journals. Fragments of poems on envelopes. Recycled school notebooks full of teenage ranting and fantasy. Beech Nut gum wrappers.

Did she look at these things? Did she read the scribbling? Flushed with fury — *fucked again* — I throw items into the most secure crannies I can find. What does it take? A lock on the door? A "Do Not Enter" sign? A German shepherd and an Uzi? I'm ready to explode.

Until, at the bottom of the box, I lift out the last papers. There, in the corner of the box, an afterthought: the severed right foreleg of a deer.

Sitting back on my haunches, I exhale noisily. Bambi. Where has it been all this time? I haven't thought about it in years, can't remember the last time I saw it. I can imagine my mother's reaction when she found it. Throw it away? Save it? Its position at the bottom of the box is deliberate. It is, quite obviously, not the first thing she turned up and, therefore, not the first thing tossed into the empty box. She found it in the course of riffling through my secrets and buried it there, to be composted under the mulch of my childhood.

I hold it in my left hand, examining it from every angle, stroking the fur with my naked stump. Memory crowds my brain for space and oxygen.

"How will my deer survive in heaven without his right foot?"

"If we believe in the resurrection of the body, then the body will go to heaven whole and well."

"Even if the hoof is missing?"

"Even if the hoof is missing."

Standing beside the dresser mirror — *poor deer poor deer* — I slip the leg up the long sleeve of my pullover, leaving the little hoof exposed where my hand should be. *The body will go to heaven whole and well.* Zoom in to that portion of my reflection in the mirror, avoiding the rest.

The Deer Woman.

It looks so natural, compared to the unwieldy prosthesis, with its gleaming metals. The prosthesis draws the eye and screams, "Accident! Accident! Pity me; I am maimed."

People would still stare if I had a hoof for a hand: *Poor child — the*

progeny of some unholy union between man and deer. But yet so graceful, so natural.
I wipe the tears from my face with the bristly fur.

A tap at my door. Push the hoof hurriedly up my sleeve, out of
sight, follow the blooming wedge of light in the mirror.

"Time for dinner, dear."

Put the hoof away safely and confine myself in the artificial contraption, ready to meet the world.

Dinner in the dining room; this *is* an event.

Dad sits at the head of the table, framed by the gleaming glass and
polished cedar of the gun cabinet. The incongruity of this piece of furniture, in this room, strikes me for the first time. The china cabinet in
the corner, the gun cabinet in pride of place. Not a Welsh dresser; not
a serving board. It is a beautiful and massive piece. But what is it doing
in the dining room? This piece of furniture requires a trophy room. It
should be flanked by stuffed pheasants, moose heads, Bambi's antlers.
My hand.

I cough into my linen napkin.

Mom has made my favourites, all especially tempting. The family's
been coached on the importance of not making an issue of my eating.
Still, I feel their scrutiny as every morsel is noted and mentally weighed,
every pea counted. The dog is banished to the backyard, conspicuous
by her absence. There'll be no clandestine feeding.

They try so hard! It's painful, pathetic. My throat closes. It's all I can
do to swallow enough food to satisfy the four of us, with our various
agendas.

My parents make a studious attempt to ignore my fumbling with silver flatware in the grip of stainless steel. Luke, on the other hand, stares
with an embarrassed sort of fascination.

"How does it work?" he whispers.

Beneath the level of the table I flex a muscle. Open. Flex again. Close.

Dad clears his throat. Luke and I grin at each other like naughty children. I reach across the table for the salt shaker, believing it to be within my capabilities. But I miscalculate. Splash! over goes my milk glass.

I brace for the explosion of expletives. But none comes. No "Jesus
Christ, Mariah!" No "Can't you be more careful?" No lecture on the
scarcity of milk during the Depression.

Mom runs to the kitchen for a cloth, Luke tosses napkins into the lake of milk. My father leaves the room. To assist in the clean-up, I think. But he doesn't return.

Tears cloud my vision. Here is one certainty: despite my best efforts, I've succeeded in destroying my family. All the years of secrecy, all the things I bore. For what? I'd give anything to hear him shout at me. This silence is a gouge on mahogany.

When I take my plate to the kitchen, I peer through the window and see him in the backyard, perched on a rusted lawn chair. One hand stroking the dog, the other pushed against his eyes, supporting the weight of his bobbing head.

Saturday on the town: girls' day out, commencing with wash-and-wear hair, followed by a shopping trip for clothing of the most utilitarian kind, clothes I can cope with single-handedly.

I used to love shopping. I'd follow my mother through the stores, stopping to examine something that caught my eye, imagining myself in a certain outfit, a certain pair of shoes. I'd fantasize a whole life around something that wasn't "me." What kind of me would wear something like that? What would she say? How would she act?

Now I am the object of scrutiny in the shops.

My mother knows every salesperson in town, it seems. "Hello, Ginny! How can we help you today?"

"We need some shoes for this young lady, June," my mother says. "Something without laces. Penny loafers perhaps."

The woman's eyes are drawn like a magnet from my mother's face to my prosthesis. She flinches perceptibly, flushes, eyes return quickly to Mom's. "Of course," she says. "Perhaps she'd like something like this."

Time after time I'm left out of these negotiations as if I'm deaf, or an imbecile. One glimpse of my artificial hand and the salespeople run, falling over themselves in their haste to satisfy us and have us out of their sight as quickly as possible.

After the shoes, the backpack to carry my school books, the "pretty" camisoles in lieu of bras, I feel erased, as if I've stepped back in time so far I've become invisible. I'm exhausted by the weight of their unasked questions, their burdensome politeness.

There are more items on the list: pull-on slacks, a few extra pullovers. As Mom writes yet another cheque, I slide away to examine articles on my own. The prosthesis chafes. Twisting it does no good; I can't get at the source of the irritation. So I consolidate a few items in one bag, take it off under cover of a now-empty bag – ah, better – and slip my wrist into my pocket. I feel lighter, more normal. Just a girl out shopping – parcels in one hand and one hand in her pocket.

With a flash of inspiration, daring, and mischief, I leave the bag with its dreaded cargo under a display of sweaters.

She'll kill me when she finds out! Not to mention the person who finds it – what will she think when she opens the bag and pulls out an instrument from de Sade's chamber?

My heart sinks. Too many of these women know my mother. How many seventeen-year-old girls are making fashion statements this season with penny loafers and a hook?

"*Virginia Standhoffer? This is Eaton's calling. Did your daughter perhaps lose a snappy little stainless-steel number while shopping today?*"

No, too risky.

I retrieve the bag; step behind a pillar and nonchalantly shove it into a large waste-basket with a swinging top. It's half full. By the time it's emptied, the item will be buried beyond detection.

Mom notices right away. "Where's the . . . you know," she asks, pointedly looking at my casual hand-in-pocket.

She can't bring herself to say the word. I love that! Everything connected with it is a "you know" – a secret, almost shameful thing. I want to supply taboo words for her to choose from: Penis? Dildo? Cunt? Fuck? Stump! There – try that one. Stump. What a gloriously final sound it has, like an axe falling on a block.

I rattle the bags. "I took it off. It was bugging my *stump.*"

Just a breath of emphasis. Just the merest wince on her face, evidenced by the cringing of one eyelid.

"Phantom limb pain," I whisper.

Or PMS. Or a "certain lack of freshness": words not spoken aloud in polite company.

I follow her to the car. Almost cheerfully.

"I've lost my hand," I say, going through the bags at home.

Mom looks at me as if I'm delirious.

"It's not here; I've lost it. The pros*thesis*," I elaborate.

"What?"

"Go through the bags yourself. It's not here."

"Maybe it's in the car." She goes out to check, returns empty-handed. "Nothing."

She glares at me, bewildered, fighting the instinct to be angry. *Mustn't upset the cripple.* She plops down on the kitchen stool, sighs deeply. "The stores are closed. I'll call around on Monday. Now what?"

"I could try going without," I suggest casually. What a dissembler I'm growing up to be.

"You'll have to go without until we can get a new one. Order another at physio after school on Monday. And try not to upset your father with − " she nods toward the stump, "in the meantime."

My father, the extraordinarily modest man, would rather come upon me by accident in the tub than be forced to look at "Elly," naked and unadorned. Give him the best technology has to offer by way of replacement − no matter how restricting, how unwieldy, how ugly. How much does his discomfort have to do with my rebellion in this regard?

I should be alarmed by these flashes of mischief, by my disregard for their feelings. The old Mariah would have accommodated them. But I find myself, perversely, enjoying my nastiness.

"Kat and Doug are waiting for you," Mom says.

Hyperventilating as the car draws near the school, I drop my backpack on the floor so I'll have an excuse to put my head between my knees for a moment.

"Luke, open the door for your sister, please." Last-minute instructions: "So, you'll walk to the hospital for physio after school." I nod. "And you'll call if you need a ride." Another nod. "Otherwise, if you feel up to it, you'll walk home from the hospital. Right?"

"Right."

"And you won't forget to order another" − the briefest of pauses − "prosthesis." She looks at me intensely. "Have a good day, sweetheart," she says, as she has hundreds of times before.

I nod again, unable to speak. Surprise myself by inclining my head to her for a kiss.

Turning away from the car toward Doug and Kat, I slip my wrist into my pocket.

"Ready to run the gauntlet?" Kat asks. "Come on, it won't be so bad. Everybody knows."

"That's supposed to be encouraging?"

She squeezes my arm. We plow ahead. Everyone greets me. My peers in Grades 12 and 13 look only at my eyes, as if they've been coached. The freshmen aren't so circumspect — their eyes are drawn to my pocket. Some of them look cheated.

"Welcome back, Mariah," the homeroom teacher booms as I cross the threshold. The room is crowded and noisy. I feel again as if I might faint, but I push through it, take my alphabetical place next to Wendy Staplin, as I have almost every school day for four years.

"It's been quiet without you," she notes as I squirm out of my back-pack. At some point I'll have to take my hand out of my pocket to accomplish it. I know all eyes are on me.

"What happened to your pros-whatsit?"

Wendy's been up to the hospital a few times over the weeks, is surprised to see me without it.

"I lost it," I hiss, without elaboration.

Somehow the day passes. I'm gratified to find that, after weeks of independent study, I'm well ahead of everyone. Good. I'll be able to coast through the semester.

"What are you up to now?" Doug asks. We're the last to leave the room.

I make a face. "Physio. Which way are you going?"

"Widener is having an information meeting for potential Danish exchange students. Why don't you come? You should apply."

"Tempting." I laugh without humour. "I could use a year away from my parents about now. But there are more practical matters at hand." The pun is intentional.

We're reluctant to part. In fact, I fear parting from him. His support has been my buttress. He senses my indecision, lingers at my locker as long as he can, helping me into coat and backpack.

"I've got to go," he says regretfully. "Sure you don't want to come?"

Shake my head, manage a smile. "See you tomorrow." I turn toward the side door, grateful that the school clears out so quickly after the last bell.

Why have I deliberately chosen not to cross at the crosswalk? I could fling myself under the next vehicle of substance to come barrelling down the hill, I think, as I wait for the traffic to clear.

Before I have time to examine this thought, my elbow is taken in a firm grip.

"Come on, let's make a run for it," a voice says.

Propelled across the street, delivered safely to the opposite curb almost against my will, I feel faint. Reaching to a telephone pole for support, I bend to get blood to my head. Large chunky boots. Sully's grinning face.

His smile fades. "Hey, are you okay?"

"I will be in a minute."

"Lucky day," he murmurs. Pulling a set of keys out of a pocket of his jeans, "Upsy-daisy," he warns, then swings me effortlessly into his arms and marches up the steps of the adjacent house.

"Where are we going?"

He unlocks the front door and continues up the central staircase. "Home."

"Whose?"

"Mine." He unlocks the door to the suite marked "2A."

"Since when?"

Sully strides across the hardwood floor and plops me down on the couch. "All will be revealed. Head down," he orders. His hand in my hair directs my body to bend. "Tea?"

His boots disappear from my line of vision. Purposeful sounds issue from the kitchen.

Eventually I lift my head, lean back against the couch, and look around. A large, bright space, the second floor of an old house, a solid house. The room is surprisingly tidy: bookshelves, small stereo, and TV. Plants, for heaven's sake, in front of the sunny window.

Sully puts a plate on the coffee table — crackers, cookies, and some cheddar cheese on ironstone so masculine it could be Neanderthal — hands me a matching mug, and sits down beside me.

A grateful sip. "Wow!" I choke. "Are you sure you put enough sugar in this?"

"I thought you might need a blood sugar boost."

I blow across the mug. "Hope you've got some insulin handy."

"You're not diabetic, are you?" His expression is so concerned it's almost comical.

"No, no. Joking."

He nods intently, not a ghost of a smile. I hold the mug as a screen for my face, my lips see-sawing between amusement and despair. Our eyes lock. But my hand starts to tremble under the intensity of his gaze.

Or the weight of the mug. He leans closer, takes it from me, and places it on the coffee table.

Suddenly I'm in his arms, crushed against his chest so hard that words are squeezed from me in a torrent like exhaled breath and water from the lungs of a drowning person. Words I didn't know I had, grief I didn't know I felt. I tell him everything: how much I hated my grandfather, how glad I am he's dead. How angry I am with my parents, how much I enjoy being a spoiled, manipulative brat. How the music's stayed with me so that I hear it all the time. How despite the music — or because of it — I wanted to end the pavane this afternoon, under the wheels of a truck. I tell Sully everything — except the secrets. Forehead to forehead he holds my face in his hands, his beautiful hands, steadfast to the squall. And when it passes we are, both of us, soaked to the skin and trembling.

What have I done? How could I have been so unguarded?

He brushes the hair back from my face. "This is probably the first time you've ever talked to me."

Floodgates clank shut; I disentangle myself from his limbs. "Don't be silly," I say. "We did nothing but talk for nine months."

"No," he shakes his head, sadly. "*I* did nothing but talk for nine months."

I can't deny this.

"You and your dad were right: we were too young. I've done a lot of thinking over the last two years. And a lot of growing, I hope."

A smile tugs at my lips: yes, he is *so* tall now.

"Emotionally, I mean." He grins, as if he's read my thoughts. "You know what today is, don't you? That's why I was following you after school; I was hoping to talk to you."

Jesus. The anniversary of our breakup. The floodgates lock and I jump up from the couch. "I'm sorry. This shouldn't have happened." I look around for my coat, my boots. "Thanks for the tea."

"Thanks for the tea?!" He reaches for my arm. "Mariah, what happened here wasn't a tea party! You poured out your soul. You told me you wanted to jump in front of a truck — I rescued you."

Anger wells within me. "So now you're a white knight, rescuing damsels in distress." I think of the most hurtful thing I can: "Maybe I didn't want to be rescued."

An inarticulate sound escapes his lips.

"I'm sorry if I led you to believe we could be involved again. I'm involved with Doug." Sort of. Tentatively.

"Involved! Involved – it's easy to stop being involved; it isn't so easy to stop loving you."

He looks at the arm he's gripping by the bicep, crumples to his knees in front of me, weeping, weeping over the stump.

Mute with dismay, I sink to the floor beside him, torn between comforting him and killing him.

"We have a shared history," I say edgily. "Old habits die hard. That doesn't make a relationship." I stroke his head.

"I'm not offering you a relationship." The words are directed to the stump. "I did that a few years ago and it drove you away." He looks into my eyes. "I'm offering you love."

I look to the ceiling, as if a solution might form from the watermarks on the old plaster.

"The last time was for me," he continues. "This time, it's for you. Whatever you need, whenever you want it. Just for you. No strings. No expectations."

My head throbs with irrationality. "If you think you'll get your revenge by making me love you!"

He brings his lips to the stump, kisses it tenderly. "No one can make you love me, Mariah. Love is something you feel, or you don't."

His words are a knife to my gut. Feel. What do I feel? To stay within the circle of his arms would be such sweet relief. Tempting, so tempting – to be soothed, to be loved, to have all the jagged edges obliterated. A calm haven in the honey-amber warmth of his eyes. Like Demerol, like drugs.

And yet, equally, to crave the pain, to control the pain. Oh, yeah, I've been doing such a wonderful job of that! Falling into the first set of warm arms that reach out to me, spilling my guts to a familiar face, complicating my life with Sully's promise of love without strings. How naïve am I? And yet, and yet: I open the floodgates just enough to peek into that future.

My decision is made for me.

The door of the suite swings open and a female voice sings out, "Honey, I'm home!" Grocery bags appear. "I had a meeting, then stopped to pick up a few things after school."

Long blonde hair swings around the door frame, followed by a model's smile: Birgitta Andersen, the most beautiful girl in school.

"I'm sorry; I didn't know you had company. Hi, Mariah. How are you?"

"Fine, thanks," I mutter. "I was just leaving. Sully, thanks for the tea."

He tries to stop me. "It's not what you think," he says.

I hold up my hand – stop. Stop. "Thanks for the tea," I repeat, more emphatically.

And I go. Fast; as fast as I can; faster. Until each breath is like a knife in my lazy eight-weeks-in-hospital lungs.

Somewhere, in the gathering gloom of late afternoon, there's a bench beside McVicar's Creek with my name on it. Literally. Carved into the wooden seat with a penknife: "M.S. + J.S.R." Mariah Standhoffer and James Sullivan Riordan.

There it is. I sit, the initials at my right thigh polished now by weather and friction. The scars of first love are permanent, I realize – no matter how brutal your efforts to abrade them. I trace the letters with the stump: M.S.J.S.R. Ow – and catch the needle-bite of a sliver. Holding my wrist up to the setting sun, I see the barb of wood where it's impaled my flesh. Pull it out, releasing two tiny drops of blood.

And a spillway of sorrow.

Waking the next morning to birdsong, I'm surprised to find I have slept, deeply.

"Sully called last night," Mom announces at breakfast. "Something about homework for one of your classes?"

I cock an eyebrow. Checking up on me, was he? We have no shared classes this semester.

"Took me back a few years," she says. "I told him you'd had such a busy day you'd gone straight to bed after supper. He said it wasn't an emergency."

"Fine," I say over a mouthful of oatmeal: a good hot breakfast, sticks to the ribs. Brown sugar and real cream. Idly calculating the calories: she'll have me porked up in no time. I picture myself wearing an elegant muu-muu to graduation.

At school I make a beeline for Wendy's locker. She's there, struggling with a book on the top shelf. I pass it down for her.

"It's useful to have tall friends," she acknowledges.

"What's with Sully and Birgie Andersen?" I ask casually.

"What about them?" A light dawns in her eyes. "Oh, that!" We're on the same wavelength at last. "They moved in together a few weeks ago."

"What's the story?"

She puffs out her cheeks. "Sully's dad was appointed to the Supreme Court so they've rented the big house to some university professor and moved to Toronto. Sully wanted to stay here, so they got him an apartment across the street." She nods in the general direction. "It's got a great view." She turns back to her locker, apparently satisfied with the explanation.

"What about Birgitta?" I ask testily.

"Her parents are in Hawaii for a month."

I try to follow the path of Wendy's logic. "So she moved in with Sully."

"The Riordans had planned all along to have her stay with them, ever since her parents booked the trip, months ago."

This is a non sequitur. I shake my head. "*Why?*"

"She *is* Sully's cousin, you know."

Ah! "No, I didn't know that," I mumble weakly. My vision suddenly blurs. Shit. I slide down the locker to a squatting position, lower my head.

"You okay?"

"Yeah, yeah." I wave her away. "I'm just fucking tired of falling into a swoon like some eighteenth-century consumptive."

She doesn't comment on the uncharacteristic profanity. "Maybe you should loosen your corset." She offers me her hand, hauls me to a standing position. "Come on, time for the bell. You can pass out in homeroom."

It's not what you think, he said. Problem is, I didn't think, I just latched on to the obvious in order to make my escape. I owe him an apology.

I watch for Sully all day, even over Doug's shoulder in the cafeteria at lunch while he's briefing me on the Danish exchange meeting.

"So, the three of us have been invited to R.W.'s house to meet the Danish Vice Consul."

"Only three of you?"

"I told you, you should apply."

"Who else?"

"John Owens. And Birgitta Andersen." He finally has my attention. "She's got a good chance; she speaks some Danish. That's a huge advantage."

I smile wryly. "Yeah, but it wouldn't be an exchange of cultures to send Birgie Andersen; it would be more like sending her *home*. I thought the point of it was to send a representative Canadian, as a junior ambassador."

Doug chews and swallows hurriedly. "You're right. They'll probably choose John Owens. Young Liberals, all that political stuff."

He stands to take our garbage to the bin.

"He really wants to go," Kat confides across the table.

"I can tell by the way he's running down his chances. He doesn't want to be too disappointed if he doesn't get it."

"You've got that right."

"You'll miss him."

She nods, shrugs. "It's not as if we're likely to go to the same university next year, anyway."

"What do you mean, next year?" I ask, alarmed. "You've got another year."

She shakes her head. "We accelerated with the semester system. We've got enough credits to graduate in June."

This news hits me like a blow to the solar plexus.

"Doug's marks are way better than mine, though. He wants to get into Harvard. Mr. Widener's filled his head with mad fantasies."

"Not so mad," I whisper, watching him make his way back.

"Hey," he announces. "Why don't we do something on Friday night?"

"Count me out," Kat says, "I have to work."

"We'll pick you up after." To me: "How about an early movie?"

"Sure." Something inside does acrobatics. "You want to meet at the theatre? Or," a plan forms in my mind, "maybe I can get the car."

They both look at me doubtfully. "Have you driven since you got out of the hospital?"

I shake my head. "No. So? It shouldn't be that difficult. It's an automatic."

Doug grabs his backpack from the table. "We'll firm it up later in the week. Going my way, ladies?"

Kat heads in the opposite direction. We climb three flights of stairs to our English class together. Panting and light-headed by the time we near the top, "I don't think I'll ever be normal again," I sigh.

He waits for me on the last step. "No, you won't." All seriousness: "Oh, you'll get your strength back. But you'll never be normal. You'll always be marked."

He smiles for reassurance. "That's a good thing, Mariah. Make the most of it. Your differences would always have set you apart anyhow, even if this," he takes my right arm, "even if this had never happened."

Shaken, I take my seat behind him in class and feign a coughing fit to cover the brimming of my eyes.

Holding back after class, I spend a few minutes blowing my nose in the washroom. Tears have been threatening all afternoon, ever since his words: "You'll never be normal."

What is normal? – especially for me. And why does it upset me so much, so suddenly, that I'll never know *that* normalcy again? Haven't I spent my whole life trying to obliterate that set of "norms". Perhaps the translation is, "You will never be whole again." Is that it?

By day's end I still haven't seen Sully. I don't even know where his locker is. It seems so strange to be on the lookout for him again. Two years ago I would have known his every move, would have planned to bump into him just to see his face light up – involuntary reflex – at the sight of me: *There she is – my mirror.*

What will I say to him? I don't know, beyond the apology.

I gather my things and leave the school. Walk down the street on the park side, just as I did yesterday, stand looking across to his sunny window. What am I waiting for? For him to sneak up behind me again and propel me across the street and into his arms? Do I want that? What *do* I want? Do I want Sully? Or do I want Doug? Both? Or neither?

Hopeless: standing on the curb, dithering like a dolt. I turn to continue down the street, but a movement catches my eye. He's standing in the doorway. Just standing. No coat, no shoes. *I'm waiting for you. Come, if you will.* I wait for an omen, as if it's not enough that he's appeared.

The traffic parts like the Red Sea. It's omen enough.

He looms above me as I stand at the bottom of the stairs. Suddenly terrified, I say, "I just wanted to apologize, about Birgitta."

"She's my cousin. She moved to town after her parents sold my grandfather's farm. I'm surprised Wendy didn't spill the beans."

I shake my head. "Not a murmur. How unlike her."

He grins. "Would you like to come in? Before you get a permanent crick in your neck?"

"I would. I don't know why, or even if it's wise."

"It's enough that you want to." He holds out his hand. "Stairs? Or elevator?"

"Stairs," I say, taking his hand. "I can't ascend so dramatically every day." A pause at the threshold. "Is she home?" I whisper.

"No. She's a whirlwind of activity. I hardly see her. Her parents'll be back on Sunday, then I'll have the whole place to myself again."

I glance around the room. "Well, someone does a bang-up job of keeping it tidy."

"That would be me." He barks a laugh. "Why do you look so surprised? Tea?"

"Thanks." He heads for the kitchen. "Only not so much sugar this time," I call after him.

There's a great view of Waverley Park from the window. And the lake. A different angle than I had from the room I shared with Luke as a child. Pie Island and the Welcomes are dark daubs against the blue, but Isle Royal's presence — normally a smudge across the horizon — must be taken on faith. Like the U.S.–Canada boundary itself.

Sully pads up behind me with a mug. "You can't see the Sleeping Giant from here," I say. "Too bad."

"You see it well from your house."

"I used to think he was God," I confide. "I used to pray to him, every night."

"And what would you say if you could see him now?"

The hairs stand up on the back of my neck. "I'd ask for guidance. For clarification of my motives here."

He leads me back to the couch. "You know why you're here."

My eyes tear up; I feel nauseated. "I'm glad you're so sure. Would you like to tell me?"

Sully leans back against the far arm of the couch, puts his feet up. I huddle against the opposite arm, knees drawn up to my chin like a child. I couldn't be farther away and yet still sitting on the same couch. His toes sneak across the cushions until they connect with mine.

"You," he points with his index finger, "you opened up yesterday." He rubs the bridge of his nose. "No, let me rephrase that. You *cracked* open yesterday. You've never done that before. Not with me; not, I suspect, with anyone else. You surprised yourself, not to mention me. Am I right?"

I nod, forced to support the weight of the mug with my knee.

"Put that damned thing down, you're shaking like a leaf again," he says gently, taking it from me. "You're like Humpty Dumpty; you can't stand the sight of your own guts spilled all over the sidewalk. You won't be happy until you get it all cleaned up, back inside your shell."

I turn away. I can't stand to look into his eyes. He sees *me*. Nine months together – and how many months apart? – and *he sees me*. Why now? Elementary – because I've let him in. How can he bear to look?

He walks around the couch, bends until we're eye to eye. "All the king's horses, and all the king's men, Mariah." Traces my eyebrow with his finger. "You can't be in control every second. Give it up. The shell's cracked open. It's going to be leaky and messy and, and," he pulls another metaphor from the ether, "it might even start to stink. *It's okay.*" He slides onto the couch beside me, takes me in his arms. "It's okay. You can't do it all alone; let yourself need me."

Pressing my nose into the nest of curly dark hairs at the V of his shirt (it wasn't there two years ago, I think), I suck his scent into my nostrils like oxygen. I feel the thudding of his heart against my ear as clearly as I can hear it.

Need. I need to need him. I crave it; oh! how I crave it. But I fear the safety he offers will prove illusory. I'll be screaming with need – addicted – and he'll laugh and turn his eyes away from me in disgust.

"Pull yourself together, Mariah," he'll say. "You're a big girl now."

And he'll strike the heel of his boot through the stinking, sticky pieces of my shell and grind them into powder.

Despite the certainty of my folly, I settle into the curve of his arm and let myself be lulled by his heartbeat: *give it up; give it up.*

"Riah. It's late, love. Let me drive you home."

An almost-dark room. My God, we've fallen asleep. My right cheek is sore, a circular imprint: his breast-pocket button. Sully runs around turning on lights, collecting my stuff while I stand paralysed in the centre of the room. He attacks my flattened hair with a brush.

"Oh, dear. Not much improvement, I'm afraid."

"What time *is* it?" I manage to ask.

"Almost six. Were you supposed to go to therapy today?" I shake my head. "Shit. Where have you been, then? Where would you go?" He helps me step into my shoes, pulls my coat on as if I'm a child. I feel a wave of tenderness toward him, almost drunken in nature.

"To the auditorium. With Doug," I say. "We've been talking for hours and hours." I gesture grandly. "Lost all track of time."

"You can pull that off?"

"Oh, yes. I have a lie for all occasions, these days.

We rattle down the stairs and out the door, around the back of the house to the garage. "All this *and* a car," I muse. "How you have come up in the world!"

He helps me into the passenger seat of his little car, putting his hand on my head as if I'm a convict getting into a police car. He slams my door, then reopens it, rolls down the window, and slams it again.

"What is this?" I ask as we roar away from his house, icy wind rushing through my hair.

"Triumph."

I nod. This makes absolute sense. "Ah, yes. It is, indeed."

"You're trying to do too much, too soon, sweetheart. Go a little slower for a while."

I've told my mother I'd gone to the library after school and dozed off there.

"I just want everything to get back to normal," I say, almost choking on the word "normal."

She pats my shoulder. "I know; I know."

I clear my throat. "Speaking of which: Doug's asked me out to the movies on Friday night."

"That's nice," she enthuses. "But wouldn't Saturday be better? You'd have all day to rest up. At this rate, you might just sleep through the entire movie."

"He's going to Widener's house on Saturday night to meet the Danish Vice Consul. So it has to be Friday night."

"How 'bout the Saturday matinee?" she teases. "Well, okay. If you're *up* for it."

I play the trump card. "Can I have the car? That way we could pick Kat up after she gets off work, go out for coffee, or something."

A huge sigh. "I've made some inquiries; it's such a rigmarole I'd hoped you wouldn't ask." I avoid her eyes. "I'll pick you up from school tomorrow afternoon and we'll have a road test. If you can manage, you can have the car. But you really should get your driver's licence reclassified."

The words are out before I can stop them: "*The Scarlet Letter*. 'A' for Amputee. A whole new episode of *Sesame Street*."

She covers her mouth with her hand. Shit, I've gone too far. But her laughter breaks through the barrier. This is new. This is okay. I find my own laughter joining hers. The next thing I know, I'm enfolded in a jolly embrace: it isn't such a bad place to be.

I pass the road test. Park. Reverse. Drive. It's a little awkward, but not impossible. I quickly develop an amended technique for left turns: hand over stump, so to speak.

"Try to avoid parallel parking," she suggests.

"Oh, I do; believe me, I do," I laugh. "Especially in this boat."

"All right then: it's yours Friday night. And if the police stop you, plead ignorance; everyone at the licence bureau has." Her smile is almost as gleeful as my own. "Home, James."

At Thursday "tea time" with Sully, he's replaced my chunk of Stonehenge with a bone-china cup and saucer of unusual translucency, replete with shamrocks: Belleek. There's a tell-tale blue Birks box in the kitchen trash. I am touched. (When I check out the display at Birks I'm shocked. Who could imagine a tea cup could be so expensive?)

"This is dainty."

"My grandmother had some like it." He smirks. "I'm tired of you passing out from the exertion of hefting that whopping great mug to your lips."

"I'm going out with Doug on Friday night," I hazard.

"That's nice." Same tone as my mother's.

"You're not upset?"

He chews on his cheek, thinks, shakes his head. "No. No, I'm not."

I gulp my tea. "You sound surprised."

"I am. Mildly." He tucks his toes under my thigh: touch time has begun. "Not so long ago I would have been murderous with jealousy. *Was* murderous with jealousy," he amends. "I could have killed him during *Richard*, sprawled out with you on that couch, day after day."

"What's different now?"

He stares at me intently over the stoneware. "I have a part of you he doesn't have."

Teacup rattles into the saucer on the table. "Which is?"

He places his mug on the table, too, rearranges his long legs like some spindly insect drawing in prey by subterfuge; I am somehow enfolded in a loose embrace.

"I have you at fifteen. Not just an unbroken shell, but," he makes a solid oval of his fist, "an alabaster egg."

I cringe. Maybe if I close my eyes, I'll disappear.

"And I have you the other day, a broken shell," the fist opens, "scrambled — and a mess." He traces an exclamation mark down my nose, punctuates it on the tip, and draws me closer.

"And I have you the other evening, sleeping in my arms like a child," he says huskily. "There will be other things, but he won't have that."

"And you're not jealous? You're too good to be true!" I accuse, sitting upright, withdrawing from him a little, yet not able to break the connection. "Are you applying for sainthood?"

He throws his head back, stares at the ceiling. "No." Sardonic laugh. "No. I promised you, no strings. Whatever you need. Whenever you want it. Keep me your secret, I don't care. I won't tell. Whatever Doug can offer, it's different than what I can give. We're not in competition. All the king's men, Mariah, jointly and severally: we're at your service. And if we can put you back together again, that's great. Or if we can help you live with the pieces, and the missing bits, that's great, too."

"And you don't expect anything in return?" I can't credit it; it's not human.

"You've given me more in these few days than you did in the nine months we were together!" his volume rises. "You've given me your self. Why couldn't you do that when we were together?" his voice cracks.

"You never asked," I answer weakly.

"It's something you give, not something I ask!" His grip on my shoulders is strong, too strong. There will be ten tiny bruises. "Even if I'd had the words then, even if I'd asked, 'Let me see your self, Mariah,' could you have let me in?"

"I wanted you to ask," I whisper. "I always hoped you'd ask."

A strangled sound: "I wasn't that smart; I was only fifteen!" He crushes me to his chest.

As I cling to him I question our sanity and the wisdom of this entanglement. Yes, some years have passed and we've grown, but still — we are only . . . *children.* Seventeen. He's tall, and has the shape and stature of a man. He's learned some things that may be, *may be,* wise.

But he's deluded if he thinks he holds no strings. He is well-intended, innocent, and haplessly naïve, my shining knight – intent on rescue and courtly love! But this exchange is no less incendiary for its innocence than an exchange of hand grenades between children: it takes only the curiosity of an instant to pull the pin – "What's this?" – and have it all explode in your face.

"Hi."

Doug waits for me on the curb outside the theatre, tickets clutched in his hand. I faithfully went straight home after school, had a nap, and drove downtown carefully. Alone. Such a feeling of accomplishment! Almost like learning to walk. I parked at the far edge of Eaton's parking lot, across the street, where I had lots of room to manoeuvre going in and will still have, I hope, when I come out.

"Hi."

We grin at each other. "I'll get the popcorn," I suggest. We draw stares from the girl at the concession stand as we struggle with the purchases. Two good arms between the two of us: a couple of freaks on the town.

The seating plan presents its own difficulties. At first I'm on his right.

"Let's swap places," he insists.

We do, with a fair bit of giggling. When we're finally settled, he places his good left arm around my shoulders.

"There," he sighs. "You realize this relationship is doomed?"

"Why?" I ask warily.

"Due to the inability of the principals to hold hands in the movies." He smiles.

Reassured, "*This* is cosy, though."

He gives my shoulder a squeeze. When the lights are dimmed for *Jesus Christ Superstar* and we're well embarked on Andrew Lloyd Webber and Tim Rice's passion play, I let the stump – "Elly" – creep over the armrest to lie against Doug's thigh, can feel his heat through his jeans like a branding iron. How bold. The rock beat duplicates the sound of my own blood crashing in my ears.

There's a sense of awkwardness to this. My thoughts wander to Sully. There we are, Sully and I – returning to the intimacy of familiar body pressed to familiar body, an intimacy that is not diminished (perhaps is even enhanced) by my missing hand. It's a familiarity Doug and I have yet to establish despite all those hours spent reclining on that backstage couch.

Can we establish it? *Will* we establish it? Or will we give it up, at some point, as being too difficult? The song is accurate: *I don't know how to love him.* Just look at the logistics involved in holding hands at the movies! There's something creepy about it, the way our lacunae draw such scrutiny. Bad enough alone: together, we're specimens under a laser beam of curiosity. *A couple of freaks on the town.*

But then, I sense he's more accepting of me than I am of him. Or of myself, even. Doug accepts the lack of physical perfection, in himself, in me; Sully accepts it. Perhaps, with time, I will come to accept it, too.

"*You will always be marked,*" he said. "*It's a good thing.*"

I try for cleverness. "The book was better, don't you think?"

"The book is always better," he grins appreciatively, then proceeds to trash the movie. He makes me laugh with his sarcasm. But something in me wanted to *like* the movie; I feel a vague resentment.

When Kat comes through the employees' exit I'm almost relieved.

"Just drop me at home," she suggests, displaying misplaced altruism. "You two go somewhere alone; I have to work again in the morning, anyway." So we drop her, but without determining a destination for ourselves.

"Where do you want to go?" I ask, directing the station wagon toward the main drag: coffee shops and car dealerships.

"Let's drive past R.W.'s house," he suggests. "I'd like to know exactly where it is, to make sure my dad gets me there on time tomorrow night."

"Think we can find it in the dark?"

"We can but try!" He directs me out to the country. "River Road."

"And would that be upstream or downstream from the paper mill?"

"Upstream from the sweet effluvia, no doubt. Where the trout still run, unmutated, and the breeze is fresh." He grunts a laugh. "As long as the wind isn't out of the east. Slow down."

I slow.

"There."

There are no other cars on the road so I pause. The familiar Citroën is in the driveway. The yard is treed and lit discreetly from the driveway to the door.

"It had to be his," he says; "it's so unlike everything around here."

"Just like the man himself."

The house is all angled fingers of glass, illuminated like an inverted chandelier planted in the earth. Not a hint of early Pulp Mill Town.

"*A la* Frank Lloyd Wright," Doug breathes.

"Impractical roofline – for this climate. Must cost him a fortune to heat, too." I sound like my father. "Car."

"Drive up ahead a bit, then turn around," he orders.

Creeping by the house again, from the opposite direction, Doug practically presses his nose up against the glass.

"It'll be lovely in the daytime. What time do you have to be here tomorrow?"

"At five."

"Perfect."

"I'm scared out of my mind; I want it so bad."

"Danish exchange?"

"No; the house."

His fantasy, I suspect, is elaborate. With what magic has he endowed the house? Its occupant? I fill in a sort of fairy tale. Poor boy from remote village fantasizes witty, urbane life. Meets a wizard who can make his dreams come true.

What will he pay to have the dream fulfilled, I wonder? What tests will he have to pass?

We drive past the house again and again until I'm jittery with nervousness that someone will have spied us casing the joint.

"Let's go to the airport," he suggests.

We choose a remote parking spot, at the far end of the field. The last flight from Toronto comes screaming in, right over our heads.

"I'd love to be on the next flight out," he says.

"And where would you go?"

"Anywhere."

"That's what our grandparents said when they left Czechoslovakia, you know. But with all of North America to choose from, why did they stop here?"

He shakes his head. "It's as if they felt they didn't deserve better than a tar-paper shack on the swamp at the edge of a great wilderness. They'd already come so far. Perhaps they felt that if they went further they might fall off the edge of the earth."

The plane taxis back toward the terminal. Doug sighs. "My father doesn't understand why I want to go to Denmark so badly. 'Your grand-parents left Europe fifty years ago without a pot to piss in, and you want to bankrupt the family trying to get back?' He doesn't get the scholarship thing. Or, at least, refuses to listen. He thinks R.W.'s filled my head with impossible dreams." He sighs. "Like Harvard."

"It *is* unusual," I admit. "How many kids from Thunder Bay even think about Harvard, let alone get in?"

"One a year, maybe," he allows.

His estimate seems a bit high to me. "Mr. Justice Riordan's the only one I can name from the last three decades."

"At least Sully's got Harvard in his blood; he'll probably be disinher-ited if he doesn't get in. My dad, though." Doug shakes his head. "He can be so pigheaded. Sometimes I think we're changelings, Kat and I. We have nothing in common with him. And nothing we do is good enough."

He turns his head – and he's gone, as surely as if he'd boarded that plane and flown away. I don't know how to get him back. Or even if I should try.

But, eventually, he returns. "Well," he says, slapping his left thigh. "I guess you'd better get me home before one of us turns into a pumpkin."

Driving across the city by the long route, I choose to define our silence as "companionable," although I'm not certain it is.

In front of his house, he's reluctant to get out of the car.

"Have a good time at R.W.'s tomorrow," I say. "You have to tell me all about it on Monday."

He stares at me so intently I suppose a kiss can't be far behind. But the porch light flicks on: parental scrutiny. We leave each other laugh-ing, but it feels forced. I have the rest of the drive across town to won-der how I ever imagined dating Doug Hassock would restore a sense of normalcy to my life.

Richard Widener beckons me into the guidance office. He makes all the usual commiserative noises about my hand, then asks, "Have you given much thought to your plans for university?"

"A little," I hazard. "I'd still like to take a Bachelor of Music, per-haps in composition."

He nods. "You do realize there's still a performance requirement for admission to the Faculty of Music, even if you plan to concentrate in composition."

"Really?" I'm mute with dismay. No exceptions for one-handed pianists? "Then, I suppose I'll major in English." My attempted smile is feeble, even from where I'm sitting.

"Now, now; don't be so hasty. Have you considered voice as your performance specialty?"

"I've always sung in choirs, but I haven't had any formal training."

"Perhaps not," he admits. "But I've heard you; you sing well. You have the advantage of a good ear and first-rate keyboard training."

"But not vocal training." Perhaps I should have taken Jim Altman up on his suggestion.

Widener leans toward me across the desk. "Here's my suggestion, if you'd like to entertain it. I have a friend in the music department at the university. You might have heard him; he was the tenor soloist for the *St. Matthew Passion* last year. John Hamner."

"Yes," I nod enthusiastically. "He was excellent."

"I spoke of you with him this week."

I flush; R.W. has talked about me? I can just imagine the exchange: *One of our budding pianists has suffered a serious mishap.* Or, more likely, *One of my silly students has shot her hand off.*

"He suggested you meet with him, have a few sessions together to assess your potential and, if he thinks it's feasible, he'll work with you in preparation for your entrance audition. You have a year."

I feel a stirring of hope. "Do you think there's a chance?"

"If I didn't, I wouldn't have mentioned you to him in the first instance." He smiles. "Shall I arrange a meeting?"

"Yes, please."

Doug turns to me after class. "Are you going to physio?"

"No." I almost add, "I'm going to Sully's," but I don't.

When I passed Sully in the hall this morning my knees nearly buckled with longing. The smile he flashed me was kinetic.

"I'm not going to physio. Why?"

Doug signals me to follow. It seems he has his own form of kinetic energy. I have no choice, put Sully from my mind.

The couch in the auditorium. What a long time it's been since *Richard!* But no, he leads me to the piano bench instead. I feel sick at the sight of it. In the ten days I've been home I haven't given my own piano more than a passing glance.

"I'm sorry," he says, alert to my reaction. "I guess this was thought-
less of me."

"No, it's okay."

I sit at his left. He pushes back the lid, starts to noodle with his
left hand.

"I've always wanted to play the piano," he says. "I used to envy you
so much. Are you sure you won't play? There's always Ravel's *Concerto for
Left Hand.*"

I lift my head. "Not enough to base a career on." Smiling reassuringly, I nod toward the keys. "Go ahead, there's no reason why you
shouldn't play."

He shoots me a glance, sees that I mean it, and starts in on left-
handed arpeggios. *The Moonlight Sonata.* Without any bass. I close my
eyes. I had it memorized at some point, how many years ago? I can see
the score inside my eyelids. Count two measures and begin: I supply the
bass chords to his melody.

"Thank you," he breathes. "That was wonderful. Like hearing it in
stereo for the first time."

"You taught yourself?"

"It's all mathematical progressions: thirds, fifths, sevenths."

I smile, surprised.

"Look, talking of progressions, there's a reason I called you here
today," he says, with mock solemnity. "I haven't even told Kat yet.
Danish exchange: I got it."

"Oh, Doug!" I embrace him, searching for words. "That's so . . ." so
terrible? so far away? "so exciting!"

"And terrifying," he adds, holding me tighter.

Nothing like the prospect of separation to bring two people closer
together.

Sully's porch light is on as I approach his house, although it's not yet
dusk. His big front window blazes with light like a beacon: "*I'm home;
I'm home.*" When I push the buzzer marked "2A" he thunders down the
stairs, throws open the door.

"It seems like for ever since Thursday," I puff. He takes the stairs
two, three at a time, kneels to clear books and papers from the coffee
table. "Homework?"

"Yup. Can't escape it. I've got three 13s this semester."

"What?" I plunk onto the couch more suddenly than I'd planned.

He cocks his head. "I'm graduating in June, if I get the three Grade 13 credits. Which I plan to." He walks around the coffee table on his knees, plants both hands on the couch at my thighs. "What's the matter?"

"Jesus!" I breathe. "Everybody's leaving me behind. You're all accelerating! Why didn't I accelerate?" Why has this option never before occurred to me?

"You were busy with music," he says softly. "How much of a load could you have carried and still had time to practise?"

"I could've handled a few 13s!" So I could graduate with him, with Kat, with Doug.

Suddenly I feel betrayed – as if I've been coerced into trust under false pretences. Need! – I've let myself need him; it's only been a matter of days! But here I am, exactly as I feared – screaming with need, addicted.

"What's the matter?"

I beat at his chest with my fist, with the stump. Completely off guard, he falls back against the coffee table. "Riah!" He tries to hold me while I fight him with the ferocity of a wounded animal.

"Why didn't you tell me the other night?"

"Tell you what?"

"That you're graduating in June! 'Whatever you need!' " Hysterical. " 'Whenever you want it!' " Mocking. " 'Let yourself need me!' " I fling all his words back in his face. "You won't even be here! None of you will be here!" This is too perfect – he's cracked me open and here I am, absolutely defenceless.

His face is flayed with dismay. "If you need me," he chokes, "I *will be here.*" He holds my wrists. "You say the words and I'll pour my heart out. I'll make a vow – and I'll keep it, on my life! But," he shakes my arms, "*you* must set the terms."

He relaxes his grip experimentally. "Whatever you need, whenever you need it: I meant that. If it means going to Lakehead instead of Harvard," he gestures up the road, "then *that's* where I'll be. You say the words."

"What are the words?" I hardly dare ask.

He presses my hand against his wet cheek. "*I choose you.*"

Three words. An enormity of commitment.

He's already said too much. Part of me wants to run and hide. Part of me yearns to say, "I *do;* I choose you."

But that would be a false choice, born of the desperation, the confusion, of the last few months, prompted by my extraordinary and undignified need for him. He would not believe such an avowal, anyhow; he's too wise for that.

We stare into each other's weeping eyes. This is too much, too soon! But I must acknowledge his generosity somehow.

"When I say those words," – is it cruel to phrase it this way? – "I'll mean them. With all my heart – a free heart, a healthy heart." My voice breaks. "I promise you that."

Drawing the stump across his cheek, I feel the stubble of each whisker clear to my womb. For once I don't turn away from the sensation but let it warm me – from the inside out – like the strength of his arms, the promise of his love.

"*Where have you been?*"

My mother's face is tight with displeasure; she knows something.

I settle for half-truth. "I was with Doug after school. He's been chosen for Danish exchange."

Her expression softens. "I got a call from the hospital. You haven't been keeping your appointments."

"No. And I don't intend to." No explosion; I go a little farther. "I haven't ordered another prosthesis and I don't intend to do that either."

"Mariah," she starts.

"No." I cut her off with a wave of my hand. "I can't feel anything with it, Mommy!" *Like the stubble of Sully's beard*, I think with a flash of desire that goes straight to my cheeks. "It's so clumsy and – "

"You can get a different model!" she interjects.

"No." I shake my head. "No."

She puts her arm around me. "What about your father?"

"He can wear it if he wants to." She hoots, holds me tighter; I smile with her. "He'll just have to get used to it."

We have our work cut out for us, I know. "I guess he will."

Safely in my room, I stretch out on the bed, my head clamouring with reruns of today's encounters. I feel like Simon Peter, denying Sully's part in my lateness these afternoons.

Why do I feel I have to keep him a secret? He's matured; he's sensitive; he's sensible, compared to the child he was at fifteen. He's so different; and yet, not different at all. *I* am different, I know that.

But I've been down the Sully route with my parents. His prospects are ever so much better now that several years have gone by and he's not in jail, has not immolated himself, has not gotten a girl (me) pregnant.

But how much less dangerous is he now that he has his own car, an allowance with a margin for Belleek teacups, and an apartment across the street from the school? Is he less of a threat, now that he's older, taller, and visibly pumped with testosterone in the timbre of his voice, the hair on his chest, the angles of his wrists? And yes, yes, in the swelling of his jeans — though we've both been careful not to notice it.

There's no comfort for my parents in this scenario. We wouldn't last five minutes under the scrutiny his "maturity" would deploy.

No, Sully must be my secret for now, the way I keep the music in my head secret from them. To avoid overreaction; to avoid appropriation. Imagine — Sully and music sharing the same secret space where, two years ago, I worked so hard to keep them apart.

On the edge of dozing I suddenly sit bolt upright. I've just heard him say, *"If it means going to Lakehead instead of Harvard, then that's where I'll be."* And Doug's words: *"At least Sully's got Harvard in his blood; he'll probably be disinherited if he doesn't get in."*

Slipping into my parents' bedroom, I pick up the phone and dial gingerly. I prepare a lie, praying Mom doesn't pick up the kitchen extension.

He answers.

I don't waste words. "When you said, 'if it means going to Lakehead instead of Harvard,' was that rhetorical?"

"No." Sully chuckles gently when he hears my intake of breath.

There are so many things I don't know; it's as if we've just met. Which, in a way, is not so far from the truth.

"I'm not sure about it yet."

"Not sure you'll apply?"

"Not sure I'll accept the offer." He fills my stunned silence with words. "I applied to all the usual places: Lakehead, Waterloo, Queen's. And Harvard. Just for a laugh."

"Not sure you'll accept the offer! Why wouldn't you?" My own memories of the place come flooding in. "Just walking through Harvard Yard is enough to make you say 'I'd sell my soul to get here.' " Doug would; and here Sully's done it, *just for a laugh.*

"You're imbuing it with too much mystery. I just want to get into university, grab three-quarters of a degree with marks good enough for law school, and get out."

"Law school, too?" I ask weakly.

"Eventually." He laughs. "The family business. Who'd have thought it?"

So many surprises!

"Not you, obviously." The laughter fades from his voice. "Why not?"

Collecting my thoughts, "A failure of imagination," I say at last. "I couldn't imagine – " *I couldn't imagine a future with you* " – couldn't imagine us grown up, choosing grown-up lives, working to achieve them."

"I did waste most of a year. I was so hurt when you broke up with me," he says quietly, "I did a lot of lashing out."

"I'm sorry."

"But then," his voice rises jauntily, "I finally found my motivation. Your dad had a lot to do with that."

"My dad?" I squeak.

"Oh, yeah. Your dad. He spewed out a lot of bullshit that night of the three-hour lecture: wild oats, getting on with my life, that kind of crap. But some of the things he said made sense to me. Eventually."

"Like what?" But I know. I replay my father's speech. "That's so wonderful," I manage, my head reeling. "Congratulations."

What have I done to deserve this, this steadfast resolve in a boy I cut loose two years ago because he was too much responsibility for me to handle? He's determined a path, taken responsibility for his future, and left room in his vision for me – *if I so choose.* It's both breathtaking and humbling.

And troubling. Troubling that he's willing to derail himself from his chosen track if I need him. He's given me so much power again. But this time, instead of abdicating responsibility – "*you're the only one who can make me stop*" – he's taken on too much. Responsibility for himself – fine; responsibility for my happiness? No – this I can't let him do.

Noble – and worthy – but so misguided. The only one who can shoulder responsibility for my happiness – is *me!* I see this self-evident truth for perhaps the first time in my life. Me – it's up to me!

I sense I was on the right track this afternoon when I made him my promise. Such a choice — *I choose you* — is made from a position of strength and wholeness — not weakness, not blind need. Any coercion I might resort to can only destroy the happiness we might someday find together.

These thoughts are revelatory, epiphanic. I feel an outpouring of — what — hope? Grace? I feel free. Light-hearted. Grateful. So grateful to Sully for this gift. His devotion will make me strong — but not in the ways that either of us might have imagined days, even hours, ago.

I will make myself strong — for myself, by myself — so that someday I might share my self, my whole self, with him.

The rush I feel is magical, musical. I will prepare a gift for him in the meantime. Take the jangled discordance of need: hear it? Jumbled brass, timpani, screaming reeds. Minor, major, atonal. Juxtapose with a patient cello — a steadfast motif, a loving motif, repetitive yet kind. Resolve into a soul-searing duet for cello and oboe — male and female — and a peaceful finale.

"Have we been avoiding each other?" Dad asks. He clears his throat, folds the newspaper away.

Taking a place beside him on the couch, "I think so," I smile.

"I'm sorry. I didn't mean to do that."

"I did."

"I let you," he sighs. "It was easier. I tried to convince myself I was giving you space."

"That's what I needed. I think I've turned a corner, Daddy."

"Good." He puts his arm across my shoulders. "I've been afraid for you. And," he adds huskily, "so very sorry."

"It's going to be okay," I assure him. I take a chance: "I've decided not to wear an artificial hand."

"Mom told me."

"I'll be a bit clumsy, but I think I'll have more control" — that word — "in the long run."

I've had the stump hidden away between the couch cushions during this exchange. I withdraw it now and lay it between us.

"It's not so bad, Daddy," I declare.

His eyes are shiny but he nods, crushing me in his embrace. "There's nothing worse than seeing your child hurt and in pain." His voice catches. "I'd do anything to change what happened."

"I know. But you can't." I employ one of his own tones: "So, let's just get on with it, shall we?" I grin at him; he risks a tiny smile.

Across the room, the piano draws his eye. I steel myself. "What will you do, now?" he asks.

"There's lots I can do in music that doesn't involve performance — piano performance at any rate. I'd like to explore those options," I hint. "And there're a few books out there I haven't read." I gesture to the wall of bookcases.

"Good. You know we've always put money aside for your education, so there's that. But there's also," he hesitates, "some insurance money coming and," he winces at the words, "a disability pension, I believe. Just keep that in mind, when you're making your plans: there won't be any financial limitations." He tweaks my cheek. "Within reason, of course: daily champagne at the Sorbonne might be another matter."

"Ah; I'll have to make other economies."

He barks a laugh; squeezes my shoulder. I hazard a definition of the way I feel: *happy, adj. (of person or circumstance) lucky, fortunate; contented with one's lot.* Happy. Imagine that.

"You caught me."

Sully grins sheepishly, his face half-fleeced in shaving cream, a towel draped around his neck.

"What's it to be — *The Barber of Seville* or *Sweeney Todd*?" he asks, wielding a straight-razor.

"Yikes! you use *that*?"

"Jimmy's idea of a close shave. Life on the edge."

"This I've got to see," I smirk.

"No way; I'd cut my throat with an audience." He decamps to the bathroom. "Why don't you put the kettle on?" he hollers. "I'll make tea when I'm done."

Bumbling around his kitchen looking for teabags, spoons, his mug, my teacup — the intimate domesticity makes me light of head. And full of heart.

By the time Sully finishes clattering around the galley and emerges with one paw looped through the handle of his huge mug and the other, open, with "my" Belleek cup and saucer perched there gingerly like fairy china, I've taken up a position on the floor at the coffee table, my books spread open before me.

"What's this?" he asks suspiciously.

"Homework." I pat the table beside me. "There's room for you."

He puts the cup down. "I have all evening, after you leave. Virtually no distractions. Come on, Riah!" he pleads, "all work and no play makes Sully a dull boy." He sees I'm serious, makes a face, and settles down across the table from me, positioning his legs so that we're forced into contact. We work. It isn't long before I find my right arm looped around his ankle companionably. *This is nice*, I note, gratified.

Stealing glances, I watch him scribble, pen dwarfed in his hand. His hands; I do so love his hands! their strength, their fragility, the way he pushes the pen across the page, the shape of his nails. Despite the size and strength of his body, these are not the hands of a hunter-gatherer or of a man who will use them to make a living. They are the hands of a man who will survive on his wit.

He catches my eye across the table.

"What?" he smirks.

I shake my head, smile.

He captures me with his legs. "What?"

"Nothing."

He lies back on the floor, lifts the table away from his torso and sits up – the contortionist! – without moving his legs.

I relax into his arms. He reads the muscles of my back, my neck, like Braille. "Hmm. This is different."

My turn to ask, "What?"

"You've had more knots than a hunk of rope at a Scouts meeting," he kneads my shoulders. "Until now. What gives?"

"Released by the great Houdini!" I grin.

He grins back, fiddles with a lock of my hair, traces my eyebrow.

Desire tugs at my heart, my viscera; a different kind of need, a happy – if perilous – need. Perhaps this will be the first visit I've made him where I will not weep. *Happy*, I think, savouring the word, the play of his fingers on my face. We've spent so much time in each other's arms – has it only been ten days since he rescued me from the street? – so urgent, so intimate. And yet we haven't kissed. This fact surprises me so much it elicits an involuntary intake of breath.

"What?" he asks, shifting his weight, instinctively thinking he must be hurting me somehow in the tangle of our limbs.

My thoughts race. Why not? Why haven't we kissed? And it comes to me: our embraces have been for the sole purpose of comfort. Comfort offered, comfort accepted. By him; by me. Despite the occasional and involuntary urgency of his erection against my leg, we've admitted no potential of sex to the proceedings; it has been love unsullied by base urges. To kiss would be to cross over, through dangerous traffic, from the park to the haven of his light-filled home. *I'm waiting for you. Come, if you will.*

I will it. I cup his strong jaw in my hand, draw his cheek to my lips. He closes his eyes. *"Only connect."* Whose words? St. Augustine's? Surely not in this context! No; E.M. Forster's. Sully too senses the hazardous crossing I've made. I place a kiss just below his eye, in the soft whisker-free zone, feel the flutter of his long lashes under my lips. Another on his neat, dark brow. His freshly shaven cheek. A dab of dried shaving cream just behind his ear – a kiss there, too.

He opens his eyes. I see myself reflected in their amber depths, an insect trapped – preserved– in the resin. He fixes answering kisses on my face, gently, ceremonially, as if there is great significance to their placement, their symmetry.

By mutual decision: the lips. I am reminded of the chaste, childish pressing of lip to lip we engaged in, that lifetime ago. So soft, so sweet – a child's lips. But now, beyond. A fierce and handsome man, endowed with incredible generosity of spirit.

In his arms, in his bed, we make each other offerings. I offer him my trust, trust that will overshadow fear – and the memory of pain. He offers me, reflected in his eyes, an image of myself that sears through all the mirror-gazing of my youth, burns away all imaged and imagined versions, leaving just his truth: me, as he sees me – desirable, beloved. Whole.

To think I thought I might visit here today and leave him without weeping! Silly girl. We offer each other tears of gratitude and joy.

I offer him my pain. It is clean pain; red pain, good pain. Brief, but sacramental. For, with it, I give a prayer of thanks. Thanks that, despite all the indignities, I am able to offer James Sullivan Riordan a small barrier of flesh. And several drops of blood to stain his sheets.

I don't want to go home. I *am* at home, here, wrapped in Sully's arms – knee to knee in bed like lost continents rediscovering each other after the Ice Age. This wonderful, sanctified mistake has drained me of my resolve to let him go. If I adopt a different self with everyone, then I've given Sully a Mariah I can't relinquish. I can be this self — this free, this loved, this *loving* — only with him, absorbing his strength and warmth through my pores like a parasite. "Hello, Mom? I can't come home — I've become attached to Sully."

Resolve returns. "An empty bed will be so lonely after this."

But it's not! Exhausted after a distracted dinner, I can't wait to get under the covers. Because *he is here*. Present — in the alien scent of my skin, the moisture between my legs. In the tiny bruises on my thighs, the dark spring-coiled hairs embedded in my flesh; in my curves and angles like the reversible presence in an M.C. Escher print.

I'm never completely alone in my bed. But Sully's presence so effectively drives the other shade away I decide Mom's unilateral decision to move me wasn't insensitive, after all; this room, once my grandfather's, is uncontaminated by memory and blood. Drawing the tactile memory of Sully's body around me like a security blanket, I fall asleep.

When I pass Sully in the hall at school he draws me aside urgently. He looks different — are we obvious to everyone? My face feels like the Odeon marquee flashing neon, ten feet high: *Made love last night — no longer virgin. Shows nightly 7 & 9 p.m.*

"Can you drop by after school?" he asks anxiously. "I have to talk to you."

"Of course." Is there any doubt? The newly hatched parasite in me wants to attach its craven lips to the exposed V of his neck. As if he's pulled a plug, blood drains so suddenly from my head to my crotch that I feel faint and drop my books in a fan at my feet.

All knees and arms, Sully bends to retrieve them. "After school," he says, then sweeps away, leaving me to a virtually wasted day.

Disengaged from everything, everyone; when Doug asks if I'm all right, I plead a migraine. "Why don't you go home, then?"

No. Not home. But I do skip my last class to hide out in a corner of the library for ninety minutes, determining a coping strategy.

Our kissing sessions, when we were fifteen, turned into endurance competitions. Despite the urgency of my current need, I don't want to spend every afternoon in Sully's bed until making love becomes something to be avoided or forestalled by other activities, like the interminable walks of our youth accompanied by the incessant drone of his voice. The possibility that we've ruined our tenuous relationship by consummating it fills me with remorse.

The coffee table, set for tea, is a signal: we won't adjourn immediately to his room. He buzzes around seriously. Nervously, even.

"Mariah, I didn't sleep very well last night," he starts.

That's funny; I did.

"I want you to know — making love with you was the most important thing I've ever done. I feel as if it's . . . changed everything."

My thoughts, exactly.

"It was something we needed to do, maybe something you needed more than I did. Affirmation? Acceptance? Healing?"

"All those things," I murmur.

"It was intense and moving," he searches for words, "maybe even mystical." He takes my hand and kisses it. "I hope you won't misunderstand when I say I don't think we should do it again. At least for a while."

I feel crushing disappointment — mixed with the helium of relief.

Shaking his head self-deprecatingly, "I can't believe this," he laughs. "Here I am, almost eighteen, telling a beautiful, desirable girl we shouldn't make love again! Am I nuts?" He places his hands on my shoulders, rests his head against mine.

"Why?" I ask, trying to keep my expression neutral.

"Why?" He looks to the ceiling as if he might have crib notes taped there, looks back to me: "Preservation."

Self-preservation? What *kind* of preservation?

"I don't want to say too much, or the wrong thing. But the other day you promised me that when you say the words," he doesn't have to say which words, "you'll mean them, with a free and healthy heart."

"Yes."

"I predict a fair bit of time passing before that can happen. Realistically? Years." He sighs. "You have an education to attend to, and so do I. When I offered you love, I also offered you freedom — freedom from the pressure of my particular needs and desires." He looks at me intently. "Last night was a magnification of my hope for the future," his voice drops. "I want that future so badly, I'm afraid I'll say the wrong things, do the wrong things, to get it." His eyes fill. "I'll prey on your need — and my own — and I'll ruin it because I want you so much!"

Face twisting, "I'm leaving it up to you," he says, resting his head once again on mine. "We can go ahead on this path, wherever it might lead. Or we can wait for that future to catch up to us, risking what might happen to us in between. But I'm not willing to make that decision for us. It's up to you."

Jesus, Sully — what a gambler you are!

To weigh a distant and nebulous future against the compelling immediacy of need, of love — and choose correctly, generously. It's terrifying. If I choose "now," I might selfishly throw our future away for instant gratification. The purity of my motives will always be suspect. In his mind; in mine.

He's afraid, as I am, that we'll be immolated by the intensity of the emotion we shared last night. Only commitment can keep it safely contained. It does seem as if one precludes the other.

The tide of certainty ebbs and flows while we hold each other. This act of faith requires as much commitment as the three words, "I choose you" — and a vision of a future that will link us in space, time, and spirit when we arrive via separate orbits. Not much margin for error.

It's a gamble I have to take, for his sake. And for mine.

"You're a brave man, Sully Riordan."

As I kiss his cheek one last time, he looks as if he'll take back all his fine words if I just incline my head a certain way. Lifting the Belleek teacup from its saucer, I hold it out to him in toast.

"To the future," I whisper, so there'll be no doubt.

Does the right decision have to feel like such a terrible loss?

Having taken a less than direct route home to avoid other people on the street, I stop and compose myself behind the neighbour's garage. I'll never get past my mother.

"I'll grab something to eat later," I promise, adding absolute truth: "If I eat now I'll throw up."

This is nuts! How can we build a future by renouncing our present? We're aware of the pitfalls; surely we can avoid them if we rein in our selfishness. If we're strong enough to give each other up, why can't we be strong enough to stay together? As together as we can be, in separate cities, separate schools.

Separate. Distinct. Yes, this is the point. We can't be separate-but-together, or together-but-separate. We need to find our way, alone. Not for us, the promises, "I'll see you at Christmas; I'll see you at spring break," when what we really need is to work, or play, with friends at hand.

The enormity of Sully's gamble empties – and fills – me alternately. Grief and promise: twin faces of the weight that drags me into sleep.

Still unable to function in the morning, I resort to the tried and true: retreat. "Just a bit more sleep, Mom. I'll feel better then."

Can I change my mind, Sully? The promise doesn't weigh much in the balance; grief is dominant. This feels childish, but it doesn't alter the pervasive sense of loss. Such a cruel choice he's forced me to make! Spiteful words niggle at my consciousness: Are you entirely sure it's not revenge for dropping him two years ago? Surely Sully of all people is incapable of such calculated cruelty toward anyone, let alone me at the nadir of vulnerability. But – a shadowy part congratulates him. If it *is* revenge, it's complete.

When Mom comes in with a lunch tray – "You *must* have something to eat," she orders – I'm at my desk with music spread all around me. I shield it guiltily as if she's caught me reading pornography. Driven more by the need to get the tray off my work space than by hunger, I wolf down the food.

Taking my work from the other night – the jangled discordance, the patient, loving cello line resolving the screaming reeds into peace – as one movement, I create another duet between cello and oboe in the second. Male and female: passionate, searing, tender. Joyful. In the third, I reprise the peaceful theme, the two instruments enmeshed in each other – and then I tear them apart. Gently. Regretfully. Themes restated: separate. Ending with the oboe, solo. Distinct. Fading off into the unknown, alone. Grief and promise. Promise and grief.

The music of offerings made, offerings accepted. The sound of moisture between my legs, bruises on my thighs. No guilt, though; no guilt. Why does this surprise me so much? Nice Catholic girl who – invoking the names of emaciated mystics, reduced herself to a cipher – gives up her virginity to young man of Danish Lutheran and lapsed Irish Catholic parentage. And feels no guilt? Listen, listen to all the other emotions she feels. Longing. Loss. Love. You'll hear no guilt.

When I've translated enough of what I hear onto the pages – enough to work from later – I scrawl a title on the first page: *Sullivan Suite.*

"You're back."

Banal observation or insight: Doug's comment covers it all. *Yes; I'm back.*
A little shaky, maybe. Especially when I see Sully in the hall and we
exchange sorrowful, sympathetic smiles. He looks as bad as I felt yesterday, which is strangely heartening. Successful revenge would surely make
for a lighter step, a jauntier angle of his head. The expression on his face
and the bags under his eyes say, "Haven't slept; admitting moral doubt."

Be brave, I telegraph with my eyes, *you were right.*

"Auditorium?" Doug suggests after class.

Unwilling to abandon my painful solitude, I hesitate. I'm also par-
tially afraid to let Doug get close. It won't be long before he, too, will
take a powder. How much renunciation is a girl capable of in one semester? Especially – I laugh a little hysterically as my mind turns from the
sublime to the ridiculous – when she needs a date for the prom! Sully
and I should have planned this better; he'd look so good in a suit.

"What's funny?" Doug asks as he steers me to Sigmund and Anna's
couch. "Share the joke?"

I can't tell him! I think, but to my amazement I do.

He hears me out patiently, dries my tears with his shirt tail, and puts
a little distance between us so he can see my face. "It's too weird,
Mariah! Sully's had time to think about the enormity of the commitment and he's back-pedalling madly."

"No."

"Then he's so afraid of losing you he'd rather detach consciously
now than face the loss later. If it works out, fine; if it doesn't, he has-
n't made a huge emotional investment."

I've considered these options and dismissed them.

"Why are you so convinced you're in love with him? It's more like
imprinting – you both fell for the first creature you saw upon hatching
from childhood."

Hasn't he been listening? "I didn't say I'm 'in love' with him," I assert.
"I said I 'love' him."

"What's the diff?" he asks callously.

"Look. When I was 'in love' with him I was fifteen and couldn't see
a future for us."

"And you're only seventeen now. What can possibly be so different?"
he demands.

I am; I am different. "I let him in." If I can't explain this to Doug, I fear I'll be unable to carry the vision. "Back then I couldn't imagine a sustainable reality around the cardboard cut-outs of each other we'd erected. But now! He's, he's," floundering, "like the Velveteen Rabbit!"

"Great realism!" Doug smirks. "A six-foot, four-inch stuffed bunny."

"*We've* become real to each other; not perfect, but real." I need to make Doug see. "And I love the reality of him — his foibles, his strengths, his weaknesses. All I can see now is the future!" I insist. "I don't know quite how we'll get there, but I see it! Not a Cinderella story, I don't want that, but real life: having children, arguing about money, laughing in bed together."

Doug flashes an eyebrow, but I press on.

"I can even see his extra fifteen or twenty middle-aged pounds; his thinning grey hair. I see him working too hard; yelling at the kids; wondering if I still love him, after all this time."

"Sounds *dread*fully suburban." Doug drawls out the words with a disaffected accent. Noel Coward, perhaps. Or Richard Widener.

I nod eagerly. "It is. I see banality, I see boredom." I gesture wildly. "And I think he sees a woman he's going to bicker with and despise at times, who might someday," I gesture to my still too-thin frame, "carry a few too many pounds after childbirth, who might laugh a little too loud or too long at another man's jokes at a cocktail party, but who will come home *still loving him.*"

"I don't know," he shakes his head dubiously. "It sounds like a different sort of projection to me: bourgeois home movies. What will you *be* in this future, other than Sully Riordan's wife or mom to a troupe of Irish Catholic kids?" A crooked grin: "That Irish gene is always dominant, you know. His mother may be Danish, but you never think of Sully as anything other than full-blooded Irish. He'll suck every particle of Slovak from your DNA."

I laugh.

Then Doug returns to the point: "So what will *you* be?"

I will be.

Isn't that enough? All these years, I've been a make-work project, modifying myself on demand for others, *dead certain* that the me inside had no intrinsic value, if it wasn't perfect: none. A cipher. Zero.

Here, I've given Sully a self — my self — that is accepted and prized. Imperfect. Inchoate. Still a make-work project, but all of my own design: Mariah Standhoffer. Composer? Teacher? Writer? Partner. Equal.

What will I be? "I'm not sure yet," I answer Doug. But I *will be*.

～～○

"All this fuss for my lab partner!" Kat laughs. "Maybe I should dab formaldehyde behind my ears instead of perfume."

Surprisingly nervous when I pick Doug up for the graduation dinner dance, I admire my friend. With her hair all pulled up and curled, Kat looks quite unlike herself.

"Shall we wait until Ray gets here?" I ask.

"No; first one there saves space at the table, though. I'll need someone to talk to while Ray dissects his dinner."

Feigning impatience, I ask, "Where's your brother? Is he ready for the ball?"

Doug emerges from the bedroom at last, followed by his mother. My heart lurches a little. He looks handsome – if embarrassed – in a new three-piece suit, the right sleeve of which is pinned discreetly into the pocket.

"Wow," he says, "you look great."

"So do you," I grin.

He removes a florist's box from the fridge, kicks the door shut. Proffering the box, he holds it for me while I fumble with the tape. A beautiful green orchid, just the shade of my dress. "Brings out the colour in my eyes," he teases.

Mrs. Hassock steps in to assist with the pinning of the corsage, since it's beyond our combined capabilities, nervous as we are. *Two good arms between us.*

"Perhaps I should have bought a wrist corsage," he suggests.

"This is just right. Thank you."

Why are we so awkward with each other? I wonder as we drive across town. Is it because Doug is hampered – face it, handicapped – by his suit coat?

"Don't worry," he says, as if he's read my mind. "I'm losing the jacket as soon as we arrive. You won't have to cut my meat for me."

"You might have to cut mine!"

He slides toward me on the bench seat, takes my wrist in his left hand. "We'll manage somehow."

A couple of freaks on the town.

Kids who never wear anything other than jeans are dressed to the nines, polished and groomed and primped. We're all bright and amusing, full of promise, facing a brilliant future. Laughter overflows each vessel like champagne.

And yet, I'm focused across the room on Wendy Staplin's table. She's with a boy from "outside school" to whom she has calculatedly given her virginity, the details of which she was quite willing to share with Carol Caldwell and I, certain she was upsetting our virginal sensibilities. Wouldn't she be shocked if she knew I'd beaten her to the punch! "It's an obstacle to dating in college," she confided. "Better to get it over with, with someone nice, someone you trust." And he does seem very nice.

Wendy's laughter, I observe, is all for Carol's date. His back is turned to me, but I can tell he's holding court: one elbow perched casually on the back of his chair, regaling the table with an obviously hilarious story, gesturing expansively. His expression is mirrored in the faces of his audience. *Sully.* I long to be at that table with him, hanging on his every word, enjoying the pleasure the others take in his company. *Isn't he appealing? Doesn't he look great in that suit?* He's solicitous of Carol, but not intimate. They're high-school acquaintances escorting each other for this occasion, like Ray and Kat.

As if he's been following my sight-line, Doug puts his arm across the back of my chair – proprietarily? I flash him a smile, returning my attention to Ray – who seems to be coming out of the shell of "science geek" long enough to be a fairly amusing companion for Kat. And not a bad dancer.

Doug excuses himself just as the band strikes up Carole King's "You've Got a Friend." Great timing, I think, over my desolation. Kat waggles her fingers at me as Ray leads her onto the dance floor. Trying not to look like a wallflower, I mumble a litany – *my date's in the john* – maintaining a benevolent expression.

"May I?" I find my elbow in a firm grip. "Come on, let's make a run for it." Propelled into the throng of milling bodies on the floor almost against my will, I look up into Sully's grinning face.

How did he arrange this? Ever suspicious of synchronicity where Sully is concerned, "I'm not sure this is a good idea," I manage, instinctively wanting to press myself against the familiar lines of his body as he holds me loosely in his arms.

The voltage of his smile dims. "I miss you."

"I miss you, too." These words don't begin to tell the tale.

"I'm giving up the apartment at the end of the month," he says.

"So soon?"

"To spend the summer in Toronto, with Jimmy and Sonja, before I head off to school."

I nod, unable to speak.

"When does Doug leave for Denmark?"

"The fifteenth of July." *Your birthday*, I think. *Eighteen.*

"You'll miss him."

"Not the same way I'll miss you."

Sully glances toward the door of the banquet hall. When he swings me around I see Doug framed in it.

"Does he know about us?"

"Yes."

A crooked smile aimed over my head. "And does he think we're nuts?" he asks, looking back into my eyes.

"No. I think I convinced him of our essential sanity at the same time I convinced myself."

I feel his grip tighten just a little. Suddenly I have a barrage of questions, the most important being, How will I know it's time? Will we keep in touch? Will we see each other?

But I don't ask. We pass the rest of the four and a half minutes in silence, letting the words of the song speak for us. When it ends, "To the future," he says, brushing his lips across my cheek.

As he turns to rejoin Carol and Wendy at their table, I rush to the washroom to see if my make-up is salvageable, and spend much too long behind the locked door of a stall ruining it further.

Waiting a discreet distance from the ladies' room, Doug holds my evening bag under cover of his suit coat, crushed in his little hand.

"Care for some air?" He drapes his jacket around my shoulders. "You okay?" Feigning bafflement, he asks, "How did he *manage* that? For me to be out of the room at the exact moment *that* song was playing?"

"He obviously had it prearranged: Doug leaves the hall for a pee, cue the band," I tease.

"You've got to hand it to him; he's always had impeccable timing. If you're not careful," he says pointedly, "he'll stage-manage your entire life." He puts his arm around my shoulders, clears his throat. "And I should get my twenty bucks back, because I had the band bribed to play that song at ten-thirty. They were ten minutes early."

"Are you serious?"

"No, but I wish I'd thought of it." He looks down, scuffs at a pebble with his shoe. "Because I mean it as much as he does," he adds.

"Thanks," I croak.

He places a tender little kiss on my lips. All these partings! In four weeks Doug will be in Denmark. No wonder everyone in that room is hysterical with gaiety: the tragic mask is lurking just beneath.

After the band packs it in, "Want to go for a drive?" I ask Kat. When she hesitates, "Bring Ray," I suggest. "He can leave his car here for a while."

We all pile into the station wagon. Ray, grateful to be included, has come so far out of his shell he's almost gregarious. He babbles from the back seat, his arm companionably around Kat's shoulders, as if they've been dating for months. Doug and I smile at each other parentally.

"What a great view!" Ray enthuses when we get out of the car at the hill that serves Chippewa Park in winter as a toboggan run. "How did you find this place?"

Who knows any more? Doug and Kat and I have spent so much time driving around, day and night, looking for places to be alone together. Looking for spring, in the impressionistic leafing of the trees around Mount McKay. A pointillist spring. A Seurat spring – each tree budding, distinct dot by distinct dot, shade by shade. Until we stood back one day, just recently, to see the big picture: a solid canopy of green.

Wind soughing gently through those leaves we coaxed into existence; the lights of the city sparkling: from this distance it looks almost appealing. *This town isn't so bad*, I rationalize. *Don't go!* Noting my involuntary shiver, Doug holds his jacket out for me. The sleeve of the right arm, pinned into the pocket, hides my stump. Just a girl out on a date – purse in one hand and one hand in her pocket.

Who are we trying to fool – hiding our handicaps, however briefly, however badly. I feel so much more fragmented with Doug than I ever did with Sully. Is it because Sully himself is whole and therefore there are fewer fragments to work around? *The whole is greater than the sum of the parts.*

The three of us — and Ray, don't forget Ray — stand looking out into the distance, trying to see a future in the crystalline sky. But the future is eclipsed, like the starlight, by the city's artificial glow.

"What the hell does *this* mean?"

I'd taken dictation from CN/CP Telecommunications on the phone. Kat looked over my shoulder at the message:

"GNIHTYREVE SI ENIF. DEVIRRA YLEFAS ETIRW NOOS. EVOL, DOUG."

"How's your Danish?" I asked.

"Looks more like Welsh. Are you sure you got it right?"

"The guy dictated it, letter by letter." My hand shook. Is this a message from some Danish Samaritan who's fished Doug's broken and bleeding body from under a Copenhagen bus?

Drawing her dressing gown around herself, Kat sat beside me at the table. "Maybe we should call the Danish Vice Consul for a translation," she said at last.

Suddenly my focus shifted. "I've got it."

"What language *is* it? Finn?"

"English. Backward. See?" I drew my finger across the words: "EVERYTHING IS FINE. ARRIVED SAFELY. WRITE SOON. LOVE, DOUG."

She snatched it from my hand. "Bastard!"

"You'd better call your mom."

"Yeah," she said, still staring at the paper. Then, "How come he sent *you* the telegram, anyway? Shouldn't he have informed his own family first?"

"He knew you were sleeping over last night!"

"Defend him, why don't you?" She tossed a huge grin over her shoulder, having chosen to read too much into things: Kat doesn't know about Sully. Still, I remained smugly flattered.

With that first communication, Doug set the precedent. If his family wants to know how he is, they ask me. Oh, sure, he writes neutral letters home, in which everything is always fine. Might pass on an amusing anecdote, or complain about the food. To Kat, at Queen's, he might ramble on about how hard it is to write exams in Danish, how worried he is about getting marks good enough to get into Harvard after all.

But Doug tells *me* the scary stuff. He tells me about the pervert who exposed himself in the washroom of a Copenhagen pub. He confides his loneliness, his fears, his bizarre nightmares. He tells me how all the kids drink Aquavit until they're plastered, and how he joins them to fit in. How *easy* it is to join them; how splendidly he fits in. The shenanigans on weekend trips to Paris and Amsterdam; the ready availability of pornography. His inability to go to confession, lest the priest misunderstand his Danish and send him straight to hell.

He doesn't tell me everything, I read *that* between the lines. But he tells me enough that I feel both privileged and burdened: privileged that he entrusts me with his secrets; burdened by the weight of his unconfessed guilt.

Doug writes often, and copiously, but he can't match me for sheer volume. I've virtually nothing else to do. Vocal lessons with John Hamner are a party — how can anyone call it work? I have the music I write for my own amusement; I spend time with Wendy Staplin, mostly on weekends; write to Kat sporadically, phone her once in a while. No other distractions.

School, too, is easy this year. I've chosen only the courses I know will gain me the highest marks and, despite working hard enough at them, I still have lots of time on my hands. Hand. Which is, more often than not, gripping a pen.

I long to write to Sully. Instead, I write to Doug as if the miles of script could form some sort of lifeline across the Atlantic. The lifeline is, ostensibly, for him — since he's so far from home, alone in a foreign country. But, at times, I wonder if it's for me.

The better part of our relationship takes place on paper. Doug professes to love my long, rambling letters. Writing to him is like talking to myself, except that I have to be somewhat ordered, logical — and spontaneous. I've developed a tone of self-parody through the reams of letters I write him that sometimes renders my most earnest introspection faintly ridiculous, even to me.

"You're so much smarter on paper," he remarks in one letter, "so much more articulate. You have a *voice* when you're writing, an authority you don't have when you speak."

Doesn't everyone? I wonder. Perhaps not.

"It's as if you pop into perspective on the two-dimensional plane of the paper," he continues. "You're more present than you ever were in my arms."

I know I withhold too much of myself when I'm with him, the way I do with my father, the way I did with Sully the first time around. Partly the old need to maintain the façade of perfection, the fear of rejection should I expose too much. More fundamental, though: I'm more articulate on paper because, when I write, *he cannot interrupt.*

Formulating arguments, discussing books and movies, describing incidents or states of mind with detail, humour, pathos – all for his amusement and edification. If he disputes my logic, two weeks might pass before I receive his response – by which time I'm emotionally distanced from the words I might have felt so passionately at the time. Free to take risks, both in form and subject, I strive for emotional honesty.

And yet I wonder if it's possible – even desirable – to achieve it. I catch myself observing everything through the viewfinder of Doug's perceptions, Doug's judgements, focussing everything for Doug's ultimate consumption. Which elements will yield the most arresting impression? Which lens length, filter, focus? Or shall I resort to a sort of psychic laparoscope – entering an open artery, an orifice, a wound – to take a diagnostic interior journey to the brain. Or the heart.

This is dangerous, I realize. Reduced to the role of observer, of mechanized receptor of experience, I am lens, aperture, film, and darkroom, all in one. I'm living a Polaroid life.

Routines evolve, like the "Song of the Day" – a little snippet of melody with a few lyrics (sometimes doggerel, sometimes poetry) that he can pick out on the piano of the home in which he's being hosted. Occasionally my letters to him become first drafts of stories or poems. I start using carbon paper, or take photocopies, before I drop the missives in the mail.

How crass can I be? I ask myself at these times. And yet I can't count on him being as reliable an archivist as he is an audience – captive and appreciative – despite his teasing.

"I'm amassing enough material for the first several volumes of the *Collected Letters of Mariah Standhoffer.* They'll fetch a pretty penny in the publishing world someday," he writes, "when you're a rich and famous composer/writer – wife to a talented barrister and mother to a horde of handsome kids."

Just as I begin to detect envy and resignation in his words, his tone shifts.

"I've decided that I don't care you're virtually married to Sully," he writes one day. "You and he have renounced each other, as you told me in a particularly poignant manner, until such time as you're ready to commit your lives to each other. Well — *over my dead body*, damn it! I'm not going to stand by and watch you ride off into the sunset with the likes of Sully Riordan. Not without a fight, anyway. *I love you, too, Mariah!* I don't know if I stand a chance against your Niall of the Nine Hostages, but you can't tell me you don't feel *anything* for me. I've got hundreds of pages in your handwriting that prove the contrary."

All this written with bold, brash strokes of his pen, underlined and forested with exclamation points. Then in smaller, humbler script: "If I'm wrong, though — say the word."

If he's in love with the voice of the letters, does that make it projection — or ventriloquism? Either way, it's a trick, not a reality.

Drafting my response, "Of course I feel something for you!" I assure him. "And I venture to call it 'love.' There are many kinds of 'love,' but English has precious few words for it. Just remember you're not in competition with Sully. You know too much to take anything on faith, but believe this: there is room in my heart for you, in some form or other. Whether there's room in my future remains to be seen."

"How'd you like to take a trip with me?" Dad proposes, pushing his chair back against the breakfast-room wall.

"A trip?" I parrot. "Where?"

"Europe."

"Europe?" Ignace, Manitouwadge, Winnipeg: sure, I might have expected one of those. But Europe? "What *part* of Europe?"

He laughs at my expression. "Well, you've been pining for and missing that boy, what's his name, Mother? Doug?" he teases. "Surely you've spent enough on postage the past few months to cover your airfare!"

"Are you serious?" This has to be his cruel idea of a joke.

"I've been wanting to get back to Czechoslovakia," he says, "before all the relatives are gone. To see the place where I was born while someone still remembers where it is. And I've been toying with the notion of taking your grandfather's ashes back, to sprinkle around the land of his birth. I don't see why we can't route the trip through Copenhagen, if Doug can meet us there. Spend a few days with him. Then visit the rellies: Bratislava, Košice, Brno, Prague."

"What about Mom and Luke?"

"We can't afford for all of us to go," Mom says. "I'm taking you to Toronto for your audition, don't forget."

"What do you say?"

My speechlessness says it all. "When?"

"March break." Dad takes a piece of paper out of the breast pocket of his shirt, hands it to me. "A tentative itinerary. See if it suits Doug." He digs through his wallet, fishes out a U.S. ten-dollar bill. "Tell him to phone, or cable us. We need to get things firmed up quickly."

I fling my arms around his neck, buss his cheek. "Excuse me; I've got a sealed envelope to steam open!"

To my carefully drafted paragraphs I add: "As for the *immediate future*, my father and I propose to be in your vicinity for a few days in March and would like to pay you a visit – if you can fit it into your busy schedule." How I'd love to see his expression when he reads this! I think, stapling the money carefully to the inside of the letter.

Doug's cable comes a week later: "Exams March 12–16. Can you postpone one week. Can't wait. Love Doug."

"If it wasn't for the fog, you'd be able to see most of Europe from up here."

"If it wasn't for the fog, we'd be on the ground!" I snarl impatiently. "There must be thirty planes in this holding pattern."

"Maybe we'll be diverted to Helsinki," Dad suggests mildly. I bop him with a rolled-up flight magazine. But when I notice one plane after another diving through a tiny break in the fog cover like threads through the eye of a needle, I come close to hyperventilating.

Leaving my nose prints on the glass in the taxi, on the windows of our rooms, I try to absorb everything.

"Now, get some sleep!" Dad insists. "His train doesn't get in until after lunch."

My father is snoring on one bed of the room he will share with Doug. When the knock finally comes, I'm in Doug's embrace before the echo fades in the corridor. Banal, excited greetings pass our lips.

"Look at your hair!" I exclaim. Shoulder-length blond locks – a

Nordic hippie.

"I know!" he raises his hand to forestall comment. "Your dad'll have a fit."

"He won't let it go without remark," I concede, "but Luke's isn't much shorter."

"Did you *have* to bring him?"

"It was his idea; his money, too," I whisper back. "Come on. Let's face the inevitable."

Sleepily putting on his glasses when I push Doug through the door, Dad stands, puts out his right hand in greeting, swaps it hurriedly for his left. "Prince Valiant, I presume?" he jokes. "Good to see you, lad; how are the Danes treating you?"

"Fine, sir; fine."

Oh my; this *will* be awkward, won't it? Whatever was I thinking when I agreed?

My father's presence is inhibiting. Especially since Doug and I can't walk hand in hand like any "normal" couple; he needs to put his arm around me to make contact. But it's not so bad. He easily assumes the role of tour guide, proud to show off his knowledge of Danish history and culture. With time at a premium — we only have the weekend — we rush through churches and museums at a frenetic pace.

"There's a Monet, a Degas, Picasso, Rodin."

Some of the world's greatest art goes by like a deck of flash cards. *Can't we stay and linger anywhere?* I'd give up seeing any number of palaces in favour of actually slaking my thirst at just one cultural fountain, or sitting down with him over a cup of coffee — alone — just to talk.

My dad is not insensitive to this. "You two spend the day together," he suggests at breakfast on Sunday. "I'll poke around by myself; we'll get together for dinner."

He takes out his wallet, fans a wad of Danish currency. "Here," he says, proffering it to Doug. "Take enough for a nice lunch and admission to all of the tourist traps we've missed. Don't be stingy; that's my daughter you've got there." He flashes one of his looks: *be cautious, be sensible, have fun.*

"The joke's on him," Doug says, watching him walk away. "I've taken enough for us to elope to Paris." He settles his arm around my shoulders and, when he's quite sure Dad is out of sight, places a deep kiss on my mouth. "Hmm," he muses, "maybe we should just go back to your room and hang out."

"The walls have ears."

He smirks. "Just kidding."

Not much.

But we do manage to break through the awkwardness of separation and the desperate ticking of the meter on this reunion, and talk. At least, Doug talks.

Meandering the cobbled streets, poking into impossibly expensive shops on the Strøget – here, at his side, I feel strangled by the weight of his personality, mute and two-dimensional. My thoughts are like Tivoli: out of season, closed. I fear he's disappointed with me in person, that he'll be relieved to have me safely back on the other side of the Atlantic. Thousands of miles, yet just a stamp, away: *I'll have so much to tell you when I write.*

Sipping take-out coffee, we sit on a bench looking out over the harbour at the statue of The Little Mermaid.

"Your audition's coming up soon, isn't it? Surely you should be practising."

I blow across my cup. "You haven't heard me in the shower the last few mornings?"

"Sing now," he invites.

"There're people around," I shake my head, embarrassed.

"And not one of them knows you, except me! What does it matter? You can put it on your c.v.," he urges. " 'Public recital. Copenhagen: March 1974.' "

Yes, I should be practising. And I haven't done more than hum in the shower, really. I fish my tape recorder and rehearsal tape out of my backpack, look around nervously.

"Forget the world!" he says. "You're here for me."

Yes, I'm here for you. "I need to warm up a little," I say, tossing back the last of my coffee. I gesture for him to wait, do some warm-ups out of hearing range, then come back. "Press play," I order.

And begin. I start off with some of the Italians, the *arie antiche* – eighteenth-century love songs, most of them – that every student does. Schubert's *Gretchen am Spinnrade.* The Aria from Villa-Lobos' *Bachianas Brasileiras,* its subtlety pretty much lost to the buzz of traffic around us.

By the time I get to the last piece – my particular favourite – I'm wound up. I begged John Hamner to let me do it despite the terrifying high "C" of the finale: Anne Trulove's big scene from *The Rake's Progress*.

"I don't know," he'd said. "We're not grooming your voice for opera."

"But it speaks to me!" I'd insisted. "And it'll set me apart from every other 'Gretchen' and 'Florindo.'

"We'll give it a try," he'd capitulated. "The part suits the bright, clear soprano you've been hiding all this time. But," he warned, "it's the first thing to go if it doesn't work."

I worked harder on it than anything all year. John conceded it made an impressive ending to the audition. "*If* you can pull off that 'C'," he warned. "If you flub it, it'll be the only thing they'll remember."

"They'll remember I *tried*," I'd insisted.

"Stop the tape." How I wish I had the orchestral version, with its beautiful oboe intro, rather than John's piano transcription. "How's your Stravinsky?" I ask. "Are you familiar with *The Rake's Progress*?"

Doug shakes his head.

What luck! Something Doug doesn't know. "At the end of Act I, Anne Trulove makes the first adult decision of her life: to leave her father and comfy home for London to rescue her lover, Tom Rakewell."

High on the expression on Doug's face, inspired by the venue, even a little driven by the appreciative nods I've been getting from passers-by: "Maestro, music please."

The recitative: "No word from Tom." The aria, addressed to the night, to the moon. And then the *cabaletta*, like a runaway horse. I'm carried along with it, bareback, hitting the "C," despite the damp March air. Doug applauds — as does a knot of people who have stopped to listen.

Doug nuzzles his face into my hair. "Mariah," he exclaims, "this isn't the voice that led the glee club, fine as it was. Your teacher's a magician!"

I'm still shaking. "Pure technique. And practice."

"Are you Anne Trulove?" he asks quietly.

I snort derisively.

"You put everything into it," he observes, kissing the top of my head. "Which one of us is Tom? Sully — or me?"

Another *frisson*. "You're being too literal."

"Have you heard from him?"

"Not since the end of June."

When I'd answered the doorbell that day, just after school got out, I found a package sitting on the porch. My name printed on the label and "fragile" stickers stuck all over the box. I took it up to my room to open.

The Belleek teacup and saucer, a note nestled in the cup: "I had the Triumph packed to the roll bars with stuff. Was afraid this might get smashed. Look after it for me; look after yourself. All my love, JSR."

I put the note in the archives, placed the cup and saucer on display on my bookshelf. When my mother asked about it, I didn't lie: "Sully's parting gift." I couldn't argue with her assessment, either: "That boy's a romantic fool." Indeed.

Still, Sully is strong, I think, while Doug is weak, like Tom Rakewell. Is that why I'm trembling – with *fear*? Having ventured to call it "love" in that letter, can I deny there's room in my heart for him? How is what I feel for Doug different from what I feel for Sully? Sully doesn't need rescuing, I determine; Doug does. What a potent, potent lure!

"I got my acceptance from Harvard," Doug confides.

"Of course you did! How wonderful!" Picturing him in Cambridge with Sully, I experience a flash of anger at the artificiality of our separation. *I miss you, Sully*; why can't we be normal kids – running up long-distance bills, sneaking in visits during breaks?

I feel myself becoming so incorporeal under the weight of Doug's arm across my shoulders that I might slip out of his grasp like a wraith. But no. Whatever I will be in Sully's future, in Doug's, I have to do it on my own.

In all our talk this March Sunday in 1974, Doug and I manage not to employ the word "love," we don't talk about the future in any concrete way, we don't discuss our "relationship." We simply are.

When my father and I drop Doug at the station on our way to the airport, the weight of unsaid words presses into my throat.

"See you in July."

We kiss. I help him into his backpack; we kiss once more. He closes the cab door for me and we wave each other out of sight.

Dad, who has been looking pointedly out of the window on his side of the cab, takes my left hand and pats it. He fishes his handkerchief out of the breast pocket of his tweed jacket, presses it on me. I make good, if silent, use of it most of the way to the airport.

~⁓

"Talk about a 'no-frills' flight!"

Grey is the hallmark of Czechoslovak Airways decor.

Picking his way gingerly down the aisle of the small Russian-built jet, "I'm surprised it's got seatbelts," Dad remarks. "It's like a school bus. And the seats look just as comfortable."

"Now, now," I scold. "It's *utilitarian*. Only the bourgeoisie need comfort."

"Please refrain from political comment," he warns quietly.

"*Me?*"

He flashes a threatening look; he's not joking.

The Bratislava airport has the same bleak, Soviet bloc decor as the plane. Dad nudges me, drawing my attention to a uniformed military guard wielding a Kalashnikov rifle.

"How can you tell you're not at home?" he mutters, just loud enough for me to hear. I'm suddenly apprehensive.

We claim our bags and proceed through the customs queue, where the uniformed official forgets he knows any English as soon as he reads my dad's passport. Place of birth: Valaska, Czechoslovakia. The conversation breaks down into charades: the guard has found "Grandpa" in the carry-on.

I stand by helplessly as Dad tries to explain, with gestures and fading linguistic ability, that the Tupperware in question contains his father's ashes. His eye lights upon a concrete ashstand; he politely begs the guard's indulgence. "*Popol. Otec,*" he says, pointing and using the words for "ashes" and "father" repeatedly. The large man refuses to encompass the subtlety: if the content of the container is ash, it belongs *in the ashstand*.

Defeated, Dad gives me a wan smile, takes the container from the man, and proceeds to the receptacle. He removes the lid and ceremoniously, slowly, pours the contents into the tray.

Poor Dad – to come all this way on an errand of filial duty, only to be thwarted by language and bureaucracy! His back turned, shoulders heaving, I can hear his sobs.

Helpless, I feel I should comfort him somehow – despite my impression that this is the perfect, if ironic, depository for the ashes of a chain-smoking pedophile.

"I'm sorry, Daddy," I say, stepping up behind him to place my arm across his shoulders.

Holding his glasses in one hand, rubbing his eyes with the other, he turns to face to me. He's not crying! He's laughing!

When he sees the look of utter incredulity on my face, he loses all restraint. His laughter peals and echoes through the barren, concrete hall, drawing every solemn bureaucratic stare within earshot. Who is this man, laughing like a lunatic, who dares disturb the Marxist decorum of this building? Surely he's been sampling CSA's fine *slivovica* on the flight from Copenhagen.

A Slovak-born Canadian drunkard, overcome by joy at returning to the fatherland; of course. Drunkenness is something these men understand. They share nods; grins break out. The official stamps our passports and visas emphatically, pumps my father's hand in a congratulatory manner and leads us through the terminal.

"Come, come."

We've suddenly become VIPs. The previously uncivil servant clears every impediment to our exit; my father shakes more hands than a politician, roaring heartily at every stop.

At the final exit, a small crowd is gathered, one member of which must be my grandfather's half-sister. The official stops, puts his arm around my father's shoulders, and announces him like royalty in a Klaxon voice: "Gabriel Standhoffer!"

Olga claims him timorously, uncertain if she should perhaps deny all knowledge. Can a firing squad be far away?

"Good, good." The man embraces him like a brother, they shake hands one more time, and the crowd applauds. *Welcome to Czechoslovakia.*

Olga embraces us. Eyes glued to my face, she reaches down to clasp my right hand in her peasant paws – and comes up with the stump.

"*Jeziš Marya Josef!*" she intones, shocked.

With Olga still holding my wrist we suffer my father's pantomime-enhanced explanation, complete with sound effects. At last she holds my cheeks in her hands, plants a kiss on each, all the while intoning, "Poor girl; poor girl."

Is it not too late to grab a plane back to Copenhagen?

Dad concentrates so hard on making himself understood he forgets to speak English. Turning to include me in conversation, he asks me a question in Slovak and – before the end of our ten days – starts receiving answers. In English, mind you, but answers nonetheless.

"I'd kill for a bowl of corn flakes," I sigh at breakfast one morning. Olga is out exchanging currency for us at a "private" bank.

Dad, too, regards the plate of heavy sausages squeamishly. "Might as well take one of these babies and plug it directly into my left ventricle," he concurs.

I yearn for Danish pastry and continental breakfast.

I yearn for Doug as tour guide as we're swept through castles and palaces without benefit of English.

I yearn for the small cramped bathroom of the Copenhagen hotel: the supply of water in Olga's Košice apartment tower is sporadic at best.

At last Olga puts us on a train to Brno. Relief is short-lived.

"You'd think, with the Utopian goal of full employment," I hiss in Dad's ear, "they could find someone to clean the damned washrooms!" There's no water either. I feel I'm permanently cured of nibbling my cuticles; I don't even want to be in the same room with my unwashed hand. I add it to the store of delights and miseries to relate to Doug.

The hotel in Brno is a haven. The water runs, and is hot. In contrast to the narrow benches throughout Olga's apartment that serve for sleeping by night and sitting by day, duvets and pillows stored under the lid, the beds are full-sized. I fall onto the mattress gratefully.

"Have a little nap, then we'll go out for dinner."

"Can't we have room service?" I moan.

"No; we'll have a night on the town."

Flashing currency – both hard and soft – like Diamond Jim, Dad is true to his word. He sifts through his wallet.

"If I'd known how much Olga could get for our money, I'd have booked us hotels all the way through."

Glomming onto us like a leech, our taxi driver chauffeurs us around the city, escorting us to dinner at a lively bistro that sports its own brewery on site.

"This is wonderful!" I enthuse. Real beer; fine Pilsner on draught. The perfect accompaniment to the meal, it enhances all the flavours of the admittedly heavy food and imparts such a benevolent buzz I forgive Dad for ignoring me in favour of conversation with the driver.

"I told Anton you're a musician," he shouts across the table. "He says there's a concert you might enjoy. Local boy: Janáček."

"*Really?*" I nod enthusiastically, all trace of fatigue extinguished.

Despatching Anton to procure tickets at the box office, "I told him I want the best seats in the house," Dad says expansively. He laughs at my cocked eyebrow. "Should set me back all of ten bucks. We could retire here," he says, gesturing to the faded opulence, "live like kings."

Box seats in the concert hall for Anton, Dad and me. I don't bother with a program. Dad translates for me: the string quartets.

"I'm only familiar with the piano works," I admit. "This will be interesting."

Interesting? Interesting! How to describe the explosion of emotion detonated by the beautiful, mysterious, sometimes dissonant music? Programmatic and unconventional, the first quartet, written late in Janáček's life, is a vivid psychological drama — a story of jealousy and revenge based on Tolstoy's "Kreutzer Sonata."

The music speaks to every drop of Czechoslovakian blood coursing double-time through my veins as I lean heavily against the railing of the box.

"Sit back," Dad warns, afraid I might counterbalance and tumble over, or that the railing will give way under my weight.

But I can't get close enough to the source of power on the stage. I can't miss a gesture of bow on string, of hand against finger-board. How do they make *that* sound? A sound like train wheels — metal screeching against metal. On the bridge of the instruments. I've never seen or heard this done before. What an effect! An atmosphere of almost unbearable tension one moment, unbearable beauty the next.

Taking the program from my father at intermission, I skim through the Czech words, looking for revelation, clues. I turn the page, draw in a sharp breath.

"What's the matter?"

"Jesus!" The page is opened to a photograph of the composer. "Janáček: Brno, 1927." Not a very tall man; almost as round as he is tall. A shock of white hair and moustache. My hand trembles.

Dad leans closer, takes the program to examine it. "He looks not unlike your grandfather, doesn't he?" he says casually as he returns the booklet.

An understatement. In this photograph, Janáček looks enough like my grandfather to be his brother. Or his father.

The house lights dim for the second quartet, subtitled "Intimate Letters" — reflecting the old man's love for the young married woman said to have been the inspiration for his remarkably productive, creative, later years.

Despite the darkness, the image of my grandfather superimposed on the composer's is burned into my mental retina. I cannot separate his essence from Janáček's. *What was that old man doing with such a young woman?* They say his love was unrequited, but they spent time together, went on holiday together with her children. And if she didn't return his love, *is it conceivable he sought his satisfaction with those children?*

There's something raw and menacing, something manipulative in the music. Beauty and terror wedded – has no one ever commented on this? Or am I personalizing it too much? The dissonance speaks of pain. Confusion. The isolation of a child who can't tell anyone her secrets. The jangled desperation of a girl with a gun in her hand. The black pain and sickly sweet smell of dying flesh.

Blow after blow the music batters me; slices me like razor blades; sears my heart like a lit cigarette. Fucks me. Loves me.

At some point I realize I'm not hearing Janáček's music any more, but my own. Tears streaming unheeded, I hold my arms tightly around my torso, trying to keep myself from fragmenting into strident chords and passionate atonality. I want to turn to my father, but how can I explain? *Daddy – listen to the music.* Hear what I hear! Know what I know; see who I am.

Our arms brush on the armrest. We're so close, surely I can transmit knowledge through the hairs of his arm, like antennae. I'm his daughter, yet he doesn't know me. Isn't that my fault? Haven't I withheld everything from him, everything suspect, everything shadowy, everything secret? Everything good! Daddy, Daddy – how can you profess to love me when you don't even know me? My fault; surely my fault.

Almost unexpectedly, the music ends and we're all on our feet. I fail to compose myself under cover of applause. Dad hands me another clean, folded hanky. He must have brought a whole suitcase full, I think with one part of my brain, while another takes a tremendous gamble.

"Can you send Anton on ahead?" I ask. "We can meet him at the cab."

The theatre empties quickly. Knees buckling, I sit while my father makes arrangements with the driver. Can I do this? Should I do this? I could drop the dice and still come up craps; I could lose everything.

Dad turns to me, perplexed. "You seemed extremely moved by that."

"It was more than just the music." I point to the picture of the composer. "Don't you think he looks like Grandpa?"

"A bit. As I said, 'not unlike.' Is this about Grandpa?" he asks gently. "Do you miss him?"

Lifting my eyes to the peeling gilt ceiling, my body shakes with indeterminate, hysterical sobs. A reversal of my father's, at the airport. He thinks I'm laughing, but I'm wracked with weeping, shattering the crumbling rococo stillness.

I bet it all: I tell my father what *his* father did to me.

Gathering that something momentous has occurred, Anton refrains from playing tour guide on the way back to the hotel. Dad grimly presses a generous tip upon him and extracts a promise of a ride to the station mid-afternoon.

There are panels missing from the mirrored lobby of the hotel. I see our partial reflections all around us, repeating brokenly into infinity. My father looks shrunken, diminished. Old. A lance of regret for what I've done to him; I wish I could take back all my words.

In our room, he empties his pockets of wallet, coins, keys and hangs his blazer up in the wardrobe. I can't stand it another second. "I'm sorry, Daddy! I shouldn't have told you!"

He turns his face to me. Sorrow; such sorrow. Sitting down beside me on the edge of the bed, "No; no. You *should* have told me, Mariah – years and years ago," he says, brushing the hair out of my eyes. "That you couldn't . . . fills me with the greatest grief I've ever known." He crushes me in his arms. "I failed to keep you safe in my own house. And compounded that failure by not seeing it, not stopping it!"

Weeping, he apologizes over and over with varying degrees of coherence. "I feel I've been denied opportunities to love you. That you needed me, and I wasn't there. I wish I could change it – I'd give anything to change it!"

Eventually, "Get ready for bed now. You've got to get some sleep."

I take my nightgown into the washroom, wash my face, brush my teeth. And wait. He'll probably change into his pyjamas while I'm in the john. I feel extraordinarily shy, as if my grandfather's depravity has spread like the shit and stench in a filthy WC. So I give him extra time. Unlock the bathroom door as a warning, brush my teeth noisily again with the door open.

When I come out, he's sitting in the armchair by the desk, smoking in front of the open window, pyjamas and toiletries in a neat heap by his elbow. He's stripped only as far as his undershirt, still fully dressed for all intents and purposes.

A loss of innocence, I think, of spontaneity. My eyes well again. He's so circumspect I'm surprised he hasn't tried to book a separate room. I feel as if I've destroyed our relationship. Wasn't that what I sought to avoid by my secrecy? Destroying him? Destroying my family? All I really wanted to do was let him in. To let him know, so we could put it behind us – like so much dust in an ashtray. To offer us both opportunity for love.

And, to his credit, he does attempt to grasp the opportunity, despite his pain. After the lights are out we are hypersensitive to each other tossing silently in the dark, awake.

"It's like exhuming his corpse and seeing his rotting flesh for the first time," he says across the space between our beds. "I have to re-examine all my memories of him, of us. Reinterpret everything in the light of knowledge." He sighs heavily. "How can you forgive me?"

"It wasn't you doing it!"

"No; but my happiness was illusory – bought at your expense. And my pride – my smug pride that I was such a good provider, such a mighty protector!" He inhales raggedly. "My whole life has been an illusion."

Somehow this has become about him. Yes, I've spoiled his image of himself and our lives together. Missing panels have been filled in with funhouse mirrors, distorting the reflection. Twisting it into something grotesque, a parody of itself.

This thought fills me with a sickly hopelessness. I close my ears to his monologue and feign sleep when he poses his next question – since I don't wish to answer it: "How long has your mother known?"

We move like geriatric tourists. Dad hands me into Anton's taxi the way he did the day I came out of hospital, as if I bear fresh wounds that may split open; supports my elbow as we board the train for Prague.

"How long has your mother known?" he asks when we're settled on the train, picking up the conversation where I dropped it the night before.

"Since the accident."

He winces. "A year. A little over a year."

Taking up my wrist from the seat between us, he examines it closely, drawing his finger along the track of scars. He can't know how often I've traced these scars myself, how often Sully has. And Doug. By now, a year later, my reaction is reflexive, involuntary. Visceral. Sexual. I withdraw gently, gradually, so as not to attract attention to the action, masking my blush with some busy ferreting through my backpack for Chapstick. Pray that my bulky sweater covers the protrusion of my bra-less nipples.

For the first time in my life I feel like a woman, a sexual being, in my father's presence. I close my eyes against the wave of disgust, clamp my sphincter shut against the pebble-pond rings of desire radiating from it. Sully. Fill the aching void with memories of Sully, acceptable thoughts, safe thoughts. Sully. Superimpose his face onto the screen of my eyelids and stare into that visage, bright as the sun. Burn its after-image into my retinas, a self-inflicted — and welcome — blindness.

"If we ever come back, we'll have to do Prague first," Dad promises in the vaulted stillness of St. Vitus's Cathedral. A Gothic God appeals to me — arms outstretched like flying buttresses. I feel as if I could join the rank of gargoyles and blend right in.

We make the pilgrimage to the house where Kafka stayed with his sister on the Golden Lane, a row of tiny cottages built inside Prague Castle's walls. It's easy to see how paranoia could overtake even the most stable soul within these cramped rooms; I feel gigantic within my scrawny body, as if I've partaken of one of Alice's growth potions in Wonderland.

At the Town Hall Clock, the skeletal figure of Death — animated by clockwork — sets the march of the Apostles in motion on the hour. It's mechanical, yet its realism draws a bony finger of dread up my spine.

Our spirits are too oppressed to muster the enthusiasm we would otherwise surely feel. So we give up, boarding the plane for Copenhagen gratefully.

Anxious to retreat, quite exhausted by two weeks of unrelenting contact with my father and, particularly, these last two days of intense, microscopic examination, I feel like a particularly odious lab specimen.

"Would you like to call Doug while we're passing through?"

I glance at my watch, shake my head. "He'd be in class now, anyway." I'll write to him when I get home, leaving days unaccounted for.

Midway across the Atlantic, Dad thumps his fist into the armrest.

"What?" I ask, wary.

He shakes his head, removes his glasses, and rubs his eyes wearily. "Sorry," he murmurs. "I'm furious with your mother."

My stomach lurches with alarm, as if we've hit an air pocket. "It's not her fault."

"She should have told me. We shouldn't have secrets like this!"

"I begged her not to," I insist, tears threatening. "I was afraid of what you might do. I'm *still* afraid of what you might do." I pull at his sleeve. "Promise me you won't do anything crazy!"

He shakes his head, over and over. "It's a betrayal – such a failure of trust!"

"Well, then, it's *my* failure." My voice rasps as if I've swallowed ground glass. "She did it for me." *She did more than that for me.*

"Stop taking on so much responsibility; stop taking the blame!" he hisses. "You're a child, for Christ's sake. Be a child! You've *never* been a child. You've been carrying the weight of the entire family on your shoulders for much too long. *I'm* the grown-up – let me *be* the grown-up, goddamn it!" he sobs, squeezing my hand until I wince.

"That's why I'm so angry – because this little conspiracy you and your mother cooked up negates me as a parent! If I'm not a parent, then I'm just the simple-minded idiot who pays the bills. And that's no basis for a marriage."

"Daddy," I start – but we thump down onto a table of cloud as solid as mahogany.

"We're in for a rocky ride," Dad says.

Does he mean on this plane? Or at home?

Either way, I can't stomach the uncertainty. I fumble for the seat pocket. My father holds the *mal de l'air* bag for me as I toss the last Danish *smørrebrød* I'm ever likely to consume.

"Leave that there!" Dad snarls.

I drop the strap of his carry-on as if it's charged. In a conciliatory tone, he says, "I'll get it later," slamming the gate of the station wagon closed. "I just have to see for myself that the place is still standing." Then he slips off to the hotel under cover of the flood of stories and gifts I have to share with Mom and Luke.

Mom accepts this untruth indulgently. "Workaholic!" she accuses.

When Luke leaves the room I tearfully explain what's happened. Embracing me, "You were very brave to tell him."

"But he's so angry!"

She kisses my forehead. "You leave him to me. That's my job."

Some homecoming. I can't bear to anticipate the impending round of Assignment of Blame.

Whatever histrionics are performed, however, all take place off-stage. No leaping cutlery, no raised voices. The only evidence — believe me, I watched for it — lies in the grey circles under my mother's eyes and the grim set of her lips in unguarded moments. And in the fact that my father's place at the table and in their bed is uninhabited for forty-eight hours.

"Dad's got a lot of catching up to do," she explains lightly.

I imagine my mother's words: "However angry you are with me, Gabe, you have to swallow it — for Mariah's sake. Otherwise, it's just her worst fears coming true. We can't prove her right about this."

Having chosen to be mature, they treat each other — when he returns — with a hyperbolic respect verging on the comical. It brings to mind the gophers on the old *Bugs Bunny Show*: "No, I insist: you go first." "Quite out of the question — after you." "All right, since you insist." Slipcovers of politeness blanketing the ragged edges of sorrow.

⁓

Another hotel room; another parent snoring in the bed beside mine. Following so closely upon the down-at-the-heels European accommodations, the Park Plaza in Toronto is sheer luxury. So civilized, so functional. I lie awake in the dark, adrift on the music for the audition, my stomach lurching and peaking on the high "C"s. The high seas. Grab that *mal de la mer* bag; it'll be a rough crossing.

It doesn't matter if I fail, I try to convince myself. There are other avenues to a career in music than here on Bloor Street. There are other schools, even other careers. *Better* careers — how many Canadian composers actually make a living at it? *Be prepared to teach.*

Just the conceit of vocalizing the dream: to be a composer! It seems so implausible, so unlikely. What makes me think I even have anything to say? What if I present my musical ramblings in class and discover it's all been done before? "Derivative." Or worse: "Juvenile and simplistic. Not an original thought in your head. Suggest you major in English."

"Aren't you going to have more than that for breakfast?"

"Just tea and toast, Mom. If I have anything more, I'll throw up. We'll have a nice lunch after it's over."

"I wish I could be in the room with you."

My hand trembles as I return the cup to its saucer. "I wish you could, too," I lie.

John Hamner waits for us outside the Edward Johnson Building, his briefcase full of music. I'm so grateful he's at the piano, a steadying influence, a focus. The music is written on his face. His lips will pantomime the lyrics, cue me to every facial expression and hand movement, every breath, every note placement — if I need it.

Eye contact with the judges, my audience, is easier than I had expected: I *am* coquette for the Italian love songs; I *am* Gretchen for the Schubert. I *am* Anne Trulove for the Stravinsky. I cast out the high notes like a fly line, watch the arc of sound spin out long and true and break the surface of the water with delicate concentric ripples. Wham! — they're hooked.

"You're in," John insists as he embraces me. "Maybe you *should* think about opera."

I waggle my wrist at him. "Not too many roles for one-handed divas. Besides," I remind him, "I'm doing this because there's a performance requirement, not from any great desire to be a singer."

"Don't limit your possibilities."

I half expect him to intone the familiar advice: *A woman should always have something to fall back on.*

Gathering the music from the piano, he says, "You have a voice. Don't be afraid to use it. You can always wear a nice little prosthesis for performance. You *can* be a singer, not just a *one-handed* singer." He smiles warmly. "Let's find your mother and put her out of her misery. I could sure use lunch!"

Mom springs for an elegant Park Plaza lunch, complete with a bottle of wine — which she begs John to choose. We are effusive and congratulatory, urbane and witty. I admire the handsome cut of John's suit, the way he lounges in his chair, long legs crossed casually. I'm in love with the world.

"Richard tells me he's off to Europe as soon as school gets out," John comments.

Richard? It takes me a beat to remember that John and Richard

Widener are friends.

"He'll be meeting your friend Doug, in Denmark, I take it."

I nod sagely behind my glass, as if this is not news.

"Lucky lads," he continues. "I love Austria."

Don't we all? I think giddily.

"Have you ever been to the Salzburg Festival?" he asks my mother.

I nearly snort into my wine. *Every year, of course! Haven't missed it since 1966.*

"Afraid not," she says, smiling wryly. "But Mariah caught part of the Janáček Festival in Brno last month, didn't you, dear?"

"Yes, it was quite remarkable."

Quite remarkable: my family still bears the scars. I've had to put up with my father's earnest overcompensation. I thought telling him would bring us closer but, somehow, it's pushed us apart by reopening the wounds.

In the past I would have retreated inconspicuously to my burrow to nurse them. But now Dad stands there like a hound at bay, eager to flush me out of hiding. To shower me with his belated love, his retroactive support. *Just let it go, Dad,* I want to tell him. I just want things to get back to normal. Or, barring that, I can't wait to escape to university. *I'm in,* I assure myself again, flushed with pride, and wine. *I'm in.*

Back in our room after lunch my mother says, "If I'd known John better, beforehand, I wouldn't have bothered coming along as chaperone. You two could have shared a room and I'd have felt quite comfortable."

I bristle. "What do you mean?"

"Well, sweetheart, it's fairly obvious where *his* inclinations lie: *Richard* this and *Richard* that." She runs a brush through her hair, speaks to my reflection in the mirror. "I detected a note of jealousy. Of Doug. Didn't you?"

My head buzzes – and not from too much wine. *Lucky lads; I love Austria.* I slip into the bathroom, sit down on the toilet lid. I'd never considered Richard Widener a "lad" before. I'd always thought of him as "*Mister* Widener" until the play – when Doug started referring to him as *Richard* this and *Richard* that, or by his initials, R.W. Suddenly I see Richard through John Hamner's eyes and John through his. Each a *rara avis.* Birds of a feather: urbane, intelligent; the same loose, elegant walk, the same disaffected accents – as if they've been to the same elocutionist, the same finishing school. The Noel Coward School, perhaps, or the Oscar Wilde.

Surely my mother has read too much into things: *Mister* Widener's interest in Doug is that of a teacher toward his protégé. Still, the fact that Doug hasn't mentioned his scheduled trip to Austria gives me pause.

When Kat comes home from Queen's for the summer she practically moves in with me.

My father has just sold the hotel in town and purchased a country pub not far outside the city where he hopes, he says, to attract "a better class of drunk." Suburban drunks; farmer drunks. And people just out for a drive along the Kaministiqua River valley.

I have no desire to spend my time out there, in the middle of nowhere, lying awake at night in "my" room over the bar while Rod Stewart's "Maggie May" — amplified by the jukebox and filtered through the floorboards so that only the bass comes through — is drummed into my brain with a sledgehammer.

"I can't stand it, Mommy!" I complain. "I can't hear my own music over the din. It's noise pollution of the worst kind."

Mom is sympathetic, but unwilling to leave me alone too much. Kat's become the sister I never had, so much a part of the family that Dad ascribes his own nicknames: "Katarina" or, more formally, "Ekatarina Hašekova."

"Do you mind?"

"He makes me feel like displaced aristocracy," she giggles.

We lie awake at night, sharing my big bed, talking as much as two shy girls are likely to, finding in each other an audience for our most inexpressible thoughts.

"Doug was always the dominant twin," she confides. "He was born first; he was bigger. He was always more demanding."

"He was *handi*capped," I point out, "so he naturally got more attention."

"There's that," she admits, "but I think he would've been the same, regardless. And I'd have been just as dominated by his personality. He's always told me what to think."

"Does Ray dominate you that way?"

"No," she laughs. "*Ray* is my identical twin. You can't imagine two people with such excruciating lack of opinion on exactly the same top-ics! Topics Doug holds dear to his heart, as you may imagine."

"Have you got an ETA on Doug yet?"

"No," she says. "I'd've thought he'd send *you* his itinerary. We're just his family," she sniffs with mock-injury. "I only know he intends to be home in time for the wedding."

Their cousin's wedding. Kat has asked Ray — also home from Queen's — to accompany her. It's a foregone conclusion I'll go with Doug, if Doug ever gets home. His last letter from Denmark at the end of June said only, "Taking a side trip to Austria before flying out of Vienna. Will call you when I get in." As Kat says, "He'll probably just turn up at the hotel in time for the toast to the bride."

The night before the wedding I have the house to myself — Mom, Dad, and Luke having decamped for the country to spend the weekend at the pub; Kat making a token appearance at home. I revel in my soli-tude, half expecting Doug to phone from the airport, needing a ride.

When the phone rings just as I'm getting out of the shower on Saturday morning, I rush, streaming water, clad only in a towel, to grab the phone in my parents' room.

"Hi."

"Where *are* you?"

"Richard's. We came in on the late flight last night. It was easier just to sack out at his place, it's so close to the airport."

"Is he driving you home later? Will you be at the church? Shall I pick you up?"

He laughs. "No: to all of the above. I'll meet you at the hotel for the reception. See you later." And he hangs up the phone before I can say another word.

Dinner comes and goes. Doug even misses the toast to the bride. Kat carefully apportions her time between Ray and me, practically apolo-gizes every time she leaves the table to dance with her date. I drink a little too much wine, just to have something to occupy myself while I watch them on the floor.

Compare their behaviour here to that at the grad dance, a little over a year ago. Ray leans to her ear, Kat throws back her head and laughs. Ray's touch is intimate, assured. He's forsaken his glasses in favour of contacts. He's grown into himself, I think, catching a glimpse of the man he'll be — given five more years of self-confidence. And Kat.

"Lovely couple, aren't they?"

I nod, not taking my eyes from them.

"Care to dance?"

"Why not?"

Draping his jacket across the back of the chair to my right, Doug takes my wrist in his left hand and, on the floor, wraps his arm around me, gripping my left bicep with his little hand. I press my face into his suitcase-wrinkled shirt.

"Sorry I'm late. Jet lag."

I lean back so I can look into his eyes. He's lying. He *knows* I know he's lying.

"Richard couldn't understand why I'd subject myself to this," he admits. "I had to spell it out for him, at last: '*Mariah's waiting for me.*' He just didn't get it."

"Do you have to go back for your luggage?"

"No, I left it at the desk." He presses his body against mine insistently, nuzzles my neck. "Jesus, you smell good! After I left you in Copenhagen, I could smell you everywhere I went. I walked into class one day and thought, Mariah's here – I can smell her perfume!"

"I wasn't wearing any perfume in Copenhagen," I recollect.

"Shampoo, soap, deodorant. Something!"

My eyes meet Ray's across the room. He nudges Kat. She looks up, grins at us. They both smile parentally. Parents. "Shouldn't you say hello to your folks?"

Doug grimaces. "Do I have to?"

"Sooner or later."

"Later, then; let it be later."

When he can no longer postpone the inevitable, I join Kat and Ray at the "young adult" table. Doug sneaks up behind his mother and bends to speak in her ear. She whirls, nearly upsetting her chair. His father stands; Doug offers him his hand to shake behind his mother's embrace. Homecoming. Kill the fatted calf.

While Doug takes his mother for a spin on the dance floor, then his sister, Ray and I chat companionably at the table.

"Do you have to go home with your parents?" I ask Doug when next we dance. They're making the farewell rounds. "Or with Kat and Ray?"

"Neither. I told them you'd drop me at Richard's later and I'd get a ride home in the morning."

I don't process this information quickly enough. "But your stuff is here."

"Yes."

"My parents are at the pub for the weekend," I offer.

"Are they?" he asks benignly.

My brain registers an insistent bulge against my leg. An idea blossoms, simultaneous with my blush. Have I had too much wine? "Maybe you could come home with me."

Our feet stop moving on the hardwood. "Maybe."

"I'll just say goodbye to Kat."

A hurried tête-à-tête. Kat hugs me, waves to Doug through the crush of a hundred bodies. "Don't do anything I wouldn't do," she mumbles, flashing an eyebrow.

He regales me with tales from the Vienna woods on our drive across town, in which Richard Widener figures more as tour guide – underling, somehow – than companion. Doug wears a badge of superiority, almost disdain – as if Richard has exposed himself as a con artist, a fake behind the machinery of Oz.

"What happened to the awestruck hero-worship?" I ask.

"I got to know him better," Doug says, his voice carrying an indefinable edge. "He's just a man."

My hand shakes putting the key in the lock of my own back door. Peering around as if he's never been inside before, Doug plops his backpack down in the hall at the foot of the stairs, strips off his jacket and tie, and hangs them on the newel post. *Like the man of the house.*

"I'm at home," I tell my mother on the phone. "Doug was tired so we left early." We grin at each other across the kitchen. "He wants to get together in the morning, though, so I thought it made more sense to stay in town than make two trips in less than twelve hours." Doug doubles over in silent hilarity. "No, no; I'm fine by myself! It's not the first night I've stayed alone!" I signal him to caution. "Right. I'll call you tomorrow. G'night."

"What a fine liar you are, Mariah!" He wanders into the living room, completely at home now, flicks on the light.

"Step away from the window," I warn.

"Why, is there a sniper out there?" he swivels his head. "Will the Sleeping Giant rat on us?" He sits down at the piano. "Play something."

"I don't play the piano," I say, suddenly agitated. "Haven't touched it in over a year."

"Not even the Songs of the Day?" I shake my head. "How do you know how they sound?"

"I *know.*"

"My little Beethoven." He plays one of the songs himself, from memory. "My luggage is full of your songs and letters. I dragged them all over Europe. I played some of the songs for Richard last night, on his grand piano. They sounded," he smiles, "well, simply *grand.*"

"What did Richard think?"

He stands up from the piano. "That they'd sound better arranged for two hands. That they sound a little thin." He embraces me, fingering the string of my vertebrae like rosary beads. "Just like you. A little thin," he breathes into the hollow of my neck, and guides me toward the stairs.

"You don't have to make a pretence of virginity for my sake," he says, with an undertone I interpret as nasty. "You told me about Sully."

Nerves rewind whatever tension his caresses may have released. "We only did it once!" I'm surprised by the strangled tone of my words.

"Yikes! I've pushed a button."

Rather unnecessarily, too. "Why?"

"Because it was there."

Was ever woman in this humour wooed? Was ever woman in this humour won? I sit up against the headboard in the rose-tinted glow from the street lamp, draw my knees and arms in as if the bed is suddenly too small. Which it is – crowded with Doug, in the flesh. And Sully and my grandfather, in memory. Not enough space for all of us. *Rub-a-dub dead; three men in the bed.*

Doug strokes my face. "He'll always be between us, won't he?"

Who, my *grandfather?* No, Sully. "He will – if you keep dragging him in!" I fall against his bare chest. "Why couldn't you leave well enough alone? I wanted *you* tonight!"

He lays me back against the pillow. "No," he whispers. "You wanted him, because he's beautiful."

I wouldn't have chosen the word "beautiful" to describe Sully myself, except for, perhaps, his hands. Handsome, yes; appealing, yes. More appealing than handsome. "You're as good-looking as he is, in a different way." Is this what he wants to hear?

Stroking my goose-fleshed arm with the fingers of his little hand, Doug works his way down until he gets to the nub of my wrist, and caresses the veins and scars until I draw breath involuntarily.

"You wanted him — because he's whole."

"No! It doesn't matter!" I exclaim, even as my brain answers, "Yes, yes it does matter."

"You're lying, Mariah. You know it," he whispers, kissing my cheek, my brow.

My ears fill with a tide of blood. *Hear the words*, Mariah. Say the words.

"It doesn't matter that he's whole!" Tell him the truth, the words he wants to hear. "I want you because you're *not*."

I can't believe I've said these words aloud, punctuated by an inarticulate wail. But before I can take them back, he crushes his mouth to mine — giving or taking breath, I cannot tell. Is it true? *Is it true?*

He kisses the salt stream from my cheek. "I'm glad we understand each other."

The morning conflagration behind the pink curtains is nauseating. My head thumps; Doug's arm around my shoulders is a lead weight. My first articulate thought: *What have I done?*

This was a mistake. I don't feel magnified in any way; I feel drained. Shall I write to you about this, Doug? Will it make you happy to read the confusion I feel examining my own words: *I want you because you are not whole?*

I bound out of bed for the bathroom, kneel retching into the bowl until my head clears. Brush my hair roughly, compose myself, and return.

Doug stirs in my bed — my bed! — looks up to see me standing beside it, naked. "My God, you're a vision in this light! As pink as the interior of your own womb."

"How would you know?" I stride to the window, pull down the shade.

Grinning wickedly, "The 'third eye' has made the journey," he says, flinging back the sheet. "And is ready to make it again." He holds his hand out to me.

A simple matter to pull on some clothes, fry up an egg, and drive him home. Abandoning all instinct for self-preservation, I slip between the sheets, sharp with the tang of his sweat, and bury my face in his golden chest hairs. "Jesus Christ! What am I doing?" And I weep.

"There, now," he comforts. "You just lost your virginity. Have a little cry." He pats my back like a child's.

"I lost that a year ago, remember? You reminded me yourself."

"No – I was wrong. You *exchanged* virginities a year ago. You gave Sully yours; he gave you his. No loss involved." He traces my eyebrow. "Like making love with yourself, it was all so noble and mystical. But now," he nips my earlobe, "*now* you've lost your virginity – or Sully's, rather – because you've been fucked by the 'other'." His voice drops half an octave. "You've fucked your shadow."

I use the word "fuck" to describe an act of violence, or violation. Is that how he sees what we've done? Panic burns in my throat like bile. "Doug – you're scaring me!"

"No! There's power in the shadow. Use it. Redefine 'normal'; redefine 'whole'. Redefine your 'self'."

The churning in my stomach – is it fear? Or excitement? Either way, he's stronger than I am – confident of his own rightness, forceful and aroused. I let myself go, despite my misgivings – aroused by his insistence.

Afterward, Doug is tender, almost penitent. I take impressions at intervals, like a surveillance camera, careful to separate my feelings from my observations. *Who is he now?* I keep my eyes fixed on his so he can't pull any sleight-of-hand – like replacing himself with a body double, perhaps – without my knowledge.

"My, you're impassive," he notes.

Impassive, adj. deficient in feeling or emotion; serene; without sensation; not subject to suffering. Ah, no; impassivity is merely the mask of the moment. My mind races behind it. Try "passive," Doug: in the sense of *suffering action; acted upon.*

The distinction I tried to grasp after making love with Sully is suddenly clear to me. *Making love changes everything* – yes. *Having* sex, or *being* fucked – these are passive constructions. But *making* love is active. Not suffering action, but engaged. Involved – as an equal. Partner – not participle.

"What?" Doug cocks his head.

The corner of my mouth lifts involuntarily into a placable little smile.

He blinks; shakes his head as if to dislodge floaters under a contact lens. "Mona Lisa," he says, in a bad Italian accent.

Mona Lisa? Is that how I look to him? Did she see what I glimpse — *the ascendancy of the seemingly impassive woman.* He's been on a little power trip here, in my bed. But two can play mind-fuck games. He thinks he's claimed a victory by forcing me to say, "I want you because you are not whole." In reality, the upper hand is mine. He's admitted his own fragmented state. But by recognizing my own passivity — and his need to manipulate it — I've turned the tables on him.

My mission: to make him whole, without his awareness that I've set myself such a task.

"This summer is too fucking short."

We watch the Perseids from the deck of Richard Widener's house, where Doug is house-sitting. The stars have aligned to provide us with almost unlimited opportunity to — well, *fuck.* I can't, in good conscience (or even in bad), refer to it as "making love" — it seems like blasphemy to apply those words to what we do, Doug and I. It's not exactly "violation" and "violence," either. Doug's definition is broader than mine. But he uses the word so freely I pick it up as part of the idiom: *sex as a second language.*

If sex is a language, though, I doubt my ability to become fluent. I can't think in this other language, I can only observe. Observe what he does to me, what I do to him, from a point just outside myself. Sex shouldn't be an out-of-body experience — I know this intellectually. Yet my observing brain is detached from the nerves and synapses, the messages hijacked along their route from pleasure centre to observation post. I'm a watchtower surrounded by barbed wire.

He's baffled. "Don't you feel *anything?*"

Yes: *pain. It hurts, damn you!*

The pathway to arousal is dark and twisted. I resist following it to this unmapped territory. There is no Sully-sunshine here, penetrating the canopy of wilderness, no safety.

Doug is so tender with the piteous parts — the stump of my right arm, the scars between my legs — I'm sure he'd be more gentle if I had been more hurt. More maimed, more scarred. Pity inspires love: no wonder we deny it. He loved the children at the psych hospital, the halt and the lame. He would love me, truly love me — wouldn't he? – if there was less to love.

Driven by the visceral thrill of darkness, I imagine diminished, nightmare versions of my body. There's precious little of me left by the time we're done. An escalating cycle: it's more and more demanding to deliver less and less.

Don't you feel anything, Mariah?

"You want me to fake it?"

"No!" he exclaims, surprisingly anguished, revealing himself as Sensitive Doug. "I want you to enjoy it. I want you to be happy."

I *feel* desired; I'm *happy* to be the object of his desire. I enjoy wielding this power over him. And yet – there's something obscene about my detachment. I know he's using me; but how am I using him? I'm no less guilty for being unable to cite the offence, chapter and verse. I've defined my mission – to make him whole – as a selfless one. So I've removed my self from the equation. I am mirror – reflecting every movement – so Narcissus can watch while he fucks himself blind.

"What are you doing here?" I opened my door to Doug's scowling countenance one evening. "I thought you were supposed to have dinner with Richard."

"We had a disagreement," he snarled, alcohol trailing like exhaust fumes as he pushed past me. "Can I come in?"

"I have company."

"Yeah. My sister."

Kat and I had looked forward to spending a rare evening together. "It's a relief from Ray's relentless maleness!" she'd sighed. To which I'd added my unspoken thought, "It's a relief from Doug's relentless sexuality." I was truly disappointed by the invasion – especially since he was in a black mood. Red in the face, his posture stiff with anger: a walking hard-on.

He drank most of the bottle of wine he'd brought, did all the talking. Kat and I sat together on the love-seat, across from him, as if distancing ourselves from some indefinable menace.

"I'm not going to Harvard, after all," he bellowed. "If all they can turn out is a generation waving the flag of fucking cultural elitism, then I'm not interested."

Neither of us was inclined to like him very much as he rambled, threatening and incoherent.

When he careened out of the room for the john, Kat and I stared at each other. *I feel more alive with her than I do with him,* I thought, letting my face crumple in dismay.

"I'm sorry," she said, reaching out to comfort me. "He's being a real prick."

Grateful for her warmth and support, I let myself linger in her arms. "I love you, Kat."

"Love you, too."

"This is beautiful," Doug sneered, kneeling at our feet.

Kat and I separated unselfconsciously.

"Have you two ever made love?" he asked and, leaning closer, drew his fingers down our faces. "I think love between women must be so beautiful. So gentle. No violation."

Kat and I smiled at each other wryly. Trust Doug to get the wrong idea.

"Why don't you do it so I can watch?"

"Don't be a dope," she said casually.

All the nights we'd slept in the same bed over the years, Kat and I, I'd never thought about it before. But I'd spent so much time this summer conforming to Doug's expectations, acting under his tutelage, I suddenly felt as if I should at least entertain his suggestion.

"Mariah, you have to learn how to come. I can't do it all for you," he said one night, leaning back in a lather against the headboard of Richard's guest-room bed. "Don't you ever masturbate?" His tone was almost hostile, accusing.

"No." I could feel the heat of my blush in the gloom. "No, I don't." Not unless you classify fingering the tracery of scars on my stump masturbatory behavior; not unless you count falling asleep with a pillow between my legs. Everything I've done with him this summer has been to please him. Follow the customs; wear the *chador*; learn from the master. Any pleasure I take is incidental, a by-product of supposedly natural processes — as excrement is a by-product of digestion.

"Don't discount anything unless you've tried it," he keeps saying. So I've kept trying, thinking, *maybe something will click; maybe I'll learn to speak the language during this sexual immersion.*

Entertain his suggestion? Do it with Kat? As I smiled at her a wire crossed, a synapse misfired, a whole grid lit up. *Don't you feel anything?* Oh, yes. Safety. Love.

"You're drunk, Doug," Kat said, standing up. "Why don't you go to bed?" Looking at me, she asked, "Shall we put him in Luke's room? Or do you want him?"

"Luke's room, definitely."

The feeling passed. Watching Kat undress, dispassionately, as I had hundreds of times before, I decided I've let Doug hypnotize me; I've become too suggestible. *You must learn to trust your instincts, Mariah!* If I failed to imagine my body entangled with Kat's, I failed equally to imagine it engaged with the sleeping young man in the other room.

Sully, on the other hand. *Safety. Love.*

Sometime before dawn Doug wandered into my room, shook Kat awake. "Swap places with me."

"Mariah? Are you okay with that?"

"I suppose so." *Wait for me!* I wanted to call as Kat padded off down the hall. *Don't leave me alone with him.*

" 'Kat creeps out on little fog feet'," he smirked at his own cleverness. "So," he said, snuggling close, "did you do it with my sister?"

"No, I didn't; I don't want to."

"Why not?" he said, disappointed. "*I* always have. I've always thought we were meant to be one, that I'd be complete, somehow, if we were."

If I'd set myself a mission to make him whole, he had his own ideas how that might be accomplished. "You're sick!" I hissed, turning over.

So close I smelled the alcohol on his breath, felt his erection prodding my buttocks. "And you love it," he added.

Do I? The visceral response to danger, the adrenalin rush – have I been mistaking it for love, too? *Not today.*

"Why don't you sleep it off – alone?" I suggested, getting out of bed.

"Have you ever considered becoming *asexual?*" he shouted.

"Fuck off."

Perhaps I *am* learning to speak the language, after all.

In the morning he was apologetic and conciliatory. "I'm sorry," he said. "I behaved badly. I was extraordinarily depressed."

"You were drunk."

"Let me make it up to you."

And he played sensitive Doug, caring Doug, for me so convincingly I relented.

His suitcase, contents rifled, on the bed; drawers open, closet ajar – he's turned the room upside down while I've been in the bathroom trying to make myself presentable enough to go home.

"What *are* you rummaging for?"

"Condoms." He grins, his erection asserting itself. "We seem to be all out."

"Well, you'll have to handle *that*," a nod to his penis, "by yourself. My mother expects me home tonight."

He pulls on some clothes deferentially. "Bring some with you tomorrow?"

"All right. I'll pull a bank job, then I'll empty the drugstore of Trojans. I hope they've restocked since last week." One thing I've stopped blushing about, at least. I seem to have spent a whole summer's allowance on latex.

A dizzying quantity of rubbers went through the check-out when I was with him one day, along with a supply of junk food and sugarless gum. The cashier, a kid our own age, watched him fumble with wallet in little hand, regarded me slinging plastic bags over my stump.

"Well," he said pleasantly. "I'm glad to see you two aren't skinny-dipping in the gene pool; *your* kids might be born with two heads."

I'd blushed a furious shade of purple. But Doug's reaction was so swift I forgot to breathe. Grabbing the boy by his crookedly knotted tie, he dragged him across the counter.

"The *lady's* problem," he intoned with barely controlled fury, "was an accident. Unlike *your* problem – terminal stupidity – which is, indeed, genetic."

After that, I'd been happy to buy condoms on my own.

"Speaking of drugstores," he walks me toward the door, arm draped over my shoulder, a fat manila envelope clutched in his little hand. "We've been together practically every day for a month. When do you schedule time for menstruation?"

"I don't."

He laughs. "You don't schedule time?"

"No. I don't menstruate. Haven't had a period since I was fifteen."

He nods knowingly. "Anorexic amenorrhea. Still?" I shrug. "It'd be nice to know if you were permanently sterile," he muses. "You could save a fortune on birth control."

I decide he doesn't mean to be insensitive; still, to deflect the focus:

"We should be going *dutch* on the birth control!"

He blanches. "Of *course* we should! I'll get my wallet."

"Forget it; I'm joking." We smooch in the open doorway. "You can make it up with a nice bottle of Richard's wine."

"I *do* have something for you." He whacks the package in his hand at a moth, then closes the door against further intrusion. "For your eyes only," he warns, stuffing it into my backpack. "Don't leave it lying around for Mommy and Daddy to find." Smiling at my cocked eyebrow, "Have a look, when you're all alone and ready for bed."

"Plain brown wrapper, hmmm?" I ask suspiciously.

"Don't be too judgemental."

"Of you — for giving it to me?"

Nuzzling my ear as he whispers into it, "No; of yourself. If something does the trick."

I check in with my mother, erect a scaffold of lies for the weekend. "Sleepovers" with Kat, "weekends" at Wendy's cottage — all of us depending on each other's alibis as we slip off to sleep with our boyfriends — it's almost too easy.

Doug's scent — sweat and rubber — clashes with my own, so I take a long shower, looking forward to a night alone, the whole bed to myself. Lights out — I'm half asleep before I remember his envelope.

Within the circle of the bedside tensor lamp, I slide the contents out carefully. Just as I suspected: pornography. A catholic assortment of pornography, I smirk, such as a nice Catholic boy might keep under his bed after a year in an enlightened Scandinavian sex capital.

I peel the first publication off the pile. Hoo haw! Amazonian mammaries undreamed of by nature for the suckling of children. The next: steroid-inflated men wielding phalluses to shame the Statue of Liberty's torch. Couples, threesomes, multiples, doing creative things to each other; perhaps I'll laugh myself to orgasm. All these things brightly coloured, air-brushed; surreal.

The next has none of the glossy frivolity of the others. Almost documentary in nature. Subdued. Yet eye-catching for its lack of hyperbole. I stop breathing. Real people, not glamorous, not perfect. Some at their daily occupations, in street clothes — as well as in varying degrees of nakedness, alone and with lovers. Real lovers, not fake lovers. Displaying true tenderness, true passion — or such truth as can be captured by the camera's eye. With a kind of dignity transcending whatever indignities have been dealt them.

Real people – not one of them with a full set of limbs.

Amputees, victims of birth defects – with and without the mechanical instruments of torture and survival that bridge their lacunae.

Turning the pages, weeping. *I want you because you are not whole.* I hear my words, I hear his. *Redefine normal, redefine whole. Don't be too judgemental. Of yourself – if something does the trick.*

Darkness can't erase the images replaying behind my eyelids. The identification is complete: I see myself splayed and displayed in my own bed for the camera: helpless, powerless, passive – acted upon.

And sticky with the fluids of arousal. *Doug, you bastard – you set me up!*

I see him, smug in his bed at Richard's, guessing my reaction. Plotting how he'll capitalize on my freakish responses and manipulate my inability to distinguish between love and loathing.

Guess again, Doug.

I've turned my rage against myself for too long, but this time no more.

I have nineteen years as a trained observer – collecting data, analysing, watching. The lens clicks on the surveillance camera catching the beloved without his camouflage, engaged in violence and violation.

Love's disguises, stripped off, unmask – *abuser in love's clothes.*

⁓

Fast forward to Kat's wedding. St. Basil's Church, Toronto. June 1980.

Spinning out over the small congregation, accompanied by our friends and housemates, Jenny Herlihy and Angela Ponti on cello and oboe, respectively, my voice carries my music – written for the occasion – text based on I Corinthians 13: *Love is patient, love is kind, love rejoices with the truth. Love bears all things, believes all things. Love hopes all things, endures.*

Kat and Ray's happiness is radiant and contagious, reflected and magnified by the other engaged couples. This summer will go down in our personal histories as a summer of weddings clustered around graduations, celebration after celebration.

As I scan the pews, I catch Doug's eyes on me, his expression unreadable.

He's dismissing the music as lightweight, I know. It *is.* The marriage songs I've written for my friends this summer have been difficult, time-consuming, and unsatisfying to me professionally. They've been true labours of love, measures of my regard for my roommates. But wholly uncharacteristic. Jenny was leery of even sight-reading the epithalamium when I presented it to her: "For the wedding? I couldn't. Your stuff is so *dark!*"

"The place I go to with you isn't healthy for me," I told Doug six years ago, when I broke off our relationship. "I don't like the self I am with you; I need to hurt her when I'm there."

Unfortunately, I had to keep revisiting that place. For the music to have any emotional authenticity, I felt, I had to have *known* it. I had a lifetime's experience exploring the dark; I couldn't quite trust the light. It had no depth.

My best work for school had a raw anger that startled people when they met me. In blind judging they always attributed ethereal romantic stuff to me and my music to a scowling depressive fellow with stringy hair who looked as if he dismembered wild cats in Queen's Park between classes. I went for maximum impact.

Of me and my award-winning choral work, *Armageddon*, the interviewer from the *Varsity* suggested that, "Mariah Standhoffer, with the willowy fragility of an anorexic ballerina" – I was still too thin – "seems physically incapable of withstanding the wind tunnel at Bay and Bloor, let alone the emotional *Sturm und Drang* sustained in her searing vision. Be warned: this woman is no lightweight."

I wish I had a copy of that article with me to pass to Doug. It seems I still need to justify myself to him, even after all this time.

"Where's James?" Brendan bellows, approaching the dinner table, trailed by Joe.

"He's got a job interview," I respond. "You know Kat's brother Doug? Doug, Brendan Maloney. Betrothed to the cellist."

"Ah, the estimable Jenny." Doug and Brendan shake hands across the table awkwardly.

"And Joe Fontina, Angela's fiancé."

Witness to Brendan's bungling, Joe has his left hand ready.

Doug, having fallen to me by default, knows none of our friends – except Ray. Even his own parents are absent, their attendance derailed by Mr. Hassock's badly planned heart attack, just ten days ago.

Masking his mouth with his hand, "Who is James?" he asks.

I smile stiffly. "That would be James Sullivan Riordan."

"Oh, *Sully!*" His eyes flash. " 'When I became a man, I put aside childish things,' " he quotes – from Corinthians and, by extension, from my song. "So, Harvard and Osgoode Hall have made a man of our *Sully*? Is *Sully* too good for him now?"

"No, *Douglas,*" I say calmly. "He's merely outgrown his nickname." Although he'll always be Sully to me.

"Where's the job?" Joe asks.

I can't help grinning. "It's a secret."

"Oh, come on, Mariah! You can tell us!"

"Even *I* don't know!" I laugh. "James wouldn't tell me – he said it might jinx it if I were to blab it all over. He would only say it was special." I take a good swig of wine. "He'll be back tomorrow night."

Doug bends to my ear. "And when are *your* impending nuptials, Mariah?"

A little shake of my head, another gulp of wine.

"You can't tell me you're not engaged – look at your face! You have Sully written all over it; Sully is the light in your eye."

"Maybe so," I hiss. "But *James* hasn't yet asked."

"More fool he," he says. "Refills, anyone?"

Eyeing his empty beer bottle, Brendan opens his mouth to speak, but is reminded of Doug's dangling jacket sleeve by the firm application of Joe's Italian-made shoe to his shin. I cough into my fist to mask my hilarity.

"First impressions notwithstanding," Brendan leans closer when Doug is safely out of earshot, "is he a bit of a prick, or what?"

"We used to be a 'thing'."

"Baggage?"

"Tons."

"James is a great guy," he says, patting my shoulder. "Time you two were married."

To my relief, Jenny and Angela join us at last. "Great restaurant, Ang!"

Angie shrugs, appraising the space. "It's nice to have an uncle in the business. Too bad it's not big enough for our wedding, eh, Joey?"

Joe rolls his eyes. "The CNE grounds would hardly do for the circus you've got planned, Angie."

The conversation devolves exclusively to wedding talk, leaving Doug an outsider. "So, Doug – taking your Ph.D. at Harvard!" Jenny says, drawing him in. "In what?"

"Psychology."

Silence – as they all check hurriedly to make sure their psyches are tucked firmly into their pants.

Brendan laughs heartily. "How's that for a conversation killer? Reminds me of that old joke: How many psychologists does it take to change a light-bulb?" He doesn't wait for response. "Only one – but it has to really, *really* want to change."

Groans: we've *all* heard it before. I blush on Doug's behalf. And Doug maintains a stony silence through the better part of a bottle of scotch.

On the dance floor, I giggle nervously, talk for the sake of talking. *How long has it been, Doug? Six years?* "I feel like an ex-wife."

He flashes a sarcastic grin. "So do I, honey; so do I."

"I'm sorry you don't like our friends."

"They're perfectly nice people, Mariah," he says. "*Perfectly nice.* I just don't have anything in common with them. Suburban day-dreams: two-car garage and two-point-five kids. We don't even have heterosexuality in common." And he dips me – self-consciously campy.

Kat cuts in. "Come on, let's dance."

"Who, *me?*"

"Relax," she laughs. "Thirty-five people in one room and we're all friends. If not now, when?"

"You've been spending too much time with your brother," I accuse, placing hand and stump loosely around her waist.

"You don't mind, do you? That he's staying at the house?"

"*Mi casa, su casa.* We have to get past it, Kat. It's a long time over."

"I wish I understood why. I mean, I *understand why*," she smiles wistfully. "But, I always dreamed you'd be my sister-in-law."

"We're closer than that, kiddo. *Sisters.* Right?"

"I'm going to miss you."

"You'll love England," I say, tightening my grip. "It's a great opportunity for Ray."

"As if he couldn't take his doctorate in North America!" she sighs.

"You'll be besieged with visitors," I smile. "I might be one of them."

"On your honeymoon, maybe," she grins. "Don't scoff, Mariah. The handwriting's on the wall!" She points; I follow her finger as if I might see her metaphor scrawled like graffiti. "Sully – James – is going to come back from that interview with a job. And you're going to run off, get married, and move God knows where yourself."

I bristle irrationally. "I'm glad everyone else is so confident of his intentions. He hasn't *asked.*"

"Not since 1971, you mean," she teases. "You've had a longer engagement than all of us put together."

When the music changes, Jenny and Angela join us for a Ukrainian dance. Laughing and stepping on each other's toes, we fall into a group hug.

"What a lovely bunch you make," Doug says. Checking his eyes for sarcasm, I detect none. "You're lucky."

As the other members of our quartet cleave to their mates on the dance floor, "To think I begged for a single room when I applied for residence at St. Joe's!" I say. "I was sure Sister stuck me in the triple with Jennie and Ang just to be spiteful, because I'd dared *ask* for a single."

"But they're musicians," Doug says. "How could you fail to become friends? I'm just surprised by how well Kat fits in. She's not exactly an extrovert."

When Kat came to Toronto to take her master's degree in nursing, it was natural she should move into the dilapidated house on the fringe of Rosedale we – Jenny, Ang, and I – called home. Sully had taken to calling it *La Maison des Belles Artistes* and it stuck.

My friends. They forced me out of my solitude to interact with them, helping me get the music onto the page so we could share it. Without them I shudder to think what a strange and lonely being I might have been. I was well on my way to obsession when they intervened.

I'd seen his name on the faculty list; hell, I'd sought it out when I applied: Jim Altman.

Jim's name was a talisman whose weight had tipped the balance of my decision to attend the University of Toronto. I'd finger the scarred "JA" on my wrist when certainty flagged. I'd missed Sully so much I'd needed something to add appeal to the span of years that loomed ahead without him.

Talk about transference! I'd transferred everything into the fantasy of bumping into Jim on campus – homesickness, loneliness, shyness, fear – a mulch of emotion fertilized longing. Those first weeks in Toronto, I'd looked for him everywhere I went. I couldn't seek him out; it would have to be an "accidental" meeting.

Part of it was active avoidance of my roommates. Getting to know them would involve an exchange of awkward intimacies. I only went back to St. Joe's to sleep, occasionally to eat.

"You must work harder than anyone we know," Jenny accused. "What do you *do* over there all day?"

Caught without a ready lie, "I'm looking for someone," I admitted. Their receptive, sympathetic faces demanded details. "My old piano teacher."

Their eyes glommed onto my handless wrist. Narrative was demanded and delivered, a friendship sealed. "What's his name?"

"Jim Altman."

"He's my oboe instructor." Angela said, slapping my shoulder. "You'd have known that if you'd bothered to speak to your roommates!"

Angie physically dragged me to her next session, with Jenny following in case I bolted.

"I can't explain to another soul," I insisted, hyperventilating. "This is a bad idea."

No beard; short-cropped hair streaked with grey; a tie, for God's sake! – I'd probably passed him in the Edward Johnson Building a dozen times without recognizing him.

"Mr. Altman," Angie began in her brash, confident way. "I'd like to reintroduce you to one of your former piano students: Mariah Standhoffer."

"Mariah, it's been such a long time!" he exclaimed, lurching forward for a hug – to which I added my right arm at the last possible second, returning stump to pocket before we broke the embrace.

"Are you studying piano?" he asked eagerly.

"Composition and voice."

"Really." His brow creased. "I *am* surprised."

"I had an accident eighteen months ago," I said quietly, seating my wrist firmly in my pocket. "I've had to adjust my expectations."

And, so saying, I discovered I'd done just that – adjusted my expectations of the meeting. Romantic fantasy fell away as Jim said all the things a concerned teacher might. It came back to me: how good a teacher he was, how truly nice a man. His offer of assistance and mentorship was generous and sincere.

As his student, my megaprojects had given me a taste for over-achievement I'd neither duplicated nor satisfied. I worked like one demented in my classes to merit his confidence in my ability and professionalism before I approached him again. He and Lesley, his wife, helped me prepare for and enter competitions; introduced me to people; shopped my work around. Some of my classmates were envious of our relationship. But the smarter ones, those whose opinion mattered to me at all, recognized that my own confidence in my work – and Jim's – was not unwarranted. I worked for the recognition he helped me attain; learned to enjoy meeting high-powered people with a mask of poise and assurance; tried not to be so self-absorbed.

Even so – "You're so *inward-focused*," Sully remarked not long ago as we worked together, "I'm half afraid you might implode."

Despite my efforts, despite his, there are times I'm so preoccupied that, even in the middle of conversations, I forget to speak. Sully recognizes these moments like symptoms of an impending *petit mal* seizure. "I'm sorry, I didn't hear what you said," he'll prompt, forcing me to articulate my thoughts, to turn outward before I'm absorbed into the nucleus of my own solitude. This inward focus is part of what Doug mistook for passivity, all those years ago. And, with this thought, I realize I'm doing it again.

When Brendan drops Doug and me at home, Jenny embraces me on the sidewalk. "Call me when James gets back. I'm dying to know where he's been!"

"Stay," I plead, surprising us both.

Holding me at arm's length, "I will if you want me to," she says, watching Doug ascend the front steps. "You're not comfortable alone with him?"

"No, no; I'm fine." *I'm a big girl now.*

"You're sure? Bren and I can both stay. Guard your honour," she smirks.

"Don't be silly." I shove her toward the car. "See you Monday." And I follow Doug up the walk to the door.

"Have the Vestal Virgins all run off to sleep with their *beaux*?" he asks as I fumble with the lock.

"Angie's gone home to Oakville to get ready for her wedding next week, right after commencement."

He walks in ahead of me, takes off his jacket and tie, hangs them on the newel post. *Like the man of the house,* I think, with a nauseating flash of *déjà vu.* "Anything to drink?"

"There's always beer in the fridge for the boys," I answer, kicking off my pumps. "And there might even be a bottle of wine."

"Will you join me, if I open the wine?"

"Why not? I'm not driving anywhere tonight." I head upstairs to pee and get out of my dress. Dither in front of the closet. Nightgown and robe? What kind of message would that send? I settle for a pair of shorts and a polo shirt.

When I pad silently, barefooted, into the kitchen, Doug is still wrestling awkwardly with corkscrew and wine bottle.

"All wine should come with screw tops," he mutters, "the purists be damned." The cork pops suddenly; he almost hits himself in the eye.

Then, taking his wine glass in his little hand, the bottle in the other, he asks, "Living room?"

"After you."

The second-hand furniture all sags badly.

"The couch is the only thing worth sitting on," I say, assuming one end. Doug takes the other. "Unless you like springs up your ass."

"It wouldn't be the first thing I've had up my ass," he comments dryly, staring me down over the rim of his glass. I blush, but do not blink. Raising his glass to me in salute, "To the 'masters' of this house," he toasts. "Another diploma for your wall next week. Congratulations."

"And to you." We clink glasses across the gulf of aged green plush between us.

"Tell me," he demands. "When did you and *Sully* reunite?"

"Last year. While he was articling."

"With *Daddy's* firm?"

I ignore his sarcastic emphasis. "No, with the Attorney General."

He grins. "Like I said, with *Daddy's* firm. Isn't Jimmy still on the bench? You can't tell me there's no nepotism involved!"

Rushing to Sully's defence, "Is it so hard to believe Sully's done very well − on his own merits?" I fume. "*Summa cum laude* from Harvard; third in his class at Osgoode Hall. Articled with the Attorney General; prosecuting for the Crown!"

Waving his little hand, "Spare me Sully's c.v.," he says.

"You asked!"

"No," he shakes his head. "I asked when you and Sully reunited; *you* offered his résumé."

So I did. I feel so baited I could cry.

Sully. Our future caught up with us almost two years ago. There he was, standing on my fringe-of-Rosedale doorstep.

"What time is it?" he'd asked.

"*It's time,*" I'd answered, swooning into his arms like a romance heroine.

Turned out he'd lost his watch and needed to be at Jimmy and Sonja's lakeshore condo for dinner at six. Still, he appreciated the sentiment — "It's time" — despite the fact that we lost all track of it and he had been late.

Since then, we've been filling in the gaps, learning about each other, laying the foundation for a life together. Discussing important issues. Like children: he accepts my infertility with hope that it will pass, or that we can adopt. Like religion: he's taken Catholic instruction in Cambridge, goes to Mass with me. Like music: some of his favourite electives at Harvard were taken with me in mind — to learn the rudiments of a common language. And, as an undergraduate, I studied ethics and the philosophy of law with him in mind, to form the basis of another.

While laying that foundation I was careful to reveal myself, scrupulous to expose all my flaws and secrets. I told him about my childhood, my grandfather, about that hideous summer with Doug.

"If I hadn't *abandoned* you," he said, wearing his pain like bad-fitting spectacles, "you wouldn't have been wide open to Doug's predations!"

"You *didn't* abandon me," I insisted. "You gave me the choice and I chose the future. Here we are."

In the interests of fairness he'd related some of his own exploits. Drinking too much; sleeping with the occasional woman for "fun" and "companionship," then backing off precipitously if anything more was demanded of him. Moments of despair when he wondered if he'd done the right thing, when he was willing to chuck it all, certain I wouldn't be there when he attained his illusory goals.

"What would it have been worth if I'd come back with my law degree, only to find you married to some fiddler in the philharmonic — or worse, to Doug? You don't know how many times I almost picked up the phone."

And would it have been so terrible if he had?

"Aren't you going to try for Doctor of Music?" Doug asks.

"Not right away. I want to take at least a year off."

"Why?" His eyes narrow. "So marriage and motherhood can inter-vene? You'll never get it, if you wait."

"I'm not sure I need it." I slurp from my glass. "I've got a head full of material; a doctorate might just add so many rarefied ideas I won't have room for my own."

"For what sort of gainful employment has this advanced degree pre-pared you?" Doug asks.

Shrugging, "On a practical level: choral director; voice coach. Less practically, I've won a few awards, had a few pieces published – " I regret this confidence immediately; it sounds so self-aggrandizing. Then I regret regretting it.

"So you can live off your royalties!" he finishes grandly. "I'm sorry. That's wonderful, of course." He studies me. "I did enjoy the song you sang at the wedding; it was quite beautiful."

Quite beautiful – I can't decide if the modifier accrues to the beauty or subtracts from it: Doug is up to his old tricks. Dousing my fury with a good hit from my wine glass, I smile graciously. "Thank you."

Doug stretches his legs out on the couch; to avoid contact I draw my knees up to my chin. "I followed Sully's career at Harvard with some interest."

I'll bet.

"He must have worked hard to take his degree so quickly," he yawns, "but don't let him tell you it was all work and no play. *Our Sully,*" God – his tone infuriates me! "made quite a name for himself. And it wasn't just James."

"Oh?"

Gesturing with his glass, "Our Sully has *lovely legs,*" he gushes swishi-ly. "Six-foot-four – legs that just won't stop! Looks wonderful in tights, and a wig, and a full set of cleavage." He leans toward me across the couch, his voice drops: "A member of the oldest, most venerated drag show on the eastern seaboard, my dear."

Staring into his green eyes without blinking: "The Hasty Pudding show, you mean."

Doug has the grace to blanch. "Yes."

"Thank you for bringing it to my attention." I leap off the couch. "You *are* a malicious bastard, aren't you?" And I turn to leave the room.

"Mariah, I'm sorry," he rises to stop me. "I thought you ought to know. I'm *glad* you know."

I measure the level of sincerity against the meter of his drunkenness.

"He was very good, I have to give him that. Always played a male lead, except for the obligatory kick line. Looked swell in a tux in *Tots in Tinseltown*. Good solid baritone, too; you could make much of that voice." He spins his wine glass in the light. "Developed quite a reputation as a drinker, though."

"And you didn't?" My own head is so fuzzy with the quantities of alcohol I've consumed I find myself forgiving him. "Not every member of the Pudding is a raging queen. You said it: the Pudding is a venerable institution, predating women at Harvard. It'd be like saying the Globe Theatre in Shakespeare's time only put on drag shows. Sully's *father* was in the Pudding."

"He's offered you all the correct motivations." Doug's smile is inscrutable.

"He *did* work hard," I insist. "The Pudding was good for expense-paid trips to New York and Bermuda. A way to have fun, to blow off steam."

Snorting into his wine glass, "I'd watch the context of the verb 'to blow'," he hoots, then sobers suddenly. "Sorry. I've offended you again."

"Did you say you were *studying* psychology or *being* psychoanalysed?" I ask nastily. "It seems you have a lot of problems, not least of which is a debilitating one-track mind! What *happened* to you? I used to ad*mire* you; I used to. . . ." *I used to love you.*

Examine these words from every angle: yes, it was true — at one time. I loved him long-distance, with an ocean between us. I loved him at the psych hospital. I loved the way he dealt with the kids. Easy, natural, giving. When did his contempt seep between the cracks like a poisonous gas, polluting all his other relationships? With his family? With me? With Richard?

With Richard! I sag back against my end of the couch. It wasn't there in his letters — the self-loathing; it wasn't there in Copenhagen that March. But by the time he came home from his Austrian summer he was consumed with it.

"What happened to me?" He reaches for the wine bottle, tops up his own glass, points the bottle at me. I decline. "I faced my own realities. I'm a *faggot*, Mariah."

"So, what was our last summer all about?" My words sound more strangled than I'd like. "*Denial?* Were you faking your constant erection?

Or are you promiscuous with both sexes?"

He looks at me levelly. "You were the only woman I ever loved."

My response: an extended vowel of frustration and disbelief. Eventually, "Bullshit. You never once used that word aloud. It was the most forbidden of four-letter words."

"Because it was the most important. I wouldn't use it lightly."

"You wouldn't use it at all – because you didn't love me. You were incapable of love. You were *abusive!*"

"Abusive! Abusive?" He looks truly shocked. "Is that how you saw it? What did I say? What did I do?"

"Everything you said was designed to distance yourself – you're doing it tonight. Outrageous. Provocative. Depraved!"

His lip curls without humour; he doesn't deny it.

"You came home from Europe so full of self-loathing and self-doubt you had to share it: 'Have you ever considered becoming asexual?' 'You have to learn how to come, Mariah!' "

He *hears* how his words echo across the years and winces in recognition.

"Giving me the pornography, knowing how it would play into my masochism."

"Your particular brand of masochism is really veiled sadism, my dear," he says sweetly, lapsing into a terrible German accent. "Uncle Wilhelm Stekel vould say you harbour ze unconscious vish to injure someone else."

At this moment he couldn't be more correct.

Laughing at my murderous expression, "Don't be so melodramatic," he says.

My voice leaves me as if he's ripped the larynx out of my throat. *How dare he trivialize me this way!*

Staring out the window behind the couch into the darkness, "Abuse!" he spits. "What do you know about abuse? With your perfect little life, in your perfect castle. With your perfect parents. Your perfect career path all mapped out. And the *perfect mate*, just waiting in the wings."

Eyes flashing like St. Elmo's fire, "You weren't a *freak* your whole life." He wags the fingers of his little hand. "You weren't a target for every depraved old fool who thought that, having been 'sent before my time into this breathing world scarce half made up'," he gestures theatrically, "I was incapable of discerning the *wrongness* of anything they might do to me. They could *smell* the 'queer' on me. *Richard* smelled it on me before I even knew what it was."

Noting the question on my face, he sighs, "No, no, he never did anything to me. I ruined that one. He thought I needed a mentor; I thought I'd found a father." He looks at me. "What do *you* know about abuse?"

A humourless laugh. *Shall I tell him now* — when I didn't trust him enough to tell him then? Six years ago I couldn't predict which Doug might respond. The gentle, caring man who could hold a handicapped child in his arms might love me and let me share my fears. Or would it be the other Doug, the one who could distance himself from anyone with a show of depravity.

Now, I *know* which Doug will respond and *I can match him* — scar for scar.

"Delicate self-cutting, *Doug!* Anorexia, *Doug!* What a *fine* psychologist you'll make! Even this — " I shove my stump into his face. "My perfect little life!" I say, leaping from the couch the way I leapt out of Richard's guest-room bed that day. "My grandfather, *Doug*, used to sodomize me on a regular basis." Waving my stump over my head, "I turned a gun on him one day, *but I missed.* My hand got in the way. So don't ask *me* what I know about abuse!" I hiss.

He appraises me as if he's found a previously unnamed specimen on a lab slide. "You would have been the same sort of pathologically introspective person, whether you'd been abused or not."

My reaction? Predictable anger. "I set myself a mission, six years ago. And I failed miserably. Brutally. I thought if I could get you to admit to love, to *feel* love, I could make you whole." A bitter laugh. "I was so naïve!" I stare at the ceiling, shake my head. "You asked me, 'Don't you feel *anything?*' That was the question you should have been asking yourself. How can you feel anything across the Grand Canyon you've formed with your erosive bitterness? We can spend the rest of our lives digging the canyon deeper. Or we can fill it in and get *over* it."

Leaning against the mantle of the fireplace for support, I find myself trembling. With anger? With relief?

He walks up behind me, puts his arm around me. Turns me so he can look into my eyes. His are pained — which fills me with an adolescent sort of triumph.

"Are you over it?"

"*Yes.*"

"Are you sure?"

Stepping to the stereo shelf, I punch a cassette into the tape player. "You be the judge."

The room fills with sound. A sort of ticking noise, played with the back of a violin bow on the bridge of the instrument. *My grandfather's pocket watch — he'd wave it in front of me when I was a baby. It was our little game.* A Slovak folk tune picked up by second violin and viola, layered over the ticking. *The song he'd sing during our game.* Happy, innocent. The ticking and the music stop suddenly. *One day I batted the watch away, angry. He held it in front of my face. Again, I batted it away. The watch had stopped. I wouldn't play the game any more.* The theme, picked up by the cello and transposed into the relevant minor key, becomes ominous, threatening, discordant. A chaos of sound out of which emerges a haunting motif.

"What is this? You wrote it?" he asks.

"I call it *The Grandfather Quartet.*"

He nods, leads me back to the couch. Puts his arm around me casually and listens intently. His embrace tightens gradually, unconsciously, as the second movement builds in intensity and tension until pow! a musical "gunshot." He jumps. Lowers his head, pressing his cheek against mine through the sound of red pain, black pain; through musical disintegration as the motifs are severed and shredded. He trembles as he kisses our mingled tears from my face.

Next — "reassembly" — like running the musical images of disintegration in reverse. The resolution of seemingly disparate, discordant motifs and fragments. The reintegration of spirit and soul. The strapping on of limbs and prosthetics. The redefinition of "whole" and "normal," and with it, *empowerment.* And beauty: the soul-searing harmony of wholeness.

Winding it up, the peaceful ticking of an old man's pocket watch and the ragged sound of Doug's sobs in his throat as we *make love* to each other — tender, regretful *love* — for the first, and last, time.

Sully drags his garment bag and suitcase out of the trunk of the cab, presses cash into the driver's hand, and leaps the walk and stairs in a single bound.

Bearing an incandescent grin so wide our teeth collide when we kiss, he crushes me — suitcase, garment bag, and all — in his embrace.

"Anyone home?" He peers around the house, cocks his head for noise.

"We're all alone."

"Good." Dumping his stuff unceremoniously at the foot of the stairs, he swings me into the living room and trips me up somehow so we're on the couch in a tangle of arms and legs, laughing and kissing, until my heart threatens to burst under the combined pressure of happiness and his hugs.

"You miss my best friend's wedding because of some mysterious mission," I say, beating his chest with my stump, "you have to tell me where you've been!"

Sitting back slightly, to see my face: "Bermuda."

"Bermuda?"

"Bermuda!" he repeats, imitating my high-pitched squeal, then drops his voice four octaves. "I've loved it ever since the Pudding days. I woke up on Horseshoe Bay at sunrise one morning, surf lapping at my shoes, throwing up onto the pink sand, and I thought, *This is heaven. I must see it sober one day.*"

"Tsk." I shake my head in mock-disgust. "And were you sober this time?"

"Yes. Sober as a judge." Neither of us comments on Mister Justice Riordan's propensity to over-imbibe. "Ask me if I have an offer."

Playing along, "Do you have an offer?"

He gestures grandly. "I *have* an offer!" Laughing, "You're speechless," he says. "Do I have to cue the entire script?"

"Did you accept it?"

"Yes; provisionally."

"When do you start?"

"Right after Labour Day."

"Labour Day?" I fall back against the couch. "So soon?" My mind goes virtually blank. "Provisionally?"

He nods earnestly. "Providing you choose to go with me."

Ah. *Time to choose.* I see now why Sully hasn't asked me to marry him: he's waiting for me to choose. Just as he said he would.

"I do."

Part Three

Fugue

"*Trust me. Jump over the edge.*"

Up along the canyon rim, climb higher. Get a running start, hang on by my toenails and try again. Exhausted with the climb, the effort, and the concentration, once more to the edge and sail over — beyond trust, beyond love. Falling, falling into — flight! On an updraft. Falling, falling. Safe. Safe in Sully's arms.

"You can't tell me people do this every day!"

He laughs. "Maybe you feel it more intensely than most people, because you've waited so long."

With time, I come to realize it's not a garden variety occurrence. We take to calling it "The Honeymoon Express," to differentiate the degree of union, the commitment involved in achieving it, from a regular weeknight frolic. It's special: longed for, feared. It's the definition of "marriage."

We'd thrown the nuptials together with such haste, "You don't think anyone will suppose it's a shotgun wedding, do you?" I'd fretted.

"No groom would sur*vive* a shotgun wedding hosted by your father," Sully had countered, "beyond the time it takes for the ink to dry on the parchment legitimizing his progeny!"

It was an intimate, informal affair. Our wedding date was bracketed by Jimmy and Sonja's annual fortnight at Silver Islet. Wendy Staplin was my maid of honour; Jim Altman played the organ and proposed the toast to the bride. Kat and Ray had already left for England, but Jenny and Angela flew into town together.

"Look at us!" Angie laughed. "Married mere weeks and already taking vacations *sans* spouses!"

Sully conscripted Luke as best man since he didn't claim sufficient intimacy with any of his Harvard or Osgoode Hall mates to compel them to Thunder Bay in mid-August.

I'd composed epithalamia for three other weddings that summer — but I didn't have time to produce one from scratch for my own. So I dragged out my *Sullivan Suite*. Its juvenile technique made me cringe but, reworked as an interlude for Jenny and Angela to perform while we signed the paperwork, it had a painful beauty. And a power born of hope.

There was a candid Polaroid Angela took of the wedding party as we convened on the steps of St. Patrick's Cathedral: Sully on the right, arm spread wide to include me and Wendy, beckoning to Luke off to one side, just slightly removed from the group. With his head angled, it's clear Luke's facial cast is all for Sully. It gave me a wrench, that photo, for I recognized in the furrow between my brother's eyes an expression I'd dismissed as childish in Sully's the day I slapped him during *Richard III:* the unmistakable scarring of first love.

"Is it everything I promised?"

Sully re-experiences Bermuda, second-hand, through me. If I absorb it like salt water through my pores, he kisses the brine from my skin. His memories are the expressions on my face as new vistas unfold: coral beaches set like jewels between turquoise sea and sky; limestone arches carved by surf. White roofs set on pastel houses like frosting on petit fours; gardens of preposterous verdancy.

The scents of frangipani, oleander, salt breezes. The blazing sun on my skin, sand under my bathing suit. The sough of wind through palms, the plash of waves, the buzz of mopeds.

"I love it," I assure him. And I do.

Yet, for someone who's spent twenty-five years in the emotional equivalent of a sensory deprivation tank, with all my faculties suddenly engaged and focused outward simultaneously, it's an assault of unrelenting sensuality. Unsure I can cope with the constant over-stimulation, I fight the urge to pull down the roller-blinds behind the hot-pink drapes of my eyelids.

Sully is burning up in bed beside me when I wake, his shin a branding iron against my foot.

"My God; you're sick!"

I pull the blankets back to expose him to the air conditioning, race to the refrigerator. Ice cubes, yes. Better yet, a package of frozen peas.

He spies me coming at him with the Jolly Green Giant. "Am I the entrée?"

"You're definitely roasting. Here."

"God, that's cold!"

"Should I call a doctor?"

"Not yet. Just let me die," he moans, stumbling into the bathroom. "Christ on a stick!" he shouts. "Grab a shoe — there's a bug the size of a cat in here."

"I brought the big guns," I say, wielding one of his boat-sized running shoes. "Good God — you're not exaggerating!"

He dives, retching, for the toilet as I jump for the palmetto bug, whacking its hard carapace until I've ground it to a paste against the tile.

"Brave girl," he says, knees trembling. "We should maintain some illusions, at least until we've been married a week."

"Too late," I grin, mopping his brow. "Any illusions that *you* will be the great white hunter in this marriage have been destroyed."

Climbing back into bed, he smiles wanly. "Sorry. Didn't mean to test the theory 'in sickness, and in health' so early on." And, rolling over, starts to snore.

I spend a day and a half of my honeymoon in bed all right, but with *The Thorn Birds.* By the time he's feeling better, I've got the bug; he reads *The Thorn Birds*, too.

The Attorney General, Shel Simpkin, smiles when he meets us. "Enjoying your honeymoon, James?" he teases, clapping Sully's shoulder. "I can tell by your pallor." We hardly have the strength to disabuse him of his notion.

The virus — or bacterium, or parasite — lingers with me. Every time I feel I'm making a comeback, I'm felled again by nausea.

It's hot in the Supreme Court the day Sully is called to the Bermuda Bar. Just one look at him in his black suit, robes, and wig, sweltering in the humidity, is enough to make me toss my cookies. But I can't leave the room! James Sullivan Riordan, the youngest Crown Counsel ever to serve in Chambers, is about to be sworn in. My heart so swells with pride that all the oxygen to my brain is cut off: I go down with a thundering crash just as Sully swears, "I do."

The AG himself whisks us off to Emergency. Sully has divested himself of gown and wig and changed into his new business attire: Bermuda shorts and knee socks.

"Bless your fuzzy knees," I croon, tickling his leg.

He takes my hand, kisses it, and holds it tightly, forestalling further tickling.

"This is so silly," I say. "I feel fine now."

"You've been saying that for two weeks. It's time to get it checked out. Especially," he says, wagging his finger at me, "after such an unseemly display in the highest court of the land!"

An earnest Irish internist named O'Grady takes Sully's history: they determine common ancestors within seconds of their introduction. He glances at my handless wrist but asks only the usual questions while taking my history.

"When was your last menstrual period?"

I roll my eyes. "1973? Or was it '72?" He gasps. "I haven't had a period since I became anorectic, about age sixteen." Sully squeezes my hand.

"Do you use any form of birth control?"

I shake my head. "What's the point?"

He covers a few other bases. "We'll take a blood test and urine sample. And then I'll perform a wee physical." He shoos Sully to the waiting room.

"Don't you go flashing those knees at the nurses, now," I warn.

"The nurses are quite immune to the turn of a shapely knee," Dr. O'Grady says. "At least, they've been shockingly immune to mine." Syringes, gloves, a speculum soaking in warm water. "All right, then. Knees up."

"*That* kind of physical!" I groan.

"Won't take but a second. Relax."

Easy for him to say, but all my reflexes are against it.

"Mmmhhm. Just as I thought." He looks at me solemnly. "Shall I tell you my findings, or do you want that great lug in here?"

The nurse fetches Sully while I dress, hand shaking.

"There's really nothing I can do for you," Dr. O'Grady says.

I hear Sully's sharp intake of breath, feel the increased pressure on my hand.

"This condition can only take its course until – " the doctor claps his hands together, smiles brilliantly " – until a few months down the road, bingo! You've got a wee babby and your lives will never be the same."

Sully, dazed and speechless: a rare enough disorder in itself.

"When?" I have the presence of mind to ask.

Dr. O'Grady shrugs. "Very hard to say, precisely. We usually calculate gestation from the date of the last menstrual period, but – " he pretends to check my chart, "eight or nine years is off the gestation scale for even an elephant." He grins. "You're about ten weeks along." He passes on instructions about diet and rest, tells me to procure a doctor.

"That shouldn't be too difficult," I say. "We just moved into Dr. McCassland's apartment."

"Perfect! Sandy McCassland's a great obstetrician. For a Scot," he winks. "Right then, congratulations!" He shakes hands with Sully, offers me a high five after the slightest hesitation, and sweeps out.

Weak with relief and excitement: how can it be? What kind of miracle is this? Sully's so silent I'm afraid to meet his eyes. It's so soon; it'll surely mess up his plans.

One thigh perched on the examination table, half-turned away from me. When I touch his shoulder he swoops his arm out and crushes me to him. "I should have decked that asshole," he sobs. "He had me scared to death. 'There's really nothing I can do fer ye,'" he mimics, exaggerating Dr. O'Grady's accent. "Jesus. Jesus."

"So you're happy?"

His kiss is answer enough.

"We can hardly tell our parents you're ten weeks pregnant when we've only been married for four!" he said.

"Oh, come on! It's the eighties. Surely to God. . . ."

He gave me a look. "Think of your father."

I did. "All right; we'll wait."

Just as well. Within days we're in our landlord's professional office. Having not had a period in years, I'm somehow, miraculously, pregnant. And *spotting*. Sully's knee bounces like a trip-hammer. I use every mental technique known to man to keep myself calm and serene. For the baby.

"James! Mariah!" Dr. McCassland greets us. "It's customary for the tenants to leave the rent cheque with my wife; you really didn't need to come all this way."

Sully bristles; he's had it with joking doctors. I pat his hand. *Calm down, calm down.*

"It's probably nothing," the doctor soothes. "You'd be amazed how many women threaten miscarriage and go on to carry healthy babies full term." He takes out a stethoscope, listens, nods. "All right." He sets up a little contraption, turns it on. The room fills with a liquid "swoosh swoosh swoosh."

"There you go. That's your baby's heartbeat. Sound and strong." We grin at each other, at him, at the imaginary swell of my belly. "Stay off your feet, Mariah, for a few days. Until there's been no spotting for at least twenty-four hours straight. And don't hesitate to call if it gets any worse. Cheerio!"

At home, Sully fusses around me like a maiden aunt.

"Don't be silly. You've just started a new job. I'll be fine."

"Maybe we should call the parents, get someone down here to look after you," he frets.

I slap him playfully. "Go to work! You'll be home for lunch, for goodness' sake."

He puts his motorcycle helmet on, then comes back to kiss me. On my side, it's like trying to kiss an astronaut.

Without him, though, it's as if the electricity's gone off. Despite the sun streaming through the curtains, it's sepulchral as I huddle under the blankets in the air-conditioned bedroom. *This is great*, I sigh. One month married, don't know a soul on the island except Sully. Afraid to get out of bed to pee, lest I dislodge the tenuous life I'm harbouring in a dysfunctional womb.

A baby! I've heard its heartbeat, yet its presence is never clearer to me than in the Rorschach blots left on the pad between my legs, the rusty message filling me – alternately – with hope (*a baby!*) and despair (*could lose it – might be your only chance*). I talk to it: a different sort of inward focus than I've ever experienced. *Hold on*, I tell it – him, I feel with some certainty; *hold on. If not for my sake, then for your dad's.*

Sully is afraid to exhibit too much – or too little – concern. This baby is as much a part of his long-range plan as our marriage, as his career. He sees it, despite the long odds of its conception, as confirmation of the essential rightness of the course he's set himself, the course he's set for *us*. I cling to Sully's vision: for your dreams to come true you need only believe long enough and hard enough.

"I've got it all arranged," he announces over lunch. "Carolyn Jackson is coming this afternoon to look in on you."

"We can't impose upon people we haven't even met!" I exclaim, dismayed.

"Not to worry." He chugs down a glass of milk. "When I mentioned our predicament to Ron, he called home, said three words, and Carolyn took over. They just live up the hill."

"Still!" I look around the room. Lunch dishes, books, magazines, wedding gift thank-you cards and notepaper strewn, close at hand, on the coffee table. Breakfast dishes in the sink; bed unmade.

Sully buzzes around the apartment. "There," he kisses me. "The Goodhousekeeping Seal of Approval." He snaps on his helmet. "I won't lock the door; that way you won't have to get up when Carolyn comes. I've left the tea things out by the kettle where she can find them."

He flashes me his grin and leaves the house. Revs the bike. Instead of roaring off, though, he pulls up to the window in my line of vision from the couch, blows me a kiss, and zooms away.

Despite my apprehension I awake to the sound of wheels on the driveway, having dozed off over my book.

"Hall-oo!" a cheery voice calls through the louvred door.

"If you're Carolyn, come in!" She opens the door, pokes her head in. "If you're *not* Carolyn," I add in a conversational tone, "come in anyway; I'm at your mercy."

"I hope you don't mind."

Manoeuvring a baby carriage through the door, she pushes it across the living room, bending to offer me her hand to shake. I hold out my left; she swaps her right for her left matter-of-factly and without embarrassment.

"Everyone calls me Caro. And this," she jiggles the carriage, "is Claire, who has just fallen asleep – leaving us a good uninterrupted hour to get acquainted over tea. Shall I?"

"Please do."

She lifts an insulated tote bag from the basket under Claire's carriage. "I've just taken a small lasagna out of the freezer; I'll pop it in the oven before I leave and it'll be ready when James gets home for dinner."

"That's very kind!" I exclaim. "How incredibly organized to have dinners in the freezer with a baby to look after. And a cake for tea! I'm impressed."

She sets the cake on the coffee table, appraises me swiftly. "You could stand a little flesh on those bones. Although, I suspect Nature will take care of that over the next few months." She grins. "I gained thirty-five pounds with Claire."

"And lost it immediately afterwards, I'd say."

Caro pinches imaginary superfluous flesh. "I have a bit more to go."

I doubt it, but don't say so. "Well, thank you for this." We toast each other with our teacups. "Cheers."

"I've been meaning to have you and James round for dinner, but it seems one or both of you have been ill every time Ron tries to issue the invitation. I'm sure you're relieved to finally know why."

"We did have some kind of virus. Either picked it up at the wedding, or caught it since arriving. Some honeymoon!"

"Honeymoon! So being a 'little bit pregnant' comes as a little bit of a surprise."

"Yes, but we're delighted. We didn't think I'd be able to conceive."

I hesitate before forging ahead. Further confidence will result in a long story. But Caro's sensible, open face invites confidence. I've learned from Jenny and Angela that friendship requires risk and, inevitably, narrative. Best to get it out of the way early.

Caro is sympathetic and outwardly non-judgemental. Still, I can see her eyeing the shambles of my life — amputation, anorexia, amenorrhea, and unplanned pregnancy — as the result of a chronic lack of organization.

Baby Claire wakes up good-naturedly. "We'll just change your nappy, shall we?" Caro coos, "Then see if you'll go to Auntie Mariah."

Auntie Mariah! I muse as I dandle the chunky four-month-old on my lap — evidence we've been accepted as part of the "family."

I feel absurdly happy relating this news to Sully over dinner. "And," I add, "Caro said she'd bring Felicity Britten and Emily Carpenter along when she comes tomorrow."

"You just naturally form quartets of friends, don't you, love?"

I answer his smile: "It's an organic form, satisfyingly complete. Not to mention handy for bridge."

"You haven't met the others yet. How can you tell you'll mesh?"

"I can tell."

And I'm right.

"If this is heavy-going for you, Mariah," Felicity runs in the door in pursuit of one-year-old Robbie, "just tell us to piss off. We can be a bit much, *en masse.*"

"Speak for yourself, Fizzy!" Emily Carpenter is laden with baby gear — all of it Felicity's — and sketch pad and pencils. "Don't mind me," she says, setting up. "I was a courtroom artist in another life; I like to keep my hand in."

"Don't be so modest, Emily!" Felicity leans toward me confidentially. "She's a damned fine artist in this life, too." Taking my proffered left hand, "Please, please — call me Fizzy," she insists. "Felicity brings back traumatic memories of a particularly horrid headmistress." Her head snaps abruptly, launching an explosion of red hair. "Robbie!" And she's off. Much of the afternoon is spent watching Fizzy chase Robbie; they're equally inexhaustible.

"We've got a pool going," Emily confides over the third pot of tea. "None of us has seen him and we haven't quizzed our mates." She looks to the others for confirmation, laughs at my puzzled expression. "Let's see how close we are. According to our calculations, James is six foot, three and a half and weighs sixteen stone."

I laugh. "On what do you base these calculations?"

"Precedent!" Leaning across the coffee table, Fizzy removes Robbie's hand from the cakes. "We think we've established a pattern to the AG's hiring."

"Tony was first in, at six-one, two hundred pounds," Caro explains. "Ron came two months later, an inch taller, a stone heavier. Now," she nods to the others, "Fizzy's Cameron broke the pattern for height — he's just under six feet, but immense through the chest and thighs and half a stone heavier than Ron."

"Why should there be a pattern?" I ask.

"It's as if Shel's hiring for the con*stab*ulary instead of Chambers," Emily explains. "He's surrounding himself with *bodyguards.* You've met him; he's just average height."

"You mean James was hired for his brawn and not his brains?" I pretend shock.

"And it doesn't hurt that Shel Simpkin and Jimmy Riordan, The Elder, were law school mates," Fizzy comments.

I absorb this speculation along with another gulp of tea.

"Are we close?" Emily persists.

Reaching to the side table for a wedding snapshot, I hold it to my chest like a playing card. "Six-foot-four," I announce. Fizzy provides a drum roll. "But only thirteen stone." I toss the picture onto the table. *Trumps*.

A groan of disappointment.

"Imposing presence, though," Emily states. "And *very* young."

It's as if I've always known them, I catch myself thinking as I laugh into my tea, more confident of the rightness of Sully's decision to bring us here than I've been since arriving.

"Here's the man himself."

Sully comes through the door, running his hand through helmet-flattened hair.

Careening across the room, Robbie throws his arms around Sully's legs at calf height.

"Who have we here?" he asks, bending to the child's level. He scoops Robbie up in one arm and stands. "Barrel-chested, ginger hair: this must be a wee Britten."

"Right you are. That's Robbie; I'm Fizzy." They shake hands across the couch. Robbie launches himself out of Sully's arms; Fizzy catches him by a narrow margin.

"Emily Carpenter," I announce; she waves from behind her sketch pad. "And Caro Jackson."

"This is Claire."

Sully shakes the baby's hand as he takes her from Caro. "My God, she's small compared to that bruiser!" he exclaims.

"She's a solid one, for four months. If you think she's small, just wait 'til you see your own!"

Turning to me with hope in his eyes, "I *can't* wait," he says softly, bouncing Claire against his chest.

"Well!" Caro says decisively. "We must be shoving off. There will be three starving Crown Counsel arriving home with nary a dinner in sight."

"That's a lie, Caro!" Emily exclaims, tearing two sheets from her pad. "I bet you've got the timer set on the oven or something in the Crockpot."

Sully tests the air. "Something smells wonderful here. Thank you."

Emily hands me the sketches casually. "I've got a thing for babies," she confides. "Don't tell the others; I'm a wee bit pregnant myself."

"How wonderful!" I smile, glancing at the pictures. A detailed drawing of me, holding Claire; and a quick sketch of Sully with Claire that so completely captures the unconscious sorrow behind his hope it makes my eyes well. I feel a strong empathy with this woman. "Thank you." We surprise each other with a hug.

"Cheerio, James! We'll have a party as soon as your bride is back on her feet."

Sully stands in the doorway, Claire still perched in the curve of his arm. "You look very natural with that," Caro says, inclining her head. "Still, I'd like to have her back. Ron's rather attached to her."

Hang on, baby! I tell my own as Sully transfers the child to her mother; *hang on.*

"Nice bunch," Sully comments, stripping off his tie. "The Merry English Wives." He settles on the couch beside me. I lean into his embrace. "Perfect mates for the Jolly English Men."

"The MEWs and the JEMs."

Kissing the top of my head, "Cameron is an honorary JEM by virtue of his marriage to Fizzy," he elaborates. "He's more accurately a JAM."

"Being?"

"A Jolly Australian Man. I can't wait for you to meet them all!"

"Nor can I. I'm tired of playing Camille."

"The only JEM you may not take to is Tony Carpenter," he warns.

"But I thought you liked him!" I exclaim. "You're always talking about what a wild and crazy guy he is."

"He's good entertainment value, love," he sighs, "but none of us admires him as a *man.* When he's not being a party animal, he's perennially in training for some athletic event or other — the Boston Marathon, the Hawaiian Iron-Man — to the exclusion of anything resembling family life. He's also a bloodless son of a bitch in court."

Raking my hand through his hair, "I've heard *you're* a bloodless S.O.B. in court, too, James Riordan," I accuse fondly. It's hard to imagine this uxorious marshmallow — currently caressing the bulge of his unborn child — taking a hard line with anyone.

A loony, cross-eyed grin: "Yes, but with Tony it's real; with me, it's all an act."

"What are these scars?" Dr. McCassland asks from behind my tented knees. "I didn't want to ask you in front of James — although I'm sure he's noticed, unless you only make love under cover of darkness."

"He knows." I hand him my standard line. "I had some problems when I was a teenager."

"The anorexia, and all."

"Yes."

"Let's talk about that."

"Why?" I bristle irrationally. "What has it to do with anything?"

He takes my hand to pull me upright, holds it while he speaks. "For one thing, your body is just now starting to recover from amenorrhea. You're pregnant by the most remote of odds." He shakes his head. "I'm your *ally* here, Mariah, not your enemy! I need to know if there have been any other effects, like heart damage, that might interfere with the course of the pregnancy and delivery. Get dressed and we'll chat."

I give him *The Reader's Digest* condensed version, but I leave nothing out. "That's my sordid tale."

"Achh," he rubs his hands through his thinning ginger hair. "That's a *sad* tale, lass. I hope the worst is behind you."

"Tell me I'm not going to lose this baby and I'll safely say it is."

"You're not going to lose this baby."

I rise to leave. "Then, the worst is behind me."

Treaty negotiations having ceased, my baby and my body have reached an uneasy truce. The child has gained the upper hand and annexed my body completely.

"So what did Doctor Sandy have to say today?" asks Sully.

"We now return to our regularly scheduled marriage," I announce, in mock-TV voice.

"Really?" Sully sounds like an excited kid. "Are you sure?" I nod. He sweeps me up in his arms and deposits me, laughing, on the bed.

Stroking his jaw, I whisper, "Thank you for your patience."

"Patience?" His face creases. "Riah, love; much as I like to share my toys with my best friend, I'd forswear making love forever if I had to. I wouldn't do anything to jeopardize your health or the baby's. You know that."

I know that. It's not just Sully's hyperbole; he's proved it once. Gratitude fans the flame of desire.

And *hormones* fan the flame of desire — seemingly in direct proportion to the increase in my girth as the pregnancy progresses.

"You're deliciously randy, Mariah!" Sully exclaims. "I can hardly keep up with you. If *this* is what causes a pregnant woman's glow, I swear we'll have twelve children. Maybe twenty."

It's almost unseemly, I think. I spend a lot of time with the MEWs, alone and in combination. I enjoy their company immensely for its own sake, yet part of me seeks it out as preoccupation against the urgency of horniness.

As close as we've become, I dare not ask Caro or Fizzy if they've experienced this second trimester carnality. My breasts (*breasts! mine!*) are tender and hypersensitive; the merest whisper of a touch – my own, Sully's, it seems not to matter – causes all my erectile tissue to stand at attention. We make love often and still I find myself masturbating two or three times a day. It's as if my entire body, from the weight of my uterus out, has become an organ of sensual pleasure.

"What do you think it feels like, for the baby?" I speculate aloud in Sully's arms.

He chuckles throatily. "Like a wave machine. Or a Jacuzzi, I imagine. Lovely, lovely contractions giving him a full-body massage. All those endorphins you're sharing: it must feel like love."

Seizing on these words like a mantra, I use them to push aside my doubts when I find my hand straying during a nap, or waking my husband in the middle of the night. I try to replicate the sensations musically; churn out much blissful, orgasmic chaff. And a few kernels of substance that capture – for me, anyway – the essence of pleasure and the amniotic fluid of love.

Thumping against Sully's hand at rest on my belly, the baby wakes me. It's as if he's using my ribs for a diving board, launching himself into the birth canal.

I should get up to pee, I think, reluctant to unmould myself from the warmth of Sully's limbs. A blustery late February morning; the bathroom tile will be cold. Quite suddenly, warm wetness floods us both. Sully leaps up when the dampness hits him, throws the covers back on the bed.

"Ohmygod!" A dark stain spreads across the front of his boxers as if he's wet himself. I giggle uncontrollably. "Contractions?"

"I don't know; I just woke up."

He scrabbles madly on his bureau for the stopwatch.

"Relax. There *is* a doctor in the house."

Our resident obstetrician makes a house call on his way to the office, at Sully's behest. "Stay at home as long as possible. No sense going in too soon; you'll be more comfortable here." He grins. "You're two and a half minutes away from the hospital; believe me, I've timed it. See you later."

Much later. Sandy stops by at lunch and again at dinner time. "Not making a lot of progress," he admits. "We'll run you over to the hospital after I eat, get you set up on a drip. Let's see if we can have this youngster by midnight."

Admitted, IV'd, monitored, drugged a little for pain. "Nice strong contractions — "

"Tell me about it!"

" — But we're not getting anywhere. Give it a little longer."

Sandy's barely left the room before the midwife assigned to us races out the door behind him. He checks the monitors. "Looks like Caesarean time. Sorry."

Sully squeezes my hand, kisses me hurriedly. "When we see each other next, we'll have a baby." I wave. "I love you, Riah!" he calls after me.

Sitting in the chair beside the bed, his eyes closed — I would have thought he was asleep, except for his knee. Bouncing, bouncing.

"Sully," I croak.

He leaps out of the chair, kneels beside the bed. His eyes are red-rimmed, as if he's been weeping. Soft thing! I think fondly.

"You have a son," he says.

"And is he beautiful?"

"He is."

"Ten fingers and ten toes?"

Kissing my hand, "Yes, my darling. Ten fingers and ten toes," he says huskily. "You'll see him in a while, after Sandy's been by." He kisses my forehead. "I've got to go now."

I'm so groggy I don't think to ask him, "Why?"

Sandy McCassland comes in, accompanied by a nurse wheeling a bassinet. "Mariah, you've got a strong, strapping lad! He was posterior," he explains, "and had the cord wrapped twice around his neck. If you'd managed to deliver him, he might not have made it. Isn't Nature marvellous? It was a good thing you made no progress."

The nurse settles him into the crook of my right arm. Oh, yes! He is beautiful. I grin up at Sandy. His face is more serious than I expect in answer to my delight.

"Now, Mariah," he says quietly. "He has a rather rare condition that will in no way affect his health."

My bowels turn to water. What? What? I unwrap him anxiously. Jesus God! I hear Sully's vow: *I will never lie to you.* He hasn't; not according to the letter of the law.

Sandy clears his throat. "It's a limb-reduction defect, sometimes called phocomelism. It means 'seal limbs'."

Grinding my eyes shut, "Which is a bit of a misnomer," I continue for him in a raw whisper, "because the hand is more developed than a seal's flipper; it's the arm that is vestigial."

"You have some experience with this?"

"The child's father is phocomelic."

"But James is quite sound!" He is flabbergasted.

I press my head to my son's. "James seems not to be the child's biological father," I supply hysterically. Oh, sweet Jesus! *Sully!*

Sandy looks stricken. "We'll leave you alone for a few minutes. Then the nurse will come to take the baby back to the nursery so you can get some rest."

A flood of sorrow. Not for the child, but for Sully.

I didn't tell him about Doug.

" 'To do no harm, to tell no lie': lovely vows, son," Jimmy Riordan said at the wedding, clapping Sully in his arms. "Did you include the legal fine print: 'errors and omissions excepted'?"

How we'd all laughed at Jimmy's joke.

Errors and omissions excepted. Errors *of* omission. *Sins* of omission. *Primum non nocere.* To do no harm. Isn't that part of the Hippocratic oath?

I didn't tell him about Doug.

Oh, sure – he knew Doug had spent the night at the house, even that we'd "had a good talk" and resolved some "old issues." But I didn't tell him Doug had passed the night in my bed.

The old lies: *what Sully doesn't know can't hurt him.* I was *protecting him from unnecessary pain.* Oh, yes, Mariah – all the answers! Even though I *knew* he'd have understood, given the circumstances. Closure. Closure with Doug, at last, leaving me free – completely free – for our future together. *He would have understood.*

But no, no – Mariah, you slut! – you had to protect your*self*. Call it the "spirit" of *primum non nocere*. But call a spade a spade: you fucked an old boyfriend on the eve of your engagement and you didn't tell your betrothed — because *it wouldn't look good on you*. Such a blemish on the image of Sully's Perfect *fucking* Mate! Mouthing words of *love* and *choice* with your crotch still sticky with another man's come — and then leaving it off the Notice of Disclosure because *it wouldn't look good on you*.

Look at you! So full of love, these months, for the miracle child — the icing on the wedding cake. Look at your fine maternal feelings for the innocent babe! You, who are so unremittingly inward-focused, focus on this: *you resent this child because he isn't Sully's*.

"What would you do if you knew your child would be born retarded?" I'd asked Doug that day at the psych hospital. *"What would you do if you knew your child would be born with only one arm?"* he'd answered. *"It's only a matter of degree, Mariah — none of us is perfect."*

None of us is perfect, Mariah — least of all yourself. You look at this tiny, beautiful baby in your arms and you'd give him up — wouldn't you? *Wouldn't you?* If you could turn back the clock, you'd let him slip out on the tide with the blood and the detritus so that Sully wouldn't know, so you could save your perfect face, so you could save your perfect marriage.

Look at you now, weeping so hard your skin splits along the fault lines of the incision. *Your* fault; your fault. Weeping, not because you feel guilty for sleeping with Doug. Not because you've destroyed the only man who loved you unconditionally, or lied by omission. But — *because you got caught*.

Taking the baby from me, Sandy puts the blood-soaked bundle in the bassinet. A firm arm around my shoulders and a Scots accent in my ear, "Hush now, lass, hush." He reaches for the call button without letting me go. "A syringe and a dose of Demerol, stat, and a suture tray; she's torn open the incision."

No, no. No Demerol, no. It'll take the edge off this pain and that's no good. I *need* this pain, I *want* this pain. *More* pain, *all* the pain. I said the worst was behind me, Sandy, but I was wrong. This is the worst. I want to die of this pain, Sandy. Sandy, *I want to die*.

I am round and bloated, egg-shaped. Swimming. Swimming in a river that suddenly diverges into two streams. Red stream. Black stream. Each presided over by a lifeguard — Sully in red, Doug in black. I feel myself going under. They both rush to my side, hold my ovoid body adrift in the converging stream. I turn to Sully. Tell him! Tell him! Choose. I can't. But by not opening my mouth, it seems, I *have* chosen. Doug holds his arms out to me and we merge, drifting off into the blackness, out of Sully's range.

Change one thing.

My son. What will I name this child? All the names we've chosen have quite fled my mind. How can I rest when I don't know where Sully is, what he's thinking, what he'll do? *He is impetuous, given to setting himself aflame on camping trips, succumbing to unusual and dangerous dares.* I throw up into the basin on my tray. The nurse says it's from the anaesthesia, but I know it's from fear.

"Emily sends her love; she's been ordered to bed," Fizzy explained when she and Caro came to visit.

"Ah, Christ." I didn't feel like visitors, but hoped they might have news of Sully. Sandy's had none.

"Word has it James is out on an epic bender," Caro offered. "The Irish certainly take their celebrating to extremes," she said with some distaste. "Ron's with him."

Relief. "He's upset," I explained, preparing them. "The baby has a birth defect."

Shocked, horrified, they tried to cover their dismay, rallied bravely. Took, and offered, comfort where they could: "It won't have any bearing on his health."

But my marriage; what bearing will it have on my marriage? And, of course, I couldn't share the reason for Sully's seemingly extravagant grief with these women, my friends.

"Women are more practical," Fizzy philosophized, stroking the baby's downy cheek. "We accept, and go on. Leave it to the men to blame themselves!"

There's no question of that, in this case. The blame is all mine.

They stepped up their visits when they realized Sully hadn't been coming by at all; it was almost more than I could bear.

On the morning of the third day, feeling stronger physically, I've determined I will bathe the baby – still nameless – on my own.

But when the nurse rolls in the bassinet, she announces cheerily.
"Already bathed!"

"You shouldn't have!" I insist. "I need the practice!"

"We didn't, dear. Daddy was in the nursery this morning. Bright and early. Gave the little tyke a very competent bath, very competent indeed."

Daddy was in the nursery!

"Said he'd be up to see you later. Left something for you."

She hands me a book, tucked between the side of the bassinet and its mattress.

"Thank you," I choke.

Name Your Baby. I open it, take out the papers nestled there. Application for Birth Certificate, filled out. And a single, folded sheet in Sully's script:

> I had some dreams for the child of my loins,
> had names picked out that would sound swell
> when hollered from the stoop.
> (Why can't we name the children precisely as we feel?
> Champion! Beloved! Brave!
> instead of veiling pride in ethnic variation:
> Niall. Casey. Dave.)
>
> In my anger I have considered many names for your son –
>   Tristram. Benoni. Arvel. Scanlon.
> When all is said and done, I've made a vow,
> can find no consolation in my rage.
> If you can but forgive me, dearest love! –
> any child of yours is child of mine:
> by love, by blood, by claim.
> And, so, I give you
>   Riordan, Anghus Gage –
> my "choice," my "pledge," my name.

Sully asking for *my* forgiveness! No, no; this isn't right. *I'm* the transgressor here; I'm the one who's slipped a changeling between the sheets of our marriage bed.

Flipping through the baby book, I look up the names Sully's included in the poem. Tristram — sorrowful labour; Benoni — son of my sorrow; Arvel — wept over; Scanlon — a little scandal or snarer. These first four names are highlighted with broad, angry slashes of his yellow pen, the one he uses to mark up briefs and statements, statutes and *All England Reports*. I feel his doubt, his rage. His pain.

And I feel his acceptance in his words — *any child of yours is child of mine: by love, by blood, by claim* — and in the names he's chosen for my child. *Our* child. Anghus — the choice. Gage — a pledge.

I press my weeping face against the open pages of the book.

When I look up, he's standing in the doorway. He looks like hell: face drawn and lined; eyes pouched, red; shoulders sagging. No jaunty Sully walk, no Sully smile. *What have I done to this man?*

Placing one thigh on my bed, he buries his face in my hair. And holds me, holds me, sobbing into my ear. When he draws away, he looks into my eyes. "Do you want to go to him?"

To Doug? "No! No!" I shake my head wildly. This is one thought I haven't entertained; how could *he*? "Not even if you leave me!"

He winces. "I won't lie to you: I've thought about it. This was very difficult for me. I'm not proud of the way I've reacted."

With his head on my shoulder, I run my fingers through his wiry hair. I want to tell him how much I love him, how sorry I am. "I wouldn't blame you," I say, stroking his dear head. "Surely, it's grounds for annulment, if ever there were any." I lift his chin so I can see his eyes. "I release you from your vow," I tell him, "if that's what you want."

He utters a strangled cry. Has he misunderstood my motive? He's a man of his word — I don't want him to be coerced by his own sense of honour.

"Is that what *you* want?"

"No!" I clutch at him like someone drowning. "I *love* you." I can't withhold the words; he has to know. "But if you can't feel the same, I won't hold you to it. It's too much to ask."

"You read the poem?"

"Yes."

"I meant those words; I meant my vows. Get a priest and a Bible — I'll swear them all over again." He nods minutely, cocks a pained, emphatic eyebrow. "If *you* will."

"I will."

His hand, his perfect hand, held out to me palm up: I press my own against it. We repeat our vows, solemn at first, sincere. By the time we finish we're grinning, drowned out by the lusty accompaniment of the baby's wails.

Sully takes him from the bassinet, holds him up for inspection. "Probably soaked," he says. Laying out all the equipment, he starts to change the child's diaper on the foot of my bed as if he's been doing it for years.

"How can you do this?"

He seems to take my words literally. "I've spent a lot of time in the nursery, in between hangovers. Have you met the head nurse?" I shake my head. "Ooo, she's vicious! But I'm her boy, now." A self-deprecating grin. "I've changed all the babies; given them all a bath. Every shade of skin in the spectrum. All different. All dear." He looks up at me. "But none more dear than this one," he adds huskily.

He takes a cotton ball soaked in alcohol, dresses the baby's umbilicus. "Oh, now, hush. That's cold, isn't it? Shh. Almost done."

Look at him, bending from such an awkward height over such a tiny child! I bite my lip.

"Before we were married," he glances at me, "we talked about children. And when you expressed doubts you'd be able, we agreed we could adopt. Right?"

I nod.

"And if the situation was reversed and I was sterile, we'd arrange a sperm donor and I'd love that child as my own. The only difference here is — I know the sperm donor because," he chokes, "because he's left a rather distinctive genetic mark."

Sully offers his finger to the baby's little hand and receives a reflexive death grip. He gently shakes his finger loose and tucks all the flailing limbs into a firmly swaddled package, something I've yet to manage.

"You are a *good man*," I whisper. The inadequacy of these words!

"No," he shakes his head. "No. I'm a selfish man," he says, handing the tidy bundle to me to nurse. "When I weigh the alternative — living without you — I have no choice."

Anghus Gage — "the choice, the only choice"; my "pledge," my vow.

He places a couple of pillows under my right arm to take the weight, rests his thigh on the edge of the bed again. "I want only two things from you: that you'll never tell Doug."

I nod.

"And that we'll never speak of this again."

My eyes flood.

"It might seem harsh, to place conditions on unconditional love, but that's the cost of this contract. I don't think it's too much to ask." He takes my free hand, holds it to his face. "I vow I'll love you and our child with all my heart, but I can't do that — do you see? — if we're always analysing it, or discussing the hows and whys."

He kisses my palm. "I realize you'll have some explaining to do when your parents come. And I'm sure I'll have words with mine. But there'll be no scenes — do you understand? — no comment. There'll be no sympathy, no condolences, no commiseration. Only congratulations. We'll all get on with it. And if your parents — or mine — can't cope with that, then we'll have to cut them out of our lives. I'll have no whispering around my son — ever." He stares, fascinated, at the infant in my arms. "Except when he's asleep," he adds, *sotto voce*.

I lean toward him; we kiss gently. "Is he Anghus? or is he Gage?" I ask.

Sully cocks his head one way, then the other. "I think he's Gage."

I think so, too.

Despite our efforts, it's not so easy to put it behind us. I ache with the need to talk about it, but I don't question Sully's prohibition; I have no right of appeal in this court. I probe conversational gaps for hints of his true feelings. No one can be so forgiving, can he? Or is forgiveness, like love — as Sully seems to think it is — an act of will?

My eyes blur when he brings us home. Home. Our first home, tainted with this terrible, terrible poison. It's as if all the walls have been painted black, but no one will mention it. Eve, surveying a defoliated Eden: *What have I done?*

The weight of it grows heavier with every ministration, every soulful glance he casts at me, at Gage, so that I'm unable to keep my head erect, my eyes open under the burden of his forgiveness. I can't bear to look, to see the effort it costs him. He planned his whole life for me and see how I repay him! *Sully.*

"Why don't you get up and have a shower, Riah," he urges. "I've got coffee brewing. The baby's asleep. Breakfast will be ready when you're done." He takes my elbow and I make the supreme effort of placing my feet on the floor. "Don't lock the door. Just shout if you need anything."

Before closing the shower door, I examine myself in the mirror. *My body is not my own*; it belongs to a stranger. The stomach's all puffy. Unbaked bread dough, zipped like a child's pyjama bag. Fuzz sprouting on my legs. I take Sully's straight razor from the sink.

The spray stings my nipples; my breasts are huge and hard as rocks, engorged with sustenance for my son. I'm not a woman, I'm a dairy product.

My uterus cramps and, with a little push, like a mini-birth, I expel slippery gobs of something the consistency of calves' liver. Clots. The water flows rusty with my blood, the colour of shame. *I will greatly multiply your sorrow and your conception; in pain you shall bring forth children. Your desire shall be for your husband, and he shall rule over you.* I am not Sully's wife; I'm his millstone. His albatross. I'm here on his sufferance, by virtue of his virtue. Not partner, not equal. *Less than, not equal to.*

More clots; it will not stop. This is somehow gratifying. I reach up to the ledge, find the razor by touch. Lower myself gingerly to the floor of the tub, press the femoral artery with my stump until it pops up plump and round, make a neat incision. One thigh, then the other, knowing that symmetry *can* be achieved. I watch while fresh blood mixes with the horrid clotted stuff. Can't keep my eyes open.

I hear him at the door. "Mariah, are you almost done?"

"Yes, my love." Almost done.

"Do you need a hand?" Jiggles the door handle. "I told you not to lock it!"

Calls my name. Scrabbling through the tool box.

Shower door slides on its track. "Jesus Christ!"

Don't take the Lord's name in vain in vein in vein.

Baby howls wailing wailing. Sully shouting, outside the bathroom window, shouting for Sandy. Shh, don't wake Sandy; Sandy brings babies. Sandy brings babies all night long. Gage. Gage. I feel my milk let down. What a mess — blood and milk all mixed.

"Post-partum depression, lass!" Sandy holds my hand. "It happens; it's not a crime. We've got you started on antidepressants. You'll feel like a new woman when they kick in." He hazards a stilted smile. "I'll be back in a bit."

I nod my thanks as he leaves.

Sully is practically in bed with me, supporting my head against his chest, his long legs stretched out. I turn my ear against his shirt so I can hear his heartbeat.

"I've told everyone you were haemorrhaging; that that's why you're back in the hospital."

Look Mariah! You've made a liar out of your sainted husband, the Last Ethical Lawyer. Brought him down to your level — a marriage of equals.

"Post-partum depression," he states.

"It's more than that." My voice is harsh.

"I know." He angles his body so he can look into my eyes.

His response catches me by surprise. I study his face carefully. Does he know? Can he know?

"Ach, the poor wee lass!" He exaggerates Sandy's Scots accent. "So pitiful, so weak; succumbing to hormones and post-partum depression." He shakes his head. "I see you, Mariah! I see you seize power. You take it in your hand like a loaded gun. Untenable positions — you turned the gun against your grandfather; you turned the razor against yourself because you couldn't use it against me."

"No! No." The truth is *I couldn't bear what I saw about myself.*

He shakes his head again, inhales deeply. "You lost control because you couldn't bear me forgiving you for something you didn't feel guilty about in the first place. You're right: you shouldn't feel guilty. And I needn't forgive. That was my mistake. It placed a hideous burden on you."

I squeeze my eyes shut against the sight of his face.

"Riah. Riah. I needn't forgive — because I *accept.* I see you three-dimensionally," he sobs, "shadow and light. I wish you could see me the way I see you."

My eyes fly open. "What? What do you mean?"

"You don't see me in three dimensions because you see only the light."

"I know you're not perfect! I didn't buy into a fairy tale."

He smiles sadly. "It's your own projected light — it blinds you to me. You've always despised me for loving you. *Always.* You can't see anything good about yourself, so anyone who loves you must be mistaken. Or a fool. That's why you broke up with me when we were fifteen."

I make a sound to stop him.

"Two-dimensional Sully, single-minded Sully – loves Mariah to dis-
traction. Plans his whole life around her. What a fool! That's what you
see even now. You think: Sully's so weak he'll forgive anything, anything,
to be with her. And so – "

He crouches beside the bed so I'm forced to look at him.

" – you take control with your razor. You remove me from the equation the only way left to you. *Because you can't get rid of me any other way.*"

He buries his head in his hand and I think he's finished. Surely he's
finished.

"I love you for your strength, Mariah!" His face is a twisted thing.
"Here – you take control. You say the word, and *I'm gone.* I'd rather forswear you, and our marriage, and our child, than cause you harm," his
voice breaks, "than have you do this, this *violence* to yourself."

Taking my hand, he traces my lifeline.

"Don't hate me, Riah! Loving you has never been simple. Or safe. It's
the biggest risk I take." He draws a ragged breath. "Let me love you –
shadow, light, and all. Sure, it's my biggest weakness. But it's also my
greatest strength. Riah."

Kissing the tears from my face, "The other day, with all my fine
talk," he says, "there was one question that didn't get asked. And it's
probably the most important one. I don't want to know the answer.
Don't *judge* yourself: just think about it."

I steel myself.

"The question is not whether *I* can love Gage." His voice comes out
a whisper: "Can *you?*"

Christ! Open heart surgery with a steak knife. *You do have a way of getting to the heart of the matter, don't you, Sully?*

"Hush, love!" he says urgently, climbing onto the bed with me. "I'm
sorry! Shh, you'll open the incision again. Shh."

Sully holds the scalpel. Go ahead, open her up – see what's inside. She's
only held together by the very finest grade of suture material, after all.
How can such an extraordinarily principled man stay married to a
woman of whom such a question needs be asked? Such a selfish,
inward-*fucking*-focused woman, compared to him, who is so selfless. So
able to get beyond himself sufficiently to see the issue, to pose this terrible, terrible question.

What's the only barrier to my love for Gage? *My ego.* My all-
consuming ego: *Gage doesn't reflect well on me.* It's not just his imperfec-

tion, his — *say it* — handicap. It's that *I* produced him, handicap and all, in an exercise of bad judgement — *skinny-dipping in the gene pool with Doug.* To have this error flaunted before my eyes, every day, every day, for my whole life and his — *can I do this?*

And what if I cannot, Sully? All well and good to ask the question, but what if the answer is "no"? Can you stage-manage this version of our lives? Are you prepared to cue our friends, our family — and feed them what line? that Gage has died? Or will you tell them the truth: that Mariah couldn't be reminded daily of her imperfections, her errors, so *we gave him away?*

There's no choice. If I can't love Gage I must finish what I started in the bathtub hours ago. Can you handle that, Sully? *Mariah killed herself and left me to raise another man's child alone.* Are these the options, Sully?

Whatever happened to the perfect woman? *What do you want her to be? She'll be it. What do you want her to do? She'll do it. What makes you angry? She'll never do that again.*

Except — I'm not perfect. He said it; he meant it. And I can't hide from him. *He sees me.* The real me, the flawed me. That he can even ask the question means he does indeed *see me,* yet he expects that I can rise above myself. *Can I do this?*

"Where's Gage?" I force myself to ask. "How is he?"

"He's with Caro." He smiles wanly. "I think she's wet-nursing him."

Another woman wet-nursing my baby! Overcome with rage and sorrow, my nipples tingle and my milk lets down, soaking the front of my nightgown. I press my arms across my bosom to keep it all in. I fail. I press my lips together to keep sound from escaping. I fail at that, too. Sully holds me; I get his shirt all wet.

"James," comes a warning voice, "you seem to be upsetting my patient." Sandy McCassland harrumphs in the doorway. "How are you feeling, lass?"

It doesn't matter how I feel. I want to spit these words out like a curse. Damn you. Damn you! But as I analyse them I realize that it does *not* matter how I *feel.* My feelings are not the issue here. What matters now is what I *do.*

I turn to Sandy. "Can I have the baby in to nurse?"

He drags his hand through his hair. "You ought not to nurse him; the antidepressants are concentrated in breast milk."

"Then take me off the drugs! I *have* to nurse him," I insist.

Taking a deep breath, Sandy blows it out in a measured dose through puffed-out cheeks, alternating his glance between us as if spectating at Wimbledon.

"You make things so difficult, Mariah!" he sighs. "On one hand, you'll bond better with the wee lad if you nurse him. And if you bond, the bonding itself might help bring you out of the depression without drugs." He clears his throat. "On the other, without medication – and even with all the bonding in the world – you might remain severely depressed. It's a tremendous risk."

"Give me a few weeks," I plead. "If I'm not getting better I'll stop nursing and go back on the drugs." Sandy's face is pained. "Please."

"All right. We'll try that. I'll speak to the psychiatrist; I doubt he'll approve. But I fought to keep you out of St. Brendan's," he exhales, "so I'll fight him on this, too." He nods to me. "James, a word in your ear."

Sully leaves the room, returns wearing a grim expression. "I just spoke with our landlord in the hallway." He offers a tired smile. "We've been evicted – with the utmost regret."

"What?"

He pushes the hair out of my eyes. "Sandy says he's happy to continue as your doctor, but he's too emotionally involved to have us as tenants. It clouds his judgement as a physician to worry about you every time he hears the shower running downstairs. Especially if you insist on going off the medication."

"Oh. Shit." I bite my lip. "Sorry."

"You're sure about this?"

I rub my eyes. "I'm not sure about much, Sully. Except this one thing."

He cocks an eyebrow. "Being?"

"Dearly as I love her, I'll be damned if I'll have Caro Jackson nursing my son one more day. She'll pass on antibodies for hyperorganization, turning Gage against me in all my disarray. I won't stand for it."

I see a flicker of light in his eyes – a light I feared I might never see again, so thoroughly had I extinguished it. The embers seem merely to be banked, however, waiting to be kindled by hope.

Suddenly I want, more than anything, to see that light flaming in his eyes. I will *do* anything to have it back, burning for me. Laughing with me. Loving me.

To see the big picture requires distance. Look at a Seurat painting. Step forward and examine the composition and you see each of his dots and brush strokes. The patch of black comprises many colours, shades, nuances. Light. Change one thing — even your perspective — and the fragments merge into a whole, of which the seemingly all-encompassing darkness is only a part.

Sully sees this; Sully *knows.* Perhaps he's right; perhaps love *is* an act of will.

⁓

"I'm off to the airport," Sully announces, bending to me from his looming height, his utilitarian words fluttering against my ear like endearment.

My arms around his neck in a death grip, I inhale the subtle scent of the plain alcohol he's always used for aftershave. Who's he trying to impress? I smile. He's already shaved today.

"Is it too late to stop them?" I plead. "Can't you have a chat while the plane is being refuelled, then shove 'em back on it?"

He sits down on the bed beside me, holds me tight. "Shh, Riah. It'll be all right. You can do it."

I'm not so sure. Whatever gains I've made in the past few days are obliterated by the prospect of my parents' arrival. Despite his assurances, Sully's aware of the danger. He won't leave me alone. Caro Jackson has been enlisted, ostensibly to help me deal physically with Gage in his absence. He's afraid.

"Your parents love you, Mariah," he says fiercely.

"I know." But what will they *think*? What will they *say*? I've been rehearsing their words since I unwrapped Gage's swaddling under Sandy's sympathetic gaze two weeks ago.

My father. How can I bear to read my failure, and his disappointment in me, in his eyes: *Haven't I taught you anything, Mariah? Weren't you the master of vigilance, well-schooled in cause and effect? How could you not have anticipated the consequences?* I'd almost rather finish off the job I started in the bath than face him. But for Sully, I might.

Relaxing my stranglehold, I draw back to let him see conviction in my smile: *I can do this.* "You'd better get going."

He kisses me gratefully, launches himself from the bed before he can change his mind. "I'll only be an hour or so. Try to get some sleep."

How can I sleep with Caro puttering around in the other room, chattering to Claire and Gage? A cup of tea and a dose of her capable calmness might set me up for the ordeal ahead. Then again, I need to marshal my strength. I tuck Sully's pillow against my bosom and close my eyes.

The sound of the car in the driveway wakes me. My breasts are leaking; Gage will need feeding soon. Or, more accurately, *I* will need Gage to feed soon.

A shadow passes across the knife of light between the curtains. I slide out of bed, drawn to peer through the gap. My father: standing on the rim of the hill looking out over the vista, wreathed in smoke.

A gentle tap. "Come in," I call.

Mom pokes her head around the door. I let the curtain fall closed on the image of my father. "Hi."

Clutching her grandson against her breast with one arm, Mom steps across the room to enfold me in the other. "Oh, Mariah!" We sink to the end of the bed, weeping over the baby between us: tears of sorrow and acceptance.

Relief — warm and sweet like Gage's baby smell — shoots through me like a drug. One down, one to go. "Daddy?"

"He's outside," she nods toward the window, "smoking himself hoarse."

"Not one word, Mom," I hear myself say, relief replaced with rage. "If he says *one word*, I swear: you'll be raising this child yourself." My mother stares at me, alarmed. "Believe me, I *know* how he'll judge me. But I've already judged myself."

Standing, I pull my nightgown up around my waist, do a little *plié* to reveal the fresh embroidery on my thighs. Her face crumples in such pain I'm forced to question the wisdom of this hasty revelation.

"Sully seems so, so composed." She looks toward the door. "Was he *cruel* to you?"

"No." I let the nightgown fall. "No. Sully's a fucking saint." Mom's eyebrow registers the harshness of the judgement. "You know what he's like," I temper. "He was en*tirely* too forgiving." *Virtue and flaw.* "But I was not. I saw myself," I point to the place where my father stands, "through Daddy's eyes."

"How can you say that?" If possible, Mom's face is even more pained than it was a moment ago. "He loves you, Mariah! He's always wanted you to be happy. If he's upset, it's only because he wonders – as I do – if your husband is strong enough to get through this with you."

"Because he's not sure *he* would, under similar circumstances!" I hiss.

"Now – you're judging *him*," Mom says quietly. "Give him a few minutes. Then let him speak for himself." Gage stirs in his grandmother's arms. "Are *you* strong enough for this, my darling?"

I stare at my son. "I wasn't a few days ago," I admit, "while I still harboured delusions of my own perfectibility." Mom's eyes crinkle minutely, giving me courage. "I have to do it – for Gage, for Sully. Sully knows what I am – and he loves me in spite of it!"

"So do I." She brushes the tears from my eyes, smiles, nods. "So does your father."

Does he really? This hope – the possibility that he might – is so important to me I suddenly wonder just whose image was last in mind as I drew Sully's razor down my thighs.

The clearing of a throat. My dad is framed in the doorway. "Hello, sweetheart."

Mom stands, gives my hand a little squeeze, then leaves with Gage.

"Hi, Daddy."

Wrapping me in his fierce embrace, he growls, "I love you, baby," kissing my forehead. "And so does James. He's a *good man*, Mariah. You're going to be all right."

"Yes. Yes, we are," I nod – almost convinced, for the first time.

In bed, at the end of the endless day, Sully rubs his jaw against my cheek.

"Ow!"

"What?"

Drawing my stump across his face, "Stubble, you Neanderthal!" I tease. "But you shaved before you went to the airport." I flick on the bedside lamp, raise myself on one elbow.

He closes his eyes against the light. I kiss his eye socket and the spidery lashes nestled there.

"I'm using an electric shaver now," he says, opening his eyes to gauge the vowel that steals breath from my lungs.

"I saw it charging in the bathroom, but I thought it was my dad's. *He* has no beard to speak of," I finish lamely. The implication – *Sully doesn't trust me.* "I'm sorry."

Shaking his head, he places a finger against my lips, and gets out of bed. A muted buzz issues from the bathroom. He slips back under the covers and presses his face to mine — "Better?" — cool from the rapid evaporation of alcohol so fresh it tingles in my nostrils, on my lips.

"You don't have to do this." *Don't treat me like glass.* "Don't change our lives."

"Just a minor adjustment to the routine," he says, missing my point. "No big deal."

I lay my head against his chest. *How many minor adjustments will compensate for lack of trust? Will we be reduced to eating with chopsticks from paper plates? Or emptying the medicine chest so I can't OD on vitamins and Tylenol? How about hiring a nanny — for me! — so that I'll never be alone?*

"Sully." I lift my head. "Sully, you can't stop me if I want to do it again." His brow furrows; I press the sorrowful lines flat with my fingertips. "You have to trust me when I say I *won't.* Otherwise, we can't go on."

"It's *me,*" he whispers hoarsely. "I can't hold my hand steady enough to shave with that razor any more, knowing how you used it."

Jesus Christ. Minor adjustments.

"Don't leave me alone with them!" I somehow forbear from speaking the words aloud, but they ache in my throat as I wave Sully off to work — his first day back since Gage's birth.

Caro takes my dad out to procure a Bermuda driver's licence. He's run out of smokes and is so antsy from the enforced relaxation he's resorted to washing all the ground floor windows of our apartment, only to find them frosted with salt spray after an overnight gale. My mother has assumed command of the kitchen. And Gage. She brings him to me to nurse, then bustles him off — "So you can get some rest." I let him go with something of the same sorrow with which I waved Sully away to the office.

But I can't rest. I lie awake, listening for Gage in the other room, desperate for him to wake so I can hold him. My breasts leak when I think of him — soaking the nursing pads in my bra, which in turn saturate my nipples so they're wet and wrinkled like fingertips too long in the bath by the time Gage is ready to feed.

After the next feeding I let Gage suckle long after he's fallen asleep, his gums moving imperceptibly, mysteriously. The suction is so strong

I gasp when I finally break the seal of his mouth. His lip is blistered, my nipple cracked.

Sully comes home from work to find me hunched over the baby's head, baptizing Gage with my tears. "Good Christ!" he breathes when he takes the child away from me, exposing a bleeding teat. He marches up the driveway to Sandy's back door with Gage tucked under his arm like a football.

"These plastic-lined nursing pads are an abomination," Sandy exclaims during his house call. "Your nipples never dry out with them. Fresh air's the best thing. Just don't let them get sunburned."

"I can't go topless!" I protest, blushing furiously.

"Keep the hatches of your nursing bra unbattened under your blouse," he suggests. "Let the air circulate. *Give* them a bit of sunlight when no one's looking."

I laugh giddily. "And a little water to help them grow?"

"If you get mastitis, you'll have to stop nursing." He looks at me levelly, assessing my mental state. I sober instantly.

"All right."

"By the way, Sandy." I hear Sully's voice as he walks our landlord past the bedroom window. "I found an apartment today. We'll move out at the end of the month, if you'll have us that long."

My heart trips over itself.

"I'll be sorry to lose you, James. Where's the new place?"

But Sully's answer is delivered out of range.

Blind fury claws at me. "Don't I have a say in this?" I hiss when Sully re-enters the bedroom.

"Sweetheart, you're not exactly in shape for house-hunting!"

"What about consultation?" I demand. "What kind of shape do I have to be in to *listen*?"

"All right, then. Listen."

But my mother chooses the moment to announce the evening meal. "Perhaps you can tell us all at dinner," I concede, letting him lead me to the table.

"It's on the north shore, Hamilton Parish." Sully waxes enthusiastic over the apartment, as if he has to sell it to us. Which he does; he has to sell it to *me*. "Not far from the water, beautiful view."

"Exposed to North Atlantic winter gales, you mean," I translate.

"We'll take long walks along the abandoned rail line," he says. "All the way to Flatts' Inlet by way of Shelly Bay." To my parents, "It's a nice shallow beach, great for kids. Or you can go as far as the causeway, to the east." Continuing his pitch, "It has central heat." He turns a benevolent expression on me. "It'll be nice and toasty for the baby. Two bedrooms," he checks points off against his fingers, "washer, dryer, all the mod cons, big yard. Garage. It's the entire main floor of the house."

"And the upstairs neighbours?" Axe murderers and child molesters who play loud music with a reggae backbeat at all hours?

"Ron and Caro."

Jesus Christ. I push away from the table – nearly upsetting my chair – and take refuge in the bedroom.

Sully flies in behind me, arms flapping. "*What?*" he demands in a low whisper. "What is *wrong* with you?"

"You *don't* trust me!" I accuse. "I'll be under surveillance, twenty-four hours a day!" His puzzlement only fuels my fury. "Why don't you just book me a padded cell in St. Brendan's? It'll have the same effect. If I'm not mad when we move in, I *will be* in short order!"

"They're our best friends, Mariah."

"That doesn't mean I want to sleep under the same roof with them!"

"Riah, Riah," Sully opens his arms to me. "It's a beautiful house. Ron and Caro saw it at lunch. They came back to get me when they found out the ground-floor apartment was available."

Mollified: "Why are they looking, anyway? They've got a great place just up the hill."

"It's not big enough. There's another baby on the way." Laughs at my expression. "You'll love it," he assures me, kissing the top of my head. "It'll be fun. If our babies keep us tied to the house, at least we'll have a live-in social life."

"I warn you, Sully." He looks at me quizzically. "Just don't say one word about the possibility that Caro's organizational skills might be absorbed by osmosis."

"No, ma'am, not one word." He grabs a book from the night stand, swears his oath on *Fifth Business.* "So help me God."

The patio is a heat trap for the watery March sunshine. Beyond the hibiscus hedge I can see down Trimingham Hill to the Dinghy Club where the yachts' bare masts bob like note-stems on a rippled staff. Some of the scooters and cars circling the roundabout trace a path up the hill opposite, where the hospital – oleander pink – is perched, or make their way into Hamilton along the harbour.

The viscosity of Bermuda light changes with the season, I've discovered. When we arrived in August – after our wedding – the summer light, like the heat and humidity, was as cloying and heavy as rendered animal fat to the palate. In the winter, when it deigns to make an appearance, the sunlight is clear. Unsaturated. Extra-virgin. The intense summer colours that so distressed me on arrival have faded to welcome pastels.

Drowsing like a cat in the *chaise longue* with Gage asleep on my chest under an afghan, I can feel his heart beating against mine, his pulse in the soft spot of his head pressed against my cheek. His little hand grips my index finger.

My son has fallen asleep to my humming as he had, in the womb, so many times. By the end of the pregnancy it seemed as if we'd had incompatible circadian rhythms. I had only to lie down and he'd wake to perform acrobatics, using my bladder for a trampoline. Sully and I started singing at bedtime, hoping Gage might settle down between us. And, perhaps, recognize our voices on the other side of the liquid divide.

I don't know how he recognized my croaking during today's session. My voice kept catching on scraps of maudlin lyrics. But there was a little theme emerging – something like happiness, something like pain – that I've inscribed in memory to be transposed later.

The screen of the patio door opens quietly. I sense my mother's lateral approach without opening my eyes. "You touch him – I'll kill you." The door draws shut.

But when the shadows are long and cool I enter the house reluctantly and let her take him.

There are boxes all over the living room. "What are you up to?" I call.

"I've started packing for you."

"Thanks."

At my desk in search of a pen and a block of manuscript paper on which to scribble down the little tune I hummed to Gage, the drawers are clean and empty. My vision goes black for a moment; I clutch the edge of the desk for support.

"Mother! You packed my *desk*?"

"I'm sorry, dear," she calls from the other room. "I didn't think you'd feel up to working."

"It's not as if I'm on maternity leave from an office job!" I never know when inspiration might strike. The middle of the night. Holding my baby in a shaft of blessed sunlight. Sitting on the loo. Speaking of which: I let the need to pee outweigh my anger.

Dad is kneeling in front of the bathroom door with a screwdriver and a Gorham's bag. He's found hardware heaven on his initial foray out in the car. "And what are *you* doing, Daddy?"

"Replacing this broken lock." He sits back on his haunches, revealing an empty circle in the door. "It should be fixed before you move."

"No!" Rage explodes behind my eyeballs like an aneurysm. "No."

Sully popped that lock a week ago and then, while I was back in the hospital, he *broke* it — deliberately and vengefully. At least, that's how I see it in my mind. As if it had been the lock's fault I did what I did. If Sully needs that lock broken for an illusion of control over our lives, then I need it, too — as a symbol, a reminder.

"Put the broken lock back," I order, my voice low and controlled. "You can replace it after I've left this house at the end of the month, and then you can re-install it in the new place."

My father stares at me, mystified. So — *my mother hasn't told him what I did.*

"Care to split a beer with me before dinner?" Mom offers. "A little bit's supposed to be good for milk production."

"Mix it in with my hay and oats, then," I sigh. I have breasts — for the first time in my life — and everyone's sole focus is their productivity.

I take my glass into the living room. Dad has his feet up on the coffee table, eyes closed. He nurses a pre-prandial nip of scotch, neat. How unlike him. Not much of a drinker, my dad, for a career bartender. Luckily. I can't imagine what our lives together in that house would have been like if my father'd been a lush, too. I sit down beside him on the couch.

"I'm sorry, Mariah," he murmurs without opening his eyes. "Your mother explained why you've . . . not been well."

He lifts his head, opens his arm like he used to when I was a child, when we'd snuggle together over a book. I scrunch up against him, lean into his warmth.

"I'm sorry you thought I'd be so harsh." He pats my shoulder. "If you had to fail at one thing, I'm thankful it was that. Life is a precious gift!"

"I *know*." My words carry an edge, since I hope to cut off further discussion.

"Who knows why things happen the way they do?"

Stupidity? Lack of vigilance?

"Perhaps there's a plan, if only we could discover the pattern of it, the intent. The opportunity behind our actions. Do we choose our accidents? Or do they choose us?"

"You're coming dangerously close to prohibited territory, Daddy," I say. "I believe Sully laid the ground rules at the airport."

"Yes, he did," he continues. His nod is a soothing, full-body action; it's like being enveloped in a live rocking chair. "Look at the opportunity here: a child, a *special* child, entrusted to special parents. Who knows? Perhaps it was the only way a child could have been born into this union between you and James."

This speculation is dangerous and exasperating. "Who knows? Time will tell." I exhale deeply. "Then again, maybe it's just blind fucking luck — and I've skewed the intended course of our lives irreparably." I squirm in my father's embrace.

"I can't believe that."

"That's awfully big of you!" I reach, with a shaking hand, across the coffee table for my allotted six ounces of beer, downing it one gulp. "You've played Assignment of Blame my entire life; to what do we owe this sudden change of rules? Assignment of oppor*tun*ity!"

"I've had a lot of time to think, Mariah, since your accident. *You* were the one who changed the rules."

I turn my head to look into my father's face.

"You were the one who made opportunity out of accident. A pianist loses her hand and becomes — a composer. Do you know how I've marvelled over that, all these years?"

"The signs were there, all along," my voice is harsh. "There's a good chance I would have found that path on my own." *Might even have found it sooner, and less painfully, if you and Mom hadn't forced me down the other one!* "But you *are* right about action," I concede. "That's the one thing I've learned from the last few weeks. What matters now is what I *do*. For Sully. For Gage."

He nods. "And for your*self*, my darling."

Sully coasts down the driveway on his motorbike. Dad squeezes my hand, salutes his son-in-law with his chin. I realize I'm with people who know the worst about me — and they haven't abandoned me, have not withdrawn their love. Not only that — despite their bewilderment, they're steadfast against my explosions of displaced rage.

"Something smells good!" Sully exclaims, stripping off helmet, blazer and tie.

"Ten minutes," Mom promises, handing him a freshly poured stein of beer. "How was your day?"

"I spent it interviewing a cadre of 'foreign *ax*-perts'," he says, imitating the local accent. "Canadians, mostly; testifying to the significance of various bits of evidence gathered in a particularly nasty rape case." He grimaces.

"They should hang the bastard by his balls," Dad calls from the living room.

Leading me into the bedroom, Sully puts the stein down on the dresser, turns to me with open arms. "Are you okay?"

"Yes, but things have been a little *strained* at times. We're all trying too hard. And I'm a bit intolerant. I'm like an animal defending her young," I confide. "I bared teeth and claws to my mother today when she tried to steal Gage away."

"That's natural." He squeezes my arm reassuringly. "Fine, they need to take care of you to show their love, but I'd be more worried if you *didn't* resist."

I smile gratefully as he steps out of his Bermuda shorts and pulls on jeans and a sweater.

"Want to go out for a while tonight?"

"*Out?*" It's like the prospect of a prison break; maybe freedom, maybe a shot in the back going over the wall.

"Don't panic, love!" Sully laughs at my expression. "We could take a run up to the new place. The landlord'll be there for a few hours, after dinner."

"All right," I agree meekly, heart thudding between my ribs. "Just us?"

"Sure; your mom can look after Gage for an hour."

"No, just *us*." This is important to me suddenly. "You, me, and Gage."

I haven't seen us as a *family* yet. Coming home from the hospital, the first time, I saw only the components — individual puzzle pieces that could never form a unit. The father piece — a big smile and an indentation where the heart should be. The mother piece, with its own lacuna. And the child piece with its obvious missing member. It fits there, against my heart. These bits will only make a family if the child piece will fit snug against the father's heart — completing him, too. *But you can't force the pieces.* Sully. I reach blindly for his hand.

"Yes," he nods, cupping my face. "I'd like us to see it together."

More planning than the Flight into Egypt and almost certainly more baggage — "We'll only be gone an hour!" — I'm trembling by the time Sully starts the car, overcome by a weird sort of vertigo. It's the first time I've been out after sunset in weeks; darkness closes around me with menace. Reverse vampirism — it seems I can only walk abroad in daylight.

"Are you cold?" Sully notices me clutching myself.

"No." Exhaling painfully, I realize I've been holding my breath. "I'm afraid."

He reaches between the seats, takes my stump in his left hand. Damned steering wheel is on the wrong side of the car; I used to love to hold hands with him while we drove.

"I remember when I came out of the hospital after the accident. I'd been in there so long it felt like home. And home was all changed when I got back."

"*You* were all changed when you got back."

There's that to it, yes. My stomach churns uneasily. "Go in a pianist, come out a cripple. Go in to have a baby, leave with . . ." *Leave with a broken man, a flawed child, and a shattered image of myself.* I start hyperventilating.

Pulling into the driveway of the Aquarium, he puts the car in park.

"Go in to have a baby," he says quietly, "leave — with a baby, a beautiful baby. *And a husband who loves you both,*" he adds fiercely. "Earlier, go in a pianist — come out a composer. Go in weak, come out — *strong.*"

I calm down, but say, "That's what I'm afraid of, Sully. It's too much responsibility to make opportunity out of accident, over and over again."

He nods. "You have permission — *be strong.* It's all I've ever wanted for you."

"But it's not becoming, it's not pretty! Strong can be *nasty* and self-serving and competitive."

"And strong can be *free*, and funny, and loving. And *alive*, Mariah." Reaching across the bucket seats, he holds me despite the gear box between us.

Alive; yes. Alive. *Look how close I came.* Look Mariah — you have to grasp the reins here and hope like hell he's along for the ride. He's ridden it out so far.

Gage mews in the car seat behind us. Sully looks over his shoulder. "We'd better get going," I suggest.

"Which way? We can see the apartment another day, if you'd rather."

I point the way down North Shore Road, eastbound toward Hamilton Parish and the future. "Home, James."

We have only a few pieces of furniture of our own: my desk, and Gage's crib, dresser, and changing table. I hold the screen door open for my father as he lugs a box in from the car.

"My God," he pants. "What have you got in here? Rocks?"

"No. Books."

"Same thing." Dad tweaks my cheek as he brushes past me, smiles wryly.

He's quoting himself. Moreover, he knows *I* know he's quoting the words we exchanged when I came out of hospital, almost precisely nine years ago. The memory is a phantom as sharp and real as the occasional synapse that still fires in my wrist. Not pain so much as a sensation that, if I roll over on waking and shake the numbness loose, the hand might be functional again by the time I'm fully alert.

Dropping the box next to the built-in bookshelves, Dad looks up to catch me twisting the stump lightly within my hand. I shove it into my pocket. Guiltily? I wonder, as I hook the door open for the procession of laughing men with boxes (Sully, Ron, Cam, Tony) that will follow.

Gage's crib is set up in the alcove of our large room for the duration of my parents' stay. I've dozed off while nursing him but when I awake to his whimpering, he's not beside me. The room is lit only by staves of light visible through the louvred closet door. Sully is pacing the room with Gage pressed against his shoulder. "Ahh!" he sighs, as if he's been suffering Gage's gas bubble himself. I discover I've been counting down the six weeks since Gage's birth in anticipation of making love with my husband.

"Leave the light on," I whisper. My invariable habit, a signal more brazen than removing my nightgown.

He settles the baby, drapes a blanket fastidiously over the crib rail. I stifle a giggle: no primal scene for Gage – at least until he's old enough for it to make a true psychic impression.

As he slides under the covers beside me, Sully groans with pleasure, "A king-size bed."

"There're acres of it; we'll never find each other."

"I'll always find you, Riah," he assures me, beginning his tender re-exploration of familiar, yet dramatically altered, terrain.

My flesh is different – not just in muscle tone, or lack thereof – but marked by three new sets of scars. Sully pays intimate attention to every suture, is weeping by the time he's attended to both legs. As am I. I draw him against my collarbone for comfort.

"Do you know?" I feel his lips moving against my skin. "Do you know I love you more than I love myself?"

How can you? – my instant unspoken response. I slam up against a wall of pain and darkness. *How can you? I don't love you that much.*

"What is it?" Sully's felt my body tense. "Am I hurting you?"

Not in the way he thinks. Here's an indictment for you, Mariah, inscribed on the flesh of your thighs: *you've only ever loved yourself.*

If I'd loved him more than myself, I would never have taken that razor in hand. But I gave no more thought to him that day than I did to Gage. The insatiable ego judges herself simultaneously unlovable *and* inadequately loved, so compensates in the only way left to her – by loving herself without limit.

The unspeakable arrogance of the victim! – so self-absorbed. It's almost enough to send me running off to the bathroom in search of a razor blade.

"Have some compassion for yourself, Mariah," he says.

And I suddenly gasp for breath. Compassion is an emotion I've rarely felt! Never for myself, seldom for anyone else – especially my parents. I've always felt that, if only I could perfect myself, I might rescue the family from its failures and excesses – thereby freeing my father and mother to become the perfect parents I demanded they should be. Their defeat was mine, and mine was theirs – an inextricable tangle of judgement and blame. Compassion was incompatible with the ruthlessness of my demands. There was not one iota of mercy for them in my verdict: *they simply did not try hard enough.*

This rage that's been erupting volcanically is suddenly clear to me. I've no one to blame but myself for this hideous and public exposure, but that hasn't stopped me from trying to displace it. My suicide attempt, as I saw it, was the logical consequence of my own actions, but *the fault was theirs* — Mom, Dad, my grandfather, Doug, Sully — everyone who'd ever failed me in any way. If they'd been perfect parents, perfect lovers, perfect mates — even if they'd been *sufficiently* good and vigilant — my life would have been so different I wouldn't have had anything to explain or prove to Doug. We wouldn't have made love that night; we wouldn't have conceived Gage. I blame you. *I blame you all.*

No mercy for them, until now — transfused through the compassionate eyes of the man who stares into my own. "You don't have to be perfect to be loved," he says quietly.

"*Sully.*"

As an act of will, I decide to dignify his words with acceptance. I won't analyse them; I will *believe* them. It's enough that *he* believes his words are true.

Gradually, beyond our mingled tears, we become aware of additional dampness.

"Look." I straddle Sully in the semi-darkness. Plip. Plip. Plip. Droplets of milk rain into his chest hair. We both shake with silent laughter. "Don't let Gage's midnight snack go to waste, now."

"Really?"

Tenderly, with uncharacteristic shyness, he takes one breast in his hand, holds it over his mouth to catch the drops. "Oh my God," he rasps, shyness abandoned. "It's *so* sweet!"

It's a miracle that a fluid produced by my own body is sufficient to sustain my son's existence and my husband's interest in this scarred and altered female form. As if that isn't gratification enough, the ripples of well-being produced by Gage's tiny mouth are so magnified by Sully's I'm engulfed in a flood-tide of desire for him so strong I'm reasonably certain I'd go through this all again to feel so loved.

⟳

"The logistics are complicated. We've got an hour before one of *them* will need a nap — " Emily nods to the children.

" — Or one of *us* will need to pee!" Fizzy interjects, assessing Caro for signs of imminent labour. The two of them are due within weeks of each other.

"Let's just move the picnic down the hill," I suggest, "to the field beside the kiln."

"What a sensible idea, Mariah!" Caro congratulates me.

Her slightly patronizing tone (as if I've never before had a practical suggestion!) is a function of her discomfort, I decide. Five days overdue can seem like a life sentence.

"Let's set up on the west side," Emily suggests, her sketch pad tucked under one arm. "I can make use of those shadows."

Fuelled by food, Robbie and Claire romp around the field. Gage is asleep in the crook of my right arm, tented by my shirt and a receiving blanket. With baby Angela at her feet in the car seat, Emily sits, angled toward the ruins of the limestone kiln, so that I can see both the old building itself and her emerging impression of it.

I envy Emily her ability to see a heap of rubble and capture it on paper to look at another day. My medium can't translate the interplay of sea and sky where they meet as backlight to forms imposed by man's hand a century ago.

After a while, Caro struggles to her feet. "I don't know about Claire, but it's time for *my* nap."

"Yes," says Emily. "We're all as torpid as drunken flies, even the kids."

We stagger back to the house, where, once dinner's on, I sit at my desk, staring out over the scene we've just abandoned. From this distance the shadows have less impact, the image is diluted.

My friends have never heard my music. *The Grandfather Quartet* is on tape, but I've never been brave enough to play it. They take it on faith when I call myself a composer. I could as easily be perpetrating a fraud.

Emily once said: "None of us can do what you do, Mariah." But it seems not even *I* can do what I do.

"There's precious little music finding its way onto paper these days," I confided to Sully recently, dropping my pencil in favour of curling up beside him on the couch.

"Why?" He put his book down warily.

"I'm happy; I'm busy."

"You need more time alone?"

"Not really. It's a shift of focus." Toward him, toward Gage, toward life. "The best music I've written has come from a deep, deep vein."

He cringed perceptibly.

"I have to dig hard to get at it." I snuggled closer. "And I'm just not willing to do that right now. I have no *need* to do it. But, as a consequence, the stuff I do write is like low-grade ore that's just strewn around the surface. Maybe I've exhausted the mother-lode."

Or is it that I'm thoroughly absorbed by "the mother load"?

"Maybe you need to mine a different material. Or use a different technique, Riah. Like open-pit mining. Or limestone quarrying."

What, though, do I *have* to mine besides my self and my emotions? An interior tunnelscape, fraught with the terrible claustrophobia of memory. There are glimmers, yes, of happiness and love seeded within the bedrock. These are the ores I must drag to the surface to be smelted into music. But what an exhausting enterprise! I give it up for the day in favour of instant gratification: feeding the household.

Steam from the pasta pot clouds all the windows. The sauce burbles audibly.

Ron comes in the back door and joins me at the stove. "Mm-hhm," he hums appreciatively. "That's the best smell I've ever heard." He pecks my cheek.

"Hungry?"

"Starving. Nothing like a round of golf to whet your appetite."

"Or your thirst," I append, placing a bottle in front of him on the counter. "See if James wants one."

"Of course he does." Ron pokes his head outside. "James!" he shouts. "I thought he was right behind me."

"I was." Sully's disembodied voice floats up from the frosted window. "Damned bike has an oil leak." He steps in the door displaying blackened hands, kisses my cheek in the place Ron just did. "How about that beer? I'll drink it outside," he says, threatening me with his oily hands until I acquiesce, laughing.

"I give him ninety seconds," Ron says, "then he'll be begging me to help. He doesn't know a wrench from a spanner."

"As if *you* do, Jacko!"

"There are altogether too many windows in this room," Ron shouts for Sully's benefit. "I can't even have a quiet moment with the wife."

"That's *my* wife, in case you've forgotten."

Ron winks at me broadly. "Your wife; my wife. Trust a tight-arsed

Canadian to be so territorial." In a normal conversational tone, to me: "How is the wife, anyway?"

"I'm fine, thanks." He grins; I blush unaccountably. "Caro's upstairs lying down."

"It's awfully quiet. Where are the kids?"

I point to the saucepan, waggle my eyebrows.

"Oh," he says mildly. "*Spaghetti del'enfantes*. My favourite."

Smiling into the pot as I stir it, I realize how well I've adapted to these intimate accommodations — four adults, and two children at last count.

Caro and I have carved out a routine peculiarly liberating in its orderliness. We each have time alone, time together, time with our kids, our friends, our husbands — *and* built-in babysitters for most occasions. Meals are frequently communal since it's pointless to duplicate our efforts, not to mention the shopping list, when we can just toss an extra potato in the pot and call it dinner. Claire and Gage are each as comfortable in the other's home as in his or her own. Despite the nine-month gap in their ages, they are content together and, when they're not, will go to any available adult for comfort.

"I'll set the table in a second," Ron passes through the kitchen, "after I wash my hands."

I hear him piss vigorously in the bathroom, bail a bucket of water out of the tub to flush with, then run fresh water in the sink. During a dry spell, Sully and I don't object to buying the odd thousand-gallon load of water to augment the supply cached in the shared cistern, but Caro is annoyingly frugal in this regard. Avid water conservation is our concession to peace.

As Ron busies himself with place-mats, plates, flatware, and wine glasses, he asks, "Did James tell you about the file no one wants to touch in the office? No? It's a bloke we all know from the squash club — nabbed for embezzling from the Bank of Butterfield."

"Yikes! How much?"

"A little less than a hundred grand."

"Ex-pat? Or Bermudian?" I ask. It's a thinly veiled race question: white? Or black?

"Ex-pat."

We grimace at each other across the kitchen. "He wasn't a particularly clever embezzler, then, was he?"

"No." Ron sighs. "I wouldn't spend a night in Casemates for a million dollars. His best hope is to be deported to a nice modern British facility. Like Brixton." He pauses to make sure I've registered this irony. "But of course the point is to make an *example* of him." His voice rises a little. "To remind all the other greedy little computer geniuses to keep their hands out of the till."

"So. Which one of you lost the toss for the file?" As if I haven't guessed.

"Shel assigned it to James," he says. "On the basis of his particular talents."

"You mean, his ability to detach his emotions from his work?"

Shaking his head — "No" — Ron's face is mock-solemn. "James is the only one of us who consistently lost to the bugger at squash!"

Sully's muffled curse issues through the window. When he storms in the door it seems as if his brows have bridged the gap between his eyes, but it's only an oily fingerprint.

"I'm going to have a shower before we eat," he says with studied control. "Can you bring me some clean clothes, please?" And he closes the bathroom door with a tad too much force.

"There goes the living definition of 'black Irish'," Ron grins. "Poor James. So much talent — but no mechanical aptitude whatsoever. Well." He gathers himself. "I need a shower, too."

"You'll be competing for the water pressure, you realize."

"Survival of the fittest." Ron's eyes flash with mischief.

By the time I drop his clothes off in the bathroom, Sully is trumpeting a passable impression of Jeremiah Clarke's "Prince of Denmark March." At least he's washed away his irritation with himself; he hates to admit defeat by mechanical objects.

As I drain the pasta awkwardly into the colander I am visited by a double image of showering men: one dark, one fair. And find myself blushing again.

Where does this weird tension come from? Familiarity? It's not flirtatiousness, not desire, that I feel for Ron. More a vitality in his presence, an energy.

We are — all four of us — like the finely tuned strings of a violin, I decide. Such tuning, of course, implies tension, a *positive* sort of tension. We pluck at each other with delight, generating unlikely associations and both humorous and creative sparks. *Interplay.*

Stepping up behind me smelling of Badedas, shampoo, and after-shave alcohol, Sully puts his arms around me and his chin on my shoulder — as he often does — to see things from my height.

"Nice sunset."

The derelict building at the water's edge has acquired a rosy glow. "Emily was sketching the kiln today," I tell him. "She has an interesting way with shadows."

"The light changes so dramatically. Infinite variations." He inhales my hair. "Mmm, you smell like dinner. Delicious."

The front door screen squeals open, then bangs shut. "Here's a cosy domestic scene," Ron comments to Caro. "Perhaps we should slip off quietly, come back later?"

Sully and I turn slowly, still entwined in each other's arms. "No need," he smiles. "Besides, I think we're all starving."

Caro looks refreshed by her nap and, I suspect, a brief shower with Ron. *Save water, shower with a friend.*

"Shouldn't we wake Claire for dinner?" Ron asks.

"No, let's just have a quiet meal," Caro sighs, settling herself in her place at the table. "It may be the last uninterrupted one we'll have for a while."

"Look!" I exclaim. "It's ablaze."

Ron and Sully stand to stare out the window. Even Caro struggles to her feet to see what's caught my eye.

The ruined kiln seems engulfed in the flames of sunset. Ears buzzing, I sit down dizzily, quite breathless.

"What's the matter?"

I wave aside Sully's concern. "Ron, what did you say when you came in this afternoon and smelled the sauce cooking?"

He shakes his head, shrugs. " 'Something smells good'?"

"No." I remember it clearly. "The sauce was bubbling audibly. You said, 'That's the best smell I've ever *heard*'."

"Did I?" he grins. "I plead guilty to mixed metaphor. Set up the gallows."

"And Sully." He looks at me expectantly. "You just said, 'The light changes so dramatically'."

" 'Infinite variations'."

Nodding, "Infinite variations." I beam as if I expect them to understand the momentous revelation I've just experienced. "Excuse me." I can hardly contain my excitement. "I've got a some new material to quarry." A liberation of the most palpable kind: I've been sprung from the prison of my self.

The others indulge me as I solidify these thoughts. I take abstract notes whose coherence will be questionable in the morning. "Planes of light and shadow," I scribble. "Blocks of sound. Shift of tonal concentration. Chromatic modulation equals the passage of time." These words don't begin to define *what* I hear, but do mark a new *way* of hearing. By the time Gage starts to stir in his room, I have a map laid out, my first claim staked.

The others are lounging contentedly amid the detritus of the meal when I rejoin them with Gage.

"Look at you," Sully remarks, "you're *high*."

I laugh giddily, confirming his observation.

He pokes at the microwave while I settle myself at the table with Gage's head tucked under my shirt.

"I've just had something of an epiphany." I feel compelled to explain my absence. "It's like a writer who's been labouring too literally with the concept 'write what you know' while ignoring the fact that there are *other ways of knowing* beyond the purely empirical," I continue with my mouth full. "You don't have to have experienced everything personally to *know* it, or to have an impression of it."

Attentive and indulgent, my audience lets me babble uninterrupted, despite my lack of manners.

"To make the leap from musical autobiography into fiction – and to recognize the point at which you've crossed the chasm!" I shake my head in wonder, laugh out loud. "The implications are huge."

"I've never heard you speak of your work with such enthusiasm, or in such detail, Mariah," Ron notes when I've wound down a little.

This is true – and not a little alarming. I look to Sully for support. He's tipped his chair against the wall, has one long leg crossed casually, ankle to opposite knee, observing with pleasure. And pride.

I've never spoken at such length – perhaps because I've always been ashamed of the inwardness of my music, afraid of exposing myself to judgement and censure. With this shift away from my *self*, however, I'm suddenly free to talk about form and impression, shape and sound.

"It's not as if it'll be devoid of feeling," I elaborate. "But it doesn't have to be *my* emotion. I'm free to *create* new moods and feelings, not merely to *re-create* what I've felt."

It's so obvious I could weep. At last — *at last!* the opportunity for true creation. I feel as if I've been handed a gift of incalculable value.

The phone had rung in the middle of the night.

"Battle stations," Sully had predicted, lunging for the receiver in the dark. "All right, mate. No, don't disturb Claire. I'll drag my blankie upstairs, sack out on the couch."

And now, hours later, here she is: Dulcie Ann Jackson. "She's perfect," I pronounce, staring into the baby's wrinkled face. I immediately regret my choice of words. Having decided perfection is neither attainable nor desirable, I hope this godmother hasn't unwittingly placed the child under a curse.

Dulcie cries, lip a-tremble. To my surprise, I'm suddenly sodden with milk.

"The power of a newborn's cry!" I marvel. "My instinct is to nurse her."

I press the heel of my hand against one breast to stop the flow.

"Go ahead, if you like," Caro smiles. "That's how I felt with Gage."

As I rock Dulcie in my arms, I feel the bite of memory. Despite understanding how Caro could have played wet-nurse to my son, I'm left only with an amorphous aftertaste of my failure that stays with me long after I've handed the infant back to her mother, unnursed.

At home, Claire is playing at Sully's feet. Gage is on his knee, solemnly attentive to the rise and fall of an expressive vocal rendering of *All England Reports*.

My heart fills. With love. And something else. *Longing*. I love Gage, fiercely and protectively. And Sully loves him, I know, without reservation. Still, when I see the two of them together sometimes, I long for something more. For the magical completion of this unit — for Gage to have Sully's blood coursing through his veins.

"Gage — look, it's Mommy!" The child strains against Sully's arms, reaches out to me with his own.

"Were you a good boy for Daddy? I bet you need your diaper changed." I hold him tight against my body; he squirms in protest.

This is self-torture at its finest, but I can't help myself. *I want Gage to be Sully's child.* I wish for it so badly it's acquired the unreality, and the logic, of a fairy-tale quest. If I can successfully pass the three tests, or answer the three riddles, the reward will be mine.

"And we'll all live happily ever after," I coo, tickling his naked tummy.

The rational part of me insists this is a dangerous waste of time. Happiness can only be manufactured by mortals doing the right thing: making opportunity out of accident, living with their mistakes, and dignifying themselves with compassion.

But, oh, what I wouldn't give for a magic wand! *Or another child,* I think suddenly, *one of Sully's own.* Another child would level the scales – though he would never say it, would never even *see* it – between Sully's expectations of our life, and the life I delivered to him.

Gage grins at me, letting loose a jet of urine and a stream of consonants: "Dadadadada."

"Charming boy! That was a clean diaper."

Surely, though, this kind of thinking denies, if not negates, Sully's determination that we – everyone, our parents, the friends who knew us all – accept Gage as Sully has: *as his own.* If Sully can do it, why can't I? Why can't I believe it as strongly as I desire that Gage should be his own?

As his own; as his own. I hum a little tune around these words, to which Gage adds his rhythmic counterpoint. "Dadadadada." I place him on the rug beside Claire, stand at my desk and scrawl down the melody.

"Sit down, darling," Sully commands.

Guilt assails me. "But I've only just come home."

"Inspiration doesn't keep a schedule."

"Caro considers it merely a lack of discipline," I exclaim, pulling out my chair.

"You need a gig," Sully had announced one Sunday morning coming out of St. Theresa's Cathedral, Gage in the carrier/car seat bumping gently against his leg. He held the church bulletin in his other hand, scanned it as we made our way to the car.

"A gig?" I'd repeated, breaking into a laugh. "What've you got in mind?"

"Church choir." He'd handed me the bulletin.

"They've got a director."

"I meant, to *sing.*" A wry smile. "I know it's a comedown, but at least it'd get you out of the house once or twice a week. It might even be fun."

Grace McCallum was the short, stout African-American equivalent of Jim Altman. A dynamo of exuberant energy and great personal warmth, she'd taken the cathedral choir in hand in addition to teaching music at the performing arts high school and directing the Musical and Dramatical Society's chorus. From a core group of unlettered amateurs, most of whom couldn't even read music, she'd formed a spirited and cohesive choir with whom she attempted brave things, both in concert and at Mass.

She welcomed me into the group. "Are you sure you don't want my job?" she teased, after quizzing me on my background.

"Your position as organist is completely safe, at least," I grinned, flashing my handless wrist. "All I really want to do is sing," I assured her, surprised to find that this was true.

When Sully slipped in with Gage to wait for me after rehearsal one day, he took a place at the back with the men. Someone pushed a book in his direction, which he managed to juggle along with a squirming baby.

At the next pause, Grace looked up over her half-glasses. "And where is that lovely baritone rumble coming from?"

Sully had grinned self-consciously; Gage burst into a cadenza of vowels while drooling all over a set of plastic keys.

"Are those two yours, Mariah?" I admitted my proud connection. "We need more men. Make sure you bring them back."

Thus Gage became a fixture of the choir, passed from one doting grandmother-type to another if he fussed, keeping himself endlessly amused by stacking hymnals like building blocks and by pushing buttons on the organ console when Grace's back was turned.

Sully kisses my ear. "I'm taking these two out for some air."

"Thanks." I lean discreetly over my work, but I haven't fooled him.

"Don't worry! I won't peek." To the children, "Do you two pups want to go for 'walkies'? Find your leashes, then."

My little tune has assumed the shape of a Christmas carol, with the mournful tug of an Irish folk song. I hear it with choir and soloists, some strings, harp, tin whistle, and uilleann pipes — of all things — underpinned by the percussive "dadada" of the *bodhrán*. Tentatively entitled "As His Own: St. Joseph's Carol."

"Are you happy here, Riah?" Luke asks.

I catch my slack-jawed incredulity mirrored in my brother's sunglasses.

With a rueful smirk, "I guess that was a stupid question," he says, glancing around the lagoon.

We've found ourselves alone for a moment, observers in a theatre-in-the-round of gentle yet pervasive activity. A tiny uninhabited island has become a private picnic ground. Two large motor boats — Cameron's and Tony's — bob at anchor just offshore. Ron serves as a diving tower for his Claire and Fizzy's eldest, Robbie. Fizzy herself is thigh-deep in the turquoise water, teaching Mark to float.

"Hold still, luv," Cam orders, examining twenty-month-old Duncan's bare posterior and brown-stained thigh. "Ah, Christ," he sighs. "Show Deddy where you went poo, luv." To the assembly, "Watch your steps, everyone. The littlest pup's not housebroken."

Sully offers engineering advice for the moat Gage and Angela are digging around Emily and an elaborate sandcastle. Caro pokes at the reluctant barbecue while Dulcie tootles on a plastic horn. And Tony, the Iron Man, is swimming determined laps marked by the points of the sandy crescent.

"One big happy family," I smile, twining an arm companionably around Luke's. "We're not too much for you, are we?"

"No. I like kids."

"As much as you like animals?" I tease. Luke, studying to be a vet, ignores the jibe. "Have you met anyone special in Guelph?" I probe cautiously.

"Not really." He cocks his sun-blond head. "But sometimes specialness doesn't show itself in an obvious way. *Life* makes people special; I'm not in any rush."

When I duplicate the angle of Luke's head I find my gaze trained on Sully. "There's something about him, isn't there?"

"Yeah; you've gotta love the guy," he says, his response as matter-of-fact as my query. Turning an enigmatic smile on me, he removes his glasses. "I'm not gay, Riah, if that's what you're thinking. I had a hero-worship thing going for Sully when I was young, but it wasn't sexual. Call it 'setting a standard of decency'. And since your marriage. . . ." He winces a little, retreating from discussion of the undiscussible. "He's a truly decent man who values love."

Luke's gaze shifts to Tony. "What's wrong with this picture?" he asks suddenly. "All the other guys are doing daddy stuff while Tony's running an endurance test. He doesn't seem to relate to the kids at all."

"He's the only man we know whose life has been completely unaffected by the birth of a child," I sigh. "He has no interest in her, but Angela adores him anyway."

Luke does a quick nose-count. "Where is she, by the way?"

"Right there," I point. "At the bow of Cam's boat. She's a good swimmer for her age."

"Daddy!" Angela's call is muted by the persistent splash of the waves.

"She's going after Tony."

"He can't hear her." Luke stands suddenly, stripping off his T-shirt. "She's in trouble."

As Luke pounds quickly across the sand, other heads lift, suddenly alert to the child's danger. Ron slides Robbie from his shoulders; Fizzy stands Mark on his feet in the water and does a shallow dive into the surf, but Luke overtakes her with his strong crawl.

Emily leaps up, destroying her creation. "Angela!"

Knifing under the water Luke grabs the girl and propels her to the surface in front of him like a figurehead on a ship.

"Wow, you're a strong swimmer!" he exclaims, when they hit shallow water. "I could hardly keep up with you." Angela coughs, then vomits over Luke's shoulder. "You shouldn't try to drink the whole ocean, though, sweetheart. Save some for us."

Caro restrains Emily gently. "Don't overreact, Em, you'll scare her."

Angela is giggling by the time Luke places her in her mother's outstretched arms, her fear forgotten.

"Did you have a nice swim, darling?" Emily asks in a steady voice – while grabbing at Luke's arm in gratitude behind the child's back and mouthing words: *thank you thank you.*

While my brother is subjected to congratulatory thumps and subdued accolades – "Good on ya, mate!" – Tony continues his exercise, oblivious to the drama. And Dulcie resumes a threadbare tune on her horn.

That warp of melody is crossed by the weft of Emily and Tony's argument. As the rest of us pack up, their words – swallowed by distance and the surf – are semaphored by their gestures, backlit by the first coloured rays of sunset. The fabric gathers mass over the roar of Cam's engine as I lean against the gunwale, holding Gage on my lap and Sully's hand in my own. By the time we've docked at the Dinghy Club, I hear the full tapestry of sound, woven of tributes to quiet heroes – my brother, Sully, my dad, Ron, Cam, Jim Altman – men who believe in love. It will be an oboe concerto, dedicated to all the decent men.

⟿

"That's very colourful, Gage. Tell me about your picture." Caro settles the girls at the kitchen table with us, passes them newsprint and crayons.

"It's a sailboat," he announces. "Like Uncle Cam's." Uncle Cam sails competitively. Gage thinks a moment. "A 'J' sailboat." He looks to me for confirmation. "There's more."

"That's right. It's a J-24," I supply.

"J-24," he parrots proudly, returning to his work.

The way children classify, categorize, and subcategorize! When he was learning to talk Gage had, at first, employed the word "car" for every moving vehicle. Then, one day, he'd noticed a lumbering pink-and-blue hulk lurching around a corner. "Bus," I'd said. And all vehicular traffic was "bus" traffic for a day or two, until some mental switch was thrown, dividing the world into buses and cars. Then trucks. Then *kinds* of trucks: garbage, fire, cement.

His delight in precision fuelled an explosion of language. And an almost unnatural pedantry. Preparing to board public transit one day, I'd said, "Let's get on the bus, Gage."

"*In* the bus, Mommy!" He'd laughed at what he considered my obvious mistake. "We ride *in* the bus, not *on* the bus!"

Technically correct, my son – as if he reads Fowler's *Usage* when I'm not looking.

"Are you ready for tea?" Caro asks. "I'll get it."

"Kettle's just boiled."

She looks over my shoulder at the manuscript paper spread in front of me. "You work best in monochrome, Mariah," she remarks.

Taking her words as implied criticism, I mull them over as I fuss with the teapot. Why can't I just sit at the table with my son, scrawling my own pictures with crayon, the way I've seen Caro spend entire rainy afternoons?

"This is a terrible thing to admit," I begin, "but I really have very little interest in *play*."

Caro smiles at me sympathetically. "It's not supposed to be intellectually challenging for the adult, Mariah; it's for the kids!"

"Am I missing something?" I mask the catch in my voice with a slurp out of my mug. "I love to be with him, but I don't think I know *how* to play with him."

Sully does; Sully spends hours on the floor with Gage, setting up Lego or the Brio trains, pushing cars around the carpet, playing soccer in the yard.

"There's nothing wrong with what you were just doing," she assures me. "Don't try so hard; just *be*. Someday he may take an interest in what *you're* doing," she smiles. "Might turn out to be a prodigy. He's already got a fine ear."

And, I think proudly, almost perfect pitch.

It hasn't hurt that Gage has spent so much time around the choir and sitting in on my sessions with his father. As we've become more and more involved with the choir, and the other musical and dramatic groups that overlap it, my casual pointers to Sully concerning breath control and tone production have turned into more formal coaching that he absorbs, exercises, practises.

A handsome male lead actor who can sing! Sully is much in demand. He sang "They Call the Wind Maria" in *Paint Your Wagon* as if meant only for me; added special poignancy to "If Ever I Would Leave You" in *Camelot*. We alternate our involvement in each production. If I'm not involved with the musical direction, Sully's on stage — always leaving one of us free to be with Gage.

And Gage absorbs everything we do.

"If I can make my diction clear and precise enough so that Gage can learn it," Sully said recently while rehearsing the Major General's patter song from *H.M.S. Pinafore*, "then I'm certain the audience will get it too."

Gage had already assimilated the Major General's nautical bearing and most of the lyrics so completely it gave me a bit of a start to see him rehearsing with Sully. I caught myself with the words "miniaturized version" on the tip of my tongue; clamped down on the phrase so painfully I had to leave the room.

"Do you want to do more work?" Caro asks. "I can take them all out for a walk, if you like."

"It's all right. I've developed an amazing facility to turn it on and off like a faucet. Do two things at once." I blow over my mug. "Like spending time with my son while pursuing my own selfish interests."

Caro looks at me sharply. "I thought we resolved this a moment ago."

"Just a mood," I sigh.

"You feel guilty because your child is not the all-absorbing focus of your life?"

"Yes."

Caro makes a face. "You interact with him much more than most working mothers do."

I open my mouth to protest.

"Aha!" She stops me before I get out a word. "You don't believe you qualify as a working mother! That's it, isn't it?"

"What I do is so *frivolous!*" I say, with more anger than I knew I felt. "It's a hobby, but it's not a job! It doesn't augment the family coffers in any meaningful way; it just takes time away from Gage and James, from us as a family."

"But it's necessary to *you!*" Caro objects. "It's *who you are.* Would you be a happier or better person if you shut your ears to your music until Gage is grown? No!" she answers for me. "You'd be resentful and bitter." Her lips twitch with amusement. "And *old.*" She turns suddenly serious. "Is *James* giving you grief?"

"No!" Sully believes in me more strongly than I believe in myself.

"Well," Caro continues, "it's not as if you're not making a name for yourself. No one will forget the Christmas concert last year. I'd have sworn Grace had enlisted The Chieftains for "St. Joseph's Carol." And before that," she continues, "the string quartet."

My cheeks flush with remembered pride. And a renewed sense of validation. Jenny Herlihy Maloney's group, All Four One, had been booked to perform at the prestigious Bermuda Festival. Their concert repertoire included my *Grandfather Quartet* under its innocuous title, *String Quartet No. 1 in A-flat Minor.* After premiering it in Bermuda, they had toured with it all over North America and parts of Europe and, eventually, gone on to record it. And Jim Altman had foisted my oboe concerto onto the Toronto Symphony Orchestra.

"What you do *is* legitimate," Caro hugs me suddenly, "even if you do it only to please yourself." She nods to the children. "They need lots of examples, if only to discover their own talents and realize it's *okay* to be different."

Ears pricking visibly, Gage's eyes meet mine. I cringe, recalling a recent preschool fracas, but smile reassuringly across the kitchen.

"What's the matter, sweetie?" I'd asked in the car that day. Gage had seemed unusually withdrawn, not bursting with the usual after-school chatter.

"What's a 'freak,' Mommy?"

My stomach lurched. *Freak, n. monstrosity. Abnormally developed specimen. Product of sportive fancy.* I realized I'd been anticipating this event, had been bracing against it — white-knuckled — like a passenger on a roller coaster, ever since Gage had started school.

"It's a not very nice word to describe someone who's different," I hazarded.

Gage ruminated on this offering a moment. "That's silly," he dismissed — in what sounded, to my ears, a very Sully-ish tone. "*Every*one is different."

"That's right," I agreed with some relief. "Everyone *is* different — and that's a good thing."

Sufficiently reassured, Gage had let the matter drop. Today, eavesdropping on adult conversation the way I used to, he appraises me to discern a shift in my opinion, or a broadening of the definition of "different."

"Gage, are you hogging the blues?" Claire asks mildly.

"No, I *amn't!*" he blusters, passing a fistful of crayons down the table from his left hand, to his little hand, to Claire.

" '*Amn't*'?" Caro murmurs into my ear.

"The Bard speaks," I smile. "It makes perfect sense, if you look at it. At least as much as 'I'm not'." I shrug. "I can't bear to correct him."

"I wouldn't. It's lovely," she sighs wistfully.

"Let's go outside and work on the flying machine," Gage proposes.

Dulcie clambers down from her chair immediately; she follows Gage, her Pied Piper, anywhere.

"I'd like to finish my pict-chaw," Claire says with her mother's clipped accent. As the eldest, she often holds out against Gage's suggestions.

"You'll need provisions," I wink at Caro. "We'll pack you a space snack, shall we?"

Claire's crayon strokes increase in breadth and velocity. "All done."

"Astronauts always tidy things away before a journey." Caro's tone stops the kids in their tracks. "In case they're gone for light years."

"We'll be back by tea, Mummy," Dulcie says solemnly.

Caro points to the table. "*Now*, please. In case you take a detour around the Milky Way."

"We won't, will we?" the little girl asks, tugging Gage's sleeve.

"We *might*," he allows, "but I think we can still be back for dinner."

After we've delivered in-flight meals to the launch pad, Caro and I tidy the kitchen. "Send them all upstairs after splashdown," she suggests.

"Oh – but!"

"Don't sabotage yourself, Mariah," Caro squeezes my arm. "None of us resents what you do as much as *you* do! Give yourself permission, for goodness' sake!" She gives me a stern look. "Off to work, now." Segues to a smile. "Cheerio."

At my desk, I hunker into my notes and sketches, trying to recapture the momentum of the work. What I do to myself *is* a kind of sabotage, procrastination raised to an art form. It's a vicious circle. The more urgent the music becomes, the more time it takes away from Gage and Sully. The more time it takes, the less comfortable I am with the process. The more I resist it, the more time I waste. The longer it takes, the more I resent it.

Yes, *resent* it. Caro's got that right. *It's the music that completes me*, that's what I resent.

It's wrong. It doesn't fit with my ideal – or, rather, what I think *should be* my ideal. I remember the image I had, just after Gage was born, of the three of us as a family: individual puzzle pieces forming a unit, with the child fitting against both my heart and Sully's, completing us both. And this is true – as far as it goes. We complete each other as a family.

But I – *I* – am not complete without the music.

When I explore this territory I run from it in abject terror. Because I invariably come crashing up against an alien and unacceptable thought: I might be complete with*out* Sully, with*out* Gage. But I can't be complete without music.

I hate this facet of myself. I *hate* it. If I could identify the part of my flesh, or brain, or spirit, that harbours this selfish, selfish need – I'd go at it with blade or bludgeon. I love them; I love them. But as *much* as I love them – my Sully, my son – they're not enough. I cannot love them perfectly, or even sufficiently, by myself.

Talk about freakish, talk about monstrous. It seems I need this attachment, this parasite. I can only love them sufficiently *with* the music, *through* the music.

Oh.

Through the music.

Jesus jesus.

Yes. Through the music.

⁓

"Where's Gage?"

This question is the one constant in our lives. From the second he became mobile, he was never again where we expected him to be. Put him down on the floor on a blanket, blink twice, and he'd rolled under a piece of furniture. Only his plaintive wail indicated he'd come up against an obstacle and couldn't roll back.

He was a world-class crawler, despite his little arm. And at ten months he was pulling up on all the furniture – until the bentwood rocker counterbalanced, rolling right over him, and he was pinned like a mouse in a trap. He was determined to walk since that day. And does; always at a run.

"He was all dressed a minute ago."

"Did you have any trouble with the tie?"

"Oh, *no*," Sully says, sarcasm dripping. "It's easy to get a tie on the Tasmanian Devil." He cocks his head. "You look wonderful."

"Thanks." I take a step toward him. "So do you." A *frisson* of desire. "I love a man in a tux, you know that," I breathe into his ear.

"Alert the philharmonic, then," he smirks. "Tell them to wear Bermuda shorts to the concert; I don't want any competition." He gives me a quick squeeze. "Gage!" he bellows.

"Right here, Dad."

"Let's go, son." Sully strides down the hall to Gage's room. "What are you up to?" An inaudible reply. "Christ on a stick! Mariah!"

I trip out of my pumps in my haste. "Oh, Gage!"

The sharpest scissors in the house are on his bed, together with the severed right sleeve of his jacket – which he's cut off at the shoulder.

"Hi, Mom." Smiling guiltily, he waggles the fingers of his right hand in greeting. "I didn't like it," he says. "I can't clap with it on."

"You could have taken it *off*, sweetheart!"

Sully coughs behind his hand, pulls on a neutral expression.

"I'm sorry, Gage." I give him a hug, make a face at Sully behind the boy's back. "I should have thought about that. But *you*," I say, helping him out of the coat, "should have asked permission before making alterations!"

"I'm sorry."

"You will be – especially if it's cool in the cathedral tonight." I tuck in the tail of his short-sleeved white shirt, straighten his waistcoat, fuss with his hair, step into my shoes. "Let's go. I heard the Jacksons leave a few minutes ago. Good thing we've got reserved seats."

"Yes," Sully agrees. "But is there reserved *parking?*"

My bowels constrict. "Well, they can't start without the baritone soloist."

We all sing in the car, joining Sully in his warm-up. By the time we've found a spot behind the cathedral his voice is smooth and mellow; mine is thin and edgy.

"Break a leg, love."

"You too," Sully says as we smooch at the north entrance, the performers' entrance.

I hold onto him a beat too long. "Nervous?" we ask simultaneously.

"Not me," he chuckles. "I've been coached by the composer herself."

"Just pay attention to the conductor tonight," I warn. "The composer has no say in the proceedings."

"Which is why you're so nervous."

"Precisely."

We stand in the yellowish light, reluctant to part.

"Mommy." Gage tugs at my sleeve. "I have to go to the bathroom."

I glance at the pendant watch around my neck. "Daddy will take you; I'll wait here."

Sully blows me a kiss. "Quick now, Gage; she can't be late."

I back away from the entrance into the shadows of a palmetto. The fronds shush each other in the breeze. A churning stomach and nerves as jangled as the orchestra as it tunes up – I wish I'd gone to the bathroom one last time myself.

It's not the première that has me so on edge. I've sat in on rehearsals.

The philharmonic is competent, the soloists fine, the choir primed.

"What's the matter?" Sully had asked after my umpteenth trip to the bathroom. "Have you got a touch of cystitis?"

No. Not cystitis. *She can't be late.* Funny he should have used those words: I *am* late. I ignored it the first few days. I've never been able to set a clock by my periods and I've jumped the gun before – picking up a pregnancy test at the Phoenix Drugstore only to have the dreaded period start in the car on the way home from town.

But, as the days click by, I keep running to the bathroom to check, bracing for disappointment. Nothing. Bought a kit thinking the purchase would be enough to bring on the flow. Nothing. Tomorrow morning I intend to use it, if there's still nothing.

It's been almost two weeks. I've never been this late. This is more than stress, more than hormonal fluctuation. My breasts are tender; I'm alert to every internal gurgle and twinge. I *know.* I want to tell him, but I need proof. I'm afraid to hope too much.

We've been through all the tests. Even though Sully tested on the low side of normal, the urologist assured us, "You have one child. No reason why you can't conceive again. It only takes one little swimmer to fertilize an egg, after all. Switch to boxer shorts."

"But – "

"I *will,*" Sully interrupted, with a black look at me that shut my mouth on my attempt to set the record straight.

Silent and brooding in the car, his brows inching toward each other like dark caterpillars: Sully – angry at me. Not without cause; I'd come close to breaking his prohibition. But Sully angry at *me.* I felt myself shrinking under his silence.

If I don't speak now, I thought, *I might be rendered permanently mute.* "I'm sorry, love," I began. "I thought the doctor should be fully informed. It might have made a difference to his advice."

"It doesn't matter!" he snapped, then softened. "If *you* want another baby, that's one thing. But don't think you have to jump through hoops on *my* behalf."

A brief glance. "Gage is *enough,*" he whispered. "I know you don't believe that. Have some faith, Mariah! Stop trying to make it up to me, damn it."

Is he right? Do I expend too much energy trying to correct the perceived wrong? *Gage is enough.* I love my husband; is it so petty of me to want to bear his child, his *own* child? How has this natural desire become yet another flaw to be rooted out of my character? *I'm not as fucking perfect as you are, Sully!* Such a spiral of despair. I turned my head and wept silently, staring out to sea on storm alert.

Reading me like a barometer, Sully reached between the seats to take my hand. "I love Gage because I love *you*. Isn't that the greatest gift you can give a child – to love his mother? Just as the greatest gift I can give the mother – is to love the *child*, Mariah."

Fine, I thought; where is the balance on my side of the equation? "But what can I give *you* – if not another baby?" I cried.

His face cleared of everything except mild puzzlement. "Another baby isn't yours to give, my darling."

"Whose is it, then?" I demanded.

"God's."

Such maddening simplicity! I felt like a dolt – an angry, churlish dolt. If I hadn't been convinced of his absolute sincerity I would have slapped his face. "You're more a Catholic than I'll ever be!"

"You taught me well."

I was breathless. And outclassed. Such simple faith in a man who can argue in front of a jury that up is down and down is up.

No, he didn't learn it from me. I don't believe, *can't* believe, so clearly. Not in God; not in Sully. *You've only ever loved yourself, Mariah.* I've made a religion of my self; I've always been the centre of my own universe.

"What can I give you?" I wanted to wail, dangerously out of balance. How can I return his love as tangibly as I receive it every day?

Home. Sully turned into our driveway, parked in the garage, walked round the car to open the door for me.

What can I give him? Only my faith. My trust. I want another baby, not just to make something up to him, but to love him through the child. As he loves me through Gage.

"Come into the house, darling," Sully coaxed.

As he loves me through Gage. My beautiful, happy, well-loved son. *There* is the proof of Sully's love for me – visible, tangible, physical – there, in Gage's smile.

Sully held the door for me. As I stepped out of the car into his arms, I felt the tug of faith like a tidal ebbing, a cleansing, leaving a pristine beach in its wake.

"Sully."

Holding my face in his hands, he saw the change as clearly as a tongue of flame ablaze over my head. *As he loves me through Gage.* Fumbled at the door with his keys, locked it behind us.

"Caro's with Fizzy and the kids at the Botanical Gardens," I murmured.

We fell into bed and made fierce, fierce apostolic love: *Sully, I believe.*

"Mommy?" Gage pipes into the darkness, so shadowed by his father's silhouette he's almost invisible against the open door.

"Right here, sweetheart." Stepping into the light, I slip my stump into the pocket of my dress and offer Gage my elbow. I stare up at Sully, desperate to speak, but there isn't time.

"Don't be late, Mariah!"

I lift my hand to wave, but he's turned back into the hall; the door closes behind him.

At the front entrance of the church, my father and brother stand smoking, waiting with Jimmy Riordan. This trip is a graduation present, of sorts, for Luke, timed so my parents can attend his commencement in Guelph on their way home. Young Dr. Lucas Standhoffer, DVM, is more comfortable with Sully and me, but the rest of the claque is too large to be lodged in our home. They've taken a suite in a nearby guest house together, and seem to be enjoying each other's company.

"Look at the size of the bug I just squashed, Gage." Luke bends to share his kill.

"I thought your job was to make animals well."

"It's an *insect*, not an animal, Gage!" Luke says, defensively. "And it's buggin' ugly, to boot!"

Dad grinds out his cigarette, kisses my cheek. "I thought you'd decided not to come."

"Hi, Pops; hi, Jimmy," Gage chirps. "Where're Sonja and Nana?"

My father-in-law squats to Gage's level. "Inside. They've saved us *front-row* seats," he emphasizes, as if the child should be impressed.

"They were re*served*," Gage says, implacably.

"Quite right," Jimmy chuckles, pulling up to his full height. "Can't put anything past you, Gage!"

The men lead the way up the aisle like mismatched bodyguards. Jimmy and Luke both have six inches and a good sixty pounds over my dad, but where Luke's weight is all in his shoulders and chest, most of Jimmy's has succumbed to gravity.

The church is packed. Fizzy and Cam, Tony and Emily – good; they've come without the kids.

"Gage!" Dulcie strains against Ron's arms, anxious to be with her hero – who scowls at her breach of decorum.

I nod and smile to friends and acquaintances with a sense of unreality. So many strangers! All these people are here to listen to *my* music? Suddenly assailed with doubt and nervousness, I take refuge in a little spot of my brain that marvels, with a different emphasis: all these people are here to listen to *my* music!

As we take our places in the front row, Sonja beams; my mother leans toward me over Gage's head. "You look lovely, dear."

Orchestra. Choir. Soloists – all except Sully. Conductor. Applause. Overture to *The Unfinished Church*.

"Where's Dad?" Gage hisses.

I hold my finger to my lips. "He'll be out in a minute."

Gage settles in beside me, his left arm still looped companionably through my right.

I'd started my oratorio, *The Unfinished Church*, not long after *The Kiln*. The site of the church, on a hilltop overlooking St. George's Harbour, was one of those places one puts off seeing, like others in Bermuda, until invaded by company from abroad. The island is only some twenty miles in area; you'd think you could see it all in a day. But there are secluded coves and isolated vantage points that one never gets to unless a special effort is made.

My parents had come to celebrate Gage's first birthday. We did St. Peter's Church with them one windy, winter-clear day. Built in 1612, tiny St. Peter's with its gleaming Bermuda cedar interior is the oldest Anglican church still in use in the Western hemisphere. Its simple lines are pleasing and utilitarian, soothing to the eye.

"Just imagine what the landscape must have looked like, forested with trunks that size!" Dad said, pointing to one of the massive beams.

A postwar blight had decimated the indigenous cedars. It was common to come across the silvered skeleton of one, reaching gnarled fingers to the sky like an anguished wraith. St. Peter's gave public testimony to the grievous loss of that resource.

"In the mid 1800s," the brochure informed us, "part of the congregation decided it was time to replace St. Peter's with a larger, grander edifice. Construction of the new church commenced in 1870, just up the hill – an undertaking so divisive the congregation was threatened with dissolution. Rather than cause more friction, the enterprise was abandoned and the building allowed to fall into ruin at the top of Church Folly Road."

We made the uphill trek encumbered with camera gear, diaper bag, stroller, and curiosity.

Most of the roof was missing. Vegetation was as lush inside as out, with palmettos growing right in the middle of the nave – a natural reclamation project.

"Strange. I feel close to God here," I said, squeezing Sully's hand.

"I've often felt that way," my father agreed, "out hunting. Nothing to separate you from God's creation."

" 'But superstition, like belief, must die'," Sully intoned, his voice filling the space.

The hairs on the back of my neck came to attention; we all turned to listen.

> And what remains when disbelief has gone?
> Grass, weedy pavement, brambles, buttress, sky,
> A shape less recognizable each week,
> A purpose more obscure.

He grinned, shrugged without embarrassment. "Philip Larkin. 'Church Going'."

"Take lots of pictures," I told him, wandering off absently. "The arches especially."

What an incestuous enterprise, this concert! One of Sully's photos forms the cover of the program because it captured visually what I'd heard that day, matching exactly my aural images of interior arches and columns weathered by the elements, backlit by sky and rampant greenery.

Overture complete, there's a moment of silence, then a cello carries a long single note. Sully enters the cathedral from the side door sheepishly, looking for all the world like a tardy concert-goer.

"There's Daddy!" Gage chirps. Quiet laughter surrounds us; Sully winks at Gage.

" 'Once I am sure there's nothing going on'," he sings, " 'I step inside, letting the door thud shut.' " And he does. Slam. He continues Philip Larkin's poem, pointing out what he sees around him. " 'Some brass and stuff up at the holy end; the small neat organ,' " the orchestra imitates it, " 'And a tense, musty, unignorable silence, brewed God knows how long.' "

He holds the last word, deep in his chest, a beat or two beyond reasonable endurance.

" 'Mounting the lectern,' " Sully ascends the stairs slowly, " 'I peruse a few hectoring large-scale verses,' " plants his hands on either side of the massive volume, leans forward urgently, " 'and pronounce "Here Endeth" much more loudly than I'd meant.' "

Audience laughter. I glance at Gage. He is rapt. This beginning section is a character piece; Sully has won them over. By the time the poet waxes philosophical, they trust his voice sufficiently to make the journey with him.

> For whom was built
> This special shell? . . .
> A serious house on serious earth it is,
> In whose blent air all our compulsions meet,
> Are recognized, and robed as destinies.
> And that much never can be obsolete,
> Since someone will forever be surprising
> A hunger in himself to be more serious,
> And gravitating with it to this ground,
> Which, he once heard, was proper to grow wise in,
> If only that so many dead lie round.

Sully's performance draws applause – as I thought it might. The orchestral suite continues with the next movement, "Folly."

"Sheer folly," my father had spat like a curse, that day. "Such resources expended to the greater glory. What waste."

We'd all agreed. Still, how many countless others had stood in the chancel staring up at the heavens, wondering if it was possible to see God in an unfinished church? And, maybe, just maybe, catching a glimpse?

The choir stands. I tense reflexively for the soloists' quartet; I worry about it most. I'm fairly confident the rest of the piece works and, if the performance had been scheduled for St. Theresa's — the Roman Catholic cathedral — with its flat cedar roof and warm acoustics, I would have no doubts. But the Anglican cathedral, chosen for this performance solely because of its larger seating capacity, has such a high ceiling it sucks the sound right up into the peak. The quartet has been a muddy, unintelligible mess in rehearsal and could be again tonight if the orchestra gets away from the conductor.

"Mommy, you're hurting my hand," Gage complains.

"Sorry!" I lift my elbow to release it, place my arm across his shoulders. He grips my wrist in his little hand.

The quartet is an inventory, of sorts. The mezzo starts lightly. "Sun. Moon. Earth. Stars. Mercury, Venus, Jupiter, Mars." A litany of stars and constellations.

Sully jumps in, low and menacing, with creatures of the deep. "Shark, squid, manta rays, angel fish all sing His praise."

"Kiskadees in poinciana, long-tails, cedar, Bermudiana." The soprano lists local birds and flora; the tenor, a who's who of common Bermuda names: "Outerbridge, Trimingham, Lightbourn, Ferreira."

A competition between disparate and warring elements, modulating in and out of chaos and cacophony. Eventually joined by chorus and orchestra united in common purpose, resolving into triumphant harmony: "Praise the Lord from the heavens; praise Him in the heights! Praise Him, sun and moon, and all you stars of light. Praise the Lord from the earth, great sea creatures and all depths, praise Him mountains and all hills, fruitful trees and all cedars."

The lyrics are an amalgam of Psalms 148 and 150. The counterpoint rallies around the cedars — the pride of Bermuda — symbol of survival despite all odds, like the ruins of the unfinished church itself. I've designed the theme to repeat just often enough that the audience will know it, and leave stirred by it — if it works — like a call to arms, after the last jubilant chord has died.

You don't know that it works when you're writing it. You hear it in your head as you put it on paper, but it's not until you hear it performed that you really know. Hear the echoes bouncing off the stones of the cathedral, hear the notes the high peaks of the roof have retained or released, hear what the audience has absorbed both intellectually and acoustically. Hear the silence. Hear the applause. Are plucked from your seat by the conductor and turned to face a standing tumult. Embraced by your grinning husband and presented with a floral bouquet of funereal, or bridal, proportions. Laughing. Weeping. *It works*; it works.

Out of the congratulatory throng in the hall an informal receiving line springs up. Sully holds Gage against his hip in the crook of his right arm, shakes hands with his own left, forestalling the awkwardness for me — as he tried to do at our wedding: "Greet Mariah with your left hand, please!" I caught him bellowing over the din into a well-wisher's ear.

My head buzzes; I feel myself blush madly. I'll never get used to this, this fuss attendant with even small, local fame, the discomfort magnified by my — *handicap*. I never use that word. But under such excruciating scrutiny, I feel naked. There are always people who do not know: "Look! She has no hand." I feel their eyes burning into me, pitying, judging. I've considered a prosthesis for these occasions. Something pretty, but useless — the sort I so disdained all those years ago.

If not for Gage I might have gone that route. *Let* people take the cold, hard, unfeeling thing in their own warm palms and watch them blush and squirm. Let it be their problem, not mine. But with Gage, I feel I cannot, *should* not, hide behind a mask. For what message would it send him? That one must hide one's differences so others won't be embarrassed and discomfited?

"Have you considered getting him a prosthesis?" our pediatrician's locum asked me once. "It'd extend his arm to normal length and he could develop quite a lot of dexterity."

"He *has* quite a lot of dexterity!" I'd replied, trembling with imperfectly concealed rage at the man's insensitivity. "He has a completely formed and functioning hand, with nerves and sensation. He uses it; he *feels* with it. He'll never be more dexterous with an artificial contrivance. Why should he sacrifice dexterity to the *appearance* of normality!"

The receiving line has broken into conversational knots. My father is outside, smoking with strangers; Gage romps around the refreshment table with Claire and Dulcie under the watchful eyes of his grandmothers and uncle; Sully's laughter rises above his father's and the Attorney General's.

"Well done, lass!" Sandy McCassland enfolds me in a paternal embrace.

I look at myself through his overly bright eyes and forgive him his self-congratulation — *she might have died, if not for me.*

Leaning toward Sandy's ear, I confide, "I think I'm pregnant."

His face lights up; he glances in Sully's direction, turns questioningly back to me. I shake my head minutely. "I haven't told James yet."

"Call the office on Monday," he says, squeezing my arm; "we'll fit you in."

Marcus O'Neill, the reviewer from the *Royal Gazette*, steps up to me proffering a glass of Perrier. I gulp it gratefully, having managed to dispose of three virtually untouched glasses of champagne without calling undue attention to myself. Marcus and I have so often shared collegial *badinage* over intermission he knows my drink, if not my opinion — often before I've formulated it myself.

"Let's see," he says, pretending to read the program. "You're the composer; James is photographer and baritone soloist. Which one of you is reviewing it for the *Sun*?"

"That would be a conflict of interest, Marcus!" I nod toward the weekly's editor and his wife. "Colin's reviewing it himself."

"He'll be more than fair toward his own reviewer."

I'm struck with unaccountable nervousness. "Perhaps you should propose a swap. He can savage me in your paper; you can savage me in *his*." Marcus has a reputation for viciousness; he thinks I'm much too soft. If he doesn't like my *Unfinished Church* he won't go easy on me, friendship or no friendship.

Sipping from his glass, he says, "Seems to me you're wasting your time reviewing, Mariah. Those who can't *do*, review."

This is as close to a compliment as I'm likely to get. "*Thank* you, Marcus."

"Tell me you weren't influenced by Samuel Barber's *Knoxville: Summer of 1915.*"

"Only insofar as we both despise gratuitous atonality."

"I can't imagine anyone other than James doing it. And nowhere other than in a church."

Bristling defensively, "That rather limits the thing's potential, doesn't it?" I don't want to defend my vision right now; I want to enjoy it.

"A little precious, maybe — coming in the side door that way," he notes absently. "Still, James's good-humoured self-consciousness plays well against the line, 'Someone will forever be surprising a hunger in himself to be more serious'."

Having thus been allowed a glimpse of the first draft of his review, I relax. It won't be all bad.

"Mrs. Riordan?" A tall, suited stranger steps up for introductions; I'm caught with the glass in my only hand. Marcus, sensing my panic, takes it from me like a butler and slips away quietly. I'm almost overwhelmed with gratitude.

"Geoff Halloway, National Film Board."

My mind stalls stupidly. The National Film Board – of which nation? Bermuda?

"Of Canada," he elaborates, as if he's read my thoughts. "I'm just here on vacation. Thought I'd test the Bermudian cultural scene, only to discover you're Canadian."

"We've been here almost six years now," I offer as a defence against a possible charge of cultural appropriation.

"I was impressed with the sense of place in your music. And I was quite amazed to hear that you come from Thunder Bay. Because it so happens I'm putting together a documentary on Silver Islet."

"Really!" His words are like an electrical charge; I scan the crowd quickly for Sully and Jimmy. "My husband is also from Thunder Bay; and my in-laws still have a camp at Silver Islet!"

"Would you be interested in doing the music for the film?" Geoff Halloway asks, then laughs at my speechlessness. "I'll take that as an expression of interest. Have you ever done film work?"

I shake my head.

"The orchestral sections of your music tonight would work splendidly with film. We usually pick a project, then choose music to suit it. In the case of *The Unfinished Church* I'd be inclined to make a film around the music, it's so visual.

"Thank you," I manage.

"Here." He takes a pen and business card from his breast pocket, scribbles hotel and room number on the back. "Can we get together over dinner, say tomorrow night? We leave on Sunday, I'm afraid."

"Let me flag down my husband." I catch Sully's eye, beckon to him, make introductions – the casualness of which belie the erratic nature of my pulse.

Turning his attention to Sully, Geoff fills him in on our conversation. Excited by his words and practically faint with elation, my vision is eclipsed momentarily by a black spot. Reaching for Sully's elbow, I affix a smile to my face — and concentrate on holding it while a knife of pain slices through my lower abdomen.

Christ oh christ oh christ. Not now. I want this baby, damn you! Have I jinxed it by telling Sandy? by wearing a pad tonight, just in case? Didn't I believe strongly enough; didn't I pray sufficiently? Wasn't my musical offering pure enough?

Praise Him, kings of the earth and all peoples; princes and all judges; young men and maidens, old men and children. Outerbridge, Trimingham, Lightbourn, Ferreira. *Praise God in his sanctuary, praise Him in his mighty firmament; praise Him with the sound of the trumpet. Fruitful trees and all cedars.*

All bloody blighted cedars and accursèd fruitless, barren trees.

I'm sorry, Sully. Another baby isn't mine to give.

"Aren't you getting up today?" Sully draws the curtains, letting in a painful stream of light.

I groan.

"Hung-over?" he smirks.

"*No.*" I think of all the wasted champagne. A hangover would be preferable to this palpable emptying. "Cramps." I press his pillow against my stomach. There will be no taut bulge there, months from now; no little Celtic chieftain playing me like a *bodhrán*.

"Let me be your hot-water bottle," he says, climbing back into bed fully clothed. He wraps his warm limbs around me. I let myself be comforted, dragged back from the abyss that looked so desirable all night.

"Come away from the edge, Mariah!" Doug had urged that summer before he left for Denmark. Kat had a white-knuckled grip on the parking lot side of the chain-link fence, yards back from the best view of Ouimet Canyon. Doug was pale and sweating with vertigo, but determined to do his masculine best not to be outclassed by a reckless female.

For I *was* reckless. Sully was gone; Doug was leaving; I'd been mere months without my hand. And my life stretched out before me like the bottomless canyon. There was no appeal to the idea of getting across it; the only pull was gravitational. Down. Down. Getting across would mean work. Bridging, buttressing, spanning. Shoring myself against emptiness, when all I really wanted was rescue: to wake up on the other side, safe in Sully's arms.

I played out a worst-case scenario that day: *the branch I'm holding breaks, the rock my foot is braced against pops out of its nesting spot — and I fall into the gaping maw of the canyon.* And I didn't care. It was a dare, of sorts; a bet with God. *Heads — the devil takes me. Tails — he doesn't. It will be an omen. If I'm spared today, it means God has won — and my life will be* all right.

What a pernicious sort of faith! If I'd known then what I know now I'd have seen I had it wrong. Heads — *God* takes me; tails — the devil has me in his grip. I'm *his* plaything.

But, then again, here I am: on the other side, safe in Sully's arms. Blessed and cursed by the Big Joker in the Sky. Heads — you're pregnant; tails — you're not.

Sully believes in the benign God, the good-humoured judge. Just like his father. My father would have capital punishment back in a flash. For murderers and brigands, jaywalkers and fornicators alike.

What did I do to warrant losing this baby? I need to blame some*thing*; some*one*; myself. But if my God, like my dad, is a hangin' judge who administers punishment wildly inappropriate to the crime — if any — then there's no way I can rationalize the loss as a consequence of my actions. If justice is not blind, random chance *is*. And so is plain, unadulterated bad luck.

"Gage and Luke are loose on an unsuspecting world," Sully stirs beside me, yawns. "And the folks'll be trekking down the railroad right-of-way for breakfast."

"I forgot about that."

"Stay in bed, if you want to," he says, kissing my ear. "I'll take care of it."

But I rouse myself, shower, dress. *It doesn't matter how I feel.*

We take breakfast on the patio, an exhausting, boisterous meal. The Riordan men are formidable alone; together they dominate through sheer physical bulk and high spirits, forcing my father and brother — dominators in their own right — to assume the uncharacteristic role of attentive audience. The only one undaunted is the least of our brethren: Gage takes his place at centre stage for an impromptu performance of *Pinafore*, missing nary a word of the patter song.

"Bravo, Gage!" A cheer goes up through the doting assembly. He takes a bow.

Jimmy grins proudly. "Christ, he's like Jamie was at that age! Isn't he, Sonja?"

She smiles reflectively, nods. I brace myself against a cramp. *Jimmy's forgotten*, I marvel. We've played our roles so convincingly even Jimmy's forgotten.

"What a stage presence!" he continues, chucking the child under his chin. "You'll make a fine lawyer, son, just like your dad."

"I don't want to mix with the criminal elephants," Gage says solemnly. "I'm going to be a veterinarian, like Uncle Luke."

"In that case you might have to *treat* the criminal elephants!" Roaring his approval, Jimmy turns to us to comment, but is suddenly silenced by something he sees on our faces. "That's a noble ambition, Gage," he says with warmth, but somewhat less volume. "A noble ambition, indeed."

Clamping a meaty paw around Sully's bicep, Jimmy gives it an emotional squeeze. "Speaking of noble ambitions, Peter Pan – when are you and your Wendy going to leave Never Land and come back to the real world?"

Sully squirms out of his father's grip. "We like it here, Jimmy."

"But it's so small – and relatively crime-free! Surely you need more challenge, son. I hate to see you wasting your potential."

"*Life* is the challenge, Jimmy," Sully says quietly. "Law just puts food on the table; it's not my consuming passion."

"What is?"

"My family," he says, tousling Gage's hair, looking around to catch my eye. I smile. "I have *time* for them here. Besides, Jimmy – "

I intercept the provocative twinkle in my husband's eye.

" – I'm not a lawyer; I'm an *actor*."

"Nonsense!" Jimmy blusters. "I've taken a few turns on the stage, too. But you can't make a living at it!"

"Maybe not," he says, winking at Gage. "But I'm good at it, aren't I, son?"

"You bet, Dad!" Gage climbs up onto Sully's lap. "You were the best Major General."

"Next to you," he says, tickling the boy gently. Looking at his father, "It's only because I'm an actor that I'm any good at being a lawyer, Jimmy. It's a role." He leans forward urgently. "My longest-running role so far," he says seriously, "but I really prefer the short runs."

Jimmy stares at his son, perplexed, gives his head a little shake. Assuming a broad, false brogue: "Who's after helpin' me clear the table, then?"

I stand quickly. "That's okay, Jimmy. I thought you fellas were planning to play nine holes this afternoon."

"Right," says Sully, clapping his hands together. "Who's on for golf?"

"Not me," Luke says. "I'm going to find a beach."

"Gage?"

"Yes, me, Dad! Me! Can I drive the cart?"

"Sure." To my father: "Dad?"

Sully calls his own father Jimmy; mine, he calls Dad. It's so rare we're all together I've never seen this particular look cross Jimmy's face.

My father sees it, too. "No, no," he demurs. "You boys go ahead. I've never spent much time on the links."

Luke roars off on a moped; Sully and Jimmy bustle around loading the car with golf clubs and gear. Dad wanders down the hill toward the kiln for a smoke; we women clear the table.

"Sit down, Mariah," Sonja urges, steering me into a chaise. "You look a little peaked." Her smile is sympathetic. "Are you feeling all right?"

I had no intention of telling anyone, with the possible exception of Sandy, but I feel the sudden need to discuss it with someone who's been there. As my mother goes into the house, laden with dishes, I grab at Sonja's sleeve anxiously.

"What's the matter, dear?"

"I think I had a miscarriage last night," I whisper.

"Oh!" She sinks into a chair beside me as if deflating, holds my hand. "I'm so sorry. I *do* know how you feel. I had at least four of my own."

"At least?"

She looks away into the middle distance, "In some ways, I felt like *every* month was a miscarriage." Turns back to me. "How far along?"

"Four weeks, maybe, from ovulation. It's the first time I've ever been so late."

Stroking my arm, "Too much stress," she suggests, "with the concert and all." Her face creases with concern — "You're not haemorrhaging, are you?" — relaxes when I shake my head.

"Were you ever given a reason for yours?" I lean toward Sonja urgently.

"Jamie was almost ten when I had the last one," she says. "Twenty, thirty, years ago they didn't have many answers. And you get tired of

people telling you that maybe *something was wrong* and it was *Nature's way*."
Rolls her eyes, smiles sadly. "By the time I lost the last one, I would
have been *happy* to have carried another child to term, even one with
something wrong." Squeezes my hand. "Be thankful for Gage."

"I am." I nod. "Have I thanked you for raising your son to be such
a good father?"

"He is, isn't he?" Sonja smiles with pleasure. "I'd like to take the
credit. But whatever he is, it's all his own doing. Jamie was the most self-
determined child I've ever seen." Qualifies her statement. "Next to
Gage." She stands.

From my perspective on the chaise, Sonja seems to tower above me
– which imparts an odd sense of personal diminishment, since she's
barely five feet tall and looks like a Doulton figurine beside her hulking husband and even taller son. "I haven't told James."

"Are you going to?"

"I don't think so."

Sorrow shared isn't lightened in any way, merely multiplied expo-
nentially. What would it serve to tell Sully, after all? Would he be happier knowing that at least one of his little swimmers stayed the course
– even if the resulting bundle of cells has been washed out to sea?

My father meanders back from his brief excursion, slouches into a
chair.

"Why didn't you go golfing, Dad?" I ask.

"As I said, I'm not much of a golfer. Besides," he stretches his legs,
crosses his ankles, "there's a father–son undercurrent humming
between those two. I thought they might need the time alone."

"I think Jimmy's a little jealous that Sully calls you Dad."

He closes his eyes, turns his face up to the sun. "We take our fathers
where we find them," he says. "Sometimes it has nothing to do with
blood. Blood can even get in the way."

Dad opens one eye. "I wasn't thinking of James and Gage when I said
that, believe it or not. I was referring to James the Elder and James the
Younger. But," he admits, "it holds for you, your brother, and me, too."

I feel a lecture gathering, steel myself for it as captive audience.

"You have so much invested in a child's life!" he marvels, sitting
upright. "You see all the genetic possibilities and familial mistakes
repeated, like eye colour, through the generations. You cannot render
impartial advice, or judgement, to a child of your own flesh!" My

throat constricts. "I've had plenty of wisdom, over the years, when your husband has turned to me. But for you? Or Luke?" He opens his hands helplessly, shakes his head. "*Nada.*"

"Not that it's ever stopped you from trying."

He cocks a wry eyebrow, nods self-deprecatingly. "Maybe I've gone about it wrong, all my life."

"What do you mean?"

Relaxing into the seat again, "I was lurking out here the other night after dinner, having a smoke, when I heard voices. So, I walked to the corner of the house. Jimmy was sitting on the retaining wall, silhouetted against the sunset; James had one knee up and was leaning on his elbow, bent toward Gage. And Gage was talking incessantly with this," Dad gestures expansively, "this pre*post*erous self-confidence – like the boy Jesus in the temple."

We grin at each other; I can picture the scene.

"Occasionally James nodded, or Jimmy rumbled a low response, but Gage went on yakking a mile a minute. Voicing all his theories, talking for the sheer pleasure of hearing his own voice – and to amuse and enlighten his audience. And he's all his own lad; a lump of clay that retains no one else's stamp or impression."

My father stares out over the sea. "James and Jimmy were surely like that with each other. They love each other; they love Gage. Yet they resist the urge to mould! To take that clay and shape it. They'll guide, yes; but they won't interfere. They allow the child to *be* himself."

It's always been obvious to me. "How did you *think* Sully got to be the way he is?"

"Quite right. But I'm jealous."

"Why?"

Turns back to look into my eyes. "Because I'm afraid I've done it wrong. I've never once heard *you* speak with such confidence, Mariah."

Is this true? Lectured, moulded, judged – yet loved. I've never doubted that love, even if I have questioned its focus. My father's love was always expressed with the urgency of hypervigilance. As if, with a cataclysm approaching, he didn't trust us sufficiently to evolve on our own.

Insecure, I always kept my opinions from him. But I *have* evolved. I've opened up – to Sully, to my friends – even if it's taken me more than thirty years to risk making a statement. To speak, in my own voice, with Gage's preposterous self-confidence, from a place of acceptance.

"Never heard me speak with such confidence? That's not quite true, Dad." I take his hand between our chairs. "It's a different language, that's all."

He looks at me questioningly.

"I think you heard me speak last night."

Joining us on the patio, "You're right," Mom concurs with Sonja's unheard opinion. They have obviously been discussing me over the dishwater. "Why don't you lie down, dear, while the men are gone. You've had too much excitement. And more to come, tonight, with this film board fellow."

I open my mouth to speak.

"Isn't that your car?" she asks. "What are they doing home so soon?"

Hitting the driveway a tad too fast, Sully scrapes the tailpipe on the incline with a shower of sparks. We trail around the house to the garage on the run.

"What's the matter?"

He offers a wan smile, opens the back door with a trembling hand. Gage clambers out of the car, displaying bloodied, grass-stained knees and scraped palms.

"Sweetheart!" I gasp, gathering him in a hug. "What happened?"

He grins. "I jumped out of the golf cart." Struggles away from me, obviously unhurt.

"Gage has a career cut out as a stunt man," Sully says, tousling the boy's hair.

"Come inside, lovey," coos my mother. "Get you cleaned up."

"A good soak in the tub will probably do it," Gage suggests, parroting someone – Sully, probably. "Can I have deep water, Mommy?"

"As long as you don't tell Auntie Caro. And make sure you save it when you're done." I watch until he's safely in the house, then turn on my husband. "What the hell happened?"

Sully walks around the car to open the door for his father.

"Gage was in the golf cart when the brakes let go," he explains.

"*You* told him he could drive," I accuse. "Was he messing around?"

Jimmy shakes his head. "No. He was sitting on the passenger side. I was whacking the ball out of the rough when – click! – we looked up to see the cart start rolling down the hill."

"Headed for a tree," Sully adds.

"So we both took off," Jimmy continues, "hell-bent for leather, but the cart just picked up speed. 'Jump, Gage! Jump!' this one bellowed."

"And he did. Just before said cart hit said tree — and flipped. It was a wreck. The foursome behind us saw what happened. They came screaming over, gave up their round to drive us back to the clubhouse."

Sully takes off into the kitchen where I find him retching into the sink. "Sorry," he apologizes, knees a-tremble. I steer him onto a stool at the counter. "Adrenalin overdose."

"All's well that ends well," I allow.

"Scares the shit out of you in hindsight."

"Scares the shit out of some people in *fore*sight." I gesture through the window to my father, straight as a sentry, smoking. His body language is obvious. "He's furious. He thinks you should've seen that one coming."

"Not everyone can see his whole life with such prescience!" Sully scowls, fear combusting into spontaneous anger. "And if *he's* so smart, tell me: did all his fucking vigilance ever stop one terrible thing from happening to *you?*"

"This isn't about me."

"No, but it's become about *him*, so I throw that out for discussion."

"Not now." Wrapping him in my arms, I feel his trembling masked by the ferocity of the returned embrace. But relief soon wins out over fear; a joke or two signals his return to equilibrium.

I can hear Gage laughing and splashing in the bathroom. My uterine muscles clench like a fist. Gage always loved his bath. I made that Sully's job, his time with Gage at the end of the day. For, when Gage was newborn, I was afraid to bathe him myself. Afraid of an image I had — one of those first black days home from the hospital — of the baby wriggling out of my grasp. And of myself — not even trying to grab him, just letting him slip away before joining him under the surface of the water.

"How're you doing, buddy?" I kneel beside the tub.

"Great! The water's deep enough for the keel," he exclaims, demonstrating with the sailboat in his hand.

"Let's see those knees."

"Nana made sure they were clean. And it didn't even hurt."

"Brave boy," I manage over the constriction in my throat.

I can weather the sight of any quantity of my own blood; always watch carefully during injections and blood tests, wart and mole removals, sutures – in case I ever have to repeat these actions myself someday. If I could have observed my own amputation I believe I would have. With dispassionate, clear-headed curiosity; a degree of distrust of the medical profession, imparted by my father; and the all-consuming need to be in control.

When it comes to my son, though, I'm not so dispassionate. I force myself not to overreact, not to alarm him with my own dismay. But to witness a spill of his blood or a laceration of his perfect, flawless skin leaves me queasy and shaken after the crisis has passed. I can't control his pain, cannot even alleviate it. He must sense my helplessness. I imagine his courage is his response to it. Then again, perhaps his stoicism is just his way, as it is mine, of being in control.

On our first Canadian vacation since our marriage, we fly to Vancouver, pick up a car, and drive to Banff where I lead a couple of workshops in choral music. After the dinosaurs in Drumheller, Gage dozes most of the way across the prairies, hypnotized by the repetitious scenery.

Crossing out of Manitoba, Sully says, "We're in northwestern Ontario, now. You can tell by the trees."

"You call them trees?" Gage asks.

Gage: a child born and raised in semi-tropical climes, who's only recently visited the towering groves of a rain forest. Seen through his eyes, the scrubby jack-pine and spindly birch are miniatures – stunted like bonsai by their arduous struggle for purchase in pockets of soil frost-hewn from the Canadian Shield. You can forgive his scepticism.

"This is home," I say, surprised to find myself overcome with absurd emotion. "I've never come at it from the west. And from such a psychic distance."

Sully glances at me to verify the tear quotient in my tone, then takes my hand.

"It's such a struggle!" I exclaim. "The climate, the rock. Settlers and trees alike: how could anything live, or make a living, in such conditions?"

Gage's logic: "Why would they even try? Why didn't the settlers just go on to the prairies. Or the coast?"

"A leap of faith," Sully suggests. "Or a complete lack of imagination."

"Or maybe," Gage grins, "the kids were screaming, 'Are we there yet?' So they decided to stay."

After a few days with my parents, we go on to Silver Islet, another first for Gage.

"You call this a beach?" Gage's face registers astonishment coupled with disgust.

"Well, yes," Sully shrugs defensively. "At least, in these parts – where we come from – this is what passes for a beach." He stoops to Gage's level. "We're living in prehistoric times, Gage." Thunks a boulder with his knuckle. "Someday, someday, this will be a beach. This rock will be a grain of sand, perhaps many grains of sand."

Gage looks dubious; Sully lays it on thick. "This is a *man's* beach, a *lumberjack's* beach: no namby-pamby corals, no delicate shells crushed in the gentlest surf. Anyone can make a beach out of that stuff! But to make a beach out of igneous rock in a fresh-water lake takes time, Gage, time! It takes the action of storms and ice. It takes . . ."

"It takes an ice age," Gage supplies.

"Right."

"So, it's not a beach."

He is right, of course. No Bermuda-born child would call this wind-blasted outcrop of rock and driftwood a beach. A beach-*head*, perhaps. But not a beach.

"This is more like it." Gage approves of the sandy beach near the old town site, runs whooping into the water; runs, screaming, back out – "*Jesus Christ, it's cold!*" – sounding for all the world like Sully or Jimmy.

"Gage, don't curse," I admonish, trying to stifle my laughter.

"It's not a curse, Mom! It's a prayer!"

"A prayer?" Grinning wickedly, Sully grabs the boy and rolls him tightly in a towel, turns him upside down and dangles him over the shallow water. "Let's hear the prayer, you blasphemer!"

"Please, God; please, God," Gage shrieks. "Don't make me go back in that water!"

We spend a few days prowling around, scrambling over the rocky shoreline, hiking to the Sea-lion. Visiting Riordan family friends who still camp in the century-old miners' houses.

Boating out to the low, flat island that once berthed the shafthouse and other structures. When the sun hits the water at just the right angle, "Look," Sully says, "there's the shaft."

Gage leans over the gunwale so far I fear he'll tumble in, head first. Peering into the black rectangle, angled hundreds of metres below the surface, I am attacked with fierce vertigo.

"Imagine the faith of those men!" I say weakly. "Heading down a submerged shaft every day, only one pump-breakdown away from drowning."

"Why do you call this the Irish Castle?" Gage asks, struggling to gain sufficient purchase to climb a little way up the sheer face of the cliff that backs the miners' cottages.

"Jimmy insists it was named by his Grandfather Sullivan," Sully says, "but it could as easily have been named by any of a hundred fanciful Irish miners."

Gage is full of questions. "Why do Jimmy and Sonja still keep the camp," he asks, "since they live in Toronto?"

"Your grandfather lived here, at Silver Islet, until he was about your age, Gage," Sully explains.

"In this house?"

"No; he bought this place when I was little. And he keeps it so that we can share it with you. Because we all had so much fun here."

Playing Scrabble and Monopoly after dark with Gage, sharing highlights of our childhood summers. A bit of a minefield for me, at best; a test of my ability to put an optimistic spin on memory. *Change one thing.* If I could eliminate my grandfather from my history I'd have a charming, if dull, story to relate: the perfect Thunder Bay childhood, a bookend to Sully's.

Absorbing impressions, brushing up on the history. And, in quiet moments, listening. Just listening. To the wind whispering the Indian legends; to the echoes of Irish and Cornish folk songs brought by the miners. To the slap of wave against rock as it works to undo all that man once sought to create here, at the very feet of the Sleeping Giant.

"I used to pray to the Sleeping Giant," I remind Sully, "when I was a child. After my grandfather would leave my bed, I'd kneel beside the window, looking out to the lighthouse, and I'd pray. Pray for forgiveness for the terrible things he made me do to him in the dark."

"Maybe I intercepted those prayers," he responds, "on this very porch."

With Gage settling to sleep in Sully's old room we stand, arms wrapped around each other, staring out over the lake.

"Did our prayers cross each other?" he asks, nuzzling my neck. "Did

I hear the cry of a little girl, weeping in the dark? Perhaps that's why I could love her without her making the slightest effort at self-revelation. Because I'd heard it all from the source, from her heart itself?"

"You've got a lot of imagination," I smile, "for a lawyer." Wonder, in spite of myself, if there is *criticism* implied in his words. "And what was *your* prayer?"

"Please, God; please, God," he shrieks, imitating Gage. "Don't make me go back in that water!"

"Are you making fun of me?" comes Gage's voice from the bedroom window.

"Big ears."

Laughing, Sully and I re-enter the cabin. "No; I was quoting you," Sully says. "Why aren't you asleep?"

For obvious reasons: Gage has half the contents of Sully's closet strewn around the room. "I thought there might be some toys in the boxes," he admits defensively.

"Did you think you might find toys in these *envelopes?*" I ask, reining in an impulse to anger.

The boy has disturbed a stack of old letters. I'm not sure if I'm more angry at his half-lie or the fact that I recognize my own fifteen-year-old handwriting on the gutted envelopes. What *did* I say to Sully that summer, almost twenty years ago?

"Honey, what've we told you about poking into other people's stuff without permission?"

"I'm sorry," he apologizes, more from habit than contrition.

"If you want to hide anything from Gage," Sully said once, "you have to leave it in full view. Put it in a box, or behind a door, and it's fair game."

This had been an endearing trait in a two-year-old. But now, at eight, Gage's curiosity still overcomes self-discipline. His inability to restrain himself bugs me.

"Curiosity is a valuable tool," I'd allowed to Sully, to our friends. "But how do you teach him to draw a line between what's his and what's not?" There's no easy answer to the question. I fear we've been too indulgent. "The child is growing up with a wanton disregard for private property."

"You're right," Sully agreed, bobbing his head seriously. "Perhaps a term in reform school is called for."

My heart tripped on itself. Sully and his father have spent their careers following the parading 'criminal elephants' with shovels. Who else knows their spoor more intimately?

"What's next?" he continued. "Trespassing? Break-and-entry?" A stern scowl: "*Cultural appropriation?*" He howled at my credulity. "Lighten up, Mariah! What's the definition of 'wanton,' after all?"

Sportive, gambolling, playful, irresponsible, capricious: not exactly criminal. Something he'll outgrow, like the construction *amn't.* I'd relaxed.

"*Ask* for permission," I tell Gage tiredly. "We rarely deny you anything; it's just the considerate thing to do. *Ask.*"

Gage looks chastened as we tuck him back into bed. Who knows if we've made an impression?

"So," my father asks as we unload the rental car. Beau and Raven, a pair of hulking Bouviers, make a nuisance of themselves as they greet us. "Were you able to pick anything up on the Silver Islet frequency?"

"Some static. Some impressions. And a few snatches of melody." I shrug casually, belying my nervousness. "I'll have a better idea how to work it all in after I've seen the rough cut in Toronto next week."

My fear is that inspiration will dry up when faced with a tight deadline. But the brain *is* at work, I realize, when I surface in mid-conversation at dinner, oblivious to topic or time.

"Your music has such a refreshing external focus," Geoff Halloway commented over our first dinner together in Bermuda.

Snorting wine through my nose, I almost succumbed to a paroxysm of choking and laughter.

"Did I say something funny?" he asked, mystified, as Sully all but administered the Heimlich manoeuvre.

"Someday," Sully grinned, "if you get to know Mariah well enough, you may realize *how* funny."

"The external focus is so new," I told Geoff, when I was finally able to comport myself with dignity, "I'm not entirely convinced it isn't temporary. It's a major breakthrough for me."

Working from Geoff's script I've developed a few themes: Discovery. Development. Depression. Dismantling. Sully steers me to solitude, managing our time with my parents so I can take advantage of the unbidden spurts of concentration as the music takes shape.

During an intense session, though, I realize I'm all alone in the house. And hungry. I stuff some leftovers between two slices of bread and step onto the deck for a breath of air laden with the scent of fresh-cut poplar. There's a chain-saw symphony. Dogs barking. A whoop of high-pitched laughter. My deduction: everyone's at Luke's. I could succumb to melancholy; instead, I let my need for company propel me down the path through the trees. I don't want to be left out of *everything*.

My brother had snatched up the hundred-acre parcel abutting Mom and Dad's spread when it came on the market. He'd been working for a veterinary clinic in town, but hated living in the city.

"It's time to strike out on my own," he reasoned. "There's not another vet for miles around."

He has a nice house (a prefab cedar job not dissimilar to my parents') on his lot and a large garage with his surgery and kennels attached, so, essentially, he works at home – or lives at work. He sees no one except his clients and likes it that way. Our folks are his only social life; Mom keeps him well-fed. "Striking out on his own" seems to have meant coming back home to live.

Luke's Newfie, Pooh-Bear ("Just me and Pooh in the Hundred-Acre Wood!"), lollops up to greet me, tail-feathers flapping, accompanied by Beau and Raven.

"I thought you were a vet, not a lumberjack," I say as Luke puts down the chain-saw and removes his ear protection. Sully and Gage wave at me from the block where Sully is splitting a heap of seasoned birch.

"Dad seems to think this clearing should be bigger." Luke wipes his brow on the sleeve of his shirt.

"You mean, he needs more wood stockpiled for the winter."

Cocking a loaded finger at me, he grins. "Bull's-eye."

My father appears from the north side of the clearing, pushing a wheelbarrow piled with poplar logs. "Jesus, man!" he roars. Abandoning the barrow he races to Sully's side. "Step back, Gage. You could lose an eye." He adjusts Sully's grip on the axe and demonstrates a "proper" swing like a golf pro. Sully turns his head slightly to meet my eyes – and rolls his own in such an exaggerated manner I can't miss it even at a hundred metres.

"Christ." Luke laughs with bemused dismay.

"How can you stand it? I'm surprised he's not in there with you every day," I say, pointing to his surgery, "advising you how best to neuter a dog!"

" 'A day without conflict is like a day without sunshine,' " he says. "And you know?" He leans toward me confidentially. "I can't take a step without seeking his advice."

"*Are you serious?*"

"I almost always do the opposite — but it absolves him of responsibility if I make a mistake." Assuming my father's facial expression, hand gestures, and tone: "It's not my fault!" he mimics, "I told him how he should do it! But would he listen?" Luke shrugs. "It makes him happy to think I'm incapable." Mom steps out Luke's back door, bearing a tray of sandwiches. "Just like it makes *her* happy," he says, jerking his chin, "to believe I'm underfed."

"Mom."

Gage and Beau wander into the bedroom where I've appropriated my mother's sewing table to new purpose.

"Yes, love."

"I've run out of stuff to read."

"That's impossible, in this house." The living-room shelves are stacked two deep.

"There's a box in the basement, marked 'Mariah's books'."

"In the rec room?" My dad had cleared the groaning bookcases of children's classics, set them aside for Gage along with Luke's quaintly antique Matchbox cars and Hot Wheels.

Gage nods emphatically.

"Fine. If it's the box in the rec room, it's meant for you anyway. You should be able to find something of interest in it." I reach out my hand to connect with him. "Thanks for asking!" I call. But he's gone in a dead run, with Beau skittering across the kitchen floor, *en pointe*, behind him.

"Slow down, Gage!" his grandmother admonishes.

Concentration broken, I glance out the window. Sully, Luke, and Dad take turns with the post-hole digger, biting into the heavy clay soil until the hole is deep enough to seat a new clothes-line pole. My parents' country retirement is exhausting to contemplate.

Sully's dark hair is as wet as a seal's. "Why don't they just get a goddamned dryer," I imagine him saying, "and be done with it?" And my father's comment: "Decorative, but useless." Meaning Sully.

Shaking my head, I smile, returning to work.

Moments later, or so it seems, Gage is back at my side. The shadows have lengthened across the deserted field; there's water running and dinner cooking. Putting down my pencil, I turn my full attention to my son.

"Is your dad in the shower?"

He nods, looks at me a long moment. He has something clutched in his little hand.

"Whatcha got there, hon?"

Gage extends his hand fully, proffering the item. When I drape my right arm across his shoulders, he shrugs it off. Eight years old, I think. So grown up.

KODAK PAPER KODAK PAPER KODAK PAPER all across the back. "Are you hungry?" Gage doesn't respond. Flip it over.

Doug.

Vision telescopes in and out of blackness. *Doug in swimming trunks, grinning, bare-chested. Waving with his little hand.* Jesus jesus. My lungs ache; I exhale gently. Deliberately. "Where did you find this, sweetheart?"

"In the basement."

"Which box?" No response. *"Which box?* Show me."

Sully's still in the shower; Mother's in the kitchen. "Dinner's almost ready," she sings.

"Good. Thanks."

Gage leads the way. Down the stairs. Into the rec room. "Mariah's books" – the box my father had set aside for Gage. Misfiled?

"Where was it?"

The boy hands me *Who Has Seen the Wind?* "Mariah Standhoffer" block-printed on the inside cover. A semester of CanLit in Grade 13. Not exactly a children's book; not entirely inappropriate. No blame accrues to my father's selection; no fault attaches to Gage's perusal. This box was set aside for Gage's use. He hasn't been ferreting through my things. He even asked permission.

Christ christ christ.

Rewind. Erase. Change one thing.

"Who is he?" Gage asks in a small voice.

Where do babies come from? What's a freak? Think, Mariah; what does the child want to know?

"His name is Doug Hassock," I say, sinking into an armchair. Pull Gage onto my knee. He doesn't resist. "We went to high school together."

"He has a little arm, too."

"Yes, he does. Many people have similar problems." *Don't ask me the statistical probability don't ask don't ask.*

"How come I've never seen anybody else?"

My breathing is so shallow I'm surprised my brain still functions. "You've lived in Bermuda all your life, Gage; you don't get a true sample there."

"I liked it better when I was the only one."

Me, too. Oh, believe me, love. Me, too.

"Dinner's ready!" Mom calls.

I look at Gage. Are we finished here? What else can I say — "Don't tell your Dad?" No. *If you want to hide anything from Gage, you have to leave it in full view.* Likewise, if you want him to keep a secret, you can't let him know it *is* a secret.

"Daddy, guess what?" Gage announced blithely, one July. "We got you a sandwich for your birthday. Only it's not the kind you eat, it's the kind you *golf* with."

"Oh, Gage! It's a 'sand wedge' and it was supposed to be a surprise!"

Sully swung the little blabbermouth into his arms, laughing. "Gosh, I hope you wrapped it well. Otherwise it might be stale by next week."

No, I can't tell him *not* to tell Sully, even if he's matured in the intervening years sufficiently to relish the surprise of others at Christmas, on birthdays. "Run upstairs and wash your hands, now."

Gage slides off my knee, stands in front of me expectantly. "May I have the picture back?"

"Sorry." I shake my head a little. "It's mine."

He thunders up the stairs and across the kitchen floor above my head. I look at the photo in my hand, my gut twisting. Damn you, Doug! Why did you have to surface now?

Holding the photograph between my teeth, I tear it first into long strips, then crosswise into tiny shreds, the taste of chemicals on my lips. Not appetizing. But if I could make it go away by swallowing it, fragment by fragment, I would. Instead, I weave my way through the house on a tour of waste-paper baskets — a few bits here, a few bits there — until my pocket is empty.

"You haven't eaten much, Mariah," my father comments, dish poised in his hand.

"No more for me, thanks."

He dips into the casserole, proffers a filled spoon.

"I said, *no thanks!*"

To Luke's questioning glance, I apply a smile as deliberately as lipstick.

All my instincts scream "flight." My right eyelid twitches uncontrollably; I notice a nimbus of light around the chandelier signalling impending migraine. I should leave the table, take a couple of Advil, and lie down for half an hour. But I assume Gage has me under surveillance and, seasoned liar that I am, I will not betray my alarm. He's found a picture; it's no big deal.

Except, it *is* a big deal.

Abandoning Sully to extended debate with my dad and brother, I take to my own bed not long after we've tucked Gage away for the night. Roll myself into a tight defensive ball, like a pill-bug disturbed under a log, so I won't fly apart with loss. For loss is the dominant emotion, no matter how I analyse it.

What have I lost? Control? – absolutely. Sully, somehow. And Gage. I've lost it all. As if by destroying Doug's photograph, I've sundered the carefully assembled jigsaw puzzle of our lives together as a family.

Over the years, I thought my wish for us had become a reality. I thought we completed each other, that the child piece fit as snugly against Sully's heart as he did against mine. But it was an illusion.

Take this photo and bring it closer to your eyes. The smiling faces dissolve in a sea of dots. Change one thing – even your perspective – on this picture of a happy normal family and it disintegrates, revealing painfully separate fragments.

I know Gage. I know how he'll pull away – from me, from Sully – when he realizes the full implications of his discovery.

"This man is not my father," he'll say, "and my mother has lied to me all my life!"

How do I defend myself against such a terrible indictment – especially since it's true?

He's not a vicious child, but Gage has absorbed qualities from everyone: Sully's ability to sprint to the moral high ground when his principles are threatened. Something of my father's judgemental tone. Jimmy's golden tongue. And a tendency, like Doug's, to know it all, to have a name and classification for everything. Palaeontologist. Phocomelic. Liar. Slut.

And what has he absorbed from me – this child, my son? Sure: eye colour, hair colour, the shape of my chin. Beyond that? Not even an IQ point or two – since Doug was so *fucking* brilliant.

It's strange. I can see traits he's appropriated from everyone else, by nurture and nature, but *I cannot see myself.* I fully believe that, had I succeeded in my attempt that day after his birth, Gage would have turned out no different than he has. Perhaps he might even have proved a happier child – alone, with Sully – than he has under my flawed, ambivalent love.

Oh, Christ.

Fleeing these last words, I force myself to turn back and look at them, even though I might be transformed into a pillar of salt for so doing. *Look, Mariah.* Ambivalent? Yes.

When I admitted to Caro that day, "I love to be with him, but I don't know how to play with him," what I must truly have meant was, "I don't know how to *love* him."

I've withheld something from Gage, all these years, against the day when he might discover exactly what he has discovered. *Yes.* I've detached myself in anticipation of the way he will turn from me and his putative father, Sully, when he finds heredity rooted in Doug. Yes. *Yes.* Christ, yes.

You fucking pathological liar, Mariah! Do you have a single emotionally honest bone in your body? You convinced yourself, when you saw you couldn't love Gage and Sully perfectly, or even sufficiently – alone – that you could love them with the music, through the music.

But you don't! You never have. It's a lie. Delusion. An intellectual prosthesis to fill a gap you've never bridged with the living tissue of selfless love.

Race to the bathroom and vomit my meagre dinner. Stand shakily, using the open drawer for support. Spy a tempting, tempting implement in it. Reach for it with a steady, determined hand.

"Are you all right, sweetheart?" Mom taps at the door. It swings open under her hand. *Damn, I've left it unlocked.* "Can I get you anything?"

"I'm fine. Just a migraine." Push the drawer closed casually with my stump. *Why don't you leave, Mom? Why don't you just fucking leave?*

She looks into my face. "You've been crying."

Determination drains away like soiled bath water, leaving only the grey residue of failure: I haven't loved my child sufficiently. *Gage.* My pathetic bulwark of control crumbles within my mother's embrace and I weep; I weep. All the while knowing I can't tell her the true reason for my tears.

"What's the matter?"

I lean in close, "Gage found a picture of Doug."

"Oh, Mariah," she sighs. "What did you tell him?"

"As little as possible without being evasive."

"It could be years before he makes the connection."

"But you know Gage!" My voice rises in despair. "It's not going to go away. He's going to think about it. Analyse it. Research it. And come back at me when I least expect it."

"Then you have to tell Sully."

"I *can't*." I shake my head wildly, blowing my nose on the hunk of toilet paper she hands me. "We're not supposed to talk about it: that was his condition."

"You must. You can't let the child have so much power." Mom strokes my cheek; her eyes fill. "It'll be like having the sword of Damocles over your head. You'll be watching Gage, he'll be watching you. And it will isolate you both from Sully."

The power of a child's knowledge. I suddenly see parts of our own family lives laid bare.

"Did you ever tell Daddy — " I whisper, *that you killed his father by serving him a fistful of Seconal with a Seagrams chaser?* "Did you tell Daddy what you did for me?"

She nods, more to her reflection in the mirror than to me. "Just after you got back from Europe," she says, confirming my long-held suspicion. "Your dad was furious at having been denied the chance to do it himself." She smiles bleakly. "Furious that he'd been excluded from parenting you. That I didn't trust him with knowing what his father had done to you," she says, brushing the tears from my face.

"How did you get through it?"

"I couldn't do it alone any more, Mariah. Not if I wanted a marriage. We had to do it, together — *for you*, my darling. Just as you have to tell Sully, *for Gage*. Because," she squeezes my arm, "whatever Gage imagines will be worse than the truth. And leaving Sully out of it will only damage what you two have together."

"But," as true as I know her words to be, I'm equally convinced of my own: "Sully will be so hurt."

"Yes," she nods, "he will. But you have to trust that he's strong enough to help you with this. You can't do it alone."

She's right. I can't. I saw that written clearly enough on the edge of the razor blade in the drawer. *What matters now is what I do.* Two options.

Use the blade. Or lay myself open to my husband and son. Take a chance on mature, *selfless* love – if only this once in my life.

Mom steers me out of the bathroom and into bed. "I'll get you an ice-pack."

Sully delivers it. "Mom used the jaws of life to pry me out of Dad's clutches."

"You mean, Luke leaped into the breach in your stead."

"Something like that." He drapes himself around me. "Feeling better? You're trembling."

"I'd like to believe it's the ice," I begin, teeth chattering, "but it's anxiety. I've got something to tell you." I brace for his reaction: "Gage found a picture of Doug."

Puffing out his cheeks, Sully lets them deflate gradually. "I've wondered when this would come up," he says equably. "It's not as if we could keep it a secret for ever."

"*I* fully expected we could!" Sully's jaw drops. "*I* took it as a personal failure that Gage found out; I thought I'd broken our *sacred trust* somehow!"

"What sacred trust?"

I stare at him as if he is dull-witted. "The condition of our contract – 'that we will never speak of this again.' "

"I thought you declared that contract null and void with your suicide attempt," he says, angry and astonished. "You obviously couldn't *live* with its terms."

"But I have!" I gesture wildly. "You said you couldn't do it if we were always analysing it, and I respected that. We've *never* analysed it; we've *never* discussed it – although there've been times I would've killed to have spoken with you about it." A cleaver of pain bisects my skull. "You changed the terms without telling me, you bastard! You've had *control* – all along."

"Shh," he hisses. "Your parents."

"*Fuck my parents!*"

"Riah."

"*Fuck you,* Sully! I kept my silence as a condition of the pardon, don't you see?"

Raising his hands to protect himself, Sully grabs at my wrists. "Riah."

"Don't touch me."

Black, black pain. I wrap myself around the core of it, holding it tight to keep it safe. *To keep it safe?*

There is no selfless love in this heart — there is only the dross of self. It's only the deep, black shaft of pain that makes me special in any way.

I must not, cannot, give it up. For, without the pain, I'm nothing.

Give it up.

After a long silence, "You have every right to be angry," he says rationally, brows knit. "We seem to have had a monumental failure to communicate."

A failure to communicate? "Is that what you call it?" *Give it up, Mariah.* Regret and relief colliding like weather fronts. Laughing and crying until I'm in danger of being sick again: I give it up.

Sully weathers the storm. "You've been a secret-keeper all your life, Mariah. You've had to believe they *could* be kept," he says, stroking me, gentling me. "And I've been on the other side, prying them out of the 'criminal elephants.' "

My lip twitches involuntarily.

"I've never believed a secret could be kept indefinitely," he continues. "*Truth will out.*"

A voice outside the bedroom door: "Mommy? Dad?"

Sully bounces up. "What's the matter, buddy?"

Gage stands in the hall, rubbing his eyes. "I had a bad dream. And I couldn't find my bedroom after I got up to pee." He yawns.

"C'mon."

As Gage places his hand trustingly in Sully's palm, *his father's* palm, I pull my robe around me and follow them to the boy's assigned room. I watch the ritual hug and tucking-in, then add my own kiss, silent blessing and thanksgiving. *Thank you for them.*

Leading me back to the bedroom, "We're together in this," Sully says. "We have to do what's best for Gage."

"He'll think so badly of me," I say, surprised and heartened by my matter-of-factness.

Sully looks at me blankly. "It's not in Gage's best interests to think badly of his mother."

"So — we'll *lie?*" The Last Ethical Lawyer will lie to his child?

"Oh, Mariah," he says, holding me tight. "I've said it before: have some compassion for yourself. Your sins aren't so special they can't be forgiven. Except by *you.*"

"It's still a function of what the child needs to know," Sully says. "You can't just come out and tell him everything; it has to be age-appropriate, if nothing else."

"But in the meantime, he's working on it. As Mom said, whatever he might imagine will be worse than the truth." I settle into Sully's arms. "What will he think? That he was abandoned by the man in the picture because he was 'bad' or 'deformed'?"

"Most kids go through a phase of imagining they were adopted," he says.

"Sometimes that feeling never goes away," I muse. "Doug used to swear he and Kat were changelings because he always felt so alienated from his father."

Sully nods sympathetically.

"Perhaps," I sigh, "all parents are doomed to fail their children, emotional or biological, in some material way. You, though." I study this man, my husband. "You made the most material of choices for us."

As Sully's brow creases in response to these words, I marvel that I couldn't have imagined such a discussion just a few short days ago. To talk about paternity issues in such a concrete way; even to speak about Doug!

"Right, or wrong. Stay, or go." He lays the words with his hands like bricks in a row. "There was choice. And yet," he opens his palms, "there was none. *I* was chosen; *I did not choose.* It was easy once I saw that," he says. "You and Doug were chosen to produce him; I was chosen to father him. Gage is the point of our marriage, its purpose, its meaning."

"We would be ordinary without him," I nod. "We'd have nothing to rally around. Without Gage, you'd have grown tired of my pathological introspection; you would have left me years ago."

I've said this without rancour, merely as a statement of fact, with — I realize — emotional detachment. Even as I note it, it disappears. Still, I'm left holding a trace of it like butterfly dust on my fingers: *this is Sully's strength.* I envy his ability to detach himself from his emotions, to see only the issue.

"Gage has brought out the best in us," Sully says.

"What would Doug have become, if he'd known Gage? Would Gage have brought out the best in him, as well?"

Sully squeezes his eyes shut. "Christ, you realize this will involve *defending* Doug — to ourselves, and to Gage! Talk about leaps of faith. I'm not sure I've got the stomach for it."

Sully has a point. How to present Doug in a sufficiently positive light so his paternity is not a negative in Gage's mind while at the same time ensuring we don't inadvertently canonize him?

"Keep it simple," Sully insists. "It was *fate*. Do *you* accept that?"

"One part of me has always thought of it as God's sadistic little joke." My throat closes. "But you've shown me the way out of that particular cul-de-sac." I smile gratefully.

Is it possible to re-invent God? A God on whom I can project my better nature and have it reflected back to me — so that I might detach from my own emotions sufficiently to accept where there is no choice. To do, rather than feel. And to love what I cannot change.

"The boys are still at the zoo," Sonja says, ushering me into the Riordan condo overlooking the Toronto lakeshore. "How did it go?"

"I'm exhausted," I admit, succumbing gratefully to tea and Sonja's need to mother. "But I'm on the right track. Geoff made encouraging noises."

I'd laid out my whole plan for him. The requirements of film are different than those of an orchestral suite. Still, I hear it both ways. As a cohesive whole, developed through several movements. And in aural images, to support Geoff's script and film without drawing attention to itself.

"This is more than I'd hoped for, Mariah!" he'd enthused. "You *are* an overachiever, aren't you?" He'd given me a quick, grateful kiss. "*The Silver Islet Suite* will help promote the film; the film will help promote the suite. On to fame and fortune!"

I was poised to make a self-deprecating comment about rising from shadow to obscurity — when my eye was caught by a shelf of awards behind Geoff's desk. *Perhaps you have to imagine these things before they can happen*, I thought, giving in to his exuberance.

I shake my head at my grandiosity. A full day's work was fuelled by the interplay with Geoff Halloway, and by that adrenalin rush. But now I'm aware only of its depletion and the need to focus away from myself lest I confuse fatigue with depression.

"Why does James call you and Jimmy by your Christian names?" I ask.

My mother-in-law smiles wryly. "I don't know. He started that when he was about ten." She sips from her teacup. "He didn't do it as a test, as some kids might: 'let's see if I can get a rise out of Mom'. No, he just assumed it; he didn't try it on for size."

"The way he started wearing Jimmy's hand-me-downs in high school?"

"Oh, Lord, yes!" Sonja laughs. "What a sight he was!"

I am pierced with memory. "I loved that."

"I know. There was something so," she closes her eyes briefly, as if replaying home movies on the lids, "so heartbreakingly vulnerable about that boy in his father's clothes. He turned them into — " searches for words, " — oversized, postwar, Ivy League *costumes!*"

"Yes, costumes," I concur. We grin at each other across the room, recalling the outlandish boy we both loved. "He's always been an actor. Gage and I are his drama; he invented himself around us."

Sonja's eyebrow lifts.

"Though we've had to rework the script lately: Gage found a picture of Doug Hassock."

Ignoring the implications of Gage's discovery, "John Hassock was a strange man," she muses. "I never understood what Lily saw in him," she turns to include me. "Doug's mother, Lily, and her sister, Myrtle, were friends of mine. We worked together at Eaton's for a while — with your mother, too, Mariah," she adds.

"Did *every*one work at Eaton's back then?"

"Every young woman of marriageable age who wasn't a teacher or a secretary," she laughs. "Landing a job at Eaton's was like becoming a debutante. On display, like mannequins, until a match was made."

Sips her tea. "A couple of English roses, Lily and Myrtle. They both had a crush on Jimmy at one time," she confides, "in the days when he cut a dashing figure in the clothes his son used as costumes."

Sonja pauses in her reverie, continues with a seeming *non sequitur:* "John was furious when the twins were born. He blamed Lily for Doug's defect. He was always a self-righteous prig: 'sins of the mother,' surely, since *he* was so perfect, so holy. He was a Catholic," she explains, "Lily wasn't. Bad enough a child is born with a handicap, without laying blame."

My cheeks colour uncontrollably. I regret having introduced the topic — since Sonja's dance around it is so intimate without addressing it.

"You've told Gage about Doug?" she asks.

I shrug. "Only the barest minimum. We'll field the other questions as they arise."

"You're brave," she sighs. "But I suppose the child needs to know. We all have a birthright, after all."

"*Sully* is Gage's birthright," I insist. "I wish the whole thing would go away. I *hate* it that Gage's focus will shift from the man who loves him to looming curiosity about a stranger. What if Gage wants to meet him?"

"Would that be so bad?" Sonja asks. "He could satisfy his curiosity and, at the same time, come to realize that paternity *is* vested in the man who loves him."

"Will he understand that? Will he get that?"

"Maybe Doug can *help* him get that. Isn't he a psychologist, after all?"

I make a dismissive noise. "*Yes.* And that's why I've avoided the species. How a man with so many problems can set himself up to help other people sort out their own!" I shake my head apologetically. "My father's always had a profound distrust of the 'helping' professions; I've inherited that with my DNA."

"You look tired, dear," Sonja says. "Why don't you lie down until the gents get home."

More for camouflage than anything, I drag my backpack and brief-case into the bedroom. Lie down on the bed. Check my watch. Close my eyes. Leap up. Juggle the heavy Metro Toronto phone book out from under the bedside table, and flick through the H's with trembling hand.

"Hello, Doug. It's Mariah."

"Tell me, Mommy. Where are we going?"

"It's a surprise, Gage, but I think you'll like it."

As we make our way up University Avenue from the subway, Gage skips along beside me, holding my elbow, content with my explanation.

I'm suffering serious trepidation. Sully is golfing with Jimmy at Glen Abbey; I've managed to escape Sonja gracefully, although I was prepared to lie. Hell, I was prepared to tell the truth, if necessary.

"A museum?" Gage asks, non-judgementally, as we mount the steps of the Royal Ontario Museum.

"Yes, love. They have dinosaurs."

"All right!" His face lights up and he commandeers the tour like a general, explaining everything to me as we proceed through the rooms. I apply my full attention to him so I won't be seen to be looking out for Doug.

But the effort becomes increasingly exhausting. "I have to sit down for a moment, sweetheart."

Gage is happy enough to poke around on his own. I concentrate on my breathing more than I did in labour.

"He's beautiful, Mariah." Doug takes a seat beside me on the bench.

Not taking my eyes away from my son, "Yes. He is," I agree.

"You look well."

I examine him for the first time. His face is haggard, but his expression is mild. "So do you."

Doug removes the coat of the expensive lightweight summer suit he's wearing, right sleeve tucked into the pocket, and lays it carefully beside him on the bench. He polishes his glasses – a necessity acquired since our last meeting – with his silk tie; takes my wrist lightly in his left hand.

I don't withdraw – although I'm tremulous with anxiety and anger. "You're late."

He shakes his head. "I've been following you."

Blushing retroactively under his scrutiny, I feel my privacy has been invaded. He has been watching me, from a distance, judging my interaction with my son. *His son.* I push this thought away angrily. *Sully's son.*

"This isn't easy for you, I know."

"Ha!" I bray, then clear my throat. "I'm sorry to spring this on you. I wouldn't, but for Gage. My mother-in-law seemed to think you might be able to help."

"I'm grateful for her faith. I wish I shared it."

"Thank you anyway." I pull away and stand.

"I didn't say I wouldn't help, Mariah; I'm not sure I can," he says quietly. "How did you think I might?"

Look at Doug, here, now, nine years since Kat's wedding. Nine years since Gage's conception. Nine years this month since my marriage to Sully. The signs of advancing age are written clearly in the man's weakened eyes, across his receding hairline, on his face – as I'm sure they must be, similarly, on my own. It's a shock. Despite seeing him that one day, nine years ago, at twenty-five, in the photo album of memory he's very much as he'd appeared in the snapshot Gage found: forever nineteen. How *did* I think this middle-aged stranger might help me with my son?

"Sully and I have done nothing but talk about this since Gage found your picture."

"Does Sully know you're here today?"

"Yes."

I'd presented Sully with a *fait accompli* of sorts. "I've spoken with Doug," I told him – wondering, as I spoke, whether the clause of our contract prohibiting contact with Doug was still in force. "Your mother suggested it."

"My mother." Sully shook his head in fond annoyance. "And what did Doug say?"

"That he'd help if he could. We're meeting at the ROM tomorrow."

He removed his glasses and rubbed his eyes. "Can't we do this without enlisting the enemy?"

"I'm sorry – I acted without thinking," I said, reaching for his arm. Was I wrong? "I had no idea how Doug might respond. You can come along, if you like. Or I'll cancel."

Sully's gaze was silent. And sorrowful. I saw – in his unguarded expression during that long moment – *an almost paralysing fear of loss*. But when he blinked, it was over; he was – detached. And with his words – "Whatever you think best" – he handed me control.

Control! What a hideous burden. My husband left the room. Left me in control of our future – and his pain. Left me with the wrenching certainty that his strength – his ability to detach himself from his emotions – is rooted in denial of his most fundamental weakness. Doug was right – damn him! – all those years ago, when he suggested that Sully's generosity was motivated by this fear.

There will be no loss for you in this, my love! A fierce determination solidified in me: that Sully's position as father be strengthened by Gage's knowledge, not weakened in any way. Even if I have to set myself up to my son as the Whore of Babylon to do it.

"I phoned you last night on pure impulse." I glance at Doug. "If I'd gotten your answering machine, there wouldn't have been a second call."

Doug waits for me to continue.

"We can't keep it a secret. Gage needs to know. How *much* he needs to know depends on him. Whatever he knows, it can't fail to impact on both his own self-image and his relationship with Sully. It has to be a positive impact on both counts. I can't stand to see either of them hurt by this, Doug. Sully is a *good man*. Sully is Gage's father; you are biologically incidental. How do I get that through to Gage?"

Doug's eyes are on the boy. "Biologically necessary," he corrects, ever the pedant. "*Emotionally* incidental."

His shoulders are hunched protectively — around his own pain, I imagine. I feel suddenly selfish and destructive, unequal to the task. Look at these lives in danger of spinning apart! Sully. Gage. Doug. Unbearable remorse is only lightened by focusing on the cheerful face of the child across the room.

"We're here for Gage," I say. "All of us."

"What will he be?" Doug asks.

I smile wryly. "At the moment, he wants to be a palaeontologist."

"Not literally," he clarifies. "I mean, what will he be in our lives?"

"He's our *raison d'être*." I answer Doug's questioning look. "Not that we have our whole lives invested in him, Sully and I. I have music — which is my work *and* my play; Sully has his work and *his* plays. But Gage is the thing beyond ourselves that gives our lives meaning and purpose."

"You speak of him like God."

"God acts on us through him."

"Oh, Mariah," Doug shudders. "This is getting too mystical for my taste! You and Sully were always on a predetermined course." He shakes his head. "Whose child *is* he, anyway? I don't see much of myself in him — other than the obvious."

"For whom was born this special child?" I ask, paraphrasing Larkin. "In him, all our compulsions meet, are recognized, and robed as destinies."

Doug flashes a doubting eyebrow.

"Sully was just a nice, amusing boy until I ruined him. Without a channel for his idealism he might have been a bored, alcoholic lawyer. And I might have been a bored housewife, giving voice lessons maybe, with mindless tunes running through my head that would never see their way to paper, let alone performance."

" 'He's a special child, Mary; I will love him as my own.' "

Doug's eyes meet mine with a profound intimacy.

"I heard the Toronto Mendelssohn Choir perform your 'St. Joseph's Carol' a couple of years ago. I opened the program — and 'Mariah

Standhoffer Riordan' jumped out and grabbed me by the throat. I was a basket case when the piece was over."

He stares at Gage, then back to me. "I think I knew then – which is why I wasn't terribly surprised to hear your voice on the phone last night. In retrospect, the Celtic element should have been the tip-off." He looks at me expectantly.

I quote his own words, " 'That Irish gene is always dominant.' "

"You remember," he smiles.

"Of course."

"There was something so personal, so immediate, about the piece. Beyond whatever regard one might have for old St. Joe."

Doug takes my handless wrist in his own warm palm.

"There was a kernel of human transformation in it. Something that might redeem a potentially alcoholic lawyer. And, who knows?" he adds. "Perhaps even a resolutely dissipated psychologist." His lips turn up slightly. "Perhaps you've got it wrong, my dear."

"Got what wrong?"

He jerks his chin toward the boy. "This isn't about how we can help Gage. But how Gage can help *us*."

My immediate response is physiological – a full, raging body blush – and emotional: *How dare you make this about you!* I want to fill the gallery with my indignation.

But Gage turns from his concerted study, spies me, and makes his way across the carpeted floor.

"This is great, Mom," he chirps. "Can we go into another room?"

"Sure."

Gage appraises Doug dispassionately, as he might a previously over-looked model on display.

I take refuge in formality. "Doug, I'd like to introduce my son, Anghus Gage Riordan. Gage, this is Dr. Douglas Hassock."

Offering his left hand solemnly to be shaken, "Are you a medical doctor?" he asks.

"No," Doug stoops to the boy's level. "I've got a doctorate in clinical psychology."

Gage glances at me. "Dad says that makes you an educated mister, not a doctor."

"That's hotly debated in some circles," Doug smiles. "You can call me Doug."

"He's an adult," Gage states out of the corner of his mouth. "Should I call him Uncle?"

"That would be fine," I squeeze my son's shoulder. "Gage has many uncles," I tell Doug. "Our friends are surrogate family."

Gage takes my elbow, steers me toward the next gallery. And takes Doug's left hand unselfconsciously in his own little right – as he might Sully's, or Jimmy's, or Ron's.

Over Gage's golden head my eyes meet Doug's. They're as bright and stricken as a wounded animal's. "Your mother tells me you're a brilliant soccer player," Doug says. "And that you like to sing," he adds, maintaining eye contact.

"Yes," Gage enthuses. "I sang *Amahl and the Night Visitors* at Christmas last year. I was Amahl. Dad was the baritone 'wise guy' – that's what Dad called himself." He grins. "And Mom was Amahl's mother. It was our 'debut performance as a family'."

You can hear the quotation marks in the boy's speech; I half-expect a footnote attributing the citation to Marcus O'Neill's *Royal Gazette* review.

Doug clears his throat. "That must have been very special. Perhaps you can sing for me later."

Gage looks around, assessing the hall's potential as a performance venue.

"Outside, dear!"

"The acoustics would be better here," he asserts logically.

"Yes," I smile across at Doug, "but you'd be disturbing other people."

"Nonsense!" Doug says, swinging him onto the staircase. "Not one of them knows you, except your mom and I." He lowers his head to Gage confidentially. "Did your mother ever tell you about her public recital? Copenhagen: March 1974."

"Gee, Mom," Gage teases. "Wasn't that before the days of the dinosaurs?" He grins. "What shall I sing?"

"Sing from *Amahl*," I suggest.

"I haven't warmed up," he warns Doug.

"That's all right."

When my son opens his mouth, the pure sweet tone that emerges comes as no surprise; it's a projection of his facial expression and features. People stop to listen, smiling indulgently, as the sound grows, as Gage recalls the hand gestures he employed on stage, as he captures his small audience with Menotti's vision of a little lame boy who is restored to wholeness by the baby Jesus — and his own generous faith.

Consummate actor, Gage accepts the forthcoming applause gracefully, smiles, and jumps down from the stairs.

"That was beautiful, Gage." Doug blows his nose surreptitiously, then tousles the child's hair.

A small girl standing nearby turns to her mother and pipes, "That boy has a funny little arm!" in a dreadful, piercing voice.

Everyone turns to stare. Beyond that, we're all paralysed.

"That's okay," Gage assures her. "Tyrannosaurus had *two* little arms and he was very strong. So am I."

More discreetly, the girl says, "That man has a little arm, too. Is he your dad?"

Gage looks up at Doug for a long beat, then back to his inquisitor. "No; he's my uncle."

When I'm able to breathe again, I fuss around the boy, tuck in his shirt-tail, comb his hair with my fingers. "That was lovely, sweetheart," I murmur. "You *are* very strong. You make me feel so proud. Your dad would be proud, too."

He leans toward my ear. "*Is* Uncle Doug my dad?" he asks quietly.

Doug bends into our huddle. "No, I'm not," he whispers. "Not in any way that counts." He looks at me. "Let's go get some ice cream, and we'll talk about that."

"I must find the ladies' room," I sniff, all a-dither, yet reluctant to leave the two of them alone for a moment. I don't want to miss anything.

Gage points with the index finger of his little hand. "That way, Mommy. I'll look after Uncle Doug."

Safely behind the door of a stall, I lean my forehead against the cool metal. *Jesus jesus give me strength*, like my son's. *Help me preserve my family — for Sully; for Gage.*

I perform emergency repairs to my make-up, take a few deep breaths. This is going well, I grimace at my reflection, all things considered — *if I survive the anxiety without having a stroke.*

When I emerge from the restroom, I glance around for the pair. Hang back a moment when I spot them. Gage tugs on Doug's left hand; Doug squats, points to something with his own little hand. It's my turn to spy. Forgiving Doug his own voyeurism as I watch them, I lean against a pillar for support.

Change one thing.

I erase ten years with Sully to imagine, momentarily, the circumstances under which this extraordinary event would be the norm. But I can't see it. A complete failure of imagination: I cannot see a way I might have placed our lives under this man's care.

With this failure comes release as pure and sweet as Gage's voice. There's an organic rightness to our lives with Sully. It's destiny.

Propelled across the room by happiness and certainty, "Who wants ice cream?" I ask.

"Then the mayor of Vienna steps up to Beethoven's grave, listens carefully, and says, 'Yes, that's Beethoven's *Ninth Symphony* — being played *backward.*'" Gage assumes a revelatory expression. "'Citizens of Vienna!' the mayor announces. 'There's no need for alarm. The Maestro is *de-composing!*'"

My son falls back against the booth, laughing that infectious laugh, spreading it to both Doug and me — although I've heard the joke a dozen times.

"Gage has performed in every comedy club across Ontario during this vacation."

"Oh, Mom! Just for Nanny and Pops and Uncle Luke," he counts off against his fingers. "And Jimmy and Sonja."

Gage cuts a swath through the rest of his ice cream like a snowplough then wriggles out of the booth and takes off at a run across the restaurant.

Doug leans toward me across the table, takes my hand. "He's wonderful, Mariah!"

"Is that your professional opinion, *Herr Doktor?*"

"Fuck professionalism; any fool can see that boy is happy and well-adjusted. He grabs people by the gut." Doug gestures with his little hand. "He's shaped by his personality, first and foremost, and only incidentally — if at all — by his *difference.*"

"Thanks for confirming that," I say, staring at our hands between us on the table. "As a parent, it's hard to tell how prejudiced you are by love."

"Love." His voice drops to a low rumble. "*I want him,* Mariah. I'm blindsided with love." He tips his head back. "I'll take you, too, if I have to," he laughs giddily. "But I want him." Stares at me, menacing in his seriousness. "Leave Sully; come with me."

I grab my hand away as if it's been burned. Doug leans back against the banquette, closes his eyes, shakes his head.

"Just testing," he says softly. "I *meant* it – it's probably the first spontaneous emotion I've admitted to in twenty years." He looks at me intently. "But don't let it worry you."

Takes a deep breath, sighs deeply. "You – *and* Sully, it kills me to say – have made a wonderful family under extraordinary circumstances." He leans toward me again. "I never thought much of Sully when we were growing up because I was jealous. He had it all – and he had you. He was easy to love, almost as appealing as Gage is. But I didn't credit him with much depth; he wasn't a tortured soul, like you and I."

He sips hastily from his mug. "He *still* has it all – and he *still* has you. And I'm *still* jealous, probably more so because of *that child*," he says fiercely, pointing across the restaurant.

"I grudgingly admit: I admire Sully." Doug simulates a tortured face. "He loves you both. I see that reflected in Gage. In Gage's happiness, in your own. You want to preserve the integrity of your family unit and Gage's love for Sully; I know that." He bobs his head. "I respect that."

Doug looks over his shoulder to make sure we're still alone. "Let me tell you: if I thought there was any hope for the three of us," his voice drops to a whisper, "*any* hope at all – I'd take it – *Sully be damned and me with him*." He nods to emphasize his point. "I could play major mindfuck games with that kid, and with you – you know I could. He'd be calling me Daddy by this time tomorrow."

He takes off his glasses, squints at me across the table. "But I won't do that. 'God acts on us through Gage,' you said."

I wait: measuring, calculating, praying.

He puts his glasses back on. "I guess I can try to determine His will just once in my fucking life."

I clear my throat to rid it of the taste of terror: I've drawn blood biting down on my tongue. "Thanks for your honesty."

"No." He shakes his head. "Thank you for yours. I was never sure you'd learn to love so well. Or I might've tried a little harder while I had a chance." He toasts me with his coffee cup. "To James Sullivan Riordan, one lucky son of a bitch."

I return the toast.

"Slow down, Gage."

He shoots past the booth on purpose, comes back grinning, and takes his place expectantly, as he might in school – waiting for a lesson to begin.

Doug drapes his arm across the back of the banquette casually.

"What did you think when you found my picture last week, Gage?"

Gage shrugs minutely, considers. "I was surprised you had a little arm, too. I've never seen anyone else. Have you? Other than me?"

"Yes," Doug says. "But I've been around."

I can practically hear Gage's mind ticking points off his agenda. I brace for his questions.

"How do you get a little arm?"

"There are several possibilities." Doug leans forward. "One way is an accident of birth. Something happens while the baby is forming. The mother gets a virus, like the flu, or takes a drug her doctor has given her."

"Like Thalidomide?" Gage interrupts.

"Yes, like Thalidomide."

"I've seen pictures in the library," he says.

"Or," Doug shakes his head, mystified, "something just happens. It's no one's fault."

"And another way?"

"Heredity. You know about heredity?"

"A little," Gage says. "A black dog and a white dog will have some black puppies, some white puppies, some black-and-white puppies. And sometimes one that looks completely different."

"That's right. Sometimes hereditary differences don't appear for generations. Sometimes a gene will mutate spontaneously, creating an anomaly, a difference. And that mutated gene might become hereditary."

"How did you get yours?" Gage asks.

"I never really knew," Doug replies. "I was born around the right time for Thalidomide but my mom insists she never took any drugs and she doesn't remember having a virus. My twin sister wasn't different in any way. So we always thought it was a random occurrence. Just luck."

I note gratefully that Doug has refrained from employing judgemental words. Not "bad" luck, not "flaws," but "difference" and "anomaly."

"You might have selkie blood," Gage proposes.

Doug blinks; I gape.

"Jimmy told me about the selkies when we were talking to the seals at the zoo the other day," he informs me.

Thank you, Jimmy, I curse my father-in-law mentally, *for clouding the issue!* But I realize Sully felt compelled to discuss our problem with his dad. We are *all* desperate for damage control.

"The selkies were half human and half seal," Gage elaborates. "Jimmy said people would be happy, if we lived in Ireland, to think a selkie woman once loved a man and left her seal blood mixed with his in their child. Seal limbs like ours might be considered a special blessing there."

Doug clears his throat gently. "The old stories helped people understand things that couldn't be explained, Gage," he says. "If they've made some folks more accepting of other people's differences, that's good."

"So, how did I get mine?" Gage asks. "You said you're not my dad — in any way that counts. What did you mean?"

My head pounds; I question the wisdom of this conversation. Sully and I should be having it with Gage, together; I shouldn't be relying on this man's goodwill — or lack thereof. Doug has been, as he admitted, *blindsided* by love for this child.

Reading my anxiety across the table, he reassures me with his eyes.

"You know lots of stuff, Gage. You know about artificial insemination, I bet."

Gage nods. "Cows, mainly. A good bull is a valuable animal. Keeps the blood lines strong."

"Do bulls make good fathers?" Doug asks.

"Calves don't need fathers," the boy laughs dismissively. "They need 'mudders' with udders."

"What about people? Do they need good fathers?"

"Oh, yes," Gage's lips twitch, "*and* mudders." He lists against me; I give him a proprietary squeeze, more to reassure myself than him.

"People sometimes use artificial insemination to have babies."

Gage looks nonplussed for the first time. "To improve the *blood* lines?"

Doug smiles. "No, when two people who love each other very much are unable to conceive a child on their own."

They lean so urgently toward each other, they're practically head to head. Excluded, I feel eerily calm – as if by surrendering all control I've somehow achieved an altered state directed by something outside myself.

"Your mom and dad have loved each other since they were kids, Gage; they *always* wanted to have children as an expression of that love. Your mom told me so herself, when she was only seventeen," Doug looks to me, then to Gage. "They had to wait a long time for you. But you were worth waiting for."

My son smiles up at me, seeking confirmation. I nod emphatically. "That's true." *That's true.*

"No one classifies donor bulls as 'fathers,' Gage. The same holds for human donors."

Gage ponders this statement, stares at Doug intently. "You were a donor?"

"In a way." Doug inhales. "I supplied part of the genetic material that formed you; your mother provided the rest. And your father – James Sullivan Riordan – provided the love and support that makes all of you a family. Without him, you wouldn't be who you are."

"Do you have any kids?"

"No."

"You never wanted to be a dad?"

"Yes. I did." Doug glances at me, moving only his eyes. I feel his thoughts like telepathy: *You were the only woman I ever loved.* "The circumstances were never right. But I tell you, Gage – " his voice drops, " – if I'd ever had a son I'd want him to be just like you."

"Little arm and all?"

"Little arm and all," Doug nods seriously, pushes himself back a little. "I've known you only a few hours, Gage, and *I* love you. I can only imagine how much your mom and dad must love you, being with you every day. Watching you learn and grow. Seeing the best of themselves in you."

Gage's arm is outstretched on the table. Doug lays his own near it; the boy's fingers naturally curve to connect.

"Donors don't usually get to meet their little calves," Doug smiles, sadness etched in his eyes. "I feel supremely privileged to have met you, Gage."

The boy nods solemnly.

The three of us stare at the hands on the table; I feel compelled to add my own. Doug's face relaxes. The current of tension between us has found a ground through our conjoined fingers and is rendered harmless, the circuit closed.

The moment is broken only by the arrival of the cheque. I blow my nose hastily on a napkin while Doug flips open his wallet to remove a few bills. Gage stands in the aisle, poised to push off an invisible mark for the hundred-metre dash.

"Wait for us, Gage. You can run around Queen's Park in a minute."

We make our way down University Avenue: hand-to-stump and hand-in-little-hand. A silent trio, each with his own peculiar compensations.

As my son sprints off to scatter a flock of pigeons at the base of the statue, I feel quite nauseous with emotion and gratitude.

Doug follows Gage with his eyes. "There's no socially acceptable role I can play in Gage's life," he says. "Not 'special uncle,' not 'godfather.' Not even mentor. Sully wouldn't stand for such an intrusion," he smiles wryly. "My appearance here today is probably more than he can bear."

I step into his arms, lean my head against his chest. "I can't thank you enough."

"Gratitude implies obligation," he says, kissing my hair. "I'll be happy, imagining you obliged to me." His voice drops. "Speak well of me to him, that's all I ask."

He releases me, looks around. "Where's Gage?"

I point to the tree he's attempting to scale.

Swinging his crushed suit coat in his hand, Doug strides across the grass, looks up at the boy, and speaks. I cannot hear his words. Gage holds out his arms, falls trustingly into Doug's. Then, with the child perched on his hip, Doug lifts his little hand to me in farewell.

For one paralysing moment I believe he intends to abduct my son. But before this fear gels into action, Gage has wriggled out of Doug's embrace and is running, running back to mine.

$\sim\!\!\!\sim\!\!\!\sim$

Hospital noises and smells assault me. When I push open the door of his private room, Sully is sitting in the chair beside the bed, glasses perched on his nose, reading *Long Day's Journey Into Night*. He looks so vulnerable in these surroundings I want to toss him his own clothes and make a run for it. Never mind the surgery; who cares if he has to use a cane for the rest of his life?

"I'm not sure I approve of your choice of reading materials," I say in a jocular tone that competes for supremacy over tears, "given the circumstances."

He takes the glasses off, puts them with the book on the bedside table, holds open his arms. "I'll be fine," he insists. "But I know you, Mariah. You're playing out worst-case scenarios."

"There's so much I want to say." I roost on his good knee.

"Use shorthand."

I nod mutely, feel his carotid artery pulse against my cheek.

"How about, 'I love you'," he suggests.

"It's inadequate for my purposes."

"It's a *symbol*, the way a pearl's symbolic of the life of an oyster. All the layers, all the accretions. I'll take it as such."

"Okay."

His shoulders shake in silent laughter. "You have to say it."

"I thought I did."

"No," he smiles. "That was me."

I press my lips to his ear. "*I love you, Sully.*"

We flash compressed, encrypted code into each other's eyes. I feel myself regaining control – as if he's right. As if nothing that needs to be said has been left unspoken.

"Where's Gage?"

I look over my shoulder, expecting him to burst through the door on cue. "He's in the waiting room; I asked him to give me five alone with you."

"How come you're getting all emotional on me now? It's only knee surgery; you're the one who talked me into it."

"You talked yourself into it, remember?"

"I did, didn't I?" He grins. "Which proves a lawyer who represents himself has a fool for a client."

"My *April* fool," I murmur, kissing the tip of his nose before I stand.

When Cameron and Fizzy had taken a larger house, they'd handed Sea Billows down to us. Ron and Caro and the girls had abandoned our shared digs the year before for a cottage fancifully named Cobbler's Race and, although we still saw plenty of them, we jumped at the chance to rent our own cottage a mile or so from theirs. It was closer to Hamilton, too, which meant less of a commute for Sully and Gage to work and school, respectively – and so near the sandy crescent of beach at Admiralty House that Gage and I came to know it as intimately as our backyard.

The move coincided nicely with the Easter long weekend. I sent Gage and Sully outside to fly kites – the national Bermuda pastime on Good Friday – while I unpacked in peace.

"Mommy! Mommy!" Gage came tearing into the house in a panic, screaming, "Daddy fell over the edge!"

I pelted across the yard behind Gage, half-expecting a set-up, some sort of belated April Fool's joke. At the rim of the excavation, I stared down at my husband, writhing amid the neighbour's mangled vegetation some fifteen feet below, his face so contorted by pain and anger it was a caricature of itself.

"You broke the banana tree, Dad!" Gage accused.

I bit my lip to keep from laughing. "Are you all right?"

"No, I'm not all right!" he snarled. "I think I broke my leg."

Not broken. "Dad's knee is FUBAR," Gage told Angela as he ushered the Carpenters into our living room to visit the layabout.

"Haven't heard of that one, James," Tony said, puzzled. "Is that something like lumbar?"

"No," Gage supplied helpfully. "It stands for 'effed up beyond all recognition'."

Sully had put it off and put it off; they don't do anterior cruciate ligament reconstruction in Bermuda. He'd have to go to Boston, or New York, for the surgery and then stay a few weeks for the first phase of rehabilitation. A month away just wasn't convenient.

But when I'd gotten a call from the Berklee School of Music proposing I do a short series of lectures ("Preferably a series of *short* lectures!" I'd responded), it seemed the time was right. I got all the ducks in a row: a booking at Massachusetts General through the surgeon; a month-long house swap with one of Sully's Harvard roommates; proposed dates and topics for the lectures; and a papal dispensation from the headmaster for Gage.

"Gage can't take that much time off school," Sully maintained.

"The autumn half-term holiday falls at the end; we'll take lesson plans and books along; he'll do a project on Boston and we'll FedEx it back to Bermuda," I insisted. "You've put off having the surgery far too long, Sully. You're just *chicken-shit*."

"The surgery's worse than the injury, for Christ's sake. So what if my knee collapses like a deck chair? I've never been much of an athlete."

"But — you've got to get the knee fixed," I growled as I snuggled against him in bed; "I'm tired of being on top all the time."

"Oh *well* — since you put it that way!"

And we'd both surrendered to the foreplay of laughter.

But, as if to make truth from jest in bed that night, a random synapse had misfired — registering as pain, instead of pleasure. I hadn't realized I'd crossed the line from enjoyment to "let's get this over with" until Sully stopped me. "Whoa, Riah. Rein in. I'm not a runaway horse, darlin'."

"Am I hurting your knee?"

"No; *you* seem to be suffering some discomfort."

When I analysed it, I saw I'd been putting such excruciating pressure on my wrist it felt as if the truncated bone could pierce my flesh.

"Let's go for it; I'll get the knee fixed," he said.

"Not on my account!" I protested — a sudden about-face. "We're getting old; we can adapt. To anything."

"True. But there is a remedy. And I'm too young to settle for old man roles."

"I thought you snagged the spring production so you wouldn't have to act." Eugene O'Neill's *Long Day's Journey Into Night*, to be directed by James Sullivan Riordan: a switch from Sully's perennial musical comedies. Something with depth, something to challenge him in a new way.

"Yes," he agreed. "I've also determined there's no one else around I trust to play Edmund. The more I study it, the more *I* want it. But I'm thirty-five — already ten years older than Edmund's supposed to be; I can't do it hobbling around with a trick knee."

The Boston accent of a voice raised in greeting in the corridor breaches the barrier of Sully's Massachusetts General door. I examine my husband carefully. Why am I getting all emotional on him now? It is *just* knee surgery; he *will* be fine. The surgeon apprised us of all the risks, but I'm certain my Sully will be restored to full athletic function to tread the boards and fly kites on into his dotage.

I'm not even worried so much about Sully, specifically, as I am suddenly alert to mortality in general. The hospital environment is awash with the chaotic swill of it, but *I* could as easily be struck by a car crossing Mass Ave. We are *mortal, adj. & n. subject to death.*

Despite my own close calls I've felt, for the past ten years, that we've become exempt, somehow, from the slings and arrows of outrageous fortune. Sully, hitherto, has always seemed physically unassailable. Oh, sure: reading glasses, the odd silver hair in his sideburns. And seven extra pounds that have only served as putty in the laugh lines — filling and smoothing — rendering his face less angular; younger, if anything.

"What's the matter?" he asks. "Are you worried about spending a couple of nights alone with Gage in a strange house?"

"No," I shake my head.

"What is it, then?"

This is not the time; I shouldn't burden him with this. God knows he's probably repressing his own intimations of mortality right now, on the eve of surgery.

"Kat called today."

"Really? How is she?"

"*Kat's* fine."

"But." He looks concerned. "I hear an unspoken 'but'."

I forge ahead. "But Doug is very ill. Leukaemia." Sully waits. "He needs a bone marrow transplant. But Kat is not a match."

He looks at me levelly. "What does this have to do with you? Other than that Kat is understandably upset."

The door is propelled open by our son. "Hi, Dad." Gage bounds up to his father. "Can I take the bed for a test drive?"

"Sure," he says. "Hop in." Gets onto the bed and bends his dark head to the boy's fair one, demonstrating the bells and whistles.

My one regret is Kat. Distance helped preserve the secret of Gage's birth. After completing his Ph.D. in England, Ray was snatched up by a multinational chemical conglomerate. Kat and I corresponded — long letters to and from the unlikely places Ray was sent: a sampling of the more progressive United Arab Emirates; Brunei; Singapore. Kat sent packets of snaps of her kids, each born in an exotic locale; I sent only professional portraits of mine in which Gage had been carefully positioned by the photographer to hide his little hand.

In the wake of the turbulence stirred up by Gage's discovery of Doug's photo, it seemed artificial to make an announcement. What would I say, after all? "Oh, by the way, Kat — I've been meaning to tell you: my son is your only nephew"? I'd assumed that, if Doug felt any pressing need to confide paternity issues to his sister, he would.

So – when I picked up the phone at our adopted Back Bay home this afternoon to hear Kat's voice on the other end, I was assailed with guilt.

"Where in the world *are* you?"

"Ray's taken extended leave. We're in Thunder Bay," she said. "I dropped by your parents' house to visit."

"That's nice!" I enthused. "I'm sure they were thrilled to see you."

"Yes; it's been a while." She paused. "They showed me some snaps of their last trip to Bermuda. It looks like a wonderful place."

A warning bell rang in my mind. "It is. You must come and see it for yourself, if it's not too tame for you adventurers," I teased.

"Mariah," she took a deep breath. "They showed me pictures of Gage."

Confirmation: Doug hasn't told her about Gage. Ten years after the fact, the secret is no longer a secret, except from Kat.

"I don't think they even realized what they'd done," she continued. "I was very careful not to reveal my shock and surprise."

"I'm sorry," I said. "One of Sully's conditions was that Doug never find out. I didn't want to place the burden of that secret on you."

"I understand," she said. "Really, I do. I've thought about how terrible a time that must've been. I even feel responsible for putting the two of you together that night, my wedding night. Right?"

"Yes. But we were adults; we did have *choice*."

She sighed. "I'm glad of that, at least. I was afraid perhaps . . . you didn't."

"No; it wasn't like that." When all is said and done, the fact remains: *Gage was conceived in love.*

"Mariah." She's steeled herself, I thought. "Such a bolt from the blue – it had to be for a reason."

"What's the matter?" I asked gently.

"Doug is dying." She continued over my strangled "Oh, shit." "Leukaemia. He's been in remission off and on for a couple of years. But he needs a bone marrow transplant and I'm not a good enough match." She laughed bitterly. "There's irony for you: we were *womb-mates*, but I'm not a match!"

"Oh, God!" Suddenly I saw where she was going.

"Don't say anything," she said. "I won't ask if this is too hard for you. I'll fax you the details and leave it up to you. Whether you have Gage tested or not, I won't think less of you. It's just a shot in the dark," her voice broke. "I have to take it."

Words failed me. "Kat – good luck. For what it's worth, give him my love." And I hung up the phone.

Doug. I feel completely powerless, realize none of us is safe. When I held the razor in my hand, I was in control. *I* was not *subject to death*; death was *subject to me*. A delusion I held on to, even as I watched my blood flow down the drain.

"All right, son," Sully says patiently. "I'm getting motion sickness. What say we 'pahk this cah in Hahvahd Yahd'?"

"There's a pop machine down the hall, Gage," I hand him a pocketful of change. "Why don't you get a drink?"

"What about you, Dad?"

"Not allowed," Sully shakes his head. "I'll have wasted away from thirst and hunger by the time you see me next."

Gage's brow creases with concern, relaxes when he determines Sully's kidding. We watch the door swing shut behind him.

"Kat wants you to have Gage tested as a donor," Sully says.

I nod.

"Jesus."

His jaw takes on its courtroom squareness; he makes a prosecutorial gesture, strokes his chin. I grit my teeth for the forthcoming indictment.

"This is why I'd hoped Doug would never find out: the fucking complications!" he rasps. "Now the whole goddamned Hassock family has a proprietary interest in Gage's genetic resources: they've staked their claim."

"*Kat didn't know.* She thinks she's discovered a terrible secret and, through it, a way to save her brother's life."

Sully massages the furrow between his brows.

"The thing of it is – and it mystifies me – *Doug knows.* If he thought Gage might be a donor, why hasn't he asked me himself?"

"What did you tell me he said that day?" Sully blows air out through his pursed lips. " 'I'll be happy, imagining you obliged to me'?"

"Well, damn it, I *am* obliged."

I gambled everything on Doug's goodwill that afternoon, fifteen months ago – and the Riordan family unit came out ahead. Gage was reassured and empowered by the meeting; Sully's position was strengthened and secured; and Doug came out smelling like a rose. I had appealed to his better nature and he pretended to have one. Or acquired one, in response to his encounter with Gage. "I *am* obliged."

"No, you're not," Sully insists. "Gage is *my* son. Doug as much as signed a release that day." Meditates a moment. "Maybe we *should've* had him sign a release: 'For good and valuable consideration, the receipt and sufficiency of which is hereby acknowledged'."

"And of what," I ask sarcastically, "would that consideration have consisted?"

But I realize, as I speak, I've already determined what that good and valuable consideration might be: Doug's better nature. Dare one even call it his soul?

Gage and I share *Fodor's Guide to Boston* between us.

"We haven't seen *everything*, have we?" he asks, kneeling on his chair to get a better look at the book.

"It feels like it, sweetheart!" I sigh. "You've worn me out."

I'm almost grateful Sully suggested we come along for his first physio appointment; it gives me a chance to be idle for a half hour after the exhausting schedule Gage and I have kept during Sully's brief hospital stay.

"Have you figured out a focus for your project yet?"

The boy nods enthusiastically. "Architecture."

"That's appropriate," I smile. "Considering one of my lecture topics is 'Music-in-Architecture-slash-Architecture-in-Music'."

Preparing for the lectures, "What the hell do I know about architecture?" I wailed to Sully during a crisis of confidence.

He forced me to look at my compositions: *The Kiln, The Unfinished Church*, "The Shaft-House" and "Stamp Mill" movements from the *Silver Islet Suite*. Even the emerging score for Geoff Halloway's current project — *A Prison Camp Journal* — based on my father's own memoirs as company clerk of one of the German POW camps not far from Thunder Bay.

"How much architecture is there in a log cabin bunkhouse?" I scoffed.

"That's not the question," Sully insisted. "How much *music* is there in it?" he proposed, thereby providing me with a hook.

"I'd like to be an architect," Gage says.

"That's great," I smile, squeezing his arm. "You can be anything you want to be."

Suddenly the subdued clinical buzz is shattered by an animal roar of pain. My heartbeats rear-end each other like cars in a freeway pile-up. *Sully*.

Burying his face against my shoulder, "That was Daddy, wasn't it?" Gage clambers over the armrest between us and takes refuge on my lap.

"Yes, love."

"They're killing him."

He survived the surgery; he'll survive the recovery. "It just hurts like hell."

"He has to do this every day — for months? Make them stop."

"It'll never be this bad again." I hope. I sincerely hope.

They warned Sully therapy would be painful initially, when it's necessary to work through the scar tissue to regain mobility. But Sully's not good at accepting limitations: our Superman has underestimated the degree of pain involved — or his ability to bear it.

When Sully reappears I'm still comforting my son. I can tell from Sully's face — as grey and creased as soiled laundry — that it's a supreme effort of will to make it, on crutches, under his own steam. He's doing it for Gage.

A therapist pushes a wheelchair along behind him. "I'm sorry you guys had to hear that," he says. He collapses, trembling, into a chair next to us; accepts an ice-pack from the therapist; admits he'll use the wheelchair for a trip to the curb to wait for a cab home.

"You were brave, Daddy," Gage puts his arms around Sully's neck.

"No, Gage; *you* were brave," he says, kissing the boy's head. "It's easier to endure your own pain than to suffer it through someone you love."

"Did you have Gage tested while I was in the Twilight Zone?" Sully asks after we've put Gage to bed.

"No." I've been lugging the faxed copy of Doug's tissue type report around in my backpack like the Dead Sea Scrolls, but I've taken no action. I've decided not to decide.

"I *am* surprised, Mariah!" he says sarcastically, manipulating the recliner like a fighter pilot. "You usually take your 'obligations' so seriously."

He sounds more like Doug than himself. I try to assess his mood by calculating an equation based on pain, time, and analgesics. "My obligations are to you and Gage," I say quietly, refusing to be baited.

Sully closes his eyes. "I came to in recovery thinking of Doug."

"I'm sorry; I shouldn't have brought it up before you went under."

"No, no." Sully waves his hand dismissively. "I got to thinking later how I might respond under similar circumstances. I'm not sure I wouldn't snatch at straws in the wind. Which makes me wonder why *he* hasn't."

The scales of justice aren't in balance; Sully is out of equilibrium. "You've always disliked Doug," I say, "yet you're wrestling with sympathy for him. I admire that."

"Fuck Doug. I'm thinking about Gage," Sully says wearily. "Don't you think he has a say in this?"

"It hadn't occurred to me."

"The parables you and Doug cooked up last summer were fine," he sighs, "as far as they went. Gage's understanding will grow with and around them; he'll apply his own judgements and interpretations. And he'll be more or less forgiving, depending on his age and the phase of the moon. But," he warns, "we might not always come off so well. Especially," Sully squirms in the chair seeking comfort for his leg, "especially if Gage determines he might've had a larger role to play in Doug's life, and Doug in his. And that he was denied the opportunity to take it."

"Oh, Sully," I sniff. "To think Doug never credited you with much depth."

Doug has rarely committed himself to anything except, perhaps, the avoidance of commitment. However, "I believe Doug consciously chose not to involve Gage," I say as I take Sully's hand. "He's been battling the leukaemia for years; he would've thought about transplants and donors."

"The Doug *I* knew would have had no compunctions about self-preservation."

Nodding my agreement, "He could have appealed to my sympathies then," I say, "manipulating me, playing 'major mind-fuck games,' until I was convinced it'd been my own idea to have Gage tested."

"Maybe he was in remission last year and didn't think his illness would progress so far."

Doug's words: *This isn't about how we can help Gage. But about how Gage can help us.*

"I'm quite sure he considered all his options, even as we spoke," I continue. "But he didn't take the opportunity, Sully," I say with some certainty. "It was his exercise of control." *As deliberate as holding a razor in your hand.* "As you said, he as much as signed a release. He *knew* he was releasing all right and claim to Gage — and to Gage's 'genetic resources'."

"How uncharacteristic," Sully sneers. "Why would he do that?"

God acts on us through Gage. "Perhaps he chose to do the right thing — just once in his fucking life."

As I prepare for my first lecture, Sully limps into the bedroom, supported only by the antique Bermuda cedar cane I bought for him just after his fall. Our month in Boston is almost over; he is recovering well.

"Do you mind if Gage and I sit in on your lecture, Professor?"

Turning away from my reflection in the mirror, I grimace, "I'd be grateful if you would. I can't imagine anyone, except maybe the department head who arranged it, turning up for the series. I'm not exactly a *name*; I can't fathom how they latched on to me in the first place." Although it wouldn't surprise me to discover Jim Altman's hand in it.

"False modesty, Mariah. What about Banff?"

"Workshops are cooperative; I learned as much as the participants. But lectures," I explain, "presuppose possession of uncommon knowledge or experience. I don't believe I have that."

Sully sits gingerly on the bed. "I shouldn't have taken you to Bermuda," he says quietly, wrapping his arms around my waist. "You were meant for a scholarly environment. You should have gotten your doctorate, then a job in academia — "

" — Where," I interrupt, "I would have churned out arrogant, intellectual music with no substance, while training arrogant, intellectual musicians to perpetuate the cycle." I rake my fingers through his hair. "You gave me a real life, Sully; I wouldn't trade that for anything. My music comes *out of* real life."

He tugs me into place beside him on the bed. "And that's both *how* and *why* they latched on to you here!" he exclaims, hugely pleased to have trapped me in his act. "They've recognized the authenticity of your voice. Your old friends are recording your work all over the place; your new friends, like Geoff Halloway, are establishing an audience. Tourists visiting Bermuda — probably the very department heads who've hired you for this gig — see someone outside the academic community quietly making a name for herself and wonder where you came from." Smiling, he shakes his head wonderingly. "Well, I'm proud as hell."

"You can't eat pride," I retort. "We'd have starved to death if I'd been supporting the family. I couldn't have done it without you, Sully."

"Money's not the only tangible measurement of success. Besides," he reminds me. "It's coming. Look at these three lectures. . . ."

"Are you sure the titles aren't too precious?" Jesus, what was I thinking? "Music in Architecture," fine. "For Film and Concert: Lights, Camera, Music." Ugh. "Mining a Deep Vein: The Geology of Musical Inspiration": I'm suddenly queasy with apprehension.

"It's too late to change the posters, Riah! Look at your collaborations with Geoff," he says. "They go well beyond music, now. He's producing your proposals!"

"Proposal, singular," I demur. "How much more mileage can I get out of my father's stories?"

"And then there's your commission for the festival. How did Marcus O'Neill put it? 'Beauty and daring – Fauré meets R. Murray Schafer'?"

"Sheer hyperbole," I scoff. I'd been commissioned to write a choral mass to be performed at the 1993 Bermuda Festival by Bermuda's massed choirs under the baton of our friend Grace McCallum. Eagerly setting to work on it, I'd envisioned a lovely duet for baritone and boy soprano – all the while hoping my boy might remain a soprano long enough to perform it on-stage with his father, the baritone wise guy.

"Yes, it's coming," I concede.

"You're not wearing that, are you?"

I cross my arms over the black dress. "What's wrong with it?"

"How about something a little brighter?" Sully levers himself to his feet with the cane, pokes around in the closet. "Like this," he suggests, pulling out a red suit.

"That's good; it brings out the colour in my eyes."

He makes a face at me and dresses quickly himself, pulling together a natty academic look enhanced by the cedar cane. We emerge from the bedroom to find Gage similarly attired.

"You two are taking this rather seriously," I note as we pile into a cab. Gage glances guiltily at his dad. "I'm quite sure all the students will be dressed in jeans – or worse."

The lecture hall, a fairly big one, is packed. A camera crew is playing at electrical snakes and ladders. And Geoff Halloway strides to the door to greet me.

"Surprise!" Gage chirps.

"Sully, you bastard!" I gape. "What've you done?"

"Hello, luv," Geoff says, kissing my cheek. "My roving camera team is going to preserve these lectures for posterity."

"You'll have to record the next one," I pummel my husband with my fist, "from behind bars — because I'm going to kill this man!" Turning back to Geoff, "Are you doing this independently?"

"On spec," he nods. "But I wouldn't if I didn't think I could flog the finished product."

My gut response: *who'd want it?* But I swallow my words; they would be ungracious.

"Are you surprised, Mom?" Gage asks, capering around us like a puppy. "It's a sort of birthday present."

"It's a week early," Sully says. "Happy thirty-fifth, my darling. Break a leg."

"Thanks." We kiss. "I'll break yours later."

As I compose myself to deliver the first of my lectures, emboldened and buoyed by adrenalin and happiness, I make eye contact with my audience. Gage. Sully. *Look at their faces*: proud, encouraging. *God, I love them!* As I determined years ago, I cannot love them perfectly by myself. I can only love them through the music.

But that's all right.

Do you hear the music behind my words? Do you hear the love behind the music? Yours for me, and mine for you.

I'm not complete without the music. I used to run from that truth, but I've come to accept it, to forgive it. Just as I've forgiven them for loving me. Sully. Gage. *They love me.* Flawed me; ambivalent me. Their love has become inevitable and necessary to my life puzzle; I'm not complete without my family. They've formed me as much as music, as memory, as accident.

As I study their faces this evening, I'm certain they know I love them. I've been groping toward this liberating certainty; it's the source of the music and light I've been using in my *Blue Sky Mass*. The recurring motif is acceptance. Happiness. Contentment. The harmony is reflective of the silvery vein of grace I've found within myself: the conviction that I've loved them *well enough*.

Another lecture topic presents itself to me. A private lecture, perhaps, for an audience of two. *Love as an expression of wholeness in the music of Mariah Standhoffer Riordan.*

⌒◠

Thunder Bay bound. Flight attendants rattle carts. Closing my book, I look over Gage's head to the window, beyond which is only the emptiness of sky, blue and blank. A metaphor for the way I feel at the moment.

"What are you reading, Gage?"

He turns out the cover of Gary Paulsen's *Hatchet* so I can see it.

"You've read that already, haven't you?"

"Pops gave it to me," he nods. "I thought I should brush up on my survival techniques."

"You never know when your grandfather might abandon you in the bush," I tease.

"This plane could go down," he pronounces, "in dense, uncharted, muskeg swamp. But I could take care of you, Mom."

The boy's seriousness makes the hairs stand up on the nape of my neck. I ruffle his hair.

"I wish Dad was with us."

"Me too." Sully's absence is the source of my own blue, blank mood.

"Think he's having a good time in London?"

"I'm sure he's very busy, taking depositions. He *is* there to work, after all."

We'd planned to go with him, until Geoff called to see if I could spare a few days in Toronto to screen the rough cut of *Prison Camp Journal*. Gage was happy enough with the prospect of a few days with Sonja and Jimmy, followed by several in Thunder Bay with my folks — and perhaps even some skiing with Uncle Luke.

"We've never spent a half-term holiday without Dad," Gage observes. I put my arm across his shoulders — to comfort myself, I decide. "But," he says, brightening visibly, "maybe he'll pick up my birthday present while he's there."

"We *were* planning to celebrate your tenth birthday in true English style." Gage turns to me expectantly. "With a tinned Marks & Spencer steak-and-kidney pie."

"Oh, Mom," he groans. "You're as bad as Dad."

I've never before been accused of that particular foible, but I accept it gratefully. Am even surprised to find it works as an antidote to the blues. Which makes me wonder: how much of Sully's humour

is deployed to counteract such indefinable malaise? Sully is my haven
of equilibrium. I can hardly bear to entertain the notion that it might
be his longest-running role; that his good-natured optimism might
often be an *act*.

The snow drifting across the airport parking lot seems to have blown
in via the Russian steppes. "Geez, it's cold!" I exclaim as we load my
parents' car.

"What did you expect for February?" My father unlocks the door.
"Hop in, Gage."

"Did you bring anything dressy?" Mom lingers with me at the
open trunk.

"The little black number Sully hates," I grin.

She overlaps me with her words: "Doug died the other day."

"Oh, Christ," I hiss. "When's the funeral?" Afraid – yet hoping – I've
missed it.

"Tomorrow." She shrugs. "Sorry."

I nod, climb into the back seat next to my son. Gage, thankfully,
monopolizes the conversation during the half-hour drive through the
frozen landscape, over the river and through the woods, past the pub,
past the gun club.

"Luke'll be over for dinner," Mom says. Pooh-Bear and a three-
legged dog race down the gated driveway as we pass the mailbox bearing the legend "Luke Standhoffer, DVM – Veterinarian."

Gage presses his nose to the car window. "Look – a deer!"

"That's one of Uncle Luke's," Mom explains.

"He has his own deer now?" Gage asks. "Does he hunt them?"

"No; you should never hunt your own land," Dad says. "You never
know when you'll need the game, for survival."

"Armageddon's coming," I wink at my son. He winks back; Gage
knows his grandfather to be an alarmist.

"Between Luke's parcel and ours, Gage, there's almost three hundred
acres of unofficial game preserve," Dad says. "The animals know
they're safe on our land. We even put out apple garlands, hay, and salt
licks for them when the snow's deep. I'll take you out on snowshoes on
the game trails; some of them will come right up to you."

"How *is* Luke?" I ask.

"He should be a millionaire," my father sighs. "There're enough animals injured on this friggin' highway to keep him busy, God knows. Trouble is, he does most of his work *pro bono.*"

"Full of ambitious ideas," Mom says. "He wants to do reconstructive ligament surgery on that deer you saw. It was barely grazed by a car; he couldn't bear to put it down."

"Hours of research and work," Dad growls. "For what? Expensive wolf fodder."

"Surely he was having you on, Dad!" Then again, maybe not. "He could have experimented on Daddy," I prod Gage as we pull into my parents' driveway.

"Yeah," he grins. "We couldn't bear to put him down, either."

"Coming home" is getting more and more difficult for me, psychologically. It's so fraught with dangers I half expect barbed wire around the perimeter and signs warning of concealed land mines. Look at the latest: I *want* to go to Doug's funeral. But what do I say to Gage? I don't really want to trouble Sully in London, so I'm on my own.

"We'll distract Gage in the morning," my mother suggests. "It might be easier if he doesn't know; you don't want to open up that can of worms again."

"Oh, great; a *secret* mission." I shake my head emphatically. "That won't work. You told me eighteen months ago that whatever Gage might imagine would be worse than the truth. Well, it holds for me, too. Dad taught me too well. That's why I dance out to the extreme verge of a situation — envisioning the worst, certain I'm teetering on the cliffs of Dover like blind Gloucester — when the reality stands on a hillock on the heath."

My mother looks at me warily.

"This family's always made mountains out of mole hills. Is there no such thing as a simple fucking truth? What are we protecting each other from?" I take a breath to reduce the volume of my voice. "Reality is less painful than the prosthetics we employ to disguise it."

In bed alone I preserve the space beside me where Sully should be. I might pinch his pillow, but I never steal his space, never enlarge the territory of my self in his absence. He, on the other hand, always annexes the whole bed when he's alone; there can never be too much room for his lanky limbs. He accommodates my presence in bed — *cleaves* to me — as he might a part of himself.

"What are we protecting each other from?" I'd asked my mother. As I see it, the secrets and subterfuges have never been selfless. We never tried to protect each other; we tried to protect our *selves*. My father thought there was a world outside he could exclude by setting up an armed camp. But each of us in turn erected our individual watchtowers and battlements within its perimeter to keep ourselves safe. Not from outsiders. But from each other.

You knocked my walls down, Sully. You and Gage.

Gage thunders past my open bedroom door, pivots, and gallops back. "Where're you going, Mom?"

Remember the simple truths. I brace myself. *Don't make too much of it.* "To a funeral, sweetheart."

"Whose?"

Patting the edge of the bed, "Doug Hassock's."

"Uncle Doug, you mean?"

I nod.

"What did he die of?"

"Leukaemia. It's a kind of cancer. He had it when you met him in Toronto."

"Did he know he was going to die then?"

"I think he did."

Gage digests this information for a moment. "Are you sad?"

Am I sad? "He was an old friend, Gage. We shared a lot of things. And it's always sad when an old friend dies too young. But you try to remember the happy things; old friends live in your memories of them."

Old lovers, too, I think – live on in a kind of revisionist fiction that endows them with haloes more golden than their living influence ever warranted. I broke off with Doug as an act of self-preservation, but I've beatified him because he behaved well once. *Speak well of me to him,* he'd said. And so I must.

"Maybe you shouldn't be alone when you're sad." Gage's ten-year-old face exhibits unnatural maturity. "Do you want me to come with you, Mom? Dad would, if he were here, wouldn't he?"

I'm not entirely sure he would, given the subject. If he did, it would be only to bury Caesar, not to praise him. In fact, my lips twitch as I recall Sully's words as Richmond upon Richard's death: "God and your arms be praised, victorious friends! The day is ours; the bloody dog is dead."

"I'm going to be with my friend Kat, Gage, so *she* won't be alone. Uncle Doug was her brother, her twin."

"Yes, she'll be very sad," he acknowledges. "So you'll be all right with her? You won't mind if I stay here with Nanny and Pop?" he asks, giving me a hug and kiss.

"Not at all, my love; not at all."

Gage is in the driveway when I pull in, throwing sticks for the dogs.

"How are you, sweetie?" I call from the car.

"Fine! Here, Beau; here, Raven." Piercing whistle. The dogs lollop to his side as I approach.

I press him against my coat, squeezing his hand through his dangling red jacket sleeve. "What did you do today?"

"Pops took me out on snowshoes," he trills. "We saw lots of deer. He let me use the Armalite; it's a good size for me — and it's a *survival* rifle!"

"Good thing it floats," I tell him, "or Uncle Luke wouldn't have survived dropping it into the creek at camp when he was your age," I smile. "What were you hunting?"

"Mice in the woodpile."

"Bag any?"

He nods enthusiastically. "A few." He lowers his voice conspiratorially. "But you have to be still an awfully long time."

"Quite a feat for you, my whirling dervish." I pull his tuque down over his eyes. He laughs.

"Grandpa said a man's home is his castle."

"I remember that speech: 'Every man is the king of his own castle'," I drone, " 'and he tries to keep it — and everyone he loves — safe. That's my job,' he said."

"Do we have a gun in Bermuda?"

I shake my head. "Not allowed. Even the police don't carry guns."

"Then, how does Dad keep *us* safe?"

Thank you, Gabe Standhoffer!

"Daddy keeps us safe with the shield of his optimism," I say, grateful for the graphic reminder that Sully is so different from my father. But this isn't concrete enough for Gage. "Sometimes safety is a state of mind," I hazard. "If you're always worried something horrible's going to happen, it's like an invitation for disaster, a magnet."

Gage doesn't buy it. Such a challenge, a clever child!

"Your dad protects us the best way he knows how. He's a much bigger man than Grandpa, for one thing."

"Yeah, but Grandpa's got guns! You could be a midget and still keep your family safe with guns!"

The little parrot — he's quoting his grandfather directly.

With a .22 in your hand and a pecker in your pants — then you'll be a man, my son! Even a small boy with a malformed arm could defend his family with a gun.

"I'll look after you, Mom."

"Your grandfather's way isn't the best way," I assert. I have to nip this in the bud. "Guns are dangerous. They can be used against the people you're most anxious to protect." I flash my handless wrist at him. "I lost my hand because of one of Grandpa's guns — he couldn't keep me safe inside his own house," I choke.

Gage nods solemnly. I feel suddenly all done in. "Coming?"

He shakes his head, waves the stick in front of Beau's face, and tears off down the driveway. "Later!" he calls.

Heaving myself wearily up the back steps, I note the apples in Gage's cheeks from the cool air and exercise. It's good for him here, developing an appreciation for nature and his grandfather's vagaries.

Dad, smoking at the kitchen table, turns from keeping an eye on Gage frolicking with the dogs, to ask "How was it?"

"It was a funeral," I say tersely. "It was terrible."

"And how was Katarina?" he asks.

Still his old name for Kat! Do any of us ever grow up, in his mind? "As well as can be expected, considering she just buried her twin," I sigh. "She hasn't changed at all. Our kids are our only tangible measurement of time." I watch Gage over my father's shoulder. "You made quite an impression on your grandson today."

"He's got a good eye. Just like his mom."

"And *her* mother before her. All descendants of Annie Oakley." Despite the jokes I feel a wave of unease just thinking of Gage with a firearm in his hand. "You did put the guns away, didn't you?"

He nods.

"I'm going to change my clothes."

Strip off the black dress and hang it in the closet. Grab a pillow from the bed and stuff it against my face to muffle the animal howl I've been swallowing all afternoon. When I'm hoarse from it, I examine my face in the mirror, pull on a shapeless peach sweatsuit over a turtleneck, and curl up on the bed.

I had set off for the funeral with gratitude in my heart. For the accident of love that gave me the two finest things in my life. Gage, of course. And Sully as I know him, elevated from the ordinary through Gage.

Was going to say "Goodbye, and thank you, Doug," for these good things. Was going to shed a tear or two of fond regret.

Despite my intentions, I was no use to Kat. She had Ray for support and the kids and her parents to attend to. She was distracted — and I was *possessed*. Self-possessed, on the surface, but seething like a hydra underneath.

Like Sully at the clinic in Boston, I'd underestimated the psychic scar tissue I'd have to work through to mobilize that chamber of my heart I'd marked, not merely "Doug," but "off limits." And when the tissue finally tore away I discovered an unholy desire and longing for Doug's curse: *"Leave Sully; come with me."*

Too late; too late.

What part of me did Doug still possess that should be buried with him? Not a healthy part, I know that much. A part that wanted to be bad. Perhaps a shadow part that enjoyed a sort of dissolution in his mismatched arms. A part that liked to be hurt, and dismantled, and *fucked.* The part that believed I deserved the things he, and my grandfather, had done to me — and not only *deserved*, but *desired*.

Come back! Doug, come back.

Desire: to be bad, deliberately bad — not just imprudent, or hapless, or mistaken — but *bad,* just once in my life. To tear this blessed, light-filled life apart, to live with a green-eyed devil who might make me sell my soul, to write a black mass, full of sulphurous emanations, to immortalize my own worst nature.

Doug was my last link to the darkness. And he's gone; he's gone.

I went back to St. Andrew's Church after the wake in the parish hall. Sat in a dark, quiet corner and wept. And prayed. And wept some more. Tried to sweep the shadows back into their box.

Give it up, Mariah.

Why this darkness? As a contrast to the light, I suppose. Redemption wouldn't be so holy if darkness held no appeal. *Give it up.*

Simply underscore the sanctity of accident, and the rightness of choices made. By me. By Sully. By Doug.

Goodbye. And thank you, Doug.

When I wander into the living room, Mom is counting a row of knitting, gestures to me to wait. I flop onto the couch.

"A hundred and fifteen," she announces. "Sorry. Was it awful?"

I'm surprised to find myself improvising yet another variation on regret. *I was no help to Kat.* Not today; not a few months ago, when it might have made a difference. Despite having determined to Sully's satisfaction that Doug had released all claims to Gage, I wasn't entirely sure I could resist Kat's appeal.

Almost four months later I'm *still* carrying a crushed fax scroll in a little-used compartment of my backpack, along with tampons and a bad shade of lipstick. I'd thought, that if a natural opportunity arose to have Gage's blood tested, it would be a sign — and then I'd be prepared. For the test. But for the ordeal if the test was positive? Was I prepared to subject Gage to a painful, invasive procedure in aid of a man he'd met only once and to whom he owes no debt?

Except his life; except his life.

Dad sits in his chair, listening while my mother commiserates. I tell her who was there, who said what, who cried. When I finish, he says, "What did you hope to gain from this?"

"Since I *happened* to be in town, I wanted to be there for my friend," I snap at him, turn to my mother. "I feel as if I've betrayed her, Mommy. I should have done more, if not for Doug's sake, then for *hers.*"

"What more could you have done?"

"Bone marrow." I strangle on the words.

"Whose?"

"Gage's."

My father leaps out of his chair. "Now, you listen to me, Mariah," he threatens, voice low. "Doug Hassock was a fucking *freak.* And I'm not talking about his hand. He was a queer, and he treated you badly. I don't know why you're so upset," he says in disgust. "It was over with Doug years ago. James loves you; he's been a better husband than you deserve. He's certainly a better man than I would've given him credit for, if you'd asked me to predict the future when you were fifteen!"

"I know." I wipe my face.

"Well, then; examine your conscience and make sure that this, this guilt you're carrying around is completely unjustified. Think of the child. Think of your husband."

I do, during the moments of separate silence we endure. Mom knits; Dad lies back in his chair with his feet up, rubbing his eyes. And I, I think about Doug and wonder if Gage might have made a difference; if the ending to his story might have been revised.

Dad clears his throat. "When are we going to eat around here?"

A blast shatters his words.

"What was that?"

It's near; too near to be the gun club down the road. Nothing in the field. Dad's out of his chair and racing for the back door.

"Where's Gage?"

My heart slams into my throat.

The closet door in the back porch is ajar. Dad swings it open fully, reaches around the frame into the space between the joists — "Jesus!" — and continues empty-handed down the steps and out the door in a fluid motion. I'm right behind him.

"Gage!"

Beau is barking at the edge of the field. The snow's packed along the tree line. My slippers sink in it, threatening to trip me up, still I manage to overtake my father. A tangle of snowshoes and the flash of the boy's red ski jacket.

"Gage!"

April fool, April fool — snow angel face down in the snow.

But, no; there's blood. Something shreds in my chest, tears in my throat. I whip my sweatshirt off, bend to the crumpled figure, wrest the rifle out of his hand. My father sees what has to be done, helps me tie the shirt around Gage's head. Releases one snowshoe from the clutches of the buried deadfall on which Gage tripped. Releases his boots from the snowshoes.

Slow down, Gage, slow down.

"Ginny!" Dad screams. "Get the car keys!"

He lifts Gage into his arms, stumbles across the field to the driveway.

"Get in," he orders.

He swings the child in through the door, places Gage's head in my lap. *Above your head! Up! Up!* My mother runs from the house bearing the afghans from the couch, a rainbow of clean tablecloths, and two pairs of boots *wordless but vocal, capable only of vowels.*

"Get the ambulance to meet us at the Rec Centre on the highway." By the time he slams his door we're spitting snow pellets in the driveway *he drives like hell.*

Jesus jesus jesus — a prayer on each beat of Gage's heart.

My father won't stop talking — *his mouth flaps and I wonder where the gun went I'd like to stop that flapping mouth* — as if the momentum of his words will propel the car down the road with greater speed.

"I told him I keep it for protection! I told him he must never use it alone," he sobs.

He will have his own way.

"He must have seen where I hide it."

He loves to play in closets.

"He must have taken it, to pretend, to go hunting."

Brushing up on survival techniques with a survival rifle. To keep us safe, while his daddy's so far away. Remembering my words of a few minutes — a lifetime — ago: it seems there is a distance limit on the shield of Sully's optimism, like on a cellular phone.

On and on the old fool babbles. Assignment of Blame, only what to blame it on? "Shut up! Shut up!" The shrieking voice is my own.

The ambulance is waiting at the arena as we come screeching in. Gently, the attendants take him from me. I stumble into the vehicle, grateful that my dad will be following behind in the car, not riding with me.

Wailing. Wailing. My voice, and the siren: a ghastly duet.

My son is dying. My clothes are saturated with his blood. They take him from me and they do what they must do.

"We should be in there; they don't know what they're doing."

My father could straighten them out: no one knows as much about everything as he does. *Shut up, Dad.*

An urgent, regretful doctor tells me what I already know: Gage's brain is dead, but his heart is strong. Will I consider organ donation?

"At least that way, his spirit will live on."

Foremost in my mind, "I have to keep him alive for his father. He's on his way." As if he's driving over from Port Arthur. "He's in England; he's on his way."

The doctor shakes his head. "Ten, twelve hours? I don't know. The tissue match may not have that long to wait. We need to harvest the organs quickly."

Harvest! What kind of word is this? Harvest. Blessed is the fruit of my womb; who will reap the bounty of my dying child?

"I'll give my consent, as long as you promise to wait. My husband needs to see his son."

My father explodes. "I'll get on the phone and arrange a fucking air ambulance. We'll get him to Duluth. They don't know what the fuck they're doing here, Mariah!"

Shut up, Dad.

Luke arrives leading a bent, grey woman. A casualty of some accident? My mother. She hands me my backpack. "There're clean clothes in there, darling."

My father draws Luke into a corner for a tête-à-tête. Luke's voice rises: "For Christ's sake, Dad — I'm a fucking vet!" And he pulls away, stalking across the waiting room to me. "Riah, Riah," he sobs, taking me in his arms. "He wants me to check on their procedures!"

The zipper of my brother's jacket is cold against my cheek. "Keep him the hell away from me." I turn to enlist my mother in the edict. "Don't let him turn this into a circus."

When I peel down my sweatpants in the washroom my briefs are so bright with blood — *I'm losing the baby I'm losing the baby* — for one instant I forget it's not my own blood. Then it hits me. *I'm losing my baby I'm losing my baby.*

At Gage's side my thoughts are all with Sully. What have they told him? "Come home, James, your child is dying"? My sorrow for him is wrenching — hours and hours to spend in confined spaces, under the scrutiny of strangers. No place to hide. I, at least, am alone with my son, my thoughts, my guilt — trying to make sense of what's happened, preparing for what I see is inevitable.

But what have they told Sully? "There's been an accident"? Will he rush home expecting to find Gage with his leg in traction? Or have they said, "Your son isn't expected to live."

Sully; Sully — I see his trip-hammer knee; I see him pacing like a caged animal, pacing across the Atlantic, walking the whole way home.

"Mrs. Riordan; we can't wait much longer."

"Then let another match move up the list!" I hear how heartless this sounds, but I'm beyond caring.

This is my child, whose hand I hold; my child whose heart beats so valiantly within his breast; beating, beating, till his daddy can get home. I watch the oscillations on the monitor, composing a cadenza for that flat line, that resting instrument. *Continue the voice, preserving the style of the opening.*

To turn back the clock – hours, days. We should have gone to England with Sully; I should have stayed home in Bermuda with Gage. But Geoff needed to see me: *I let the music get in the way.* I should have been more vigilant. I should have made sure Dad had locked the guns away in the cabinet. Oh, to change one thing! One thing. Sully, Sully, how can I look you in the eye – I've killed our child, as surely as if I'd pulled the trigger of that gun. *The cursed music got in the way.*

Sonja and Jimmy slip in lugging carry-on baggage. Who has made all these calls? Who called Sully in England? Who called Toronto? Who has the presence of mind for details – my mother or my brother? If I'm mute it's only because I don't know which question to ask first.

"It must be soon, Mrs. Riordan. His vitals are slipping."

No; no. No. "How long will the harvest take?"

"Only a few minutes. They're ready in OR; we have a helicopter and two charter flights standing by."

"Where will they go?"

"We don't usually say," he begins – then, compelled by my expression, "His heart will go to Toronto," he confides; "the liver and kidneys are going to Calgary."

I glance at my watch, have no idea what it says. "Give me another half hour." Beat on, brave heart.

Suddenly I'm filled with words he must take with him on his way. How many things have I left unsaid? A lifetime – God! I'll be talking to him every day, trying to make it up. This is no ending; this is the beginning of a lifetime without him.

But his heart will go on beating. I can speak to this phenomenon. And do: scribbling a few words on a piece of paper. Catch myself midway with one part of my brain: *What the fuck are you doing, Mariah? Detached at a time like this?* Receive permission from Gage with another: *It's okay, Mommy; you have to do it your own way.* Gage. When they come I press the piece of paper on them.

"You must give this to the child, to his parents. Promise me. Please. You must let him know." They promise.

It isn't long before I hear the helicopter swooping from the pad, beating, beating its way to the airport to catch the flights.

Minutes later – can it be? – Sully comes through the door. His face; his face – this will be harder than I thought.

"Where's Gage?"

"You must have passed him on the way."

Sully doesn't play Assignment of Blame by the Standhoffer rules; to that extent, he's an outsider, even after all these years. But when Dad attempts to catch him in an embrace of sympathy – "Son, I'm so sorry" – Sully's face blackens as he spits out the words: "You keep a loaded gun in a house with *children*?!" then crumples into my father's arms as if he's been shot himself.

Fumbling an alien brand of cigarettes and a pack of machine-dispensed matches, Dad leaves the building for a smoke. As Jimmy and Sonja approach us like suppliants, I step aside to let my husband have a moment with his parents and join my mother on a bench to observe the trial: *Riordan v. Riordan.* In this unprecedented case, the Judge's expressive hands present an appeal to the Prosecutor – which motion the Prosecutor dismisses with a sweeping gesture. *Jesus, Sully! Don't reject them now!*

Mom, hard-wired for automatic-hostess, voices my own question: "What are we going to do with them?"

"There's no room at your house."

Luke lifts his head from between his knees. "How about mine?"

Where to go? What to do? I don't want to go home with my parents; why can't Sully and I stay at Luke's? But Sully is holding the door open for Sonja and shrugging off Jimmy's attempted embrace.

I race down the corridor. "Where are they going?"

"The Valhalla."

A hotel? "Sully, they shouldn't be alone! What are you thinking?"

Outside on the sidewalk, my father approaches them, trailing smoke. Sonja reaches up to Jimmy; I can hear his wounded-bull bellow through two double-paned doors: *"I've lost my son to you, Gabe, and my grandson as well. Get the fuck out of my way."*

"Sully." I drag him away from the door so Dad won't see we've witnessed the exchange. Even so, he re-enters the hospital bearing the Judge's verdict like a ball and chain.

"We'll see them tomorrow. Let's go."

We go. My parents have placed an old bedspread across the back seat of the car, covering Gage's blood. Sully whips it off like a magician, searching the Rorschach pattern of it for meaning, for revelation.

I can't do this, I think, observing him. *I can't do this.* Yet I must.

I catch my dad's eye in the rear-view mirror as he accelerates on the approach to the overpass just west of the city limits. *Take us out, Dad.* I surely would. *Just a little more gas and a wrench on the wheel to escape the grasp of inertia right at the crest of the arc — and through the barrier to the railroad tracks below.* Sully turns to me as my grip on his hand tightens in anticipation. As if he's intercepted my demand, he presses my face to his so I cannot turn away: I can't tell where his tears leave off and mine begin.

He unfolds his legs into the driveway. Crumpled suit, Burberry raincoat, dress shoes. "Show me."

My parents stand on the porch, their own heads pressed together, reluctant to enter the house. I lead him to the spot.

"Here."

It's obvious, unmistakable, preserved bright crimson by the snow. Sully falls to his knees, utters a strangled cry. Reaching blindly for my legs, he puts his arms around my knees and weeps. And weeps. I kneel beside him in the snow, at this altar formed by a snow-covered deadfall. And a snow angel's impression. My snow angel; my son.

Framed by the kitchen door, Luke is as uncomfortable as a stranger, his shoulders hunched around his ears as if to muffle the sound of Sully's voluble pissing in the back porch loo. Dad clatters under the sink, comes up with the Christmas Crown Royal. He puts a couple of tumblers on the table, pours himself three fingers, and leaves the bottle out. Straddling a chair beside me, Luke gestures with the bottle.

"*Por favor,*" I say, initiating an old joke out of habit and desperation.

"Sure. Pour for four," he responds on cue, smiling weakly, as he sloshes liquid into glasses for Sully and me, then screws on the cap.

"I can't believe you, Mariah," Dad says, leaning over the sink. "You sold your son to the butchers."

An explosion of pain, like an angina attack. Luke covers my arm with his large warm hand and my intake of breath with his words. "Daaadd," he growls warningly. "Don't go there, Dad."

As if he hasn't heard, "Some rich cat's kid in Toronto needs a new heart," my father continues, "and you aid and abet a *murder* by giving your consent! Did you think they'd do their best by Gage if they could sell him for spare parts?"

Luke stands so suddenly his chair falls over. "*Shut up*, Dad!" he shouts. With his eyes on mine, "Do you think you can deflect the blame this way?" he says. "Whose *fucking gun* was it?"

My own angry words issuing from my brother's lips: I seem to have become a ventriloquist. But my brother is no dummy.

"I'm sorry," Dad rasps, lifting his glass to his lips with trembling hand. "I was out of line."

The toilet flushing, the squeak of the bathroom door. "What?" Sully asks, realizing he's missed a scene.

"Let's go to bed," I urge. "We need to be alone."

Taking up a position where he can look out over the field to the crimson stain, he lifts the poured tumbler. I turn to my mother for assistance.

"We've all been up too long," she says. "Come, Gabe."

"I've got a menagerie to feed." Luke pulls on his jacket, palms Sully's shoulder, hugs the rest of us awkwardly. "I'll be back in the morning."

Silent hugs all around. "I'm sorry, Mariah," Dad presses his stubbly cheek against mine. "I'm sorry."

Unable to speak, I nod, then sit at Sully's right. Silent. Silent; my heart a smashed thing in my chest. I loop my right arm around the bottle for a grip, twist the cap with my left. It's too tight, damn it; too tight. Sully takes it from me, a reflex refined in our decade together — how many cans has he opened? How many jars? He removes the cap easily, pours a few glugs into my glass, into his. He tosses it back, pours out more.

"We have some decisions to make," I begin.

A nasal consonant, undefined.

"Where will we bury him? Here? Or in Bermuda?"

"Here," he drains the glass again. "Bermuda was always temporary."

"Open coffin? Or closed?"

Wincing, "Jesus! Closed!" He opens his eyes. "Open!" He turns to

me. "Can they – oh, God!" He buries his face in his sleeve and sobs.
He takes my hand across the table. "How can you sit there and ask the
practical questions! All I can ask is, 'why?' "

"I've had twelve more hours of 'why?' than you."

The shadows lengthen along the field in inverse proportion to the level of
liquid in the bottle. The object of our vigil is obliterated in the darkness,
but I know it's there. At some point, Sully falls asleep with his head in the
crook of his arm. I slide my hand out of his, find my mother's scrub pail
in the laundry room, fill it with hot water. Clutch the rechargeable flash-
light against my breast with the stump of my right arm and go out, boots
flapping on my feet, to melt my dead son's blood into the snow.

I place an afghan around Sully's shoulders. Then, after returning the
pail to the laundry, I wander into the basement recreation room. A wall
of photographs. Me. Luke. Gage, at various increments of growth. A
box of toys – antiques, almost – reserved for Gage's use on our visits.
A box of books. Children's classics, most of them. And one misfiled –
Who Has Seen the Wind?

Change one thing.

Gage. Was it the axis – this misfiled book? harbouring a photo of a
misshapen man? Is this where the change took place?

Maybe I didn't take my obligations seriously enough. My smug reading of Doug's silence may have been wrong. *Jesus jesus – what if I was
wrong?* Perhaps Gage was not intended to be the agent of redemption
of Doug's soul; perhaps he was meant to save his father's life.

To make full opportunity out of the accident of Gage's birth – is
that the action I overlooked? My focus was too narrow, my vision
flawed. *This isn't about how we can help Gage – but how Gage can help us.* I
missed it; I missed it. I sealed our fates by not seeing the big picture.
We fenced off the cliffs of Dover, but we let Gage stumble on the
heath. In snowshoes, with a .22 in his hand.

Tired; so tired. I flick the light off and huddle into the couch, the
book tucked under my arm. Not expecting to sleep, just unable to keep
the weight of my head upright any longer.

Tell me a story, Mommy.

Gage. What story could I tell you if I knew it was the last?

There is no last story, Mommy; there is only the next.

But I do sleep. For the rectangle of window is grey with winter dawn when my eyes are forced open by the noise of someone stoking the wood-burning furnace. Instead of going back up the basement stairs, though, the someone — my father — steps into the rec room without noticing me in the shadows, opens the closet door, reaches around behind the joists. And closes the closet door with one hand, a shotgun in the other.

"So, there's a gun in *every* room?"

He whirls, homing in on the sound of my voice. "Jesus, Mariah! You scared me half to death! What are you doing here, sweetheart?"

My book falls to the floor. "I was waiting for you." On speaking the lie, I am instantly convinced of its veracity. "What are you doing with the gun, Dad?"

An absent glance at the weapon, as if he's surprised to find it in his grasp. "I was going to lock it away."

"A little *late* for that," I accuse. *"Tell me what the fuck you're doing with that gun, Dad."* Impelled by rage, I stand. Too quickly. Fatigue, low blood pressure, low blood sugar — Christ, when did we last eat? — the smouldering fuse is snuffed by dizziness. "Go ahead," I say, flapping my hand dismissively. "Take the easy way."

"Mariah." His face shifts along the grain like a log split by an axe. "I was worried about *you*. And James."

"The way you *didn't worry about Gage?!*"

We stare at each other dumbly. My words cannot be retracted; there is no response he can make. I collapse to my knees beside the couch, braced for perdition. But it seems I will not be immolated by my anger, nor he by my blame.

"Don't sit on the concrete, sweetheart, you'll get piles," he says gently. He takes my elbow, helps me to my feet, crushes me in his arms. Expels the inarticulate sorrow from my very soul.

Daddy, I want to die!

Have I said this aloud — or just communicated it telepathically? Either way, he knows. He knows.

Scrape and swish; scrape and swish. There's no solace in some repetitive tasks. I should like to find the answer in the pattern of holes down the middle of the double-edged Wilkinson Sword blade, but no revelation comes.

Surely I've failed my son in the most material way. As my father failed me.

Sully. Gage. Look at their faces. God, I love them!

And yet, within the slag of failure, there's a silvery vein of grace I've found within myself: the conviction that I've loved them both *well enough*.

My hand shakes and I'm stopped by an unearthly noise echoing against the tiled shower stall. Only gradually do I recognize the wild uncivilized sound as my own voice, keening for my son.

In a few minutes I'll turn off the water and dry myself. My clothes are laid out on the bed: black stockings, black dress. Black shoes wait on the floor. I'll dress carefully and, at the funeral, I'll be in control — for Sully. But here, with the spray thundering down on my head, I'll weep. And I will finish shaving my legs.

"Will you stop your mother?" Sully pleads as we collect dishes from the living room. "She'll kill us with hospitality."

That's her way. She will feed, and pamper, and render comfort to every waif and stray — Jimmy and Sonja among them — who come to the door. She will buttress us all.

I find her in the kitchen — where else? "Mom."

"This is the third time I've run the dishwasher today," she says, pouring detergent into the cup. "I just hope there's enough water in the well." She straightens slowly, wiping her hands on her apron. "What can I do for you, sweetheart? More glasses?"

"Everyone's gone, Mommy."

I've meant this as a measure of our privacy. But she uses it to gauge our loss. As my mother's face crumples I feel the high ledge I've been clingling to break away under my feet. *What will shore up the buttress when it crumbles into disconnected stones?* But even as we tumble into each other's arms, it seems possible two heaps of rubble might somehow support each other's essential structures — achieving the precarious equilibrium of catastrophe.

"Come to Bermuda with us," I beg. We will have to go back. But I'm scared to death. The child in me wants to linger in the comfort of my mother's arms, to merge with her warmth until this icy sorrow melts away.

"No," she runs her fingers through my hair, "not now. I'll be *with* you, but you and Sully need to find your way together. It won't be easy. Getting through it will be exercise of will, enough for a lifetime."

Part Four

Requiem

*T*he child is gone.

Gage's absence is a tangible thing, like the reek of mildew in our cottage when we unlock the door. I have the dehumidifier running before Sully drags the bags in from the taxi, a load of clean towels rebaking in the dryer, the heating cycle of the air conditioner turned on in the bedroom, and the covers thrown back to dry the clammy sheets. *I hate Bermuda*, I think, for the first time ever.

"Don't you have anything to declare?" a surly inspector asked as we came through customs.

Anything to declare? I might have filled the arrivals hall with my declaration – a feral howl that threatened to overtake civility – even as Sully leaned closer to the man and mitigated our suspicious lack of acquired consumer goods by quietly declaring our son's death.

The child is gone.

Sully performs the welcome-home maintenance chores: opens all the shutters, checks the cistern, primes the pump. Plugs in the hot-water tank. Sprays for ants outside the kitchen window. Collects the mail from a neighbour. Whacks a palmetto bug with his Topsider at the back door as it scuttles in ahead of him.

"I should mow the lawn before it gets dark," he says.

"Can't it wait?"

"It's been three weeks. Otherwise I won't be able to get to it until the weekend."

"Whatever. We need milk for breakfast. Where're the keys?"

"Don't take my set; I need the suitcase keys. The water should be hot enough for a shower when I'm done."

Good Christ; we throw ourselves furiously into the sanity of routine! And yet, there is no routine without Gage.

When I get back from Miles' Market (a fifty-dollar trip for milk and bread and fruit, "a little something" for dinner and maybe for Sully's lunch, a six-pack of Bass Pale Ale, and a large tin of Baygon for the ants), the lawn is neatly clipped, the lawnmower put away. A deflated beach ball is draped over the barbecue at the back door like a Dali clock. The door to Gage's room – which I know was open when I left – is closed. I intend to take Sully a towel, warm from the dryer. But, at the *en suite* door, I stop with my hand on the knob. He is sobbing. I leave the towel on the bed.

"Why are you bothering with dinner? We've done nothing but sit on planes all day." Still damp from the shower, his dark hair sleek like an otter's. "I'm not hungry," he says. Peers into the meagrely provisioned fridge, grabs a Bass.

"I'm not sure that's very cold yet."

"Doesn't matter. Where's the opener?"

"*Daddy, it's on the fridge!*" Gage would have said. Their standing joke. As if the magnetized opener would ever be anywhere else.

I cover his intake of breath: "You must have been Speedy Gonzales out there with the lawnmower!"

"Why, is it uneven?"

"No, just . . . fast," I finish lamely.

While he opens a bottle of wine for dinner, I surreptitiously remove the third chair and Pimpernel place mat from the table. We push some food down our gullets – all substance, no taste. The wine bottle magically empties itself, despite the fact that only one glass is poured for my consumption.

I clear the table.

"Do I have a shirt for tomorrow?"

"In the closet."

"Have you got any dirty laundry?" he calls from the hallway.

"Side pocket of my suitcase," I holler back, as after every vacation. I continue loading the dishwasher, mindlessly, somnambulatory. Suddenly, I awake. "*No!*"

Too late. Clutching the blood-stained peach sweatsuit to his chest, he reels back against the louvred linen closet doors and sinks to the floor.

"I'm sorry!" I fling my arms around him. "I forgot it was there! I didn't know what to do with it – burn it? Throw it out? Preserve it like the Shroud of Turin? Sully!" Thumping my head against his chest, "Sully, I'm not strong enough for this!"

His grip is fierce. "No, Riah. You're the strong one, always have been."

God help us! If I'm the strong one, then we're doomed.

"It hurts too much to imagine what you went through," he says, clutching the stained garments in his hand. "At least, you got to say goodbye."

I long to tell him everything, every detail. Would he then feel less left out? Sully — can I tell you my fears: can we share this? Can we survive it?

Gage was with us every minute of our married life. He was the secret wedding guest, the anticipation of our first months together and — at his birth — our first heartbreak, our first test. He was Sully's choice, Sully's pledge. Anghus Gage — the blessing of our days, the cornerstone of our union.

How can we go on without him? What are we without him?

Will Sully even want me, without Gage? We've invested so much together for Gage, we've forgotten what it was we were before, what brought us together, what it was about each other that we chose. *I chose you, Sully,* then Gage chose us. We are nothing without Gage. Two lacerated hearts, bleeding with loss.

Sully falls asleep while I'm in the bathroom — helped along, no doubt, by his share of the dinner wine. My side of the bed is still clammy when I slide in; it takes me longer to fall asleep than it does to warm the sheets. I wake when he gets up sometime later, to pee, I think. But he leaves the bedroom.

When I wake again he has still not returned. I pad down the hall in bare feet. The light is on in the living room. He's asleep there, under one of my mother's hand-knit afghans. Bank statements and bills, a few flyers, and the complimentary *Globe and Mail* from the plane are strewn on the coffee table, on the floor. As are five emptied bottles of Bass. The cardboard carrier is on the kitchen counter; I fill it with the empties in the living room, leave it by the back door. I file the mail in the den, collect the sections of the paper, and take them to the back door, too.

On the final trip to turn off the light, I notice something on the couch under his elbow; slide an envelope, letter, and creased photographs away gently.

Forwarded to us through the transplant registry, one photograph bears the smiling face of a young boy. I lean against the armchair for support as I scan the letter. Remarkable recovery; doing well; heart is strong; parents grateful. The other photograph is of a cross-stitched sampler bearing my words, framed and hung over the child's bed:

> *Beat on, brave heart. Long may you beat*
> *and carry this sick child into a life of joy and strength*
> *while we who're left behind gauge*
> *the love you brought us, not life's length.*
>
> *And in your beating may there be an echo of the life that passed.*
> *May you do fine things, animating a gladdened host.*
> *Beat. Beat and measure out the days*
> *remembering, sweet heart, we loved you most.*

This, at least, is something to cling to: Gage's heart still beats. I wish I could say the same for my own.

When the alarm goes off I feel as if I've just gotten to sleep. Sully's still in the living room. Why should he bother being at work on time? He's not slept well either. I turn it off, fall back to sleep.

"Why didn't you wake me?" he storms in angrily.

"I thought you needed the rest."

"I've got a job to do, damn it!" He thrashes around the bedroom, pulling on knee socks, shorts, shirt, tie.

"What do you want for breakfast?"

"Don't bother. I don't have time." He storms out, knocks around in the coat closet for his helmet, starts the Honda 90 with seven kicks and revs off down the lane. No kiss; the first time in ten years?

When I wake again the clock reads 1:19. Can this be right? I bury my head deeper in the pillow. A car door slams in our driveway. A knock at the back door. Shit. I know who it must be: Merry English Wives. If I ignore them, will they go away? Not likely. Caro and Fizzy both have keys. The JEMs will have seen Sully at the office, will have alerted the women that I'm home. Brave Caro — has she brought the others along for moral support?

I dither around the room trying to find my robe, punch my arms into it.

"Mariah!" Caro's voice through the back door's jalousie window. More knocks. Key in the lock.

"Coming!" I shout.

We meet in the kitchen, embrace. "Sorry. I had firm instructions to enter."

"I knew I should have put the chain lock on after James left this morning!" I tease.

"Wouldn't have kept me out long. I'm nothing if not resourceful. Besides, I know every way to break into this house. Fizzy's been locked out more than once! I'll just get the others, shall I?"

The question is rhetorical. There's no derailing Caro Jackson from her appointed rounds.

"Put the kettle on," I call after her. "I'll jump into some clothes."

The MEWs are in a tight, whispering huddle when I return, scuttle apart like roaches in the light.

"Mariah!" Fizzy hugs me and kisses my cheek. "I'm so sorry."

Emily steps up for her turn. Like a receiving line at a wedding, I think. This is an ordeal for them, too, I remind myself. They're here under orders – Sully's – to make sure I'm all right, as well as by virtue of social convention. We are "sisters-in-law," the sorority of wives of the Crown Counsel. Surrogate family, expatriates all. In our decade together we've shepherded each other through most of our pregnancies, assorted biopsies, tubal ligations. Adversity brings out the best in them. I steel myself to their good intentions.

We take our tea in the living room, making me doubly glad I'd tidied up in the middle of the night. What impression would that brigade of dead soldiers have conveyed?

"Come to our house for dinner," Caro urges. "I'll have everybody. The children are traumatized about Gage."

"We're *all* traumatized," Fizzy amends.

I shake my head doubtfully. "I don't think James can cope."

"Cope? Cope!" Emily stands clutching her elbows against her bosom. "You're supposed to grieve! People expect you to cope far too early, if you ask me. As if there's a statute of limitations on the grieving and you're supposed to be coping before it runs out!" She walks to the sliding glass door, stares out at the sea. "I'm sorry."

"No, Emily's right. You need to grieve; we need to grieve with you."

"James won't want to break down in front of the kids." Not to mention his colleagues, his friends.

"Why not!" Caro demands. "This is our children's first brush with death, death of a friend, an age mate. It raises all sorts of questions in their minds. What does it say to our children," she continues urgently, "if we cannot mourn them? If we're so controlled it appears we're able to cope with grievous loss as if it hardly matters? It undervalues them, it undervalues us." She takes my hand. "They need to see our pain, to understand our loss, and their own. They need to know their presence, or their absence, makes a difference in our lives. . . . Will you come?"

How can I refuse?

Sully, on the other hand, is furious. "How could you commit me to such an ordeal without consulting me!"

"They're our friends. The children need us. Gage was like a brother to them." I try to reprise Caro's arguments.

But he won't hear. "No," he holds his hand up for me to stop. "No; you've no idea what it was like for me today, trying to carry on in Chambers, in the 'halls of justice'," he says sarcastically, "with – everywhere I turned – an awkward attempt at sympathy and commiseration. I wished I'd had a button that said, 'Thank you for your condolences – but let's get on with it, shall we?' No. You go, if you can bear it, but leave me out of it."

"How long do you plan to avoid our friends, then? For ever?"

He looks at me stonily. "As long as it takes."

By the time I pull the car into the driveway at Cobbler's Race I'm trembling with dread. The other cars are there already – Tony and Emily's; Cameron and Fizzy's. Ron answers my knock by engulfing me in his arms like a giant Yorkshire bear.

"You have to know," he says, his eyes welling, "how sorry we are. Gage was as close as one of our own."

I know he's sincere, yet I pick up a distant echo of his prayer, "*Thank God it isn't one of mine.*" I forgive it willingly; I'd have done the same.

He looks questioningly over my shoulder to the car.

"I'll talk with the kids for a while, but I can't stay," I say. "James wouldn't come, and I don't want to leave him alone."

"Ah, Christ! Poor sod," he hugs me again. "We can't have this. Caro!" He goes into the kitchen to confer with her.

"Shit, Mariah," Cameron greets me in his urgent, awkward manner. "Life just isn't fair."

"Something like this shakes us all up," Tony says, taking my arm. I shoot him a glance, wondering if he's mouthing platitudes – or if there's actually been seismic activity in the bedrock of the man's selfishness. He leads me into the kitchen where the women bustle around, packing up food.

"If Mohammed won't come to the mountain," Ron says, "then the mountain must go to Mohammed."

"Now," Fizzy warns them, "don't be *men*; be friends."

"Felicity, love; you misjudge us," Cameron says sweetly. "We'll do just what we'd do in Oz – won't we, lads? – Take the bloke a case of cold and frosties; give him a cuddle and a pat on the bum; say 'Hard on ya, mate.' Git him out back for a rousing match of no-rules football – where we'll beat the crep out of him – then git him pissed." Cameron winks at me. "It never fails."

The kids have assembled solemnly in the lounge: Caro's girls Claire and Dulcie; Fizzy's lads Robbie, Mark, and Duncan; and Emily's demon Angela.

"Uncle James was too sad to come," Caro explains. "Sometimes people don't realize they might feel better if they talk about how sad they are."

Led by Claire and Dulcie, they all present me with handmade cards – "What We Will Remember Most About Gage." *It should have been birthday cards last week. Balloons and presents. And, for a joke, a tinned Marks & Spencer's steak-and-kidney pie ablaze with ten candles.* Gage.

Fighting my instinct to run, I remember Caro's words and let myself both laugh and cry over their sublime, preposterous presentation. I hug them all, wipe their tears, let my own fall unabashed. It's reassuring, in its special way. They're young, but they *will* remember Gage, however imperfectly. I wish Sully could be here.

After dinner, we wait for the men to return. It's a school night; eventually, Emily and Angela go home with Fizzy and the boys in the station wagon. Tony will take Cam home later.

As Caro and I put the girls to bed, Dulcie asks, "Is Gage in heaven, Aunt Mariah?"

Children! Gage in a plane: *When will we be high enough to see God?*

"I believe he is, sweetheart. I have to believe he is."

Caro and I are huddled over our umpteenth cup of tea when Ron returns with Tony and Cam. They all look grim and bruised.

"We succeeded in one pa't of our mission," Cam confides.

"Which part?"

"To git him pissed."

This is not the encouraging breakthrough I'd hoped for.

When the alarm goes off he rolls over toward me, pressing himself against me like a spoon. Is this habit or design? Either way, I'm gratified by the contact.

After a few minutes of radio chatter he stirs, rolls onto his back. "Oh, man," he murmurs, rubbing his eyes. I roll with him, reluctant to let him go. I mark the second it hits him – he gasps, then is suddenly tense all through. Tense, and gone.

"You wake not knowing, don't you?" he growls. "Like you have 3,650 mornings before. Then – blam! – it hits you fresh."

"Yes."

"How long does this go on?"

Is it rhetorical or does he expect an answer? "Until it's habit to be battered every morning, I suppose."

He lets out a long breath, gets out of bed. "I'm sorry about last night."

"Maybe it worked out best."

"Women have it easier, I think," he poses. "You have it bred into your DNA to gather with the crones in front of the fire – "

"Crones! Thank you very much!"

"To share your stories, your joy, your pain. Men are outsiders," he says, pulling on his knee socks, "looking in on the domesticity of that scene. Unable to couch their pain in terms other than, 'Looks like rain' or, 'How about Manchester United?' " He looks at me a moment. "I'm quoting from the Book of Ron, by the way, lest you mistake these for original thoughts."

I smile. "Sensitive guy, Ron. What would we do without him? We've been lucky in our friends."

"I'd much rather not have need of them at all," he says hoarsely.

Yes; well, that goes without saying.

"Any Tylenol?" he calls from the bathroom.

"In the medicine chest." Where it always is. Except that, like his friends, he hasn't had much need of it lately, either. I make a note to see we're well-supplied.

I put on a pot of coffee, pour him a bowl of raisin bran, and toast a hunk of bread, aching all over like a convalescent.

"What about you?" he asks, picking at his food.

"Not hungry. I'll get something later."

"What are you going to do today?"

Standard mornings buzzed with Gage and Gage's plans for the day. Sometimes the logistics rivalled the Normandy landing: soccer practices and matches, chorus, play dates – all to be sandwiched in around our other commitments.

What *am* I going to do today? "I don't know," I strangle on the words. "I just don't know."

Pulling my robe tighter around me, I watch from the front door until Sully's out of sight around the bend in the lane. *Don't go; don't go!* For the first time I wish, irrationally, for a "regular" job to go to that would take me quite away from myself, from the house, from the memories.

Other mornings, other days, I would have waved them both off down the lane. Sully would drop Gage at Saltus on his way to the office and I'd face a few hours at work in the den with a clear head, a sense of anticipation.

Hear the music? Yes – capture it! Get it all down on paper, those first years, and – more recently – on the computer. What a wonderful thing, the computer: my official, if extravagant, gift from Sully for my thirty-fifth birthday, lugged back from Boston and *declared*. MIDI keyboard, sequencing software, the works. It betrayed a certain lack of understanding, on his part, of my methods. Still, it did make orchestration a great deal easier, being able to copy and paste sections with one click of the mouse. And Gage loved it. He could record the bass of a piece on one track and synchronize it with the treble on another. *Like hearing it in stereo for the first time.*

The silence is oppressive. Not just because Gage is gone (*Gage is gone!*) and Sully has left for the day. *But because there is no music in my head.*

How, then, can something so empty, so vacuous, weigh so much I can't hold it erect? In the bedroom I wedge my head between the pillows so it won't fly apart, crush Sully's pillow to my face so I can smell his scent, hold it to my heart as if it will stanch the wound.

The phone wakes me to terror. Three-seventeen, according to the clock radio. Jesus!

"What were you doing?" he asks.

The ready lie: *Just having a little nap.* Instead, I force out the truth, "I seem to have slept all day."

"I'll be late for dinner. I've got a lot of catching up to do."

"What time?"

"Seven. Seven-thirty."

"Why don't you come home for dinner and then go back?" *Like you used to, when you had to.*

"I'll be too tired; I'd rather work through." *I did that for Gage* – his unspoken words – *I won't do that for you.*

"I'll shoot for that, then."

"Don't fuss."

I fly into the shower, race down to Miles' for provisions. Something prefabricated, but tasty. I'm uninspired, despite not having eaten all day. Staring into the butcher's display, engulfed by indecision: it's just dinner, for Christ's sake! Pick something, anything. *Sully won't even care.* A couple of stuffed chicken breasts, a head of romaine lettuce weighing in at a dollar a leaf, some carrots and a few rolls: I'm so exhausted by the effort I want to sleep in the car.

At eight I break and butter a roll, force down half a chicken breast and a few carrots.

At nine, I wrap the food and put it in the fridge.

By ten I'm in bed sobbing into his pillow because, after its hours crushed against my breast, it smells more of me than it does of him.

About eleven, I hear him at the door and wait for him to come into the bedroom. But he doesn't. He pisses copiously in the main bathroom; flushes; doesn't shower. Looking for him later, I find him huddled under the afghan, his clothes heaped on the armchair. I clutch his shirt to my face: the salty tang of sunshine and dried, deodorized perspiration. *Sully.*

"Come to bed," I urge, kneeling beside him. At this range I can smell the cigarette smoke in his hair, the beer on his breath.

Stirring, he draws the afghan more closely around his shoulder, his wedding ring glinting in the faint light from the street lamp down the road. Taking his hand in my own, I press it against my face, not caring that I might wake him.

"What?" His hand goes to my hair.

"I was so worried," I choke, but get stuck on the "I." No words, just vowels. Vowels of loss and loneliness.

He lifts me onto the couch beside him, joins in my wordless lament. If God has any mercy, we will die now – together, this instant – married by our grief. There isn't room in the world for this sorrow. This pinnacle of loss cannot be shared with living people. It is a holy thing that must be presented to God – and Gage – on a different plane.

Does he understand this? Will he take me to the sea, a few short yards away, and hold me in its depths, where our tears will mingle with the sea's own brine as we float out on the tide – to Gage? Do you see this, Sully? Will you come with me, to the sea?

He stands, holds out his hand to me. "Come."

Oh, yes! He sees. He knows. I stand joyfully. *I will come with you, my love!*

"Let's go to bed," he says.

My heart shatters into pieces as I take his hand and follow him down the hall to bed. Where the living sleep.

"Don't leave her alone." He's on the kitchen phone, his back turned to the hall, his voice low. A damp towel hangs around his neck. "She's had a very bad night." Silence. "Yes, I'll be there by five. Thanks."

Turning, he looks guilty when he sees I've heard. "Caro and Ron. Ron brought me home from the club last night. He's going to pick me up on his way in."

"And you've consigned me to the seventh circle of hell for the day," I accuse, "where reside the fornicators, and the compulsively organized!"

He folds me in his arms. "I shouldn't have left you alone so long yesterday, Riah. It was selfish of me. You seemed so, so together. Going off to dinner with our friends when I couldn't stomach it." Kisses my hair. "Caro will keep you busy."

That's what I'm afraid of: Caro will have me busy and organized, the grief all tidied away and disposed of in no time. Dearly as I love her, I'd rather be alone than at Caro's mercy all day.

New Year's morning: right here in this kitchen. Was it only two months ago?

"What was your resolution?" I asked her.

"I resolved to be more organized."

A peal of laughter. You've got to love that dry British wit! Then I saw her puzzled, slightly hurt expression. She was serious!

"You're the most organized person I've ever known."

"D'you think so? *I* don't think I'm particularly organized," she said forlornly.

I hugged her. "Caro, an anorexic doesn't think she's particularly underweight. Believe me, you couldn't *be* more organized."

A day with Caro! Lingering in Sully's arms, "Be it on your head then, James Riordan!" I say, "when you come home tonight to find we've added a wing to the cottage, and been conscripted by eight different committees! Anything could happen."

Ron roars up our lane on his Suzuki. Sully kisses me goodbye. "Have a good day," he says sardonically, pulling on his helmet.

Ron says to me, intently: "Caro'll be here in fifteen minutes."

Is that a threat or a challenge?

Caro has the kettle whistling by the time I get out of the shower, a coffee cake sliced up and three mugs sitting beside the teapot.

"Are we expecting company?"

"Fizzy's coming after she drops the boys at school."

Oh, good! I think disloyally. Fizzy will add a touch of levity to the proceedings; she's been known to sabotage Caro's most sensible and organized activities by dint of her sheer exuberance.

She comes through the kitchen door, bringing in the sun with her untameable red hair. "Thank God! Tea! I haven't stopped since I got up. Morning's such a battleground: why can't the boys be more organized?"

Caro doesn't comment, but I can hear her thoughts: "Because *you* are less than organized, my friend!"

Putting her feet up on the coffee table, Fizzy sinks into the armchair gratefully. "I say; I've always loved this room, but you've got it so nicely arranged. Remember your first place?" Sandy McCassland's apartment had had one big room — living room, dining room, kitchen — all open to each other. "There just seemed no sensible way to place the furniture."

We both look pointedly at Caro, who snorts into her cup. "Until Caro broke in and moved it all about!" We laugh; Caro aspirates her tea. "Imagine, Mariah coming home from town to find the whole house reorganized!"

"Victim of a B & D — break and decorate," I grin. "I wonder if that's in the *Criminal Code?*"

Pounding Caro on the back, Fizzy says, "Just signal if you need the Heimlich manoeuvre."

Caro waves her away. "Laugh if you will, but you must admit," she croaks, "it looked much better when I was done!"

We do; it did.

"So," she says, standing, "what say we tackle Gage's room?"

My lungs deflate at the same instant Fizzy inflates hers, sharply. "Caro!" she exclaims. "Perhaps Mariah's not ready for that."

Stricken speechless — how can I be laughing with my friends one instant and be beaten the next? — I feel as if I've developed multiple personalities. I'm Mariah, friend to these women. And Mariah, childless mother. Will I ever be able to predict with certainty which woman will open her mouth to speak?

"I don't want to turn it into a shrine," I decide. "The door's been closed for days; James can't bear to look."

"What do *you* want?"

What do *I* want? I want Gage to come back! To fly in through the kitchen door, letting it bang against the wall in danger of smashing the glass. I want him to race through the house in his muddy sneakers, to fetch something from that room — "Hi, Mom!" — and then drop it somewhere for me to trip over. I want him to leave the water running in the bathroom until the cistern is drained; to stand in front of the open fridge to cool off on a ninety-degree day; to pick all the blossoms off the hibiscus and bring them to me in a glass jar. I want him to use the silver serving spoon to dig a hole to China; I want him to keep that chameleon in his room for a pet; forget about the live snails in his pocket when his pants go through the wash. I want him to make so much noise I can't hear myself think. *Gage!*

"You don't have to do it all at once," Caro says gently. "Think of it as a ceremony. Examine each thing, decide what Gage would want you to do with it. Relive the memories."

Caro sounds so sensible, but can it be right? To dismantle his room and assign each object a new home? *Like his heart, his liver, his kidneys.* Will it all live on, transplanted into someone else's life? Lego blocks reanimated by Fizzy's lads. Stuffed animals cuddled by Claire and Dulcie's sleepy limbs. Which of them will most value the Brio trains? The complete set of Roald Dahl?

I'm too weak to resist. Caro brings the cartons in from the trunk of her car. We commence.

True to his word, Sully arrives at Caro and Ron's a little after five, despite having stopped at home to fetch the car. The girls are playing on the lawn. I watch from the window as he stops to talk to them, bending his great long legs until he's down at their level. *Is it true the biggest men make the most tender fathers?* He straightens at last, pats them on the head, shakes the kinks out of his bad knee. I meet him at the door.

"How was it?" he asks. "As bad as you thought?" Laughs gently at my answering expression, gives me a squeeze.

"Stay for supper," Caro orders, embracing him.

He looks to me. "Do you have anything in?" I shake my head. "All right. Thanks." Caro hands him a bottle of beer and a stein. He strips off his tie, unbuttons his shirt collar. "Ron won't be far behind. He was just finishing up when I left." Opens his throat and quaffs from the bottle.

"I didn't see the wing on the house," he comments dryly when Caro leaves to call the girls. "Is it the eight committees, then?"

"No. It was Gage's room." He winces. "I told you anything could happen."

Pushing back from the table, Sully rests his elbow on his chair. "I have some news," he announces after the girls have left for baths. "I think I've found a new job."

"Where?" Ron says.

"Vancouver." He takes my hand under the table, holds it in his own resting on his thigh.

I feel a sickening shift in balance. *Thank you for discussing this with me!*

"I've spent most of the last few days in the office on the phone," he admits, "following up leads."

"Ah!" says Ron. "Your door's been uncharacteristically closed. But I attributed it to," he breaks off lamely, "you know."

"I think our lives here are at an end. Surely the change will do us good."

It's hard to dispute this logic. He constrains my hand.

"Well!" Caro says, too brightly. "Do tell!"

Yes, Sully; do tell! I urge silently. *Do explain this unilateral decision.*

Leaning urgently into the table, "I've been in touch with every one of my law-school mates of any integrity and/or intelligence," he begins.

"Then your phone bill won't be quite so bad as I feared!" Ron interrupts. "What would that be? Two calls? Maybe three?"

Caro slaps at him warningly. "Hush, Ron!"

Sully grins. "I articled with Lee Delarey. He's looking for another trial lawyer to go into partnership with." He drains his beer bottle. "Looks like I'm the man."

"So, this decade's experience on a desert isle has not been all for naught!" Ron says, handing him another beer.

Sully toasts him with it. "This decade's tax-free *savings* have not been all for naught," he says, drinking deeply.

"When?" Caro asks my own question.

He glances at me. "As soon as we're ready."

Silent in the car, I'm unsure how I feel about his announcement. Gage is gone. Our lives here are at an end. Is it possible to move too fast?

"What do you think?" he asks.

Looking for something positive, something neutral, "At least the weather's better than Toronto," I decide.

At home, he leans against the frame of Gage's open door, draining a Bass he's taken from the fridge. "Caro's thorough, isn't she?"

I survey the room from his shoulder. Labelled boxes: The Barn. Claire. Dulcie. Duncan. Keep. "We should go through it all," I say, "make sure you agree with our assessments. It's not too late to change anything."

He shakes his head blindly, closes Gage's door. "It's fine. Whatever you think, it's fine. Especially if we're moving. We can't take everything."

"But there might be something else you think we should keep," I insist, anxious for his approval, his input.

"*It's fine*, I said!" closing the *en suite* door with just a tad too much force.

Two *faits accomplis* in one day – his; mine. Is either one easier to take
than the other? I don't ask, *What about me? What about my commission?* My
work – if I had any going on in my head right now, which I don't – is
portable. *If* I finish it – and this was never in question before – I can
send it in to the festival committee. My career goals won't be weighed
in the balance of his decision. But – *if only he'd asked!* I feel so insignifi-
cant – an afterthought in my own marriage.

Up. Down. Round about. They say the aftermath is like a roller
coaster, but this is wrong. On a roller coaster, at least, we'd be strapped
into the same carriage. And would scream with terror at the same
points, experiencing it in tandem.

This is more like bumper cars in the dark. No highs, no lows: on
level ground, spinning out of control. Two separate vehicles on random
paths through the darkness, we only feel the same emotions in collision.
Trajectories of grief colliding, side-swiping. The physics of motion
bash us off course, apart. Only to come together again, head on, when
least expected.

How does any marriage survive the separateness of sorrow?

Phone conversations with my mother are impossible: "How are you,
darling?"

"Oh, you know: *fine*. And you?"

"*Fine.*"

I miss her with a screaming urgency; we sense each other's pain over
the wire, but can't communicate our own. "How's Luke?"

"He's inherited his father, I'm afraid."

"*What?*"

"Your dad's over there all the time; he can't stand to be at home. At
first, he'd wander back to sleep – or, rather, *not* sleep," she sighs. "And
then he started nodding off on Luke's couch. He's graduated to the
guest room now."

"Surely they both race back to the house at meal time, when they
hear your spoon clattering in their dinner bowls!" Like Beau and Raven,
Pavlov's dogs.

"They're fending for themselves," she says. "Gabe talks; Luke listens.
We can only give it time."

Ah, Christ! Poor Luke. "But, what about *you?*"

"*I'm fine.*"

My brother, the Perfect Child. He's been there to help haul the logs and fix the roof and plough the snow and pick up the pieces. He's been there – all I've been is *away*.

Frantic, I call Luke on his office line, hoping to catch him alone. "How are you?"

"Fine."

"How's Mom?"

"She's not sleeping well; neither is Dad. So, rather than disturb her, he's taken to sleeping here. Temporarily," he emphasizes.

"They have a guest room, too," I point out.

"Whatever gets you through the night." His shrug is almost audible. "How are *you*?"

How am I? *The memorial service was worse than the funeral,* I want to tell him. *At least the Catholic "Rite of Christian Burial" revolves around a Mass – you can chime it off by rote with just a thin sliver of the conscious mind engaged, even anaesthetized with shock. Weeks later, though, the anaesthesia has worn off, leaving all the amputated nerve ends shrieking with loss. Those little boys in Saltus uniforms! – they all looked like Gage. And then there were our friends with their kids. And the soccer team. And the choir, with a girl soprano singing the Pie Jesu instead of Gage. And Sully's legal friends, Sully's theatre friends, Sully's squash and golf friends: under their scrutiny Sully achieved such distance he might have been receiving a satellite feed from Mars. Battered by waves of extended eulogy, the pathetic dike of control I'd erected was inadequate to the task. I lost it; I fucking lost it.*

It's like using a telecommunications device for the deaf: it takes all of us to relay each other's emotional states.

How am I? *"I'm fine."*

Sully determines we'll leave by the end of May, before it gets too hot. A goal, something to work toward: it helps.

Not that I don't spend an inordinate amount of time bawling into boxes as I pack. Not just for Gage, but for the passing of our era together. Article by article, the life goes out of our home. The walls are white where once they were ablaze with reflected colour and life: flaming sunsets; blue sky, blue water; flowering vegetation. Music in our hearts. And Gage.

"Why did you pack the stereo already?" Sully asked. "We're not leaving tomorrow!"

I have no words to explain. He wouldn't understand if I told him: *I've become a deaf-mute.*

The cranium walls are white, an inviolable space. *There is no music in my head.* Nor can I bear music from an external source. All of it is fraught with associations; all of it impinges on the purity, on the vacuum, of perfect silence. I'm afraid: if the seal is broken I'll have no control over what may rush in to fill the void.

The labelled boxes in Gage's room are distributed, the furniture given to charity. His room has become the depository for our packed possessions.

"Here."

I hand Sully a carton. He's been standing in the arch of the dining room watching me wrap the good china, swigging a beer. *When did a long brown bottle get to be a permanent extension of his hand?* I wonder, annoyed. It's already hot, for May. I'm barefooted and in shorts, wishing we had central air conditioning.

"Why don't you make a stab at packing the den," I suggest, trying not to sound irritated.

He takes the box, turns on the TV to accompany his task. *Jeopardy* theme music is replaced with static.

"Shit!"

Ignoring him, I go on with my own chore.

Silence. More static. "Jesus Christ!" The sound of something being thrown into a box. Static. An inarticulate cry of anger and anguish. A tremendous crash.

I run to the den. "What the hell are you doing?"

Standing amid the scattered contents of a shelf of videotapes, he punches them — one at a time — into the VCR. Static, coloured snow on the screen. No sound, no recognizable picture.

"What *is* the matter?" I demand.

Throwing each video into the carton with increasing fury, "Fuck! Fuck, they're all ruined! Fucking mildew!" he sobs.

The family videos. Most of them of Gage.

"Sully."

I take a few steps toward him, but he's on the move. He grabs the shelf out of its brackets on the wall, swings it in a wide arc with all his considerable might as if it's a baseball bat.

"He's gone!" he shouts.

Clipping the TV, the computer monitor — and my cheek — in his follow-through, he seems not to notice. Backing out of the room, I run into the bedroom and lock the door behind me.

The noise continues in the other room, the sound of determined destruction. Grief run amok. Jesus Christ! What to do? Shaking, I dial the number at Cobbler's Race.

Ron answers the phone with his musical "Hall-oo!"

"Can you come? It's James."

He gasps. He can hear the noise, through the door, over the phone. "What's the matter?"

"Please come! I'm so. . . ." What? terrified of my own husband? "Can you come?"

"Yes! Are you able to drive?"

"I think so — but I won't leave him alone. I'm in the bedroom; he's in the den."

"On my way."

Trembling, I tiptoe into the *en suite*, examine my face in the mirror. My left cheek is split like a peach and throbbing. I wipe the blood with a face-cloth, apply pressure. Sit on the bed and wait for Ron. He roars up the lane in the car, having broken land-speed records for the one-kilometre run.

"James!"

He blocks the doorway to the den with his own substantial bulk as I race past him, grab the car keys from the hook by the back door, and run to the car. I drive slowly and deliberately to Cobbler's Race.

Caro runs out. "You can't sit here sobbing all night," she says, leading me into the house.

"The girls?"

"In bed."

Good.

She sits me on a stool in the kitchen, puts on the kettle, takes out the first-aid kit. "Let's get some ice on that. I think it'll close without stitches with a butterfly bandage. But I'm quite sure you'll have a lovely shiner."

Great.

My teeth are chattering, despite the heat of the evening. She leads me into the lounge, hands me two Tylenol and a mug of tea, wraps me in a mohair throw.

"Want to talk?"

I shake my head.

"Can you sleep?"

I shake my head again. But I do — the sleep of denial and despair.

Awake to strange surroundings with a double-whammy: the much-too-familiar blow to my heart — *Gage!* — and this new one, to my face. *Sully.*

Ron's car's not in the driveway. He's stayed with Sully through the night. What a friend! I think gratefully.

"I'll send Ron home," I tell Caro when I join her in the kitchen, "assuming all's well."

Wrapping me in her arms, "Are you all right?" she asks.

"He didn't mean to hit me; I got in the way."

She holds me by the shoulders, looks into my eyes. "That's not what I asked." She repeats, "Are you *all right?*"

"Seen better days, Caro."

A sisterly kiss on my good cheek. "Take care. Call me later."

There's a packing crate full of glass and eviscerated electronics at my back door. Ron — shirtless, in his boxers — is making coffee in my kitchen as if he belongs there. Tilting my chin like a child's — "Ah, Christ!" — he kisses the laceration on my cheek, presses me against his chest.

"How is he?"

He sighs. "Have you thought about grief counselling?"

"We talked about it. But this is such a small place! He has to face all the psychologists on one side of the courtroom or the other, you know that." I clutch at straws. "Maybe once we're away, where nobody knows us." *Where we'll be friendless and at each other's mercy.*

"What about a priest?"

"Christ, no!" I shake my head vehemently. *Angry; too angry at God.* My eyes fill. "Did he sleep?"

Ron hands me a mug of coffee. "I sedated him with the last of the Chivas."

"Thank you, Dr. Jackson."

"I'll tell them not to expect him at work today."

I blow across my mug, nodding.

"Try to get him to talk." He looks at me earnestly. "I mean *really* talk."

"Okay."

Pulling on his clothes in the living room, familiar, unselfconscious. A brother; a friend. *I'll miss you more than anyone, Ron.*

He kisses my cheek again. I watch from the door as he folds himself into the car. Then I go into the bedroom to meet my husband, the stranger.

Sully. He looks so peaceful, so innocent. Making sure the alarm is turned off, I slip off my shorts and polo shirt, and crawl into bed in camisole, panties. And socks. His arm goes around me. The reflexes of marriage! To give comfort and accept it, no matter how unconsciously. We sleep.

When he stirs, I roll over to watch him wake. It's a struggle, his surfacing from oblivion. He fights it. I used to love to watch his eyes flutter open, focus on mine, crinkle in a smile. *Good morning, love!*

Today, when he finally awakes, sees me watching him, sees my face: "Good Christ!" He sits bolt upright, falls against my bosom with a wail. I wrap my arms around him to contain the squall.

"I'm sorry; I'm so sorry," he says when he's capable of forming words at last, "I didn't mean to!"

I stroke his hair. "I know."

He plants tiny kisses tentatively all over my face, "Riah, Riah." Wets me with his tears. "Make it stop!"

"I can't. I'd give my life to make it stop."

Two weeping bodies, colliding with need, with loss. Somehow, in the urgency of our pain – for the first time since Gage's death – we rediscover the reflexes of love. Tender, tender, sorrowful love.

"It's as if he's been erased! Don't you see?" He's brought two mugs of tea to bed. "All his things given away; all his pictures packed; all his videotapes ruined." He sucks at the steaming cup. "Eliminated from the face of the earth."

"I feel the same way; I do." *But I haven't resorted to destroying the den.*

He sits cross-legged on the bed, the mug on the sheets next to his right thigh, his head supported by his left fist. "There's more."

I stroke the back of his neck with my stump. "What is it?"

"I don't want to hurt you – I don't think I'd speak if Ron hadn't insisted I should."

Steeling myself, "What, Sully; what?"

He lifts his head, inhales harshly. "The worst thing about losing Gage . . ." He opens his fist, hides his face behind the five open fingers. "He was mine while I had him. But now that he's gone," he sobs, "he's Doug's!" Face creased with pain, "He's not mine any more. As if he ever was! We let Doug into our lives — and he stole Gage away."

The betrayal in his words hits me like a body blow; I reel away as if I've been kicked. I don't feel it on my own behalf. But on Gage's.

"No! You're wrong, Sully. We let Doug into our lives and he *gave* us Gage in the truest sense."

He scowls at me, hurt and confused.

"Doug was the *donor*; a donor gives. And the donee accepts the gift. Not God's sadistic little joke — God's gift. I didn't truly accept it, Sully, until we let Doug in."

I can't deal with this. The fist in my throat that's rendered me mute these last weeks gets in the way; my ears roar, impacted with the build-up of words unspoken.

"Until Gage found Doug's picture, until we started talking about how we were going to handle the problem — God help me, Sully — I felt like Gage was a mistake, my *unholy* mistake. Talking about it with you helped tremendously." I stroke his leg. "We broke the sound barrier."

Kneeling at his feet, "I wrestled Doug for Gage, and *I won*," I insist. "I refused to lose to him, Sully! because I finally saw Gage's birth as our salvation, not our undoing. The final barrier: I tore it down. I fought for us — because we are worth fighting for. I accepted the gift and I *would not change one thing*. Not you, not Gage. Not *one thing* about our lives."

I place my forehead on his scarred knee. "That was the last wall, Sully. If we hadn't broken the sound barrier then, I wouldn't have learned to love Gage, finally, completely, *well enough*." His hand goes to my head. "And if I hadn't loved him well enough you'd be alone right now."

Fingers close around a handful of my hair. "Mariah." He draws me onto the bed.

"Gage was our challenge and our opportunity. We invented ourselves for him. He brought out the best in us. He was our spotlight of grace, Sully."

"Yes," he nods. "He *was*. But now!" he sobs. "Ten years ago I chose — or *was* chosen — to make a life for the three of us. But where are we today?" His voice is hard, broken: "It didn't count! It didn't matter. Gage is gone and our lives are shattered."

"You were the only father Gage knew," I say. The words sound flat, emotionless. "Doug didn't steal him away. But he will, if you let him."

Sully looks at me doubtfully.

"We have to talk about him," I whisper. "We have to break the sound barrier again, Sully. We have to keep a place for him. Or *he'll be gone*. It's up to us. We have to preserve *us* for Gage. Otherwise, what was it all for?"

"I didn't mean to imply there was nothing to keep us together!" he exclaims, anguished at this apparent misunderstanding.

"I know; I know," I say gently. "But marriages are destroyed by mourning, by separateness. We need a code, a shorthand to the other when one of us has spun off into an orbit of grief alone." I stroke his hair. "Something to pull us back into the gravitational field."

He nods, pinching his eyes shut. "I miss him; I miss him," he says raggedly. "I can't stand how much I miss him." Presses his ear against my midriff as he did when Gage was growing there, listening for heart-beat, waiting for movement. "I accepted the opportunity of his birth, Mariah. But — Jesus God! — where's the opportunity in this loss? This gap can't be filled."

I can't see how our lives are going to go. *The bottomless canyon stretches out before us. Until this moment, the only pull has been gravitational. Down. Down.*

"You're right; the gap can't be *filled*, Sully." I've tottered on its brink before. But gravity suddenly has no hold on me; I feel weightless, free. "Getting across will mean work. Bridging, buttressing, spanning. Shoring ourselves — and each other — against the emptiness, when all we really want is rescue." *To wake up on the other side, safe in each other's arms.* With Gage. Intact in memory.

I'm suddenly convinced: "The opportunity is in the survival, Sully. In the carrying on. In the preservation of our selves — our best selves — and the place we made for Gage." He looks doubtful. "Come. There's something we have to do."

The vacuum must be broken; I *can* control what rushes in to fill the void.

"There's only one thing I want to hear," I say, pulling the box marked "Tapes" out of the pyramid in Gage's room. "One thing I've been afraid to hear. Need to hear. Must hear." Sully slices open the sealed box, waits beside me — solemn as an acolyte — as I select the hand-labelled cassette.

Near despair, "The stereo's *packed*," he reminds me.

"The car. Grab your pants."

The "Benediction" of the *Blue Sky Mass* translates as: "Blessed is he who comes in the name of the Father, Son, and Holy Spirit. Where there is charity and love, there is God. We are bound together in one by the love of Christ."

He plugs it into the deck, waits to adjust the volume.

My voice off-mike: "All right, you clowns. I want to see if this works. Are you ready?"

"Mimimimimimi!" Gage warbles.

Sully: "Who's Mimi?"

"I'm cueing the accompaniment. In three, two, one."

Sully reaches across the gear shift as music fills the car and the yard beyond its open doors *Benedictus qui venit* Gage's amplified voice over-lapped by Sully's *in nomine Patri et Filio et Spiritui Sancto* entwined and engaged *Ubi caritas et amor, Deus ibi est* in a peaceful harmony *Congregavit nos in unum Christi amor* a duet of love between father and son.

Do you hear the music in the words and the love behind the music? Yours for me and mine for you? Do you see our world taking on colour? There are blue dots in memory; there are red. Together, they give the appearance of purple; together, they give the appearance of life.

"We are together in this," he says, kissing the tears from my face. "For Gage. For us."

When Sully starts to sing, duplicating his own recorded voice, I'm flooded with such tenderness for him I bend to absorb the tonal vibrations in his breast against my ear. He puts his arms around me and — still singing — holds me, holds me, as I weep. For Gage. For him. For me. In a musical space where we can be together, honouring the gap in our lives.

Queued along a narrow strip of shade in front of the terminal are our friends. Cameron, Ron, and Tony help unload the taxi of enough luggage for ten people; their mates — Fizzy, Caro, Emily — stand stiffly, holding their elbows. We smile tentatively, as if meeting for the first time, while four hulking specimens of manhood rough-house like puppies, collide with passengers trying to make their way to the doors.

"Don't forget to write," Fizzy says quite unnecessarily. The other MEWs hug me in turn, issue their own last-minute instructions.

One last round of handshakes, slaps, and hugs.

"Right, then." Caro the drill sergeant organizes the departure. "Cheerio. These people have a plane to catch. And I have to rescue my parents from seven children."

Six. She's included Gage in the count. Which, in a way, is as it should be. For when I remember these people, our friends, my favourite memories will be of our children all playing together. Dulcie. Claire. Robbie, Mark, Duncan. Angela. And Gage.

Goodbye, Gage.

I entrust his frolicking shade to their care.

AFTERWORD

While I would be delighted to credit "Laura's Story" from Dusty Miller's *Women Who Hurt Themselves* (BasicBooks, A Division of HarperCollins Publishers, Inc., 1994) as a source of inspiration (Mariah considers the Zapruder home movie of the Kennedy assassination an informing metaphor in her life), I didn't read Miller's excellent study until after I'd finished the novel. It gave me a bit of a start (to say the least!) to read what could have been Mariah's words in someone else's book but, since Miller takes pains to point out that "the voices of the women are not actual transcriptions, but rather representations of the many voices listened to and learned from," I've come to accept the synchronicity.

I am indebted to Louise J. Kaplan's *Female Perversions* (Doubleday, 1991) for providing a name for one of Mariah's more extreme behaviours.

I share with Mariah a delight in word play and the precision of language. All definitions quoted within the novel are extracted from my venerable, battered copy of *The Concise Oxford Dictionary* (Oxford University Press, 1964; Fifth Edition, 1974).

ABOUT THE AUTHOR

Loranne Brown grew up in Thunder Bay, Ontario, then took her B.A. at the University of Toronto. During a decade in Bermuda she was an arts reviewer and weekly columnist. Her short story "Repetitive Tasks," which is adapted from *The Handless Maiden*, was chosen as a finalist in the 1996 Writers' Union of Canada competition. Loranne Brown lives in Langley, British Columbia with her husband and two children.